HOLDING FOR THE QUEEN
THE SOLDIER'S SON
BOOK V

MALCOLM ARCHIBALD

Copyright © 2025 Malcolm Archibald

Layout design and Copyright © 2025 by Next Chapter

Published 2025 by Next Chapter

Cover design by Lordan June Pinote

This book is a work of fiction. Names, characters, places, and incidents are the product of the author's imagination or are used fictitiously. Any resemblance to actual events, locales, or persons, living or dead, is purely coincidental.

All rights reserved. No part of this book may be reproduced or transmitted in any form or by any means, electronic or mechanical, including photocopying, recording, or by any information storage and retrieval system, without the author's permission.

For Cathy

"There is no doubt they [The Gordon Highlanders] are the finest regiment in the world."
Winston Churchill (attributed)

"We are not interested in the possibilities of defeat: they do not exist,"
Queen Victoria

"I hold Ladysmith for the Queen."
Sir George White, during the siege of Ladysmith

GLOSSARY

Afrikaans: the language spoken by the people of Dutch descent in South Africa. It originated in the Dutch language spoken by the original European settlers in South Africa.

Biltong: air-dried cured meat.

Boer: Afrikaner countryman, although most British used the term for any citizen of the two South African republics who fought against Britain.

Bundook: British rankers' slang term for their rifles, from the Hind word banduq, meaning 'gun'.

Burgher: Afrikaner townsman.

Bydand: Steadfast – the motto of the Gordon Highlanders.

Commando: gathering or group of Boers and/or Burghers for the purpose of war.

Dorp: village.

Great Trunk Road: major road across Northern India.

Grim, on the: British rankers' slang for service on India's Northwest Frontier.

Gun cotton: or nitrocellulose, a flammable mixture of cellulose and nitric and sulphuric acids; it was used as an explosive.

ILH: Imperial Light Horse.

Kerk Predikant: Church Minister.

Khaki: a term for British soldiers, named after the colour of their uniforms.

Kloof: steep-sided valley or ravine.

Kopje: hill.

Koppie: small hill.

Laager: encampment, often of wagons placed in a rough circle.

Majuba: a battle fought on 27th February 1881, where the Boers defeated the British.

MI: Mounted Infantry.

Nek: a col, a dip between two peaks on a mountain range.

PBI: Poor Bloody Infantry.

Publics: Public Houses.

Rinderpest: highly infectious viral disease of cattle.

Rooinecks: literally, Rednecks, a derogatory term for British soldiers, probably referring to their tendency to burn under the sun, unlike the tanned Burghers.

Shabash: well done, congratulations.

Shine: noise.

Stoep: veranda.

Spruit: a small watercourse, usually dry.

Swaddie, swaddies: slang term for British soldiers, normally men from the ranks.

GLOSSARY

Taal, the: an alternative name for Afrikaans, the language spoken by the Boers.

Transvaalse Volkslied: Transvaal national anthem.

Uitlander: a non-Boer in either of the Boer republics. Many were from the British Isles.

Voortrekker: person who migrated northwards from British-controlled Cape Colony to help found the Boer republics.

Zarp: Transvaal Police.

CHAPTER 1

SOETWATERS

TRANSVAAL, THE ZUID-AFRIKAANSCHE REPUBLIEK

OCTOBER 1899

Michal Rheeder jabbed in his heels and leapt his horse over the fence, landing with a shower of dust on the far side. He dismounted with a flourish, pushed back the broad-brimmed hat from his long blond hair and strode towards the farmhouse of Soetwaters.

"Hendrik du Toit!" Michal shouted. "Hendrik! Are you there?"

Pushing open the front door, Michal peered inside. The interior was sparse, with little furniture on the beaten earth floor, while the plates on the antique dresser gleamed with cleanliness. The long Martini-Henry rifle on the wall was old-fashioned but well kept, with a faint whiff of gun oil. "Hendrik?"

When he realised the house was empty, Michal left quickly,

jumped on his horse and trotted to the fields, acknowledging the servants with a careless wave.

"Hendrik du Toit!"

"Ja?" Hendrik was in his late thirties, but a lifetime spent outdoors, coupled with hard labour and recent grief, had carved deep lines in his tanned face. He lifted his hat politely when he saw his visitor. "Michal? What is it?"

Michal lifted his hat and shook Hendrik's hand. "A commando!" Michal shouted. "We are raising a commando! Will you join us?"

Hendrik surveyed the younger man briefly before replying with a slow nod. "Ja, I am no warrior, but I will join you. I buried my wife and my son last year, so all I have left is my farm and war. Who are we fighting?"

Michal swept back his hair and grinned. "I don't know," he admitted. "It might be the native tribes or maybe the Rooinecks."

Hendrik rubbed a hard hand along his jaw before he replied. "Ja, the Rooinecks. I fought them twenty years ago when I was a boy, even younger than you, and we will have to fight them again."

"Get your rifle, Oom Hendrik, and three days' supply of biltong and flour." Michal grinned with excitement. "I have never been on commando before."

Hendrik sighed. "Maybe it is time you did. It is not a good thing to kill a man or to see men killed," he said thoughtfully. "Yet sometimes it is necessary to do a little evil for the greater good."

Michal waited impatiently while Hendrik gave detailed instructions to his servants, saddled his horse, added a second and brought food, his rifle and ammunition.

"Where and when are we assembling?" Hendrik asked.

"Two miles outside Vereeniging," Michal replied. "Tonight."

Hendrik glanced over his farm to ensure everything was in order, gave final orders to his servants and turned his horse's head. "Lead on," he said, and rode away, leaning well back in the saddle. Hendrik looked to his right as they passed the simple church with the surrounding graveyard where he had buried his wife and son, mouthed a silent prayer and rode on. Hendrik could blame neither the native tribes nor the British for his wife's death of fever, and he refused to put responsibility on the Lord, yet his feeling of smouldering resentment against the world needed an outlet. Hendrik patted the stock of his rifle. Somebody would have to pay, and the Rooinecks had a history of interfering with other people's business.

The veldt spread around them, dotted with small farmhouses and decorated with trees, singly and in neat plantations. Above, the abyss of God's sky stretched forever, cool blue except for a handful of distant clouds.

"Somebody is coming," Michal nodded to the north, where rising dust indicated a rider. "Three men, riding hard."

Hendrik could read the dust as well as Michal. "Ja," he agreed. "Three riders. Unless their horses flounder, they will be here in ten minutes."

The riders emerged from the dust: an older man and two younger companions. The older man was bearded and rode slightly in front, with one of his companions having the facial fluff of a teenager desperate to achieve maturity, and the other smooth-faced as a girl.

"Louis Grobler and his sons," Michal said, lifting his hat in welcome.

"We are joining the commando," Louis said. Tall, slender and wiry, he took position behind Michal and Hendrik, with the two youngsters making up the rear.

The farmers rode easily across the veldt with the horses' hooves the only sound, and the openness extending as far as they could see. Hendrik examined each farm they passed, instinctively checking the condition of the livestock and wondering about fresh water and grazing. His mind wandered back to Soetwaters and the quiet graves where his wife and son rested.

"More riders are coming," Michal said, as another band rode from behind a *koppie*, three mature men and five youths who announced their arrival by firing rifles in the air. Hendrik knew them from the *nagmaals*—the quarterly farmers' gatherings—and greeted them with handshakes and raised hats.

The newcomers tagged on behind the Groblers, and the enhanced commando trotted forward to Vereeniging. Other riders joined them, occasionally as individuals, more often in small, tight family groups, sometimes of three generations: grandfathers, fathers and sons.

"You are collecting quite a commando," Hendrik said, as they halted to rest and water the horses.

"It is not my commando," Michal said, shaking his head. "I have no experience to lead. I am only helping gather the men."

"Then who will lead?" Hendrik asked.

"You know how we arrange a commando," Michal said. "The men from a district gather under a commandant with two field cornets, each above several corporals."

"I know the system," Hendrik replied patiently.

"Adriaan Wessels is the Commandant, and Dannie van Niekerk will be our field cornet," Michal replied. "We will vote for a corporal at Vereeniging. You will meet Adriaan and Dannie later."

"I know them by name and reputation," Hendrik said.

They assembled beside a farm a mile outside Vereeniging with the sky ominously dark and the noise of the bustling little town reaching the Boers. The men found places to settle for the night, either in the open or inside a barn, and Hendrik lit a fire to combat the chill of the coming night. Most of the commando gathered around.

"Have the Rooinecks attacked Vereeniging?" Hendrik asked.

"They have not," Michal replied cheerfully.

"Then why are we here?"

"Ask the Field Cornet," Michal said.

Dannie van Niekerk was a serious-faced man in his forties

with a neat beard and sad eyes. "You men all know how the Rooinecks are treating us," he spoke without preamble.

The men nodded.

"The British are moving their soldiers to the western borders of the Transvaal and the Orange Free State, with troopships already at sea for Cape Town and Durban. We will soon muster on our borders with Natal and Cape Colony. They want to annex the Boer Republics to their empire."

"Remember that the British are taking the gold from the Witwatersrand," Dannie continued. "They take our gold from under our land and transport it from Johannesburg to British-owned banks."

Michal nodded vigorously. "The British are stealing our gold," he said. "They stole our land in Natal and the Cape, and they steal our gold and try to tell us how to govern our country."

Dannie nodded. "President Kruger has ordered that we should recover some of our gold. This commando will reverse the Rooinecks' theft." He raised his voice. "We will commandeer what is ours!"

Michal joined some of the others in cheering and looked at Hendrik for support.

Hendrik's expression did not alter. He watched Dannie, concentrating on every word.

"How will we commandeer gold from the Rand when we are thirty miles away at Vereeniging?" Hendrik asked quietly.

Dannie smiled grimly, expecting the question.

"The gold is loaded onto the mail train at the Rand and sent down to Cape Town," Dannie explained. "The railway line, as you know, passes through Vereeniging." He gave another taut, humourless smile. "We will stop the weekly mail train and commandeer our gold."

Michal led the cheering, waving his hat, his long blond hair rippling down his back.

"When is the mail train due?" a large, dark-haired man asked. Hendrik eyed the speaker with suspicion. He knew everybody in the area and was wary of outsiders. The speaker was not local and did not look like a Boer—a farmer. He was alert, wary even, with a .577 Express hunting rifle over his shoulder and two ragged dogs beside his feet.

"What is your name, *meneer*?" Dannie asked, lifting his hat.

"Piet Stoffberg," the man replied.

"Where are you from?" Dannie asked.

"Everywhere," Piet replied vaguely, holding Dannie's gaze. "I have been hunting in the low veldt and the north, and I did not know the Rooinecks were causing trouble until I joined your commando."

"They hide their actions behind politeness and a pretence to care for the Uitlanders," Dannie replied. "But Oom Paul * knows them and will forestall their plans. The mail train is due tomorrow afternoon." He gave instructions to the men, who listened and nodded to show they understood.

Michal grinned at Hendrik. "We'll show the British they can't take liberties with our Zuid Afrikan Republik, the Transvaal."

Hendrik nodded slowly. "Ja," he said. "If they try to take our country, we will retake our gold." He began to fill his pipe, thinking of his dead wife and son and hoping the servants were caring for his farm.

COMMANDANT ADRIAAN WESSELS WAS AN OLDER MAN WITH grey hair and a long beard. He passed responsibility for the mission to Dannie while he disappeared on an errand of his own.

Michal watched Adriaan ride away, tossed back his hair and asked Dannie about his plans.

"Listen," Dannie said, and positioned his men around the station at Vereeniging, with Hendrik and Piet at one end of the platform and Michal in a small group at the other. Dannie took

---

* Oom Paul: President Kruger.

charge of Michal's group. Ignoring the station master's protests, Dannie sent a man onto the roof to watch for the train coming. Hendrik watched impassively, unconcerned if Dannie's plan succeeded, yet determined to do his duty for the Republic.

The commando waited under the serene blue sky, with a slight wind rustling the branches of the trees. Passers-by either hurried past or watched these armed men, wondering what would happen.

"Here she comes," the lookout on the roof called. The station master automatically removed the silver watch from his waistcoat pocket, checked the time, and nodded approvingly.

Hendrik shouldered his rifle and stepped back, watching Dannie and Michal edge forward at the far end of the platform. Dannie had sent Louis Grobler into the station master's office, and now everybody waited for the results. Hendrik could nearly taste the tension in the air. He checked his rifle was loaded, leaned against one of the iron pillars that supported the roof, and waited. A few railway servants scurried away, sensing trouble.

The station master signalled for the train to halt, and it began to slow a few hundred yards before reaching Vereeniging, with steam hissing and smoke gushing from its funnel. Hendrik heard the brakes squeal and saw the steam increase as the train neared the station, with the driver watching from his cab, wondering what was happening.

The train eased to a stop, with the boiler steam and smoke dissipating on the platform. All the railway workers had fled, and only the armed Boers remained with the station master. Dannie, Michal, and two other men approached the driver. While Dannie spoke, the others held their rifles ready. The driver and a uniformed guard left the engine, speaking quickly and staring at the armed men.

Hendrik turned his attention to the goods carriage that stopped opposite where he waited. The sliding door was closed, barred and double padlocked, a sure sign that it contained something valuable. Hendrik looked up as Michal ran towards them with a bunch of heavy keys in his hand and his rifle bouncing over his shoulder.

"Open the locks!" Dannie ordered brusquely.

Michal chose a key from his bunch and inserted it into the first padlock. After twisting it for a few moments, he cursed, withdrew the key and tried another. Hendrik moved slightly, keeping his rifle trained on the driver in case he decided to jump into his cabin and move away. The driver was middle-aged, bald and sweating, with a cigarette dangling from the corner of his mouth. He did not appear like a man ready to chance being shot.

"That's better," Michal said as he turned the third key. He yanked the padlock open, threw it on the ground, and tried the next, laughing as it clicked the first time of asking. He released the heavy iron locking bar within a minute and threw the door open. The armed guard inside stared, open-mouthed, as three Boers pointed their rifles at him. He stepped back to the pile of heavy money boxes, each stencilled with a bank's name.

"What's all this?" The guard swivelled, unsure at which man to aim his revolver.

"Out!" Michal ordered.

"Stand aside!" Dannie said. "We're coming in."

"You can't come in here! This is the Royal Mail!" the guard waved his pistol uncertainly.

"Drop the pistol and hands up!" Dannie prodded the guard with the muzzle of his rifle. "We are four to one."

When the guard hesitated and reluctantly obeyed, Michal picked up the revolver and thrust it inside his belt. Hendrik guided the guard away, pressing the muzzle of his rifle against the man's back.

Dannie jumped into the carriage and began hauling out the locked money boxes. "Put them on the cart!" he ordered.

Michal lifted the first box, with the name *Bank of Africa* stencilled on the front. He carried it to the flat cart that waited beside the platform as others carried away the other boxes. Hendrik read the names: *African Banking Corporation, National*

Bank of the South African Republic and the *Natal Bank*. As a God-fearing man, Hendrik was not happy about the robbery, but he also knew that the gold had been destined to make wealthy foreigners even richer at the Republic's expense.

Dannie pointed to the mail sacks piled in the corner, some labelled *For Her Majesty's Soldiers in Natal*.

"Take these as well," Dannie ordered. "They might contain valuable information."

Michal nodded and tossed the mail sacks onto the cart.

Dannie lifted his hat to the staring guard. "President Kruger thanks the government of the United Kingdom for allowing us to commandeer gold that we rightfully own," he said. Reaching up, he removed a rifle from its brackets and tossed it onto the cart beside the bullion boxes. "In case you have any silly ideas about being heroic."

"You won't get away with this," the guard spluttered.

Dannie pushed the man back, slid shut the carriage door and replaced the padlocks. "Tell the driver to move on," he ordered. "And we'll get out of here."[*]

---

[*] The Boers stopped a gold consignment at Vereeniging, taking an estimated half million pounds worth of gold. The method and names in this account are fictional, although the robbery was one of the first acts of the Second British-Boer War.

CHAPTER 2

TRANSVAAL, THE ZUID-AFRIKAANSCHE REPUBLIEK

OCTOBER 1899

"Like rats leaving a sinking ship," Leslie grunted as a uniformed Zarp, a Zuid-Afrikaansche Republiek policeman, jostled a group of nervous men and women off the pavement and onto the dusty road.

Dressed in civilian clothes and trying to hide their military bearing, Captain Andrew Baird of the 2nd Battalion, Royal Malverns, and Lieutenant Damian Leslie of the Imperial Light Horse slouched through the streets of Johannesburg. They watched the people hurrying to the railway station to catch the trains to Durban, Delagoa Bay or Cape Town, spoke to those who could spare the time and gleaned what information they could about affairs in the Transvaal's gold city.

"Are you leaving as well?" a plump, well-dressed man asked Andrew, his eyes darting nervously from side to side. He clutched a bulging canvas bag to his chest with white-knuckled hands.

"I am not sure what I am doing," Andrew replied, watching the hurrying civilians leave a wide arc around the police.

"Leave!" the plump man urged. "It soon won't be safe for any Uitlander – any non-Boer – in either of the Boer republics. Unless you are a Dutchman or a German, you'll be hounded out or thrown in prison on a trumped-up charge." He lowered his voice. "I saw the stolen gold arrive yesterday. There were three wagonloads, with the Zarps and some rough, ragged-looking back-veldt Boers guarding it. I heard that Oom Paul Kruger rubbed his hands and gloated when he saw the gold. Kruger appreciates the value of gold, especially when Uitlanders have done the hard work of tearing it from the ground."

"Gold is always welcome," Andrew said solemnly. By the look of the plump civilian, he had never done anything harder than wash his hands or scan his bank balance.

"I'll have to run," the plump man excused himself. "I have to catch a train out of here." Crossing the road to avoid the Zarps, he scurried away, still holding his bag as if it held all his worldly treasures.

"He was scared," Leslie observed.

"This whole town seems either scared or very tense," Andrew observed.

They stood at a street corner, watching a constant stream of civilians—men, women and children—head towards the railway station. The Zarps seemed to be everywhere, watching the crowd, occasionally pulling a man aside to question him, asking for papers or hustling him away. Andrew kept a wary eye on the police, ready to move away if they seemed interested in him.

"This place is even worse than when I left," Leslie said. "It's more like Russia than Africa."

"Have you ever been to Russia?" Andrew asked.

"No, but I've heard the stories," Leslie said.

"So have I," Andrew agreed.

"What will we do if the Zarps approach us?" Leslie asked.

"I don't think they will," Andrew told him. "We're dressed

like back-country Boers rather than Uitlanders. If a policeman comes close, walk slowly away, speaking in Afrikaans."

A young family scurried past, with the husband carrying two heavy suitcases and the wife dragging an infant by the hand while cradling a baby in the crook of her left arm. The man was red-faced and looked prosperous, with good-quality clothes and glossy boots, while the woman's long dress was fashionable, with a bright ribbon around her straw hat.

"You lived in Johannesburg before you moved to Natal, didn't you?" Andrew asked.

"I did," Leslie confessed with his ready smile. "I emigrated from England to Johannesburg to make my fortune in the gold mines."

"Did you make your fortune?"

Leslie laughed bitterly. "The gold mines are not for men working on their own. They are for immensely rich people employing others. You are risking your life to make a fortune for the already wealthy, and then the Transvaal Government, Oom Paul and his cronies, got jealous and began to lean on non-Boers —Uitlanders. I got out before the situation got worse. The Transvaal is a police state."

Andrew watched two Zarps from under the brim of his hat. Although they pulled up the occasional man, they seemed more interested in talking to each other. Neither glanced at him.

"The Pretoria Executive promised to issue permits to all Uitlanders who wish to remain in the republic," Leslie reminded him. "Yet now that war seems inevitable, they have broken the promise."

"That's how I see it," Andrew agreed. He shifted away as a third Zarp joined the others, who stiffened to attention.

"That one is a sergeant," Leslie said casually. "Now the non-Boers are fleeing Johannesburg in their hundreds. The poor things don't know what best to do under Kruger's repressive regime."

Andrew nodded as the Zarp sergeant faced them. "Let's go

into the railway station and see if things are as bad as people say. We must make a report, after all."

Leaving their stance on the street, Andrew and Leslie joined the crowd that crushed into the station. Two mounted police kept control with a mixture of words and muscle.

Andrew was unprepared for the scene that greeted him as railway officials crammed the frightened refugees into carriages that were already packed to overflowing.

Leslie stepped forward. "For God's sake! We can't allow this!"

"Stand back and watch," Andrew ordered. "We are not here to interfere, and trying to help will only attract attention to us and do more harm than good." Despite his words, Andrew had to restrain himself when he saw burly Afrikaans-speaking officials thrusting scared civilians into open cattle trucks. He saw one uniformed railway worker roaring abuse at two cowering women trying to shield their children.

"That'll do!" Andrew put a hand on the uniformed man's shoulder. "Back off there!" He spoke in Afrikaans, the language of the Boers.

The uniformed man turned, opened his mouth to blast the interfering stranger, saw the expression in Andrew's eyes, and rapidly retreated.

Andrew stamped his boots on the concrete ground. "Any sympathy I had for the Boers is rapidly diminishing." He glared after the official. "I don't like bullies of any breed or nationality."

"I agree," Leslie said quickly. "I don't care a twopenny damn about the Boers stealing gold from the banks, but mistreating women and children is beyond the pale."

Andrew nodded slowly. He found it hard to reconcile such a callous treatment of women with the Boers he had encountered during the Transvaal War. *Maybe town Burghers are a different breed from the Boers from the veldt.* He stepped forward again as a couple of young Burghers pushed a Uitlander woman onto one of the open carriages.

"Have a care there!" Andrew pushed the most vocal of the Burghers back. "You can't treat a woman like that."

"They are Uitlanders," the man retorted. "Rooineck women come to steal our gold and our land."

"Leave her!" Andrew snarled, controlling his temper with an effort. He felt Leslie step beside him as more Burghers gathered, shouting at the civilians on the cattle truck as they supported their aggressive comrade. Some yelled at the Uitlanders, with a few teenagers throwing rotten fruit at the scared passengers. One man, bearded and grim-faced, shouted he wanted to shoot everything that speaks English—until another uniformed railway official hurried over, but rather than join the aggressors, he pushed them back from the train. "Leave these people alone."

The woman passenger faced Andrew for a moment, mouthed her thanks, and squeezed into the open truck. The official noticed a young girl in a thin dress crushed in the farthest corner of the truck, slipped off his heavy greatcoat and passed it to her.

"Keep warm," he said in a thick accent. "It is cold at night."

"Good man," Andrew said, nodding his approval.

"Come on, sir," Leslie escorted Andrew away.

"I should have known better," Andrew said as the train moved off in a hissing cloud of steam. "I don't like bullies." He watched the train leave the station and into the overcast morning. "It's threatening rain," he said. "Those women in the cattle trucks will have a torrid time. If all the Boers feel like this lot in Johannesburg, I can see their journey being very unpleasant."

"That's what we'll say in our report, sir," Leslie told him. "I am sure you have seen worse along the Northwest Frontier."

"I have," Andrew agreed, "but that doesn't make the situation here any better."

They heard a commotion and saw a pair of Zarps holding a revolver to a short civilian's head. One Zarp threatened to shoot the man as the other screwed on a pair of heavy handcuffs to his wrists.

When the railway official moved to intervene, the Zarp shoved him roughly aside.

"No," Andrew prevented Leslie from intervening. "Your accent would give you away. Best leave now. The Zarps have been watching us since I intervened with the lady."

Leslie grunted. "I hope this nonsense turns into open war, sir. I'll enjoy shooting these people." He lowered his hat to hide his face and glared at the closest Zarp.

Andrew shook his head. "I don't understand it," he said. "The Boers I met twenty years ago were decent, hardworking men of the soil and not at all vindictive. I can't see them treating women and children in such a manner. This cruelty is a side of their character I was unaware of."

Leslie stirred uneasily. "Let's get back to Natal, sir. I think we've seen enough here." He glanced at the fast-disappearing train. "Thank God the British don't make war on women and children."

Andrew led the way from the station, ignoring the Zarps. "Please, God, we never stoop that low to fight a war. We'll get back to Natal yet, Leslie. We still have places in the Transvaal to visit."

"Yes, sir," Leslie said, smiling again.

CHAPTER 3

TRANSVAAL, THE ZUID-AFRIKAANSCHE REPUBLIEK

OCTOBER 1899

"Twelve wagons," Andrew said quietly. He leaned back on the slope of the *kopje* with his binoculars steady in tanned hands.

Leslie pencilled the number in a small black notebook. "That makes thirty in the last two days," he said.

Andrew nodded. "We'll go down after dark and see what they're carrying."

Leslie closed his notebook and replaced it in the breast pocket of his jacket. "Probably the same as all the others," he said.

"Probably," Andrew agreed, "but we'll make sure."

They remained where they were, surveying the limitless expanse of the veldt. Andrew saw mile after aching mile of dun-coloured grass, broken by the occasional eruption of a *kopje* or the green streak that signified a riverbed. A few farmhouses and the associated barns were scattered across the land, with the fields spreading around, grazed by fat cattle.

A team of eighteen oxen pulled each wagon that creaked past. Skilful native drivers wielded long whips and addressed each beast by name, encouraging the lazy, praising the hard-working and moving with the confidence of men who knew their worth. The ox-wagons seemed to belong to this landscape: slow, enduring, nearly as natural as the sharp cracking of the whips, which sounded in contrast to the patient endurance of the beasts and the turning wheels of the vehicles.

In such wagons, the Boers had ground north in the Great Trek, escaping British rule to carve out their independent states in the heart of Southern Africa. Andrew watched the rolling wagons, with the same pattern in use seventy years later, when steamships controlled the seas and steam railways sliced through continents on steel rails.

As the sun eased to the hazy horizon, the long wagon train stopped. The dust gradually settled, and the oxen relaxed in response to the drivers' whistles. As if by instinct, the wagons laagered, forming a rough circle with the beasts inside. The escorting riders slipped off their shaggy ponies and spoke for a few moments, their rough voices carrying through the clear air of the veldt. One man laughed, with others joining in, and the servants made a fire within the laager.

"Give them a couple of hours to settle down," Andrew said. "Then we'll have a look." He leaned back against the rock at his back, content to wait. Campaigning in Africa and Asia had taught him patience and the necessity to rest whenever possible. He felt his companion fidgeting and smiled. Leslie was new to such ventures and would learn, as all young officers did.

The laager was a full mile from Andrew's position on the *kopje*. He waited until the sun had dipped beyond the world's rim and the campfires flickered across the velvet-dark night, with the scent of cooking fires and coffee drifting on the wind.

"Follow me," Andrew said, lifting a bull's-eye lantern from his saddle pack.

Leslie grunted and raised himself from the ground. They checked their horses and slid down the slope and onto the veldt. Andrew took the lead, walking slowly and listening for any sounds. He could not see any sentries but heard the low rumble of men's voices, with occasional loud laughter. A horse whinnied, and Andrew stopped, remaining static for three minutes as he watched the outline of the wagons against the rising stars.

"Sir?" Leslie said.

"Quiet!" Andrew hissed him to silence.

When he judged it safe, Andrew moved again, placing each foot carefully on the ground as he neared the laager. One of the oxen bellowed, encouraging his companions to join him, and for a few moments, their calls filled the air. Circling the laager to the side furthest from the oxen, Andrew selected a heavy-laden vehicle.

"Watch my back," Andrew whispered.

Leslie nodded. He looked nervous, with his eyes flickering from side to side.

Andrew unfastened the laces that closed the wagon's canvas cover and slid inside. He lit the lantern, sliding the shutter nearly shut so it only emitted a thin thread of light. As he expected, the interior was packed with wooden cases, with barely room for him to fit.

Andrew positioned the lantern so the beam shone on the fastenings of the nearest case. The top was screwed down and secured with heavy metal bands. Rather than struggle with the screws, Andrew inserted his knife between two of the rough planks that made up the side of the case. He shaved off a sliver of wood and tried to insert his fingers into the case. When the opening was too small, Andrew sliced off more wood, scuffing the shavings away with his foot so there was no visible evidence. He halted when he heard a noise outside, closed the shutter to block the light and crouched down, swearing when a gust of wind flapped the open wagon cover.

The noise ended. Andrew counted a slow hundred and began work again, easing open the lantern shutter and shaving off another sliver of wood. He tried his fingers again, gasping as the rough wood scraped his knuckles. He squeezed out a single brass cartridge, grunted in satisfaction, slid the bullet into his side pocket and dragged the case around so the damaged side was not visible.

"Sir!" Leslie hissed. "Are you all right?"

"Yes. Keep watch!"

The wagon held a score of similar cases. Andrew counted them before he left, blew out the lantern and left the wagon, securing the cover before he climbed to the ground. Leslie was outside, fidgeting with nervous impatience.

"Any luck?" Leslie whispered.

"Ammunition," Andrew replied. He led them fifty yards from the wagons and lay prone to examine the cartridge.

"What kind of bullet is it?" Leslie asked.

"Rimless bottleneck rifle cartridge," Andrew replied. "Point two-seven-five calibre, or seven millimetre if you prefer."

"Mauser bullet?" Leslie asked.

"Mauser bullet," Andrew confirmed. "German-manufactured. They come in clips for the Mauser Model 1895."

"We haven't found any rifles yet, sir," Leslie said.

"We'll try another wagon," Andrew decided.

With the Mauser cartridge safely in his pocket, Andrew led them around the circumference of the laager. By now, the campfires were dying down.

"Choose a wagon," Andrew invited.

"This one is as good as any."

The cover was laced tightly shut, so Andrew spent nervous minutes on the driving step before he slipped inside and relit the lantern. He immediately saw that Leslie had chosen well, with long wooden cases piled in the back of the wagon.

Fortunately, the lid of the topmost case was loose, possibly because somebody had already checked the contents. Andrew slid it open and nodded at the strong smell of gun oil. A dozen bolt-action Mauser rifles, packed in straw, lay inside.

"1895 pattern," Andrew murmured, lifting one of the rifles. He found it beautifully balanced and ready for a clip of cartridges. "It's a lovely weapon." He sighted on the neighbouring wagon, with the weapon sliding against his shoulder as if made for him. *I would not like to be on the wrong end of this rifle.*

Andrew quickly replaced the Mauser and eased the lid back into place. He froze and doused the lantern as somebody spoke a few yards outside the wagon. Sliding to the floor, Andrew lay still, hoping nobody had seen his movement through the thick canvas wagon cover. The man spoke again, the words clear to Andrew, although he spoke in Afrikaans.

"Only five more days, and we'll be in Pretoria."

A second man laughed. "You're missing your wife."

"Not as much as she's missing me."

The voices died away as the men sauntered past. Andrew remained still for a moment, counting the cases in the wagon. When he judged it safe, he slid out and crawled into the darkness outside the laager.

"I was getting worried, sir," Leslie said.

"So was I," Andrew replied. "That wagon was full of Mausers."

Leslie nodded. "As we thought. What now, sir?"

Andrew considered for a moment. "Now we return to the horses, grab some sleep and see what else we can find before we file our final report."

"I'LL BE GLAD TO GET BACK TO NATAL," LESLIE SAID, stretching as they rode slowly across the endless dun veldt. He looked around him. "I hope we return to the Transvaal with an army to bring these people to heel."

"Do you want a war with your neighbours?" Andrew asked.

Leslie hawked and spat dust-laden spittle on the ground. "I hate the Boers and everything they stand for," he said. "You saw how they treated the Uitlanders in Jo'burg."

"I saw," Andrew replied briefly. "A war will bring more suffering, not less."

"A war will end their insolence, sir," Leslie insisted. "We've put up with them for far too long."

Andrew glanced at the younger man. "Have you ever been to war, Lieutenant?"

Leslie hesitated before replying. "Not yet, sir, but I'm willing to do my bit for the Empire."

"I've seen a few wars," Andrew told him quietly. "None of them were pretty."

They rode in silence for the next few minutes, looking around them. A *kopje* rose in the distance, appearing a few miles away, although Andrew knew the clear air of the veldt made distances deceptive. "How far would you say that *kopje* is?"

"About twenty miles," Leslie said. "We might make it by nightfall, with luck." He adjusted the bandoliers that crossed his chest. "Are you looking forward to getting back to Natal, sir?"

Andrew nodded. "I am," he said and smiled. "I hope there's a letter from my wife. I haven't heard from her for a while."

Leslie grinned. "I understand, sir." He chuckled. "You have to keep an eye on these women. When the cat's away, the mice will play, eh? Out of sight, out of mind!"

"Nothing like that!" Andrew snapped. "We've been married for nearly twenty years, damnit! I just want to hear from her."

"Of course, sir, I do apologise," Leslie said smoothly.

They were quiet again, with Andrew thinking of Mariana and his left thigh beginning to bother him. He had been wounded on the North-West Frontier two years previously, and the injury ached from time to time. As he slowed to rub the pain away, he saw a ribbon of dust rising in the distance. "Slow down," he said.

"I see it," Leslie said. He shifted in his saddle, placing a hand on the butt of his rifle.

"We won't need that," Andrew told him.

"It could be a Boer commando. We don't know if we're at peace or war," Leslie said.

Andrew shook his head. "More likely, it's a group of men riding to market, or to a wedding, or into town to buy supplies."

Leslie reluctantly released his rifle. "If you say so, sir." He narrowed his eyes, peering into the distance.

"I say so," Andrew said. "Just ride slowly and acknowledge them as they pass."

Leslie took a deep breath. "They could shoot us as spies."

"Why should they think we are spies?" Andrew asked. "We are just two men riding across the veldt."

The dust came closer, and Andrew watched as a body of riders emerged. A man with a long, untidy grey beard led, with three middle-aged men next, followed by half a dozen younger men, some with the immature faces of youths.

The oldest man acknowledged Andrew and Leslie by raising his hat and speaking a few words of greeting. When Andrew replied in kind, the men rode on. The youngsters examined Andrew and Leslie until one of the older men snapped at them to mind their manners, and they looked away.

"They don't look like farmers going to market," Leslie said. "I wonder where they are headed."

"So do I," Andrew replied, trying to hide his concern. "We'll follow them. Keep a distance between us so we create less dust."

THE VILLAGE OF VOGELBURG HUDDLED IN THE MIDDLE OF THE veldt as if the surrounding space overawed the seventy-eight houses. There was a broad main street with a market square where a second road intersected at right angles, a church that stood in simple pride, two stores and half a dozen lesser streets with a few individual houses. Each house boasted a stoep, where men, women and children watched the riders arrive.

"We'll stay here." Andrew guided Leslie to a side street with a view of the market square. "Dismount and watch."

Two women watched Andrew and Leslie dismount, discussed them briefly and moved on to a more interesting subject.

The horsemen gathered in the square, with others joining them singly and in small groups. Everybody seemed to know each other, with the grey-bearded elders greeting each other with formal hat-raisings and the youngsters boisterous and loud. Andrew felt a sense of *déjà vu* as he watched, transported back nearly twenty years to the months before the Transvaal War.

"It's a commando gathering," Leslie commented. "They're gathering for war."

"It looks very like it," Andrew said. "But I think it's a *weaponshaw*—a meeting to show every man is willing to fight and to check they all have a rifle." He lowered his voice in case the English language betrayed him as a Uitlander.

Andrew observed the men. Some were townsmen in sober dark suits and bowler hats, and a few wore tailed coats and top hats as if they were attending a funeral or a wedding. However, most were countrymen, farmers from the veldt. Often shaggybearded, with tanned faces, corduroy trousers and flapping jackets, they wore floppy-brimmed hats and rode sturdy ponies as if born to the saddle. Every man present, from youngsters in their early teens to lined ancients, looked familiar with the rifles they carried and the heavy bandoliers strung across their chests.

"They're a wild-looking bunch," Leslie said. "Only one degree above savages."

"They certainly look wild," Andrew agreed, mentally comparing them with the quiet farmers from his home on the Scottish-English Border. "But they are very capable fighters." He remembered the Boers advancing at Majuba Hill, driving back some of Britain's best soldiers.

As Leslie studied the riders, he began to look angry. "Will they fight against us? They look confident."

"They'll fight if they feel the need," Andrew replied. "I hope we don't go to war."

"It looks like they're thirsting to attack us, sir," Leslie said. "We weren't ready for them last time. They caught us by surprise."

"Count the numbers," Andrew said, refusing to be drawn into a discussion about a war that ended nearly two decades previously. "See what kind of rifles they carry."

"What's happening now, sir?" Leslie asked as the horsemen parted to allow a wagon to creak into the square.

"Watch and see," Andrew said. He ignored the group of women who had returned, evidently wondering why they were not in the square with the rest of the men.

When the wagon stopped outside the church, a tall, dignified man beside the driver stood up. Wearing a black frock coat and a top hat, he addressed the suddenly silent crowd, although Andrew was too far away to hear the words.

"What's he saying, sir?" Leslie asked.

Andrew shook his head. "I don't know."

The dignified man spoke for fifteen minutes, with men in the crowd responding with an occasional nod or an approving growl. When the speaker gave an order, the driver dismounted and stepped to the back of the wagon.

As the farmers and townsmen moved forward to the wagon, the driver handed each man a brand-new Mauser and a packet of ammunition.

"What the devil?" Leslie asked.

"You were right. The Boers are arming for war," Andrew said. "These German Mausers are superior to anything we have. They are as accurate, and the Boers can reload them with a clip of ammunition while we must reload our Lee-Metfords one bullet at a time. That will give the Boers an advantage, and if each Boer carries an identical rifle, they can share ammunition."

Leslie grunted. "The war will come soon, then."

"I'd say so," Andrew agreed. He became aware that the crowd of women was growing, openly asking why they were not with the other men. "Time we were out of here," he said.

"Uitlanders!" one of the women shouted, pointing an accusing finger. "Rooinecks!"

"Mount and ride," Andrew ordered. "We've overstayed our welcome."

Leslie was astride his horse before Andrew finished speaking, glancing at the women and kicking out at one who came too close.

They left at a trot, with women shouting insults after them and one throwing handfuls of mud and small stones, which all fell short.

"Do we have sufficient information now?" Leslie asked.

"I should say so," Andrew replied. "Time to head back." He glanced over his shoulder. "Nobody is following, but we'll put some distance between us and Vogelburg before we stop."

CHAPTER 4

TRANSVAAL, THE ZUID-AFRIKAANSCHE REPUBLIEK AND LADYSMITH

OCTOBER 1899

"It will be war soon," Dannie said, stepping aside and lifting his hat to a passing woman. "Oom Paul has exchanged angry notes with the British government, and the Orange Free State has a fixed alliance with us. The Zuid-Afrikaansche Republic will not fight alone this time."

Hendrik nodded gravely, looking around at the streets of Pretoria. The Transvaal capital was busy, with batteries of modern artillery rattling through the broad streets. Hendrik nodded to the men in unfamiliar uniforms who sat alongside the shining guns.

"They do not look like Boers," Hendrik said. "Are they foreign mercenaries?"

"They are the States Artillery," Dannie explained. "Citizens like you and I, but trained by German and French experts. They will give the Rooinecks a hot fright."

Hendrik watched as a small commando—a mixture of mature men and beardless boys—rode past, all carrying rifles. The younger men were laughing, enjoying the excitement of going to war, while the older men looked serious, knowing what lay ahead.

"Where are they going?" Hendrik asked. "Everybody seems to be going somewhere. Nobody is content to remain at home on their farm." He lifted his hat as Michal joined them.

"They are going to the Natal border," Michal said. "Ready to invade."

"We are not at war with the British yet," Hendrik reminded him.

"We will be soon," Michal replied. "Then we will drive the Rooinecks into the sea and reclaim the Cape. The land will be ours again."

Hendrik pulled a tobacco pouch from his pocket and began to fill his pipe. "That might take some time," he said.

"It will be worth it," Michal told him. "It will be worth it to regain what is ours."

"Ja," Hendrik lit his pipe, puffing out thick clouds of smoke. "Holding what is yours is good. I will hold my farm."

Dannie laughed. "If the Hollanders of Cape Colony and Natal join us, we will defeat the Rooinecks before Christmas."

Piet stood a few feet away, listening without speaking. He looked at the bright sky. "If the Rooinecks try to take our land, we must drive them away," he said, deep-voiced. "I will fight for that."

Colonel Robert Graham placed Andrew's written report on his desk and leaned back in his chair. His face was as tanned as any Boer, and his hands as meaty as a labourer as he surveyed Andrew and Leslie.

"Thank you, gentlemen," Graham said without any change of

expression on his face. "You have added to our store of information and confirmed the reports of others." His Ulster accent seemed to add emphasis to his words.

Andrew and Leslie stood in front of Graham's desk, a breeze from the window rustling the map of Southern Africa that occupied most of the wall at his side. "What have other people discovered, sir?" Andrew asked.

Colonel Graham considered the question before he replied. "Without going into details, Baird, I can tell you that the Transvaal Boers have some modern artillery—French 75mm and 155mm Creusot guns—which outrange anything we have in Africa."

"Trust the French to arm our potential enemies," Leslie said.

"The French are still smarting over the Fashoda affair," Colonel Graham reminded.* "But the Germans have also provided the Boers with 120mm Krupp howitzers, in addition to the Mauser rifles and ammunition you discovered."

Andrew grunted; he remembered the German connection during the Transvaal War. "I expected the French and Dutch to favour the Boers but not the Germans. We have fought shoulder-to-shoulder with them for centuries. All of Europe seems to dislike the United Kingdom. They're rushing to aid the Boers."

"Not only the Europeans are aiding the Boers," Colonel Graham said. "The Boers have purchased more than twenty 37mm Vickers-Maxim quick-firers—pom-poms—from us."

"From Britain?" Leslie gasped.

"Yes indeed," the Colonel said. "To some businessmen, money matters more than patriotism or the lives of British soldiers. The Boers also have Maxim machine guns, which means we will face an enemy as well, if not better armed than ourselves

---

* The Fashoda Incident of 1898 was a territorial dispute between Britain and France in what is now South Sudan. Both nations tried to claim a section of land, but eventually, France withdrew.

—an enemy who knows his land like the back of his hand and is an expert shot and horseman."

"Maybe armed, maybe," Leslie said. "But can the Boers fire the damned things? Most are back-veldt farmers—rustics still living in the seventeenth century."

Graham nodded sadly. "Pretoria has hired foreign experts to train them to fire the damned things."

"There was foreign support for the Boers in the Transvaal War," Andrew reminded them. "It threatened a lot without amounting to much."

"President Kruger has sent ambassadors to European countries to elicit support," Colonel Graham said. "In particular, they want the Dutch, Germans, French and Russians to help them—diplomatically if we remain at peace, and militarily if this nonsense ends in warfare."

"Will it end in war, sir?" Leslie sounded almost hopeful.

"Almost invariably," Graham replied.

"How are we placed, sir?" Andrew asked. "How strong is our army in Natal and Cape Colony?"

"We're placed badly at present," Graham replied with brutal frankness. "Our stores only have scarlet and blue uniforms—nothing in khaki—and you know how the Boers love pipeclayed belts across bright scarlet."

"That's a bad start," Andrew admitted.

Graham shook his head. "Oh, there's worse," he said. "We know that the Boers are probably the finest mounted riflemen in the world, yet our powers-that-be have neglected to build up a reserve of horses, horseshoes or saddles." He forced a wry smile. "Maybe the War Office expects us to be bareback warriors."

"I hope the War Office sees sense soon," Andrew said. "The Boers with modern Mausers will be even more formidable opponents."

"Modern Mausers and modern artillery," Graham murmured. "I hope our politicians can at least delay any war until reinforcements arrive from Britain."

"In the Transvaal War, the Boers had a couple of ancient pieces of artillery they dug up from under the ground, with a local blacksmith as the armourer," Andrew reminded them.

"What do we have for ordnance, sir?" Leslie asked.

"Over 80 million rounds of rifle ammunition," Graham opened a file and read the contents. "Plus 66 million rounds of illegal dumdum bullets that we can't use. We only have 200 rounds of artillery ammunition for each of our guns—barely sufficient for one decent battle."

"How about men, sir? How many do we have?" Andrew asked.

Colonel Graham stood up and paced the length of the room before he replied. "In the summer, we had ten thousand regular soldiers and twenty-four field guns."

"In Natal, sir?" Andrew was surprised to learn there were so many.

"No, Baird. In all of South Africa."

"Ah," Andrew said. Ten thousand men would be spread very thin to defend such a vast area. "But we also have local forces."

"We have," Graham confirmed, "but even so, the Boers will outnumber us—and if things deteriorate, the Hollanders, the Dutch in Cape Colony and Natal, may join their compatriots."

"You said in summer, sir," Andrew searched for good news. "I believe Milner has brought in reinforcements since then."

Alfred Milner was the British High Commissioner for Southern Africa and Governor of Cape Colony. He was a recognised imperialist who supported British expansion in Southern Africa.

"He has," Graham said. "Including local forces, we now have 22,000 men. The regulars are trained, but most of the colonials are not. Between 11 and 12,000 are in Natal, which, as you know, is the colony most vulnerable to Boer attack."

"How many men can the Boers muster, sir?" Leslie asked.

"If the Orange Free State joins the Transvaal, as seems likely," Graham said, "their combined forces could top 50,000 riders.

Men between sixteen and sixty are expected to fight—and most will. They are naturally hardy, ride like centaurs, shoot like marksmen and have a natural eye for cover."

"They are a formidable people," Andrew agreed.

"We have a score to settle with them," the Colonel said. "If it comes to war, we will recreate the natural order and wipe something off the slate." He sat down and nodded. "Well, gentlemen, you have done all I demanded of you. Now, you may return to your respective regiments."

"Yes, sir," Baird saluted, and they left the office. He shook Leslie's hand as they bid each other farewell, but he was glad when the lieutenant marched away.

I did not take to you, Damien Leslie, and I hope we never serve together.

LIEUTENANT-COLONEL GEORGE SYDNEY NEWLAND OF THE Second Battalion, Royal Malverns, poured himself a South African brandy, tasted it, screwed up his face and added more to his glass. "They call this stuff Cape Smoke," he observed casually to the gathered officers of his regiment. "It is a drink without class, like the people of this damned country. I'll be glad when our time here ends, and the War Office posts us elsewhere."

The officers either nodded in agreement or said nothing. Andrew sat in the middle, observing his fellows without feeling part of the battalion. The Royal Malverns were an ancient regiment with a history that stretched back centuries and a fighting record second to none, and the Second Battalion, once the 113th Foot, were a later addition. Andrew's family, the Windrushes, had been part of that history from the beginning, with his father having spent much of his career in the Malverns. Andrew had carved out another path, and only his father's influence had found him a place in the Officers' Mess. Although most of his peers treated him with civility, Andrew sensed a reserve, as though they resented his presence.

Newland perched on the edge of his desk and surveyed the men before him. Tall, spare and gaunt-faced, Newland was the ideal of a British infantry officer, with his athletic figure, his bristling moustache and a row of medal ribbons that proved his experience and courage.

"We daily expect to be at war with the Boers," Newland said. "When that happens, we will do our duty like gentlemen and soldiers." He slid a cold glance around the officers. "We will win, of course. We are British. As the Colonial Secretary, Joseph Chamberlain, said, I believe in the British race. I believe that the British race is the greatest of governing races the world has ever seen, and there are no limits to its future."

Andrew felt vaguely uncomfortable and stirred uneasily in his seat. He had travelled sufficiently to have learned to distrust the prevailing tide of jingoism and supreme nationalism.*

"We will win the war," Newland continued, "and the Royal Malverns will prove themselves the best regiment in the best army in the world."

Some of the officers responded with a hearty "Hear, hear!" One man, clean-shaven amidst a host of moustached men and slightly old for a lieutenant, caught Andrew's gaze and quickly looked away.

Newland sipped at his brandy. "We have a couple of new officers in the Mess, gentlemen. Some of you will know Captain Andrew Baird."

About half the officers glanced at Andrew, who rose to acknowledge the murmured greetings.

"Captain Baird has joined us by a circuitous route," Newland explained. "He is a veteran of the Zulu War and Majuba, as well

---

* Jingoism was a peculiarly British word that was current at the latter end of the nineteenth century. The phrase came from a popular song when war with Russia seemed likely: "We don't want to fight, yet by jingo, if we do, we've got the ships, we've got the men, and got the money, too!"

as facing King Theebaw in Burma. More recently he fought the along the Khyber with our First Battalion, before being transferred to us because of his local knowledge."

Some officers nodded acknowledgement at Andrew's record, with the veterans assessing him through narrowed eyes. The subalterns looked impressed.

Newland continued. "Baird brought a score of veterans from the First Battalion who preferred to remain abroad rather than return to Blighty. He is the son of General Jack Windrush, who has a long association with the Malverns," Newland concluded. "Both battalions."

"We also have Lieutenant Sinton," Newland said as Andrew sat down, and the clean-shaven lieutenant stood.

"Lieutenant Sinton was educated at Eton before working in civilian life and then attending Sandhurst. He comes from one of the best families in England and chose to serve in the Royal Malverns, although he could have joined the Guards."

Andrew studied Sinton. The lieutenant was tall, slender and as elegant as Newland. He surveyed his fellow officers through laughing blue eyes, with a slightly embarrassed smile on his lips. He acknowledged Andrew's nod with a quick grin.

"Sit down, Lieutenant Sinton," Colonel Newland ordered.

The officers faced their front, where Newland finished his brandy before resuming his speech.

"We are fortunate to have some of the best officers in the world in the Royal Malverns," Newland said, "and must ensure the rankers are up to scratch."

Most of the officers accepted the praise as their due.

"We cannot expect much in the way of individual intelligence from our men," Newland continued. "They come mainly from that part of the population which is poorest, worst fed from infancy, least educated and brought up largely in crowded towns. The remainder are country lads, not naturally men gifted with intelligence."

Again, Andrew stirred uneasily. He knew the faults of the

British soldier. They were unimaginative, often poorly educated and from a deprived background, but they were stubborn, as brave as any soldier in the world and loyal to a fault. In Andrew's opinion, the men deserved better leadership, pay and conditions, but that was true for most sections of the British working class.

"We must do our best to mould them into soldiers," Newland said. "That is your job, before and during the oncoming conflict with our Boerish neighbours."

"They will follow us, sir." Major Cradley was grey-haired and vastly experienced, having been with the Malverns since his youth. He had long since given up any thoughts of promotion and contented himself with being an efficient officer and writing a history of his regiment.

Newland treated Cradley to a cold stare. "Of course they will, Major. We are their officers." He stood up. "That's it, gentlemen. I leave it to you to train the men." He walked from the room, leaving Andrew to wonder if the gathering had been worth his time.

More importantly, if the battalion was going to war, he had to find a couple of new horses. His previous mount was not suitable for the hectic energy of battle. Andrew examined the horses in the British lines, discarding some with hardly a look and examining others with more care.

"What are you looking for?" The lieutenant in charge of the remounts was old for his rank, and had long decided he would go no further in his career, so he could treat senior officers as he chose.

"A sturdy horse that can stand the hard usage of the veldt," Andrew replied. "My last animal wearied quickly and curtailed my activities. Speed is less crucial than endurance, and stamina is better than looks."

The lieutenant recognised a man who understood horseflesh. "I may have some beasts that interest you over here." He nodded to a field on the outskirts of the town. "Most officers want a tall thoroughbred, an Arab with an infusion of English or Irish blood."

Andrew grunted. "A thoroughbred will be grand in a charge or to show off in Hyde Park," he said, "but not as good in a long patrol across the veldt. If I know anything about the Boers, we will do more hard riding than close fighting, so I'll need a couple of horses to suit."

The lieutenant eyed Andrew up and down. "Come this way," he said, stepping towards the field. He walked with the peculiar swaying motion of a man who spent more time in the saddle than on foot.

Eight horses roamed in the small field, most grazing but with two running around the fringe as if hoping to escape.

"These are the ponies we bought from the local farmers," the lieutenant said. "They may be what you are looking for."

Andrew examined the horses for a few moments before he moved forward. One pony had already caught his eye, an ugly, scarred animal standing alone in a corner of the field.

"Are they all salted?" Andrew asked.

The lieutenant nodded. A salted horse was one which had caught distemper and recovered, so it would not suffer from the disease again.

"As far as I am aware."

"Where did that horse come from?" Andrew nodded to the pony standing alone.

"God knows," the lieutenant said. "It came with the rest. It's a morose, cantankerous brute more suited for the glue factory than anything else."

Andrew grinned. "That's a Basuto pony," he said, and walked forward.

Andrew had been riding ever since he could walk and understood horses as well as he knew men. When he moved to Berwick-upon-Tweed, he had spent time with the local farmers, including the Horsemen who ploughed the Berwickshire fields. These men had all been trained in horse management before the

Society of Horsemen accepted them. One man passed on some of their secrets to Andrew.

"Hello, my little friend." Andrew stood a few yards from the Basuto, speaking in Afrikaans and English. The horse laid back its ears, reacting better to Afrikaans than English, and the treats he carried in his pocket also helped.

Within ten minutes, Andrew led the Basuto back to the watching lieutenant. "He's an ugly little beast," he said, "but he won't let me down."

The lieutenant eyed Andrew with new respect. "You managed him well enough, sir," he said. "It looks like you've found yourself a horse."

Andrew noted it was the only time the lieutenant addressed him as sir. "I want another," he said. "Ride one, rest the second."

The lieutenant nodded. "I have a second Basuto," he said. "Come this way, sir."

CHAPTER 5

TRANSVAAL, THE ZUID-AFRIKAANSCHE REPUBLIEK

OCTOBER 1899

"We are the van Niekerk Field Cornetship of the Wessels Commando," Dannie van Niekerk announced grandly. "Together, the Republics have an army of nearly 70,000 men, mostly well mounted and with better weapons than the Rooinecks possess. We also fight for a better reason: to ensure we remain free."

Hendrik listened without much interest. Three of his cattle were sick when he left the farm, and he wondered if they had recovered. He saw Michal hanging on Dannie's words, his eyes glowing with patriotic fervour. Simultaneously, Piet cleaned and examined his new Mauser, gazing down the barrel and making minute alterations to the sights.

"We were part of the parade in honour of President Kruger's birthday," Dannie announced. "Now we shall reclaim Natal for the Republics."

The Niekerk Field Cornetship had attended that parade,

where the commandos had ridden past President Kruger, *Oom Paul*, the man the people hoped would ensure the continued independence of the Republics by defeating the British Empire. While other men had lifted their rifles to salute the president, Hendrik had merely examined the man who had given the British an ultimatum: withdraw your soldiers from near the Republic's borders, or he would declare war.

The assembled Boers had cheered at Kruger's words and celebrated all night, singing, drinking and shouting around their campfires. Michal joined in the jubilation, encouraging the members of the commando to sing the national song and moving from camp to camp, shaking hands with his fellow warriors and introducing himself.

Hendrik could still hear the national anthem, with the rousing words echoing through his head.

"Ken jy die Volk vol heldemoed
en tog so lank verkneg
Hy het geoffer goed en bloed
vir Vryheid en vir reg
Kom burgers! laat die vlae wapper
Ons lyding is verby
Roem in die sege van onse dapp'res
'n Vrye volk is ons!
'n Vrye volk, 'n Vrye volk
'n Vrye, Vrye volk is ons!"

"Know ye the folk full of heroism,
And yet, so long oppressed?
It hath offered property and blood
For freedom and for righteousness.
Come, citizens! Let the flags wave
Our suffering is over;
Praise the victories of our braves:
That free folk are we!

That free folk, that free folk,
That free, free folk are we!"

Piet had raised dark eyebrows at Hendrik. "Youngsters welcome the excitement of war," he said. "But they do not understand the reality."

"Not only youngsters are cheering," Hendrik replied soberly as he saw grey-bearded men wiping damp eyes as they sang.

Piet nodded again. "God willing, we will all still be cheering in a year's time."

"God willing," Hendrik said quietly.

The day following Kruger's birthday, when the British refused to agree to Kruger's demands, the two Boer Republics declared war on the British Empire. Commandant-General Piet Joubert, *Slim Piet* – cunning or smart Piet – took command of the army to invade Natal, and rations of biltong and meal for five days were issued to each man. As the Republics' women braced themselves for war, the flying columns, the vanguard of the Boers' army, rode forward to the Natal border.

"Do you wish to become a corporal?" Dannie asked Hendrik. "You are the most experienced fighter here. You fought the Rooinecks at Majuba."

"*Nee*," Hendrik shook his head emphatically. "That was twenty years ago when I was a young man. I am a farmer, not a fighter, and never a corporal."

"As you wish," Dannie said. "I thought I would ask, but you are right. We would be better with a dynamic, more thrusting man."

Despite his young age, Michal was appointed corporal in Wessels' commando. Hendrik was first to shake the young man's hand.

"You are the best man for the corporalship," Hendrik told him as Michal grinned proudly.

As the commandos merged, the Boer army moved to the Natal border in a mass of horsemen, guns, wagons and cattle.

"We are part of history," Michal shouted, watching the host head to the border. He removed his hat and tossed back his blonde hair. The sun caught his profile, glinting on his bright blue eyes and highlighting his jaw with its neatly cropped beard.

You set out with such hope on this crusade to return our land, Hendrik thought. *I hope you find what you seek.*

The Boer army poured around the village of Volksrust, where Joubert split them up before they ventured into the mountains of northern Natal.

"Our commando will stay together," Commandant Adriaan Wessels told them. "We are large enough that we do not have to merge with another." He looked over his men. "I know most of you personally. We are neighbours and farmers; I know your sisters and wives, and you know my wife. Some of us fought side by side against the Rooinecks twenty years ago."

The men nodded in agreement. They knew and trusted Adriaan Wessels as a good farmer, a husband and father, and a man blooded in battle.

"This war will be different, though," Adriaan said. "The Rooinecks no longer wear scarlet, so they do not give us such a fine target."

Most men laughed, although few had fired at, or ever seen, a British soldier.

"We can still shoot them," Wessels said. "Rooinecks are easier targets than eland or springbok!"

The men laughed again, easy in each other's company and confident of a quick victory against the ponderous, infantry-heavy British army.

Adriaan lifted his voice to carry to every man in his commando. "Come on, men! Let's push the Rooinecks into the sea and regain our land!"

Even Piet cheered, with only Hendrik reserved in his reaction. He joined his fellows in moving forward, yet his mind was still busy on his farm.

"Was that the mail?" Andrew asked Smith, his soldier-servant.

"That was the mail, sir," Smith assured him. "Letters for you." He stood at attention, pink and peeling with sunburn. "I heard that the Boojers stole a hundred bags of our mail when they robbed the gold train, sir. Maybe your other letters were there."

"Maybe so," Andrew agreed. "Dismissed, Smith."

"Thank you, sir!" Smith threw a hasty salute that would have disgraced a second-day recruit and retreated, leaving Andrew with his mail.

There were only two letters where Andrew had hoped for at least half a dozen. His mother wrote one letter a week, always two pages of immaculate script with every word carefully crafted and written in perfect copperplate. In contrast, Mariana could write two or three letters daily in her wild, undisciplined scrawl. Andrew could always judge his wife's mood by her letters and hear her voice between the words. Andrew held Mariana's letter, savouring the pleasure of reading the contents. He did not know the writing on the second letter and pushed it aside.

Settling down in the cane chair he had brought from India, Andrew opened Mariana's letter.

The Boers, Kruger, the regiment, and all Southern Africa can go hang for the next half hour.

"As I said in my last letter," Mariana began, "I've been having fun with Charlie. We've been riding together and visited Berwick market. Next week we plan to take the train to Edinburgh to go to the theatre. Won't that be grand?"

Andrew looked for a date at the top of the page, but Mariana neglected such formality.

Who the devil is Charlie? And what right does he have to spend time with my wife?

"Mrs Lightfoot is such a joy in looking after the children

while Charlie and I go out. Sometimes we take the children, and don't they have fun with the two of us?"

I'll have words with Charlie and Mrs Lightfoot when I return.

Andrew found references to Charlie in every second paragraph of the five-page letter, lauding Charlie's prowess in riding, singing, croquet, rowing on the Tweed and even his affection for the children.

"Charlie is quite taken with the children, especially Simla. They are becoming quite close."

Are they, by God?

"Charlie is even more interested in the Arthurian legends than I am and is an authority on Border history."

As Andrew read, Lieutenant Leslie's words returned to him, "while the cat's away, the mice will play."

Andrew shook his head. *No,* he told himself. *Mariana would never do that. She is as faithful to me as I am to her.*

Andrew finished reading the letter and folded it back inside the envelope. He had never doubted Mariana during nearly twenty years of marriage and shook the idea away.

I wondered why she was determined to return home rather than come with me to Natal. After all, she grew up here. Did she rush home to meet this Charles fellow, whoever he is?

Nonsense!

Andrew scanned the second letter, which proved to be from his factor. Three paragraphs contained business news about the upkeep of the farm and livestock. Only the last paragraph troubled him.

"I am happy to say that Mrs Baird is keeping well, and her new friend keeps her occupied. Major Dixon looks after her adequately."

Andrew put the letter down and took the pipe from his pocket. Only then did he realise his hands were shaking.

Charlie? Major Dixon? What the devil is Mariana up to?

※

"GENERAL WHITE HAS DECIDED TO MAKE LADYSMITH THE British Army's headquarters in Natal," Major Cradley said.

General Sir George White, VC, was a veteran soldier who commanded the British troops in Natal.

Andrew nodded, with his thoughts more on Mariana than Southern Africa.

"What are your thoughts on that?" Cradley asked.

"Ladysmith is not a large place, but the most important town in northern Natal," Andrew replied. "It will be difficult to hold if the Boers invade."

Cradley looked up sharply. "Oh? Why is that?"

"Ladysmith sits in a bowl surrounded by hills," Andrew said at once. "We'll have to garrison the hills, or the Boers will overlook the town. That will mean a large garrison."

"The Boers will have to reach Ladysmith first," Cradley pointed out. "We can stop them at the frontier."

"We might," Andrew agreed. "That would depend on General White in Ladysmith and General Penn Symons in Dundee." He squeezed out a smile. "Ours not to reason why."

"I know little about General White," Cradley said, watching Andrew through bright, intelligent eyes.

"General White is a fighting man," Andrew said. "An Irishman who served through the Indian Mutiny and won his Victoria Cross in the Second Afghan War. Afghanistan was good to him: he was promoted to brevet lieutenant colonel and a CB. After that, there was no stopping him. He was a major general before 1890 and then commanded the army in India before he came here."

"And Penn Symons?" Cradley asked.

Andrew wondered if Major Cradley was testing his knowledge. "Penn Symons is a Cornishman, I believe," Andrew said. "He and I have been through the same campaigns, fighting the Galekas and Zulus, campaigning in Burma and the North-West Frontier."

Cradley nodded. "Yet he is a general, and you languish as a captain."

"Penn Symons is a career soldier," Andrew said. "I resigned my commission and only returned to the Colours a couple of years back."

Cradley nodded. "You should be more advanced in your rank," he said. He looked up as the door banged open, and Lieutenant Sinton burst into the Officers' Mess.

"The Boers have declared war!" Sinton nearly shouted. "They've invaded Natal and the Cape Colony with thousands of men!"

Andrew took a deep breath. Some of the officers cheered; others looked thoughtful.

"That's it, then," Cradley said. "The die is cast now."

"At least all the uncertainty is over," Andrew said. "As they've declared war and invaded us, nobody can say we were the aggressors."

"They will, though," Cradley said. "Every European Power will blame us for everything that happens. They always do."

Andrew produced his pipe and began to fill it with tobacco. "Let's hope we put up a better show than last time we fought the Boers."

"There will be no Majubas this time," Cradley said grimly. "I guarantee you that."[*]

Andrew smiled faintly. "I wish you had some way of guaranteeing your guarantee." He lit his pipe and leaned back, but rather than contemplate the coming war, he thought about Mariana.

Who the devil is Charlie?

---

[*] The Battle of Majuba, 27th February 1881, was the last battle of the First Boer or Transvaal War. The Boers defeated a small British force on Majuba Hill and retained their independence.

CHAPTER 6

LADYSMITH AND DUNDEE, NATAL, SOUTH AFRICA

OCTOBER 1899

Major Crawley thrust his head into the Officers' Mess. "Get your men ready, gentlemen! B and C Companies are going to Dundee to reinforce General Penn Symons' force!"

"That's our companies, Baird," Captain Boswell said, smiling.

"I know." Andrew was already on his feet. He had barely spoken to Boswell but thought him a competent, if unimaginative, officer.

"The colonel is also sending a platoon of Mounted Infantry," Crawley added.

Andrew liked the idea of Mounted Infantry, men who rode to battle and fought on foot, but thought they seldom reached their potential. He suspected many men volunteered for the unit because they thought riding a horse was easier than marching.

By the usual skill British soldiers possessed, Andrew's C Company already knew they were on the move. The NCOs had passed the news to Lieutenant Sinton before he mustered the men, with busy corporals ensuring each man had the correct equipment.

"You have a forty-mile march ahead of you," Andrew said when C Company were on parade. He searched every face, wondering that so many were very young men. "Make sure your boots are sound, and you've filled your water bottle and ammunition pouches." Andrew took Sergeant Kenny aside. "Make sure their canteens are full of water and not spirits," he said quietly.

"I will, sir," Kenny replied. Of average height and broad-chested, the sergeant sported a chestful of medal ribbons. Andrew judged him to be around forty years old.

"And every man should carry a biscuit at least," Andrew said. "God alone knows when the commissariat wagons catch up."

"I'll ensure they do, sir," Kenny assured him.

The Malverns marched before dawn the following day, with Andrew riding ahead of his company. He sent scouts ahead and on the flanks, with warnings to watch for bodies of Boer horsemen.

"Many of these men have never experienced a march in wartime conditions," Boswell walked his horse beside Andrew's. "They look excited."

"They'll soon get into the swing of things," Andrew said. "The first skirmish will settle them and sort the men from the boys. And there are a lot of boys in the ranks."

"Too many," Boswell echoed Andrew's earlier thoughts. "The army looks younger every year."

Andrew pulled his horse aside and watched the khaki-clad column march past, kicking up the dust and with the sky vast and blue above.

I wonder how these youngsters will cope with the hard-riding horsemen of the veldt. Some of them have only learned which end of a rifle sends out the bullet, and the city boys are nervous outside a street.

Hills dominated Dundee, with the 1500-foot-high Impati to the north and the flat-topped kopjes of Lennox and Talana, eight hundred feet high, two miles to the east. The Malverns set up their camp beside General Penn Symons' base three-quarters of a mile west of the town at the bottom of a shallow depression. Andrew and Boswell posted pickets, had men dig latrines, and checked their surroundings.

"Where are the Boers, sir?" Andrew asked as the general held an officers' conference.

"They invaded Natal on the 12th," Penn Symons said. "On the 13th, they rode into Charlestown, in the north of Natal, and pushed on to Newcastle."

"I know Newcastle well," Andrew said. "My wife's parents are buried there. And her sister."

Penn Symons did not hide his smile. "Then you are the right man for the job, Captain Baird. Take out a patrol of Mounted Infantry and see what you can find. I want to know if the Boers are still advancing and what force they are in. No heroics, Baird; it's a reconnaissance, not a fighting patrol."

"I'll take a dozen men," Andrew decided, interested in observing the Mounted Infantry at first-hand. "Veterans, though, not youths fresh from the publics. But I want Lieutenant Sinton."

"Take him, by all means," Penn Symons said.

The patrol left two hours before dawn, each man with a spare mount and carrying extra ammunition. Andrew had them muffle the horses' hooves and ride in extended order, with each man visible to the next to ensure nobody strayed in the dark.

"I don't know how good you are," he told them. "But obey orders and stay on your horses, and we'll be fine."

The men looked at him, eyes gleaming in the night. Only Sinton mustered a laugh.

Andrew led, moving slowly until he had assessed each man's riding ability. When he was satisfied the men were capable on horseback, he increased their speed and headed north towards Newcastle, listening for the sounds of hoofbeats in the night.

"How far are we going, sir?" Sinton asked.

"Until we find something positive," Andrew replied. "I want to ride at least halfway up that hill," he pointed to a bulky hill ahead, dark against the greying sky of dawn, "and scan the land from there."

"Yes, sir," Sinton said.

"Make sure nobody strays," Andrew ordered and pushed on, watching the sun gleam beyond the eastern horizon. He had seen that same sun rise over Burmese jungle and Khyber hills, but here in South Africa, it always reminded him of his early campaigns when he met Mariana.

Damn that man, Charlie, intruding into my thoughts!

Andrew halted on the flanks of the hill and lifted his binoculars. He swept the horizon, where the great mountains swept down to the plains, grunting when he saw movement.

"There they are," he said.

The wagons coiled from the north, wagon after wagon pulled by extended teams of bullocks, with armed Boers riding on either side. Even with the binoculars, the figures were tiny, seemingly ant-like, yet Andrew knew each mounted man would be an expert horseman and a more than capable shot.

Sinton nodded, adjusting the focus of his binoculars. "How many are there, for God's sake?" he asked.

"Thousands," Andrew replied soberly. "It's up to us to discover just how many thousands. We'll move closer. Remain here with the men, Sergeant!" Taking his spare horse, Andrew pushed closer, blessing the clear air that enabled him to see into the distance.

The columns of wagons extended for miles, a steady Boer encroachment into Natal. Each wagon held fighting men or supplies, with some carrying women and children in the strangest invasion Andrew had ever seen. He focused on one wagon, where a woman in a long dress drove the team, and bright yellow wheels flashed in the burgeoning sunlight.

"The Transvaal and Orange Free State must have drained all their men into Natal," Sinton said quietly. "Are they trying to colonise us?"

Andrew examined the wagons through his binoculars. "Maybe so," he replied. "If I recall, the Boers were in Natal before we took over. They might aim to reclaim the land."

The wagons rolled on, grimly determined men guiding them through the mountain passes and shaggy, bearded riders leaning back in their saddles as they pushed further into British territory. Andrew thought the scene could have come from the seventeenth or eighteenth century, except for the very modern rifles each man carried.

"Sir!" Sinton pointed to the left.

Andrew saw the ribbon of dust that warned of riders approaching the hill. "Time to leave," he said. "Let's get the MI back to camp."

Andrew led the Mounted Infantry at a canter, with the horses kicking up dust and Sinton acting as rearguard. Glancing over his shoulder, Andrew saw the riders following, still distant but slowly drawing closer. "Pick up the speed, MI!"

The Mounted Infantry pushed harder. Andrew aimed for a line of small hills a few miles away, hoping to lose the pursuers among the kloofs and gullies.

"They're getting closer, sir," Sinton warned.

Andrew nodded. His men had been riding for hours with one change of horses. The Boers, with their hardy ponies, would be fresher and vastly more experienced horsemen than most of the British. Andrew calculated the distance to Dundee and knew the Boers would catch them long before they reached the British camp.

"Slow down," Andrew ordered. He knew a fast canter could soon become a gallop, and then both horses and men would be blown. Men could panic in unfamiliar situations, and any retreat would become a rout. If he kept the men together, he could fight his way clear, which would do wonders for morale.

Andrew scanned the land ahead, searching for a suitable defensive site. "Ride for that little *kopje*," he ordered.

The *kopje* was little more than a rocky knoll covered in thorny scrub. Andrew led his men to the base and ordered them to dismount.

"Jenkins, hobble the horses. The rest find defensive positions. We'll see off these Boers."

Andrew had deliberately chosen veterans from the First Battalion, men who had fought along the Khyber, rather than young recruits who had never faced an enemy. The men settled behind rocks or patches of scrub, hefting their rifles without visible emotion.

"Form a circle for all-round defence," Andrew ordered.

With only a dozen men, defending the entire knoll was impossible. Andrew knew the Boers could surround them. He focused his binoculars, watched the dust creep closer and then ten men emerged from the cloud.

Andrew nodded with satisfaction when he saw they were beardless youngsters. They would be eager to prove themselves and more reckless than their experienced, cautious elders.

"Let them come close and give them a volley," Andrew ordered. "Wait for my word."

The Mounted Infantry waited, watching through the narrow, callous eyes of veterans. Andrew saw them pull the Lee-Metford carbines close to their cheeks and aim. Jenkins chewed on a lump of tobacco, Albright kept both eyes open, and Jones breathed a brief prayer.

Rather than spread out as more experienced men would do, the young Boers advanced in a tight group, peering at the knoll but holding their rifles ready.

"Wait!" Andrew ordered. He had been in similar situations in South Africa two decades before. He felt a tickle as a questing fly explored the sweat on his cheek. "Pick your man!"

The veterans did not need the order.

"Adjust your sights to two hundred yards!"

The Boer horsemen came closer—four hundred yards, three hundred, two hundred and fifty. Andrew could make out the features of each man. Lowering his binoculars, he lifted his rifle and targeted the leading rider, a man with a broad face and downy whiskers on his jaw.

Two hundred and thirty yards; two hundred and twenty; two hundred and ten.

The Boer on the extreme left squeezed the trigger in what Andrew thought was the first shot of the Second Boer War. The bullet whizzed above his head with a familiar, unpleasant whine.

"Fire!" Andrew ordered and squeezed the trigger.

Andrew saw his man stagger back in the saddle with an amazed look on his face. The other Malverns fired a second later, and two more Boers jerked, with one screaming and holding his stomach.

"Another volley!" Andrew yelled, working his rifle bolt. The Boers looked astonished. They returned fire, still pounding forward. Andrew did not know where their bullets landed as his patrol fired again. One of the Boer ponies whinnied, high-pitched, and flailed at the air. The others scattered, with only one man still advancing, shouting, his hat thrust well back on his head.

"Cease fire!" Andrew roared as the advancing Boer realised he was alone and turned away. The survivors fled, leaving three men and one horse on the ground.

"Anybody hurt?" Andrew asked.

None of the Malverns were injured.

"Check the Boers," Andrew ordered, grimly satisfied with the skirmish.

First blood to us.

The horse was too severely injured to save, so a merciful bullet ended its agony. One of the Boers was dead, and the others were only wounded, one badly.

"Dress their wounds and leave them in the shade," Andrew ordered. The Boers were even younger than Andrew had thought, with one of the wounded around fourteen years old. The boy sobbed as Sinton put a dressing on the bullet hole in his shoulder.

"Your friends will be here for you soon," Andrew told him, placing a canteen of water at his side.

"Best leave, sir," Albright advised. "The next Boer force won't be so accommodating."

"Take the Boers' rifles and ammunition," Andrew nodded to the casualties' weapons. "The fewer rifles they have, the fewer they have to fire at us."

Sinton gave a twisted smile. "I've never seen a dead man before," he said.

"It's not a pretty sight, is it?" Andrew asked. "That's the glory of war the newspaper reporters and romantic poets write about. Now, get the men ready. His friends will be here soon, and they won't be pleased."

GENERAL PENN SYMONS LISTENED TO ANDREW'S REPORT WITH interest. "I'll heliograph your information to General White in Ladysmith," he said. "I had not expected such a large invasion force."

"No, sir," Andrew agreed. "The Boers have prepared for this war." He bit off the "Better than we have" before he spoke.

Penn Symons stroked his impressively waxed moustache. "So it seems, Captain; so it seems."

Both sides moved cautiously, neither eager to precipitate a full-scale battle until they assessed the other's strengths. On the 13th of October, General White led a powerful force in a reconnaissance, which the Boers easily avoided. Two days later the Boers retaliated when they captured six men of the Natal Police at a drift of the Buffalo River.

"Things are hotting up, Baird," Boswell said.

"So it seems," Andrew copied the general's words.

The minor encounters continued, with British and Boer patrols meeting at Besters Station on the 18th of October and more Boers reported at Hadders Spruit, a few miles to the north.

"Each sighting is closer to Dundee," Captain Boswell said, reading a week-old newspaper. "They'll be on us soon, and then we'll see how brave they are."

Andrew nodded to the surrounding hills. "I'd be happier if we had pickets up there. I've suggested that to the general, but he's convinced the Boers won't dare attack a full British brigade."

Boswell laughed. "I agree with Penn Symons. They'll only attack small detachments they can overwhelm."

"I think you underestimate the Boers."

"They're only farmers," Boswell casually turned a page. "Why, the very name Boer means farmer. They surprised us at Majuba, but we're ready for them now."

"I hope you are right," Andrew said and left the tent to check C Company's pickets. Cloud covered the surrounding hills, blocking the sun and casting a grey shadow across the British camp.

CHAPTER 7

DUNDEE, NATAL, SOUTH AFRICA

OCTOBER 1899

Andrew opened his eyes as he heard the distant crackle of musketry. He glanced at his watch, blinking away sleep to see the time. Half past three in the morning of the 20th of October.

Who the devil starts a fight at this ungodly hour?

"Smith!" Andrew slid out of bed, calling for his soldier-servant. He dressed and was outside the tent within two minutes, sniffing the air and glancing around to see what was happening. A few moments later, the flashing of a heliograph from the picket at Landmans' Drift informed the camp that the Boers had fired on them.

Penn Symons reacted immediately. "Bugler!" he snapped. "Sound the Stand-to!" When the silver notes sounded clear and urgent through the dark to wake the camp, the general ordered two companies of the Dublin Fusiliers to march in support of the picket.

"Come on, C Company!" Andrew chivvied his men. "No more lazing in bed! Johnny Boer wants a fight!"

C Company assembled, with Sergeant Kenny roaring as they came to sleepy attention, rifles held in right hands and sun helmets at every angle.

The Dublin Fusiliers marched boldly out, full of confidence and fighting spirit, their boots sounding hollowly on the ground.

"Right, lads," Andrew addressed C Company as they paraded in the misty morning. "We might be fighting Brother Boer this morning, so follow orders, trust your NCOs and officers, and we'll be fine." It was not the most inspiring speech, but C Company accepted it. The mist altered to a dismal drizzle that could have dampened the men's spirits, but they were keen to fight, to show the Boers that British soldiers were superior to shaggy-bearded farmers.

The NCOs marched around the ranks, adjusting a tunic here, snarling at them to set their hats at the right angle and ensuring their rifles were clean, bright and slightly oiled.

"Now we'll see, Baird," Boswell lit a cigar and exhaled a plume of aromatic blue smoke.

"Now we'll see," Andrew agreed.

The garrison waited in orderly ranks, the khaki-clad infantry looking stolid as the 18th Hussars and the Mounted Infantry stood beside their horses and the eighteen pieces of artillery, already limbered, waited for the order to move.

Andrew paced with his company, speaking quietly to Lieutenant Sinton and the NCOs, judging the temper of the men. They were quiet but calm, watching the surrounding hills.

"Are we going to stand here all day?" Boswell asked.

Ten minutes later, Penn Symons gave his answer.

"Dismiss!" the general barked, and the men returned to their quarters, except those engaged in other duties. They removed their equipment and grumbled about the pointlessness of mustering in the middle of the night. The gunners unlimbered and led the horses away, and the cooks prepared breakfast.

Private Conway was on fatigues and began to whitewash rocks as Corporal Harwood barked instructions.

Andrew watched the bustle die down, re-read Mariana's last letter and thumbed tobacco into his pipe. He checked C Company's sentries, Sergeant Kenny at his side, and the men stiffened to attention.

"Stand easy, men," Andrew said quietly. "You're not on parade."

"Sir!" Lieutenant Sinton opened a long brass telescope and focused on the hills. "I can see movement up there!"

Andrew lifted his binoculars. "So can I," he said. "The Boers have occupied Talana Hill during the night." He grunted. "They're overlooking the camp."

As the rising sun burned away the mist and the drizzle eased, Talana Hill became clearer. Dull green rather than the more common brown, it curved to a steeply round summit, sharply defined against the hazed blue sky. About halfway up, an extensive area of woodland hugged the contours, with farm buildings and stone walls on one side and above.

Andrew felt his tension rise when he saw men moving on the hill. "They've stolen a march on us."

General Penn Symons was also studying Talana Hill, muttering comments to his staff officers as they took notes.

"Sound the Stand-to," the general ordered for the second time that morning, and the men assembled, with the veterans glancing at Talana Hill and the youngsters grumbling.

The Boer numbers increased until they darkened the crest of Talana.

"They've got a gun!" Sinton warned.

"Indeed they have," Andrew replied. *Why did we not occupy Talana?*

"We'll have to push them off the hill," Boswell said.

Andrew did not hear the crash as the Boer artillery fired but saw the fall of the shot outside Dundee. The younger men on parade twisted their heads to watch the Boers on the hill. The

Boer artillery fired again, and everybody heard the scream as a shell passed over them, rising horribly the second before it crashed into the ground on the far side of the British camp.

Andrew saw some of his younger men flinch, lowered his binoculars and moved to them, walking slowly to calm any ragged nerves. He knew being under fire for the first time was an unnerving experience.

"Keep in your ranks, lads! They're only ranging shots."

A third shot followed the second, and then a fourth and a fifth, all landing outside the camp. Some exploded in the soft ground, while those that did only raised a fountain of earth.

"The damned cheek of it!" Sinton said. "Firing on a British camp!"

Andrew grinned despite the situation, for Sinton sounded genuinely outraged. "Yes; how dare they!"

Penn Symons gave rapid orders. "Limber the guns, move them to the front and keep the Boers busy. Cavalry, circle the hill and threaten the enemy's left flank."

The gunners needed no encouragement to hitch up their horses. Two batteries rattled forward, galloping out of the camp and through the streets of Dundee, where the gunfire had wakened the now-alarmed inhabitants. Andrew watched through his binoculars as both batteries unlimbered on a rise outside the town. The drivers moved the horses to the rear, out of danger, as busy gunners loaded and aimed. Officers gave smart orders, and the British artillery soon replied to the Boers. The orange-red explosions climbed up the hillside, tossing dust and smoke to the sky and scattering shrapnel among the attackers.

Within a few moments, the Boer fire slackened as shrapnel burst above and among them. Andrew saw the Boer gunners rapidly withdraw, with many riflemen diving for cover from the sharp steel shards. A few ran to their ponies and retreated, already having had enough of war where the enemy retaliated.

"Leicesters!" Penn Symons snapped. "Remain behind with

the 67th Field Battery to defend the camp and guard the road to Newcastle. The remainder of the infantry, follow me!"

Ignoring the disappointed Leicesters, Andrew mounted his horse and rode to the head of C Company. "Here we go, men!" he said cheerfully. "We'll be one of the first to have a crack at the Boers."

"Come on, you lucky buggers!" Sergeant Kenny shouted. "Let's be having you! Heads up, chests out, stomach in! Keep in step, Conway!"

As the infantry marched through Dundee, many inhabitants stood at their doors and cheered them on.

"Give the Boers what for, boys!"

"Show them what Britons can do!"

"Give them toco, boys!"

"Kick them back to Pretoria, lads!"

"They've fired on civilians, boys! Show them the bayonet!"

The Malverns responded in kind, waving to the children and shaking the men's hands.

In peacetime, half of these civilians would slam their doors on swaddies. Enjoy your popularity, boys; you pay for it with blood.

Penn Symons pushed on, with the civilians' support raising the infantry's morale. Both British batteries of fifteen-pounders, the 69th and 13th, edged to 3,000 yards of the enemy, fired a few rounds and advanced another 700 yards. They engaged the Boers in an artillery duel, firing at enemy gun emplacements on neighbouring hills to support the advancing infantry.

By seven o'clock, the infantry was arrayed at the foot of Talana Hill, staring up the olive-green slope at the Boers on the summit.

When the bugles ordered the advance, the men moved forward and immediately slithered into the deep bed of a stream. The men nearly fell over each other, NCOs cursing them with foul oaths and officers bawling orders to their men.

"Come on, C Company!" Andrew dragged out a cursing Conway by his collar. "Get out of there! Form up! Extended order! Corporal Harwood! Get your section in order! Sergeant Kenny! Organise your men!"

Eventually, the infantry extricated themselves and looked upwards, where the British artillery continued to fire at the Boer guns, ripping up the hillside and spreading a haze of dust and smoke interspersed with lethal bright explosions.

"It's a reversal of Majuba," a man shouted. "Remember Majuba!" Others joined in, so the chant rose to the Boers waiting on the heights above.

Andrew remembered Majuba well. He had been on the summit of Majuba Hill with Lieutenant Ian Hamilton of the Gordon Highlanders in February 1881 when the Boers scaled the heights. The Boers had pushed the British off in a major disaster and a defeat that helped end the war in the Boers' favour. Now, the British would try to advance against the Boers in a similar position on top of a hill.

"Open order!" Andrew ordered, glancing to the left and right to see how his men reacted. C Company extended to ten paces between each man. The Malverns were in the second line beside the Rifles, with the Dublin Fusiliers in front and the Irish Fusiliers in the third line.

General Penn Symons walked his horse around his men, spoke to the senior officers and called to a bugler. Andrew dismounted and knee-haltered Letsie, hoping he did not stray too far during the battle. He intercepted Penn Symons' disapproving glance and looked away. He had no intention of making himself an easy target for Boer riflemen, who always targeted the officers first. The general had no such caution and had an orderly holding a red pennon at his side so the infantry could always see him.

When the bugle sounded the advance, Andrew checked his watch. It was seven-thirty in the morning, and the first battle between the British and Boers had begun.

I wonder if people will remember Talana Hill as well as they recall Majuba?

Andrew checked his men. They moved steadily through tall, dry grass that matched their khaki uniforms. The Boers were firing, with the distance well within the 2,200-yard maximum range of their Mausers, but firing downhill at a moving target was never easy. A few British fell without upsetting the momentum of the advance.

Andrew stepped in front of his men and paced uphill. He focused on a dense blue gum tree plantation that spread across the hillside, hoping the Boers had not thought to position a strong garrison there.

That plantation will provide cover for my men.

"Come on, C Company!" Andrew shouted. He saw B Company on his left, Boswell encouraging his men, and an occasional Boer shell bursting among the advancing infantry.

As the first British line approached, a succession of muzzle flashes came from the wood. Men fell, thrown backwards by the force of the bullets, or crumpled to the ground, spinning, coughing blood, with stomachs and chests torn open. The rest, a line of Dublin Fusiliers and Royal Malverns, moved on, bowing their heads or slitting their eyes as instinctive reactions against the storm of Boer bullets.

"Push on!" Andrew encouraged. He increased his speed, very aware the Boers would try to kill the officers first. A bullet ploughed into the ground at his feet, raising a small fountain of dirt. Another plucked at his sleeve.

To the left of the wood, a dry *kloof,* a deep gulley, stretched toward the hill's summit. Andrew saw some men jump into the *kloof* for cover, only for Boers at the upper end to fire down the length, making the gulley a killing ground rather than a sanctuary.

"Push on!" Andrew shouted again, but with casualties mounting, the men sought cover from the increasingly accurate Boer musketry. "Get into the trees and shove the Boers out!"

Only then did Andrew remember the farm steading beside the wood. He saw Colonel John Sherston lead a platoon of the

Rifle Brigade to one of the defending stone walls. As Sherston clambered onto the wall, a Boer marksman shot him.

The Boers always aim for the officers. The leaders, the best and bravest are always the first to go in every war.

While some British infantry hugged the ground under Boer fire, others advanced to the fringe of the forest.

"Come on, the Malverns!" Andrew roared. "Come on, C Company!" He stepped over a groaning man, hunched his shoulders and sped forward to the trees. He heard men at his back, some encouraging themselves with yells, others moving in desperate silence or gasping with effort. Until the British reached the wood, all the advantages were with the defenders, firing at men advancing uphill across open ground. Andrew glanced over his shoulder, seeing the hill littered with khaki-clad dead and wounded men. Conway was swearing, running with his pith helmet bouncing at the back of his head and his eyes wide and glaring. Sergeant Kenny was shouting at the men, with Corporal Harwood silent, weaving from side to side to spoil the Boers' aim.

Every regiment present now had contingents in the British first line as they struggled through the wood, snapping twigs and firing whenever they saw the enemy. The Boers withdrew before them as more British infantry entered the plantation. Men found cover and fired upwards at the Boers, who sheltered behind makeshift sangars, isolated rocks and farm walls as the British infantry settled at the edge of the plantation.

"Come on, lads!" Andrew ordered. "Form a firing line!"

C Company lay among the trees, exchanging fire with the Boers. They fired, worked the bolt, aimed and fired again.

Andrew studied the ground ahead. If they advanced beyond the trees, the British advance faced another stretch of open ground. Boer musketry swept the clear space, lifting the dust to create a waist-high haze. The infantry hesitated to advance.

Brigadier General James Yule, commanding the infantry, bellowed to the men to move forward. When they remained static, Penn Symons sent a brace of staff officers to spur them on.

"Assault!" the staff officers ordered Yule, gesticulating forward. "Get your men up that hill!"

"I will when I am able," Yule replied.

"Come on, the Malverns!" Andrew stepped forward, hoping C Company would follow him. He stood alone for a moment, with Boer bullets kicking up the dust around him and whining past his head.

Sinton joined him, standing beside a tree, smiling nervously. Andrew swore and withdrew quickly as bullets thudded into nearby trees. With so many marksmen shooting at him, a lone target would not last long.

"Brigadier Yule!" General Penn Symons was in the rear. He spurred his horse uphill, leapt over a wooden gate and pushed to the wood, urging the third line of infantry to advance.

"Get your men forward!" Penn Symons ordered. "Get up the hill!" He dismounted, shouting at officers and men alike.

Andrew tried again, stepping into the open to encourage his men. This time, most of the men followed, with the NCOs snarling the privates forward.

"Come on, Malverns!" Andrew ran forward, jinking from left to right to dodge the Boer riflemen. He heard the pad of boots behind him and moved on, running towards a low stone wall. Penn Symons was on his right, striding for a gap in the wall with his orderly at his side. The general stepped through the gap and looked upward towards the Boer positions.

Andrew saw Penn Symons stiffen and fall as a Boer bullet plunged into his stomach. The orderly dropped his red pennon and leapt to the general's side, desperate to help.

Penn Symons struggled to a crouch, with blood already soaking through his uniform and dripping to the ground. He motioned to a staff officer. "I am severely, mortally wounded in the stomach," he said calmly.

The staff officer motioned to a group of soldiers, who carried the general away from the front. "Have they got the hill?" Penn Symons asked. "Have they got the hill?"

Andrew glanced at his men. C Company had reached the wall, and the men sheltered behind it as they fired at the Boers. Bullets flew in both directions, splintering the upper courses of the wall and burrowing into the ground.

Beyond the wall, the upper hillside was terraced, with a series of stone walls, and another wall stretching at right angles.

That's a retaining wall to hold the farm cattle in place, Andrew thought. *We have the same on our farm. The techniques are the same the world over. Well, it's time to earn my pay.*

"Come on, C Company, let's capture this hill. Charge, lads!"

CHAPTER 8

TALANA HILL, NATAL

OCTOBER 1899

"Come on, C Company!" Andrew yelled and dashed forward, using the cattle wall as shelter from the Boer bullets. A trickle of men followed, with the Malverns mingling with the Rifles and Irish Fusiliers as they ran in single file, keeping their heads beneath the top of the wall. The men slammed down behind the welcome shelter, gasping as they thrust their rifles through chinks between the stones to fire at the Boers.

Andrew glanced over the wall, with the Boers waiting behind sangars at the crest of the hill, only two hundred yards away, but over open, bullet-scoured ground with only a low wall between. On Andrew's left, Captain Connor of the Irish Fusiliers shouted to his men, vaulted the stonework and ran forward with a dozen Fusiliers at his back. The Boers greeted him with a torrent of musketry, and he fell beside half his men. Lieutenant Nugent of the Rifles tried next, only for the Boers to wound him within seconds.

Dear Lord, help me survive this day.

"Come on, Malverns!" Andrew yelled, rolling over the wall. He felt another tug at his sleeve, saw the rapid fountains of dust where the Mauser bullets landed, swerved right and left and threw himself behind the low wall, surprised he was still alive. Men joined him, some gasping with effort and others with fear.

Sergeant Kenny grasped a stubby pipe between his teeth as he shouted to the men. "That's the way, lads! We're pushing them back!"

Boer bullets knocked chips from the stone, leaving a blue lead smear.

"Well done, C Company!" Andrew shouted. He peered through a crack between two stones and saw a line of dark slouch hats behind the sangars, with the long snouts of Mausers poking forward.

"They'll slaughter us!" a heavily acned teenager shouted.

"We're pushing them back," Sergeant Kenny repeated.

A platoon of Dublin Fusiliers leapt the wall and rushed forward, to lose three men in as many seconds. The rest spread out, then threw themselves down and began to return fire.

Despite the officers' encouragement, the advance faltered again. The Boer marksmen picked the British off, crashing bullets through the infantrymen's heads until the 69th Battery of the Royal Artillery fired in support. A hail of shrapnel exploded over and around the Boer positions, rattling from the stones and knocking down men.

"Thank God for the guns," Private Hobart said.

"Thank God be buggered," Conway replied. "The gunners are firing at us!"

When the artillery stopped, the British pushed forward again, rushing past the final wall to reach the summit. Some of the Boers remained, and for a few moments the British infantry fought them hand-to-hand. However good their marksmanship, the Boers could not face bayonets wielded by angry British infantry.

Andrew lunged at a tall man, saw him raise his rifle in self-defence, then shout something in Afrikaans.

"Drop the rifle!" Andrew snarled. The man obeyed, his mouth open in horror as Conway rammed his bayonet hilt-deep into another defender. More Boers surrendered, while others fled downhill away from the stabbing bayonets.

Lieutenant Sinton ran past, firing his revolver, chasing after the rapidly retreating Boers. "We've done it! We've captured the hill and defeated the Boers."

"Majuba!" an Irishman shouted, although Andrew was unsure if he was a Dublin or an Irish Fusilier. "We've avenged Majuba!"

Andrew glanced back at the khaki bodies scattered over Talana Hill and realised the Boers on neighbouring Lennox Hill had been shooting at them for some time.

"Colonel Gunning of the Rifles is down!" Captain Boswell shouted.

This war has already cost us some good officers and scores of men, and it's barely begun, Andrew thought.

He did not expect the sudden crash of shells on the hill summit and the spread of vicious shrapnel.

"The Boer artillery is firing again!" Conway shouted.

"That's not the Boers!" Corporal Harwood replied. "That's our bloody guns!"

Andrew realised that the corporal was correct. The British artillery, seeing men on the summit of Talana Hill, thought the Boers had repulsed the attack and opened fire. The cheering ended, and men dived for cover behind the Boer sangars or threw themselves to the ground.

When the vicious shards of shrapnel spread from above, the infantrymen realised a sangar was no protection from an air burst and quickly withdrew downhill.

"Do we have a heliograph?" Andrew shouted. "Can anybody signal to those idiots to stop shelling their own side?"

With the British in temporary disarray on Talana, the Boers on Lennox Hill increased their firing.

"Keep down, C Company!" Andrew roared, although his men had already huddled into whatever cover they could find. When another shell exploded nearby, more of the men scrambled back down the hill.

"I'll gut these gunners when we get back down," Conway snarled.

"If we get back down," Private Hobart replied.

"Hold tight!" Andrew shouted.

If the guns force us from the summit, the Boers might return, and we'll have to capture the blasted place again.

"I've had enough of this," a signaller from the Royal Irish Fusiliers muttered and, daring the flying shrapnel, clambered onto a rock in plain view of the British artillery less than a mile away. He waved his arms in a semaphore message, jumped down when the guns fired another salvo, returned to his post and continued to signal, swearing profusely.

The artillery stopped. As the smoke and dust cleared from Talana, officers and NCOs began to organise their men.

That Irish signaller deserves a medal, whoever he is, Andrew thought.

"To me, C Company!" Andrew shouted, standing on the signaller's rock. "Lieutenant Sinton, bring me a list of casualties. Sergeant Kenny, where's Corporal Harwood?"

"I don't know, sir."

"Then find him," Andrew said. The Malverns gathered, some shamefaced at running, others jubilant at surviving, and a few with minor wounds.

"Sir!" Sinton approached Andrew as the British artillery fired again. The men, already nervous after the last bombardment, scattered, abandoning the bare crest to find cover further down the hill. Andrew flinched as something screamed past his face and hurriedly joined his men down the slope. The shellfire increased, hammering at Talana Hill for a murderous half hour before ending abruptly.

Andrew raised his head from the rock he had hidden behind. He had no recollection of diving; self-preservation had driven him. Now, duty took over as the smoke and dust cleared once again.

"Sergeant Kenny!"

"Sir!" Kenny adjusted his pith helmet as he marched to Andrew's side. His tunic was torn, and something had opened a small cut on his right cheek, so blood trickled to the point of his jaw.

"Get down the hill and tell the gunners we've captured the hill." Andrew fought to keep the anger from his voice.

"Yes, sir," Kenny saluted and descended the slope, avoiding the dead and injured men.

The Malverns made their way cautiously to the summit, with men glowering nervously over their shoulders at the British artillery.

"Sir!" Sinton said. "Would you look at that?"

On the east, the Boers were in full flight. Horsemen and wagons were heading away from Talana Hill, some in apparent panic, others in the rough formation of their commandoes.

"Now there's a perfect target for the guns!" Sinton said.

Andrew watched as the British artillery, fresh from shelling the infantry, limbered up, moved to Smith's Nek and unlimbered, with a splendid view of the Boer retreat.

"Open fire, gunners!" Andrew intoned. "If we inflict a major defeat now, we can end this war without further bloodshed!"

Lieutenant Colonel Edwin Pickwood's two batteries were on the *nek* between Lennox Hill and Talana Hill: twelve artillery pieces with the entire Boer army spread out before them. However, rather than fire, Pickwood sent a messenger to General Yule asking for instructions.

"Fire, gunners, damn you, fire!" Andrew said as the Boers withdrew unmolested.

As the guns remained mute, Major Eustace Know led two squadrons of the 18th Hussars around the Boers, attacking a few isolated groups and taking some prisoners.

"Sir!" Sinton extended his large telescope, staring into the distance. "Try this, sir; it's more powerful than your field glasses."

Andrew accepted the telescope and peered past the retreating mass. Half obscured by rising dust, he saw Colonel Moller with 120 Mounted Infantry and Hussars riding hard to try and stop the Boers. Slightly behind them, a cart carried a Maxim machine gun. Andrew grunted, wished them luck and returned his view to the guns. He learned later that a Boer commando captured most of the force, while the Boers also wiped out the Maxim team when their cart bogged down.

"Why don't the guns fire?" Sinton asked, scanning the plains through Andrew's binoculars. He focused on an old iron church that crouched on the flank of the hill. A Boer stood outside, holding up a white flag. "Have they surrendered? Or do they want a truce?"

Andrew studied the building. "Neither," he said. "Look at all the wounded outside the church. The Boers must be using it as a hospital." He handed back Sinton's telescope. "The Boers are asking the gunners not to fire on the hospital. The gunners must believe we have a general truce." He watched as the Boers streamed away. "What a waste of an opportunity."

GENERAL YULE STOOD ON THE SUMMIT OF TALANA, SHAKING his head. He lowered his binoculars. "Where is the heliograph? I must send a message to General White in Ladysmith."

"We don't have one, sir," a staff officer replied.

"Don't have one?" Yule repeated. "Damn it all, we must have one. How can I send a message without a helio?" He looked around in irritation. "Look here, who knows this area?"

"Captain Baird does, sir," the staff officer replied. "He was here in the Zulu War and at Majuba."

"He'll do." Yule beckoned Andrew over. "Baird! Take a message to General White in Ladysmith. Tell him we've defeated the Boers on Talana Hill, and they're running like rabbits before a fox."

"Yes, sir," Andrew said. "I'll tell Lieutenant Sinton to look after my company, sir."

"What?" Yule looked up. "Yes, yes, of course."

With a pleased Sinton in temporary charge of C Company, Andrew mounted Letsie, took Moshie as a spare and set off for Ladysmith through the increasing rain.

CHAPTER 9

LADYSMITH, NATAL

OCTOBER 1899

"Thank you, Baird." General White listened to Andrew's report. He smiled briefly. "I already knew of Yule's battle at Talana, but confirmation is always welcome. Did you have any difficulty riding here?"

"A little, sir." Andrew was tired and dusty from his long ride. "I had to detour around a large Boer commando near Elandslaagte."

White nodded. "I'll send a patrol to investigate. In the meantime, you'd better rest, find something to eat and return to your company."

"Yes, sir," Andrew saluted and left the general's office. Immaculate staff officers looked at him disapprovingly as he rode to the Malverns' camp, with one major commenting on his scruffy appearance.

"You're letting the side down, Captain. An officer should at least try to show his men an example."

Andrew did not reply but wondered if the major had ever met an enemy in his career. Some soldiers served for years in quiet postings in southern India, Malta or Canada, while the War Office sent others to the hotspots of the North-West Frontier or Burma. Andrew had long since stopped trying to understand the workings of the War Office.

Colonel Newland greeted Andrew's reappearance in the regiment with news of their position.

While you were toodling about on Talana," Newland said, "the Boers have been busy here. A mixed commando of Transvaalers, Orange Freestaters and German mercenaries thrust through Botha's Pass and cut the railway line between Ladysmith and Dundee."

"I saw some of them at Elandslaagte, sir. They're more active than I expected," Andrew said.

"They're at Elandslaagte," Newland continued as if Andrew had not spoken. "General White has sent Sir John French with a force to dislodge them."

Andrew was impressed with the speed of White's response to his information.

"Have you met General French, Baird?" Newland asked.

"No, sir," Andrew admitted.

"He's an interesting fellow, our man Johnnie French," Newland settled comfortably in his seat. "Major-General John French started his career as a naval cadet until he discovered he had vertigo, which precluded him from climbing masts. Imagine a ship's officer unable to climb aloft, eh?" Newland smiled. "Well, the Navy's loss is our gain! He joined the 8th Hussars, where he's had a quiet career, only seeing action during the Sudan War of 1884."

Newland chuckled. "He is quite a man, though, famous for his amorous exploits and monetary problems. Now we'll see if an officer lacking in wartime experience is the best man to face an enemy as capable as the Boers, eh?"

"General White must have confidence in him," Andrew remarked.

"Indeed," Newland said. "Now, Baird, I don't think you should return to Dundee just yet, not with the Boers on the rampage. It's best you remain with the battalion at present. I'll send a note to General White to that effect."

"Yes, sir," Andrew said.

After checking his empty mail basket, Andrew joined Major Cradley in watching French's little army leave Ladysmith. A battery of Natal Artillery, with tiny seven-pounder mountain guns, rattled beside five squadrons of Imperial Light Horse and a few companies of the Manchester Regiment. The Light Horse only carried outdated single-shot Martinis, which gave them a grave disadvantage compared to the Mauser-armed Boers. The Manchesters were smiling and joking as they boarded an armoured train to go to battle, with the men wondering at this novel method of transport. They left in the dark before dawn, with the Mancunians cheering as they departed.

"They look very confident," Andrew remarked.

Major Cradley nodded. "They've heard of Yule's victory at Talana and know they can do even better."

"It wasn't an easy victory," Andrew said. "The Boers fought well, and we lost some good officers and too many men."

"We won," Cradley said quietly. "That's more than we did in the last Transvaal War."

Andrew grunted, remembering the khaki corpses strewn across Talana Hill. "The Imperial Light Horse look determined," he agreed. "I worked with Lieutenant Leslie of the Imperials. He disliked the Boers." Andrew watched them ride out, each man looking more determined than the next.

"I know about Leslie," Cradley replied. "The Imperial Light Horse are nearly all Uitlanders, refugees from Johannesburg and the other towns in the Transvaal. They are the men the Boers have been abusing and exploiting for years. Now they have a chance to retaliate, and, by God, they will take it."

Andrew began to fill his pipe. "I see," he said.

"That's John James Scott-Chisholm in command," Cradley nodded to a man of less than average height. "He's Scottish, though, rather than a Uitlander, and what he lacks in inches, he makes up for in grit. He fought at Ali Masjid in the last Afghan War. Behind him is Major W. Karri Davies, who helped raise the regiment. Davies is an Australian Jew, and as the Boers dislike Jews as much as Uitlanders, he had a rough time in the Transvaal. Kruger jailed him for struggling for Uitlanders' rights and supporting the Jameson Raid in '95."[*]

Andrew studied the Imperials. "Quite a man," he murmured.

"That's Major Aubrey Woolls-Sampson at his side. He was a gold miner and took part in the Jameson Raid. Kruger threw him in jail, too."

"There seem to be many scores being settled in this war," Andrew said.

"Maybe too many," Cradley replied quietly. He lifted his chin as Lieutenant Leslie rode past, his neatly clipped moustache looking very military and his uniform sufficiently immaculate to impress any drill sergeant of the Brigade of Guards. Andrew remembered the bearded ruffian he had worked beside and wondered at the transformation.

"There's your Lieutenant Leslie," Cradley said quietly. "He hates the Boers more than anybody I've ever met. He leads a troop of the most desperate fellows you could ever hope to avoid. God help the Boers if they slip the leash."

Andrew studied the men riding at Leslie's back. They looked rougher than even the average irregular horsemen, men from the fringes of the colony who would never fit into a civilised society. He had met the type before, footloose wanderers, adventurers,

---

[*] The Jameson Raid of New Year 1895/6 was an abortive attempt to raise the Uitlanders against the Boers. Led by Leander Jameson and backed by Cecil Rhodes, it was 500 men strong. The Boers easily defeated the incursion.

wild men searching for something; the unwanted dross of the Empire.

"They seem a disreputable bunch," Andrew agreed.

"The Boers know all about the Imperial Light Horse and who rides with them," Cradley continued. "Only yesterday, the Jo'burg Commando sent a message to Ladysmith asking what the Imperials' uniform was so they could face them in battle." Cradley scratched his head with the stem of his pipe. "I heard some Uitlanders have thrown in their lot with the Boers, so they'll know the ILH men well. I wonder what personal grudges will be played out if the two meet."

Andrew grunted again. "This should be a war between professional soldiers," he said. "It sounds like a blood feud between rival tribes."

Cradley laughed. "Things are different here in Africa."

"They shouldn't be," Andrew said. "We're at the end of the 19th century, for goodness' sake, not the blasted Middle Ages."

"You're testy today," Cradley said. "You need some sleep."

"I'm worried," Andrew admitted. "The Boers are in more force than they were in the Transvaal War; they have more modern weapons and are more prepared for a war than we are." *And Mariana has not written to me, but I won't mention that.*

"Do you think Kruger can defeat us?" Cradley sounded incredulous.

Andrew considered before replying. "No," he said. "I don't think so. I don't believe the British public will allow their army to lose another war. The Boers are quite capable of giving us a few bloody noses, though." He watched the last of the ILH ride past. "Worse, if they persuade one of the Powers—Russia, Germany, or France—to get involved, or the Cape Colony or Natal Dutch to join them, we could be in for a rough time, sir."

Cradley laughed. "Any European power would have to get their men to South Africa first, and the Royal Navy would have something to say about that."

They walked back to the camp, side by side in the misty

morning, with the army's normal activities continuing as though the war was thousands of miles away. A heavily moustached sergeant drilled his platoon, a corporal shouted at a defaulter, the cooks prepared breakfast, and a farrier shoed an officer's horse.

"The French have forces already in Africa, sir," Andrew reminded. "And the Germans in German South-West Africa are blood brothers to Kruger's men."

Cradley thrust his pipe into his mouth and looked at Andrew sideways. "You know South Africa well, don't you, Baird?"

"My wife is from Natal, sir," Andrew replied. "I fought three wars here before this one."

"It's my first time here," Cradley admitted. "What do you advise I do when we meet the Boers?"

"Keep your head down, sir," Andrew said immediately. "They are excellent shots and fine horsemen. They don't seem to understand the concept of a white flag, though, so be wary if you see one."

"Ignore it?"

Andrew shook his head. "No, sir, but watch your back. If one Boer decides to surrender, that doesn't mean his fellows will also lay down their arms."

"I'll bear that in mind," Cradley said seriously.

French periodically heliographed news to Ladysmith. The garrison cheered when they heard the Imperial Light Horse had skirmished with Boer scouts, easily pushing them back.

"The Imperials would enjoy that," Cradley said gleefully.

Without a company to command, Andrew waited near the heliograph and followed French's progress. When they neared the hills at Elandslaagte, French's men saw the main Boer camp, with the green-and-white tents and clumsy wagons somehow incongruous near the railway station. As the British approached, the Boers emerged from the buildings they had commandeered. The Natal Volunteer Artillery fired their seven-pounders, inadvertently hitting a Boer ambulance.

Within a few moments, the Boers retaliated with a pair of

powerful Krupps. They fired from far beyond the range of the muzzle-loading seven-pounders, with well-directed fire slamming onto the British batteries. Frustrated but not defeated, the Natal Artillery spotted the Boer position on a distant hill and cranked their barrels to fire at their extreme range. When the British officers watched their shots fall short of the Boer guns, French ordered his force to retire. It was better to withdraw rather than waste lives in a pointless duel against superior artillery and a greater Boer force.

Cradley shook his head. "We'll have to do something about these Boer guns," he said. "We're not used to facing an army with greater firepower than we have."

"We may get our opportunity," Andrew said as the bugles sounded the Stand-to.

General White sent reinforcements to French, with battalion after battalion packing the troop trains that steamed from Ladysmith. The Devons were first to leave, carrying their rifles and with pith helmets angled against the sun. The Gordon Highlanders were next, determined to avenge their defeat at Majuba Hill nearly twenty years before but which still rankled. The Royal Malverns followed, squeezing onto the small train, sweating in the confined space yet eager to fight the enemy.

"Here we go, lads," Andrew said. "We beat them at Talana, and we'll beat them again. Forward the Malverns!"

The officers travelled in less crowded conditions. They sat in near silence, watching the land roll past, with each man lost in private thoughts. Andrew loaded his revolver, closed his eyes and lay back, trying to catch a few minutes' sleep before they detrained.

"General Ian Hamilton commands the infantry," Major Cradley said. "You know him, don't you, Baird?"

"We fought together at Majuba," Andrew confirmed. "He is a good soldier, brave as they come."

Cavalry supported the infantry—Lancers and Dragoon Guards, eager to show the Boers that British horsemen were equal to anyone from the veldt. Two artillery batteries also rattled out of Ladysmith, hoping to match the Boer Krupps.

As soon as they detrained, Colonel Newland marched the Malverns to General French and ordered them to halt.

"Send out sentinels," Newland ordered his officers, "and find water for the men and horses. Forage for whatever food we can locate."

Andrew glanced around. Elandslaagte was on the plain, with higher ground to the south. It would hardly count as a hamlet in the United Kingdom, yet here, the location mattered more than size. He saw General French counting the men and nodding in satisfaction.

"We outnumber the enemy," French told the officers. "And our artillery more than matches theirs. However, the Boers are defending hills, so we will advance into deadly rifle fire. They will also stay hidden behind rocks and in trenches."

"My men can take it," Colonel Newland said.

Colonel Ian Hamilton addressed the infantry. "We will advance in an extended formation, moving in short, disciplined rushes when we come close to the Boers." "The enemy is there," he said, gesturing to the hills. "I hope you will shift them before sunset." He hesitated for a moment as he stared towards the Boer positions. "In fact, I know you will." Hamilton paused again, gauging the mood of his men. "In the morning," he said, raising his voice so every man could hear him, "newsboys in the streets of London will be calling out the news of your victory!"

Andrew expected the resulting cheer. British infantry responded well to a charismatic leader, particularly one who shared their danger, as Hamilton did. They raised their helmets, waved, stamped and shouted as Hamilton watched them fondly.

The sun was already well past its zenith when French ordered the advance. Andrew saw a flurry in the rear as White arrived with an entourage of staff officers, but the general allowed French to fight the battle without interfering.

For the first few moments, the infantry advanced in columns

of companies, tensely waiting for the hidden Boer riflemen to fire.

"Extended order!" Newland shouted. "Let's show Brother Boer what the Malverns are made of!"

The Malverns opened up, moving steadily forward. Andrew heard the men muttering as they advanced, with the soft swish of grass and the rhythmical thump of their boots somehow sinister under the forbidding sky.

"E Company, take the lead," Newland ordered, "F Company in support, extended by sections."

Andrew took his place on the extreme left of the Malverns, with the long lines of infantry advancing in a slow, methodical and impersonal movement that seemed more mechanical than human. He looked up, smiling with memory as the Gordons' pipers began to play and the strains of *Cock o' the North* carried across the British lines.

"Oh, God," a Malvern said. "The Jocks are strangling a pig!"

"Good!" another man replied. "The Boers will shoot at the bloody racket and leave us in peace."

"I can't stand the skirt-wearing bastards anyway," a third man snarled. "They think they're the only regiment in the army."

The advance continued, with the pipers encouraging the men and the Boers waiting in silence above. After ten minutes, the Boer pom-poms fired, the quick-firing guns they had bought from British manufacturers now firing at British troops.

"Remember Majuba!" a man shouted, and the Gordons responded with a loud cheer. "Remember Majuba!" They extended the final vowel, so the word became "Majubaaaa," echoing across the advancing men.

Some distance behind the infantry, the British artillery opened fire, with the shells arcing over the advance to explode in fire and fury on the Boer positions.

"What's French doing?" Major Cradley asked. "Are we just going into a frontal attack? I wish he'd let us know."

"I think he's trying for a simultaneous attack on the Boer

front and flank, sir," Andrew replied, "but as we can't see their positions, it's impossible to see where their flanks are."

Andrew peered ahead. The infantry advanced against a low rise, with higher hills behind. Hamilton ordered the remainder of the men into open order, and they marched over the first hill unopposed by the enemy.

"Where are the Boers?" Cradley asked. "You know how they work. Have they already run away?"

"They'll be here, somewhere," Andrew replied. "Watching us."

Cradley studied the hill ahead. "I can't see them."

"No, sir," Andrew agreed, "but they'll see us."

Andrew heard a youthful laugh and glanced to his left, where a young Gordon bugler dodged a rough cuff from an irate corporal.

"Try that again, and I'll tan your erse, you wee imp!" the corporal roared as the bugler halted a safe distance away, grinning.

Andrew looked away, glad boys could still be mischievous and suddenly missing his children. *I've hardly seen Simla and Iain. They'll be quite the youngsters now, beginning to be as cheeky as that bugler and not knowing who I am.*

The infantry pushed over the first hill, with the artillery firing ahead, targeting the Boer guns and sangars. The explosions flared, orange-red beneath spreading smoke. With the hill behind them, the British marched into a wide valley of thin, yellow-brown grass that stretched to two hills, one a long green ridge and the second smaller and more distinct, a sugar-loaf-shaped *kopje*. The Boer pom-poms fired, with the rapid explosions targeting the Gordons without silencing the pipes or slowing the advance.

"I can feel them watching us," Major Cradley said, puffing at his pipe.

Andrew nodded, feeling very vulnerable as the khaki lines marched slowly towards the double hill. Behind the ridge, the dark storm cloud rose higher, as if nature were copying the actions of humanity.

The Malverns were quiet, with only a few grim jokes as they marched toward the distant ridge. Their boots thudded hollowly on the ground, their clothes rustled, and their equipment rattled softly, accentuating their harsh, nervous breathing.

"Where are they?" a man asked. "Why don't they show themselves?"

"Come out and fight, you bastards!" another man shouted in a strong West Country accent.

The Boers did not reply as the British marched on, each step bringing them closer to the Boers' Mausers.

Into the valley of death, Andrew quoted silently. His hopes rose. *Maybe the Boers have retreated before we arrived. No: if they had, our scouts would have seen them. They're there, watching and waiting.*

Some of the infantry flinched when the Boer artillery fired again but relaxed a little when they realised the enemy was aiming at the British guns. When the British batteries replied, an artillery duel continued for a few moments before the Boers fell silent.

"They can't compete with the Royal Artillery," Cradley said.

The British guns altered their target to the long ridge ahead, firing shrapnel to discourage the Boer riflemen and support the infantry's advance.

A red-faced and wildly excited subaltern nearly barged into Colonel Newland.

"General French sends his compliments, sir," the subaltern gabbled. "He says the Devons and Malverns are to advance against the enemy's front and hold their attention while the Gordons, the Manchesters and the Imperial Light Horse launch the main attack from the flank."

"Very good, Lieutenant," Newland replied calmly. "Could you kindly tell me where the Boers' front is and where lie their flanks?"

The subaltern looked confused. "I don't know, sir," he confessed.

"No more do I," Newland told him. "Go back to General French and tell him the Malverns will advance as ordered."

"Yes, sir," the subaltern said, evidently pleased to escape.

"Here we go, men," Colonel Newland shouted. "On to glory!"

CHAPTER 10

ELANDSLAAGTE, NATAL

OCTOBER 1899

The Malverns marched on, expecting the Boer riflemen to fire at every step. Instead, the heavy cloud drove lashing rain into the faces of the advancing infantry.

"Welcome to sunny Africa," Major Cradley said, slithering on the wet grass.

Andrew grinned sourly. "I could get wet back home, thank you, sir."

As the infantry ducked under the driving rain, hidden Boer riflemen finally opened fire. Andrew saw the quick spurts of muzzle flares and heard the rattle of hundreds of Mausers.

"Here we go," Andrew said. He estimated the summit of the ridge was eight hundred feet above the plain. A man grunted and crumpled near him; another spun in a half-circle, holding his left shoulder from where an ugly red-brown stain spread. Colonel Newland strode in front, seemingly impervious to the bullets that splattered around him. Rather than dust, the Mauser bullets raised muddy fountains in the sodden ground.

"Keep going, men!" Andrew shouted. "The sooner we cover the ground, the quicker we can be at them!"

Andrew thought this long-range warfare was very impersonal, with the enemy largely hidden and artillery performing the killing. He peered through the rain without seeing a single slouch hat or Boer rifleman, while the scale of the battlefield dwarfed even a battalion of British infantry.

From beneath, the hill slope had appeared smooth, but now Andrew saw it undulated in dips and rises. The hollows protected the advancing British from the defenders; the Boers hammered them with rifle fire when they ascended the rises.

"Get down the slope!" Andrew shouted as the Malverns negotiated a hollow. "Don't linger on the side that faces the Boers."

Andrew saw a Malvern fall to lie still on the grass, looking as peaceful as if he were asleep. A youngster staggered back, staring in amazement at the spreading blood on his tunic.

"The recruiting sergeant never told me I would get shot!" he said as he slowly sank to the grass.

"Push on!" Andrew shouted. When another youth threw himself behind one of the ridges, fiercely moustached Sergeant Madron lifted him by his collar and landed a hefty kick on his backside.

"Move!" the sergeant said. "Get forward!"

Andrew saw a farmhouse ahead, squat and functional with its wide stoep and whitewashed mud walls. A group of men emerged and opened fire on the Imperial Light Horsemen, acting as infantry to the Malverns' right.

"Boers!" a Malvern shouted, pointing wildly. Glad to see the enemy, he began to fire, swearing loudly.

"They're not Boers," Sergeant Madron corrected. "They're mercenaries. German volunteers!"

The Imperial Light Horse met the Germans with a torrent of

well-aimed musketry, firing their Martinis like professional soldiers. Leslie shouted abuse as he dropped to his knees, firing and reloading like a man in a fury.

"Mercenary bastards! This isn't your war!"

His men followed him, spreading out as they fired. The Germans stood to fight, but within minutes, the ILH wiped them out and marched on, jubilant at their small victory.

"Advance, Gordons! Bydand!" Andrew saw a Gordons' officer lying on the grass, bleeding profusely from a bullet in his thigh, urging his men on. The officer lit a pipe, dragged himself to the top of an undulation and pointed to the summit. "Get them, Gordons! Remember Majuba!"

"Majuba!" the Gordons roared. "Remember Majuba!" They pushed energetically forward, losing men and with some firing upwards at the hidden enemy. "Come out and fight, you cowards!"

A barbed wire fence stretched along the ground, delaying the advance as the infantry clambered over the top or searched for a passage through. Boer riflemen waited until the British approached the gaps and fired into the crowd.

"Avoid the gaps!" Andrew warned the Malverns. "Climb the fence as quickly as you can!"

The musketry became more accurate as the British neared the Boer positions.

"They're getting too good at this!" Crawley gasped.

"They are," Andrew agreed, "but they're not as dangerous as they were in the last war. We're facing town Boers, rather than the country-bred men."

Colonel Newland strode in front of the Malverns, straight-backed and refusing to duck or flinch from the bullets that whined and screamed past him.

"Look at the colonel," a man shouted. "The Boers can't touch him. He's charmed, that's what he is."

Colonel Chisholm of the Imperial Horse was not so fortunate as he hurried forward, bearing a bright sash to encourage his Uitlanders. A Boer marksman aimed for the sash and fired, with Chisholm falling, a second bullet crashing into him as he crumpled. The Imperial Horse growled and pushed on, determined to avenge their leader.

"Come on, boys!" Leslie stopped to load his Martini.

"Keep together, Malverns!" Andrew shouted as the advance became ragged. Men moved in short rushes, panting for breath as they ascended the seemingly interminable hill. Units began to merge as some men moved faster than others, with a few lagging behind, reluctant to face the musketry that tore holes in the ranks.

"With me, Malverns!" Andrew gathered his men, shouting at those in the rear. "Keep moving!" He knew it was better to arrive at the enemy in a concerted rush rather than in small groups the enemy could pick off. "Sergeant Madron! Keep your platoon together!"

"Sergeant Madron's gone, sir!" a tousle-headed corporal said. "Shot through the head. He's lying back there," he indicated the crest of the last undulation.

"You're in charge of the platoon, Corporal Reeves!" Andrew said, ducking as a bullet hissed past his face. "Keep the men together!"

Colonel Newland marched ahead, not deigning to glance behind him, confident that his battalion would follow. He drew his revolver when he was a hundred yards from the summit, still not breaking stride.

"After me, Malverns!"

As the Boer fire increased, some infantrymen hesitated, searching for cover rather than pushing forward. Andrew saw Ian Hamilton gathering the stragglers as he strode around the infantry with his staff officers.

"Keep on, Malverns!" Andrew urged. The Highland pipes were still sounding, their high wails encouraging the Gordons.

The Boers were closer now, remaining behind their rocks as they fired at the exposed British soldiers.

"Come out and fight, you Boojer cowards!" Corporal Reeves shouted. "Fight like men rather than skulking behind shelter!"

Andrew saw the muzzle flash of a Mauser, aimed at the spot and fired his revolver, with the bullet raising chips from the rock.

"Sound the charge!" Hamilton ordered. "Buglers! Sound the charge!"

The bugles sounded, with the young Gordon bugler raising his bugle to the sky as he blew. The Highlanders pushed past, their bayonets extended, and pith helmets tilted back on their heads.

"Don't let the Jocks beat us, boys!" Corporal Reeves shouted. His platoon followed, shouting and swearing as they ran. The Manchesters and ILH also charged, losing a few men to Boer musketry as they forgot their fatigue and loped forward.

"Come on, Malverns!" Andrew shouted, ignoring the bullet that zipped past his head. He powered on, long-striding towards a sangar. He heard a roar as the British and South Africans reached the summit and dashed forward, eager to avenge their dead in that long ascent.

A Boer rose in front of Reeves, fired a last shot at the advancing men and threw up his hands in surrender.

"Too bloody late, chum!" the corporal said, and plunged his bayonet into the man's stomach, twisting the blade before he withdrew. "That's for Sergeant Madron."

Some Boers turned to run, others continued to fight, while a few lifted their rifles above their heads in quick surrender. The British infantry flooded over the plateau on top of the hill. The Boer guns stood there, with the crews dead or wounded around them.

"Majuba!" the Gordons shouted. "Avenge Majuba!"

British soldiers ran to the guns, waving their pith helmets and cheering at this proof of their victory.

Andrew saw one group of Boers resisting. They wore black frock coats and tall hats, so some British hesitated to fire back.

"They're civilians!" one Gordon shouted. "We cannae shoot civilians!"

"They look like seedy businessmen," another man said. "What are they doing here?"

"They're shooting at us, you blasted fool!" a Gordon corporal replied. "Shoot back at them!"

As the Malverns, Manchesters and Gordons advanced across the summit of the ridge, they met the Devons, who had experienced an easier passage with fewer casualties. The two converging British forces occupied most of the hill, except where the frock-coated Boers held on behind a natural sangar of rocks.

"The stubborn buggers refuse to accept that we've beaten them," the Gordon corporal said as Mauser bullets hissed past. He ducked behind a rock. "Surrender, you silly buggers! We've defeated you!"

In reply, the Boers fired again, hitting an unwary Devon, who fell, mouthing insults and obscenities as he held his arm.

"Move to the right flank, men," Newland ordered. "D and E Companies, advance on that Boer position. F and G Companies, give covering fire. Who's playing the blasted bugle?"

Andrew heard the bugle call, the thin notes sounding high above the deep-throated roars of the British soldiers.

"Listen!" Corporal Reeves shouted. "Listen to the bugle, boys!"

The calls were urgent, insistent. The first was "Cease Fire", and the British soldiers listened in disbelief.

"Cease fire? The buggers are still shooting at us!" Reeves said. "Where's that bloody bugler?"

"I'm damned if I can see him!" a Devon sergeant said. "Can anybody see the bugler?"

After the "Cease Fire", the notes of the "Retire" sounded over the ridge.

"Retire! Get back off the ridge!"

CHAPTER 11

ELANDSLAAGTE, NATAL

OCTOBER 1899

"Retire?" Men stared at each other in disbelief. "Retire? We've only just got here! Why the hell should we retire?"

"Orders!" a sergeant of the Manchesters shouted above the crackle of Boer musketry and the intrusive notes of the bugle. "Obey orders, lads! The officers know best."

"What's happening, sir?" Corporal Reeves asked Andrew. "Why are we retiring?"

As confused as the rest, Andrew shook his head. "I'm damned if I know, Corporal."

Officers gathered their men as the British began withdrawing from the hill they had gained at such cost.

"To me, Malverns!" Andrew shouted. "Withdraw by sections. Don't rush, and don't let the Boers see your back!"

"How about them?" a truculent Gordon private pointed to

the Boers who clung to the fringes of the ridge. "Are we going to leave them in possession of the hill?"

"Follow orders!" a heavily moustached sergeant snarled. "Do as you're told!"

The men stepped back, cursing and swearing. They were unhappy at leaving the hill but obeying orders as their training had taught them.

"I can't see the bugler!" Reeves said. "Who's giving the orders?"

The young Gordon bugler ran forward with his bugle dangling from his belt and his face red with effort. "I don't think that's a British bugle," he said. "That's a dirty Boojer playing a trick!"

A few men around him stopped, with the Gordon corporal eyeing him disapprovingly. "What's that you're saying, lad?"

"Retire be damned!" the bugle boy said, lifting his bugle to his lips and sounding the Advance.

"Good lad!" the Gordon corporal said, lifting his chin towards the last Boer stronghold. "Sound it again, lad."

The young bugler blew again, with his cheeks bulging with effort, and men nudging each other as they turned around. Some grinned, one man spat on his hands, and another muttered an obscenity.

"Let's get these bastards!"

Andrew lifted his voice. "Obey the bugle, boys! Advance! Drive the Boers back to Pretoria!"

"Do the bloody officers know what they're doing?" a Malvern grumbled in a broad Herefordshire accent. "Advance, retire, advance." He turned around. "Come on, lads, before they want us to move sideways and dance the bloody polka."

The infantry returned, some cheering, others unsure what to do. Colonel Newland strode to the captured Boer guns, shouting to the Malverns to rally to him.

"After me, boys!" Andrew shouted. "Don't lose momentum!" He led a mixed group of Malverns, Manchesters and Gordons in a surge over the plateau, shooting or bayoneting any Boer who still resisted. The British poured over the ridge and down the other side—Malverns, Gordons, Devons, Manchesters and dismounted Imperial Horse in a mad scramble to chase the enemy.

The Boers had camped on the far side of the hill with wagons, green tents, horses, bullocks, and a scattering of women and servants. Andrew saw panic hit the camp as the Boers ran down the slope with the British infantry in pursuit. Servants scrambled to yoke the oxen, women lifted their skirts and ran to the wagons, and men leapt onto horses or tried to help their wives.

That young bugler won the battle for us, yet nobody will ever remember him.

Andrew saw a group of Boers raise a white flag, and then the entire camp seemed to be on the move—wagons, horsemen and organised commandoes racing to escape the pursuing British.

"Sir!" an excited lieutenant shouted. "Look! British cavalry!"

A squadron of the 5th Dragoon Guards and another of the 5th Lancers had ridden around the hills and witnessed the Boers' hurried withdrawal. As the day eased to a close, they cantered forward, then charged. The lancers lowered their lances, and for a moment, Andrew saw something that lived with him forever—a scene that could have come from the Sikh Wars of half a century before or even the Napoleonic Wars. He saw a line of mounted men, with the dying sun glinting from the lance tips and the pennons flapping with the wind of their passage. They charged into the retreating Boers.

Some of the enemy threw up their hands in surrender, others tried to flee, and a few turned to fight. The lancers crashed through, dipped their lances to skewer their targets, withdrew the weapons and continued. Andrew saw the Dragoon Guards ram into the Boers, their heavy horses knocking down the smaller Boer ponies and their swords slashing and thrusting into the homespun clothing.

"Give them quarter, for the love of God," Andrew prayed as the lancers wheeled and returned, spearing the hapless Boers, either on their ponies or when they lay on the ground, wounded or not.

At that stage, mad with battle-lust, the cavalry gave no quarter. They hacked and speared, thrusting at terrified men until the anger cooled and sanity returned, and they began to round up Boer prisoners, who dropped their rifles and raised their hands.

The British cavalry charge completed the rout of the enemy.

That's two battles we've won now, two more than the last time we fought the Boers.

"What price Majuba?" a jubilant Gordon asked. "What price Majuba, eh?"

The British captured around two hundred prisoners and inflicted an estimated two hundred and fifty dead and wounded.

"A lot of these Boer casualties were Burghers from Johannesburg," Major Cradley said, puffing on a cheroot. "Others were Hollanders from Natal and the Cape Colony who joined the enemy." He removed the cheroot and grinned. "The Imperial Light Horse destroyed the German mercenaries."

"How about our casualties?" Andrew asked.

"About 41 killed," Cradley replied quietly, "and over 220 wounded, with the Gordons and Imperial Light Horse the worst hit. Not bad for an attack uphill on a defended position. The boys did well."

"The Gordons have avenged Majuba," Andrew said soberly. He remembered the sick despair of that earlier battle.

"Do you know what happened up there?" Cradley asked Andrew. "When we nearly retired after capturing the hill?"

Andrew shook his head. "I think the Boers imitated our bugle calls," he said. "But a young bugler saved the day."

"It wasn't the Boers," Cradley blew out a ribbon of smoke. "Did you see a Boer with a bugle? I didn't, and I doubt anybody else did either. It was Ian Hamilton's doing. He saw a group of Boers raise a white flag, believed the whole jing-bang of them had surrendered, and ordered the Cease Fire. The men close by obeyed, but some of the Boers fired, hitting a few men, who fell back."

Andrew listened, understanding the sequence of events.

Cradley continued. "An Imperial Light Horse officer shouted, 'Don't retire! For God's sake, don't retire!' but in the confusion, the men only heard the word retire, and a Light Horse bugler sounded the retire."

"I see," Andrew nodded. "Battles are confusing at the best of times."

As the British settled for the night in the Boer camp and some of the Imperial Light Horse patrolled to find stray Boers, General White summoned Andrew.

"Did you lose your horses in the battle, Baird?"

"No, sir," Andrew replied. "I knee-haltered them and allowed them to rest at the bottom of the hill."

"Good. Can you find your way back to Dundee without falling into the Boers' hands?"

"I'll try my best, sir," Andrew said.

"You'll have to. Grab a couple of hours' rest and then return to Dundee. Give Yule my compliments and tell him to withdraw his entire force to Ladysmith. With the Boers rampant in Natal, he's vulnerable up there and liable to being cut off."

"Yes, sir," Andrew said.

"Tell Yule I will do what I can to help when he comes nearer." White nodded and moved away, with his staff at his heels.

It was a little over 26 miles from Elandslaagte to Dundee by road, but with Boer commandoes on the loose, Andrew chose a more circuitous route. He rode Letsie, his favourite Basuto pony, and led Moshie on a long rein. Andrew was familiar with the area but rode cautiously, watching for any Boer patrols. Although the main Boer army had fled, Andrew knew that individuals or small commandoes could still roam this section of Natal.

Andrew eased up a slight slope, halted in the shade of a mimosa tree, and peered ahead. In the clear air, he saw a static wagon a couple of miles ahead, with a rising ribbon of dust approaching from the south. The wagon had distinctive yellow wheels and a patched canvas cover, while the extended team of oxen stood patiently waiting.

Boer or British? That wagon might be trouble, Andrew told himself and lifted his binoculars to see what was happening.

A woman knelt beside the wagon, peering intently at the rear left wheel. She wore a long dress and a broad terai hat, and Andrew could not see any men around.

It's unusual for a lone woman to drive a wagon, especially during a Boer invasion. Have the Boers left her behind when they retreated?

As Andrew watched, he saw the woman move to the rear of the wagon and take something from the interior. With her back turned, Andrew could not see what she was doing, but a few moments later, he heard a hammering that carried across the mile between them.

It looks like she's got trouble with her wagon.

The ribbon of dust moved closer to the wagon, then drifted away as the riders moved around the woman and halted. Andrew watched through his binoculars until he made out five men. They dismounted, with one holding the reins and the others surrounding the woman. She looked around and stood up with a hammer in her hand. Andrew could not see the expression on her face.

"That's Lieutenant Leslie and some of his troop," Andrew said. He took a deep breath. "Come on, Letsie. Let's see what's happening."

It was an easy downhill ride to the wagon, with Andrew conserving the strength of his horses while he watched what was happening ahead. As he drew nearer, he heard the woman's raised voice and the raucous laughter of the men.

"What's all this?" Andrew remained on horseback, with one hand on the butt of his rifle.

The men glanced at him, with one swarthy, long-chinned trooper stepping closer. "Who are you?"

"Captain Andrew Baird, Royal Malverns," Andrew replied. "You men are with the Imperial Light Horse. What's happening here, Leslie?"

"This woman is a Hollander, maybe a Boer sympathiser," Lieutenant Leslie explained with his easy smile. "We are finding out what she is doing here."

"What are you doing here, madam?" Andrew asked in Afrikaans, lifting his hat politely.

Andrew judged the woman to be about thirty, with a smooth, tanned complexion and dark hair above fine brown eyes. She wore a multicoloured scarf around her neck, with horizontal red, white, and blue stripes broken by a vertical stroke of green. "I am fixing my wagon," she replied in the same language, nodding to the rear offside wheel, which had a broken spoke.

"Thank you, ma'am," Andrew kept his voice level. He changed his language to English. "The lady has a broken spoke," he explained to Leslie.

Leslie grunted. "Why is she here at all?"

"Do you speak English, ma'am?" Andrew asked.

"No," the woman's gaze darted from man to man, examining them calmly.

"She's either a Boer or a Hollander," Leslie said. "Look at her scarf! It has the colours of the Vierkleur, the Transvaal's flag. We should take her to General Yule for questioning."

Andrew shook his head. He could feel the tension in these men. "She's a lady and a civilian with a damaged wagon. We don't make war on women or civilians. You men get about your business."

Leslie frowned. "You can't order us around. We're not in the Malverns."

"I outrank you, Lieutenant," Andrew reminded coldly. "Get about your business, whatever that is."

"We're not in the Transvaal anymore, Captain Baird. I am a lieutenant in the Imperial Light Horse," Leslie said. "We don't take orders from an infantryman."

"I was in the Natal Dragoons," Andrew countered, putting an edge on his voice. "Long before you even came to Africa. Now get on with your duty and leave this woman alone."

Leslie stepped back as his men hesitated. The swarthy man stepped to his horse and put a hand on his carbine. Andrew tightened his grip on his Lee-Metford, hoping he did not have to use it.

Leslie smiled and raised his hand in a casual salute. "As you say, sir. Come on, boys." He strode to his horse, mounted with an easy swing, and touched a hand to the brim of his hat. He looked from Andrew to the woman. "Be careful, sir. She might not be as innocent as she pretends."

The others followed Leslie, with the swarthy man favouring Andrew with a mirthless grin. Andrew watched them gallop away, raising a dust cloud that drifted towards the wagon. He relaxed his grip on the rifle and drew a deep breath.

CHAPTER 12

NATAL

OCTOBER 1899

"*Danke,*" the woman said quietly. "*En wat over u die van, Meneer?* And what name do you bear?"

"I am Captain Andrew Baird of the Royal Malverns," Andrew told her.

The woman held Andrew's gaze with clear, steady eyes. "I am Jacoba Fourie, once of Verdraaide Bome."

"Twisted Trees," Andrew translated. "Is that a farm?"

"It is a farm," Jacoba replied.

Andrew nodded. "Is it in Natal?"

"It is northeast of Pretoria," Jacoba continued to hold Andrew's gaze. "In the Zuid-Afrikaansche Republiek."

"You do realise we are at war?" Andrew asked.

"Yes," Jacoba replied evenly. "I was visiting my sister on her farm near Ladysmith when the war started, and now, I am trying to get home." She indicated her wagon. "Could you help me with the wheel, Captain? I have a broken spoke."

Andrew thought of his duty to recall General Yule's force but knew he could not allow Jacoba to remain stranded in the veldt. As well as the danger of wild animals, there might be wild men. "Of course, ma'am," he replied.

"I heard the wagon making strange noises a while back," Jacoba said. "I wasn't sure what it was until I checked." She nodded to the wheel. "A spoke splintered, and I have to replace it."

Andrew saw Jacoba had already fashioned a spoke for the wheel. "You've done a good job," he approved.

Jacoba ignored the compliment. "I'll have to take the wheel off to replace the spoke," she said. "I'll need you to help."

"I've never taken off a wagon wheel," Andrew admitted. "Do you have a jack?"

Jacoba shook her head. "I don't need one. I want you to take the wheel off when I lift the wagon. I've already outspanned the oxen."

"How the devil can you lift the wagon without a jack?" Andrew asked.

Jacoba favoured him with a glare. "Just take off the wheel when I tell you."

"As you say," Andrew replied.

Jacoba lay on her back under the rear axle, glanced sideways at him, and brought the back of her skirts and petticoats between her legs up to her waist. "Don't look," she warned.

"I won't," Andrew reassured her after a guilty glimpse of a white thigh. He knew that Boer women did not wear anything under their petticoats.

Jacoba pushed upwards with her legs, lifting the wagon to allow Andrew to remove the wheel. He worked as quickly as possible, laid the wheel on the ground, and loosened the rim sufficiently to slide in the spoke. He used Jacoba's hammer to bang the rim back into place before replacing the wheel.

When Jacoba allowed the wagon to return to the ground, Andrew hammered the wheel in tighter.*

"Are you all right, Jacoba?" Andrew asked as she crawled from under the wagon, stood, and brushed down her skirt.

"Thank you, Captain Baird," Jacoba said, as though lifting a heavy wagon was as easy as milking a cow. "That was helpful. I'll inspan the oxen and get on my way."

For a moment, Andrew was twenty years away, when he first met Mariana and her sensible, practical sister, Elaine. He had fallen for Elaine almost immediately and saw echoes of her in this stocky, self-assured Boer woman. He watched her inspan the oxen, calling them together with stylised hoots and whistles, and addressing them by name.

"They know their names," Jacoba explained, "and each has his position in the span. They get jealous if another beast takes their place."

Andrew nodded, produced his pipe, filled it, and lit the tobacco. Jacoba cracked her long whip, and the wagon lurched slowly onward. Andrew watched the wheel for the first hundred yards.

"It will hold," Jacoba told him. "I checked your workmanship."

Andrew hid his smile. Elaine would have said the same thing. "You're very handy, Mrs Fourie. I've never seen a woman lift a wagon before or inspan a team of oxen. Where did you learn such skills?"

"I am a farm girl," Jacoba explained, as Andrew rode close to the slow-moving wagon. He looked ahead, measuring the time it would take to reach Dundee and hoping General Yule's little army was ready to depart. "My parents wanted boys to work the farm, but all they produced was me." Her smile made her serious

---

* Mr Douglas Doyle, a native of South Africa, told me about Boer women using this technique to change a wagon wheel in the 1930s Transvaal.

face more attractive. "They named me for the son they never had: Jacoba."

"Jacoba is a fine name," Andrew said. "Can we make this wagon move faster?"

"Maybe a little," Jacoba said, giving a long whistle and a series of cracks with her whip. The oxen increased their pace from a crawl to a trudge, with the great wheels creaking and thudding on the ground.

"Thank you," Andrew said, glancing back at the spoke.

Jacoba intercepted his look. "It will hold," she assured him again. "Are you in a hurry, Captain?"

"I have a message to deliver in Dundee," Andrew told her.

"If I am slowing you down, Captain, you can ride ahead. I will follow at the speed of the wagon." Jacoba smiled again, crinkling her eyes at the corners.

"We will ride together," Andrew said. "I won't leave a woman alone with the country in such a disturbed state."

Jacoba negotiated a dip in the ground, whistling to her team before she replied. "Even when I am from an enemy country?" She raised her eyebrows as she spoke, so Andrew wondered if she was mocking him.

"Britain does not wage war on women," Andrew told her. "Besides, your husband will no doubt be anxious for your safety."

"My husband?" Jacoba's face lost all expression. She whistled, and the oxen avoided a soft patch of ground. "Well done, Shaka! Well done, Tugela!" she congratulated one of her leading oxen.

"Your husband will be with the invading army," Andrew said. "You arrived with them." He smiled. "I watched them arrive in Natal, and your wagon has distinctively coloured wheels."

Jacoba allowed the lead pair of oxen to pull the wagon around an eruption of anthills. "It was sensible to travel with the commandos," she said.

"It was," Andrew agreed. "I'll stay with you until we're close to the Boer army, and then we must part."

"They would shoot you on sight," Jacoba told him bluntly. "They shoot anything khaki."

"They would," Andrew said. "There must be thousands of Boers in the army."

"Many thousands of Boers," Jacoba said, smiling again, "and I will tell you no more, except that none of them is my man, and your probing for information will not work."

Andrew knew that the terms "man" and "husband" could be synonymous to a Boer woman. "Is that so?"

"I am a *Bokkeoppas*," Jacoba said with a defiant lift of her chin. She looked at Andrew as if expecting derision or disdain. "A *Bokkeoppas* is an unmarried woman over thirty. It signifies I am good for nothing except herding goats."

Andrew recognised the bitterness in Jacoba's voice. "I would disagree with that," he said. "The way you handle the wagon and fixed the wheel was impressive."

"These are a man's skills," Jacoba said. "A woman should keep the house and raise children. What man wants a woman who is as strong as he is?"

The wagon jolted up a slight rise, and they both halted to peer at the landscape ahead. "Any decent man," Andrew said quietly. "I am sure many men in the Transvaal would welcome a woman like you."

"Would you?" Jacoba asked.

"I have been married for nearly twenty years," Andrew replied, smiling.

"And if you were not married?" Jacoba persisted, with her eyes sharp.

Andrew held her gaze, recognising her hurt. "I would have been honoured to meet a woman like you," he told her.

"Oh." Jacoba looked momentarily nonplussed. She opened her mouth to reply, closed it again, and whistled to her oxen, who pulled again. Andrew rode at her side, hoping they were not much longer on the trail.

When they neared the British camp outside Dundee, Andrew spoke again. "I will have to leave you soon," he said. He pointed to the ground, where horses' hooves had churned the mud. "That was a Boer commando, and I'd say they rode that way less than an hour ago."

"Can you track?" Jacoba sounded surprised.

"A little," Andrew said.

Jacoba eyed him thoughtfully. "I did not know *Rooinecks* could track," she said. "I didn't know they could be like you."

"We are not all the same," Andrew replied. Suddenly, he did not want this woman to leave. He lingered for a moment, trying to read the expression in her eyes. *Don't be an idiot!* "Do you want me to take you to your people?"

Jacoba hesitated before she replied. "My people?" She gave a quick smile. "They'd like nothing better than to shoot or capture a *Rooineck* officer." Her smile broadened. "Especially one carrying a message for the garrison of Dundee."

"You guessed?"

"It was not hard to guess," Jacoba told him. She dropped her smile. "Thank you for the escort, Captain Baird, and your help with the Uitlanders."

Andrew nodded. "These men were no gentlemen. They did not act like British soldiers."

Jacoba eyed him again. "You had better return to your General Yule, Captain, and I will return where I belong." She unravelled the multicoloured scarf from around her hat. "Here, Captain. Wear this for luck." She hesitated again. "It may keep you safe in times of trouble. And it may help you to remember me."

"Thank you," Andrew said, accepting the scarf and standing awkwardly, wondering at the expression in her brown eyes.

"I'll never forget you," Jacoba said. She smiled again, turned to her team, and whistled, turning the wagon to follow the commandos' tracks.

Andrew watched her for a moment, stuffed the scarf in his

pack, and kicked Letsie towards the British garrison in Dundee. The image of Jacoba Fourie remained in his head. *Don't be stupid, Andrew. You have a good wife in Mariana and only met Jacoba briefly. Forget her.*

Yet the image remained: a stocky, capable woman who was so like Elaine.

CHAPTER 13

DUNDEE, NATAL

OCTOBER 1899

"You have a message for me from General White?" Fifty-two-year-old Brigadier-General James Yule spoke through his walrus moustache as Andrew stood before him. "Spit it out, man!"

"General White sends his compliments, sir, and says he cannot reinforce you without sacrificing Ladysmith and the colony behind," Andrew repeated the message word-for-word. "He says you must try to fall back on Ladysmith, and he will do what he may to help you when you come nearer."

Yule drummed his fingers on his travelling desk as he heard the order. "Thank you, Captain Baird. You may have noticed that our victory at Talana only temporarily discomforted the Boers. They are already drifting back towards us and have their huge Creusot gun on Impati Hill."

"I noticed signs of Boers on the journey here, sir," Andrew replied.

"No doubt that is why you took such a time to reach me with General White's urgent message," Yule said dryly.

"The Boers did delay me, sir," Andrew did not give details. He was already regretting neglecting his duty to help Jacoba.

"You arrived safely, which is the main thing," Yule said and looked up as an explosion sounded outside the town, for the British had left their original camp. "The Boers are also sending us a message," he said.

"It would appear so, sir," Andrew agreed.

"I probed towards Glencoe Junction this morning," Yule said, "trying to capture the fleeing Boers from Elandslaagte. However, the enemy artillery on Impati Hill soon found our range. We withdrew through the mist, thankfully with few casualties."

"The Boers are a resourceful people, sir," Andrew said.

Yule stood up, looking worried. "I knew we had two possibilities. We either stick it out in Dundee and hold off the Boers that will besiege us or withdraw to Ladysmith. I had decided on the latter before you brought your message."

Another shell landed, this time inside the town, sending up a tall fountain of mud and earth. Andrew heard a man cursing and wondered if the Boers had hit him.

"Tell me of any Boer dispositions you noticed on your journey here, Baird," Yule ordered. He listened as Andrew pointed to the evidence of Boer activity and the number of fugitives from Elandslaagte. Yule marked Andrew's information on a large-scale map.

"Thank you, Captain. Return to your company," Yule ordered. "My staff and I will decide the best route to Ladysmith."

C Company greeted Jack with smiles and nods. "We thought you were dead, sir," Sinton said. "Were you involved in that battle at Elandslaagte?"

"I was," Andrew admitted.

"You lucky dog, sir," Sinton said enviously. "Two battles in two days!"

"I am not sure that lucky is the best word," Andrew replied.

"I'd have given everything to have been there," Sinton said. "Not that I have much to give."

Andrew raised his eyebrows. "I thought you were a scion of the nobility, a member of one of the oldest families in England, with blue blood in every vein."

"Oh, that's true enough," Sinton said. "I'm probably related to half the nobility between the Tweed and the Tamar, but I am the fourth son with no chance of inheriting."

"Don't you have a title?" Andrew asked.

"I am the Honourable Lionel Aubrey Sinton, sir," Sinton said with a smile. "I never use my title and never will inherit anything more than a fond farewell or a what-the-hell-are-you-doing-back-here?"

Andrew smiled sympathetically. "I see your point," he said.

"I tried civilian life and failed miserably, sir," Sinton said. "I must sink or swim in the army, and as I have no desire to sink, I seek action, bloodshed and glory to rise through the ranks to become a Field Marshal."

"Hence your envy," Andrew said.

"Hence my envy," Sinton agreed. "Some men serve for years without seeing action, and you were in two glorious victories in two days."

"I am sure you'll see your share of fighting before we win this war," Andrew reassured him. "Now, I must visit my men."

As Andrew spoke to his company and visited the wounded in the makeshift hospital in Dundee, Yule organised moving the garrison to Ladysmith. Information that Andrew and various patrols brought told the brigadier that the Boers occupied the direct road-and-rail route, so he worked out a longer alternative. Yule decided to take the garrison along the road to Helpmakaar until they reached Beith, then head south through the Van Tonders Pass.

"That pass would be a fine place for the Boers to ambush us,"

Andrew said, remembering his experiences on India's North-West Frontier.

"Yule will send out pickets to control the peaks," Sinton said.

"That's what I would advise," Andrew agreed. He hesitated for a moment. "You know your way around the Army List, don't you, Sinton?"

"Pretty well, sir," Sinton replied. "I study the *Naval and Military Gazette*, looking for openings for promotion, sir."

"Have you ever come across a Major Dixon? Spelled with an X."

"I know of two Major Dixons, sir," Sinton replied immediately. "Major Stuart Dixon from Hampshire and another Dixon from your neck of the woods."

"Do you know his Christian name?" Andrew tried to sound casual.

Sinton screwed up his face. "It will come to me in a minute, sir. Hang it all; I know the name. Oh, yes. Charles Dixon, sir. He's distantly related to the Duke of Buccleuch, I believe, and got a degree at Oxford. He's quite a scholar, sir, with an interest in Arthurian literature."

He would have. "Thank you, Lionel," Andrew said, pushing away his personal worries to concentrate on the route to Ladysmith.

With the pass negotiated, Yule planned to march his men to Ladysmith, fording three major rivers.

"I remember fording the Buffalo when we invaded Zululand twenty years ago," Andrew reminisced. "We lost a few men in the current." He looked upwards at the threatening sky. "Let's hope the weather clears up. I don't relish crossing flooded rivers."

On the Sunday night, Yule sent Major Wickham of the Indian Commissariat and a column of wagons to strip the now-deserted British camp of anything useful. With two companies of the Leicesters as escort, Wickham filled a convoy of wagons with ammunition, food, and clothing for the journey to Ladysmith. Andrew imagined the frantic scenes in the old camp that dark night as men raked among the sagging tents and stores while nervous sentries watched for the Boers. Busy NCOs organised men to light candles inside the remaining tents to fool the Boers into thinking the British had returned to their old camp.

Simultaneously, Brigadier Yule gathered the garrison south of Dundee, with the Malverns joining the 4,500 men, including infantry, cavalry and three field artillery batteries.

"Keep quiet, lads," Andrew warned C Company. "The less noise we make, the less the Boers will know we are departing."

"Why are we retiring, sir?" Corporal Harwood asked. "We defeated the Boers. We gave them the devil of a hiding."

"We're returning to Ladysmith," Andrew replied. "If we stay in Dundee, the Boers will cut us off."

"Yes, sir," Harwood said. "I am sure we could defeat them again."

"I am sure we could, Corporal," Andrew agreed.

Sinton returned from inspecting the company. "All the fit men are present, sir."

"Thank you, Sinton," Andrew said.

"I heard the brigadier has spread false information that we're heading to Glencoe to meet reinforcements," Sinton said.

"I heard the same," Andrew said. "Yule is sending the Boers the wrong way. A garrison in column is very vulnerable to ambush, so the brigadier is ensuring we have a few hours to get away from Dundee before the Boers follow."

"What about the wounded?" Private Conway asked. "Where are they?"

"We've left them in the hospital at Dundee," Sergeant Kenny replied. "The Boers will take care of them. The Boers are Christians, not savages like the or Burmese."

"We should have taken the wounded with us," Conway complained. "It's not right, leaving them to the enemy."

Andrew agreed, although he also appreciated Yule's strategy.

The column had to move fast to escape the Boers, and the sick and wounded would slow them down. The journey on jolting wagons would also be agonising for injured men. Yule was sensible to leave the wounded behind, but Andrew was unsure if he would have made the same decision. The brigadier had also abandoned the Dundee Town Guard, who now had the choice of facing an overwhelming Boer army or laying down arms and surrendering.

You had difficult choices to make, Brigadier.

Yule pushed the column out of Dundee, with his cavalry and mounted infantry scouting ahead and watching the flanks and rear for the enemy. The men slogged on, stumbling in the dark, unsure why or where they were marching but obeying orders like soldiers.

"Are you sure we won at Talana?" Private Hobart asked. "This rushing feels more like a retreat."

"We're consolidating the units at Ladysmith," Sergeant Kenny said.

"Consolidating?" Hobart repeated. "Is that another word for retiring?"

"No. It's another word for I'll boot you up the arse if you ask any more bloody stupid questions." Kenny was not known for his patience.

"Yes, Sergeant," Hobart said, relapsing into moody silence as his colleagues hid their smiles.

The column marched through heavy rain showers, with the officers urging the men on and ensuring nobody fell out. The ground rose before them, rough underfoot, as the darkness eased, and the stars above faded.

"Keep moving, men," Andrew encouraged. "We're bound for Ladysmith, dry beds, and hot food!"

Yule's small army wound on before him, men marching in quarter column, stumbling over loose rocks, with the outside files glancing around in case the Boers swooped down on them.

On the early afternoon of Monday, 23rd October, Yule's force arrived at the entrance of Van Tonders Pass, footsore, sodden with the rain and wondering what lay ahead.

"That's the first twenty miles covered," Sinton said. "And not a whisper of a Boer."

"Only forty miles to go." Andrew raised his binoculars to study the hills that rose on either side of the pass.

"Can you see anything?" Sinton asked.

"No," Andrew said. "But that doesn't mean the Boers aren't there. These lads can hide an entire commando behind a blade of grass."

"Best get a team of mowers out, then," Sinton said with the ghost of a smile.

The bugles sounded the halt, allowing the men to find the driest spot on the ground they could and stretch out. Some were asleep within minutes despite the rain. Andrew organised the company cooks to feed C Company, sent out pickets, and checked his men. Boswell did the same, with a damp cheroot clutched between his teeth.

"Nobody's dropped out, sir," Sergeant Kenny reported. "We have a few men with blistered feet."

"Have them report to the medical orderlies," Andrew ordered. "We are only a third of the way into the journey."

"Yes, sir." Kenny saluted and marched away, bellowing for the footsore men.

Yule allowed the column to rest that afternoon, with the men recovering and the officers concerned about a Boer attack. After an evening meal of biscuits and half-heated tea, Yule led them into the Van Tonders Pass shortly after dusk.

"Come on, C Company," Andrew said. "Take the rearguard, Sinton, and round up any stragglers."

The pass was narrow and undulating, with a track that bent and looped between scrubby woodland. Andrew relaxed slightly when he saw the hills were further from the road than he had expected. After his experiences on the North-West Frontier, he had visions of an ambush by Boer marksmen hiding on steep slopes only yards from the path.

"Keep the men moving," Andrew ordered. He could feel something watching from the trees and twice saw the glint of moonlight on yellow-green eyes. "Don't let them stray. God knows what's waiting in the bush."

"Lions and tigers and things that go bump in the night, eh?" Sinton said.

"There are no tigers in Africa," Andrew replied pedantically.

"I was speaking figuratively, sir," Sinton said.

"I know," Andrew told him. "But the men could hear you, and the less intelligent might take you seriously."

The sound of boots thudding on the damp ground mingled with the creak and crash of wagons, the soft bellows of oxen and the whistles of the drivers. The pass was only six miles long but seemed endless as Andrew ushered C Company through, with his nerves screaming at every twist and bend of the track. He expected to hear the "buck-up" report of a Mauser at any moment and nearly envied the less imaginative of his company who plodded on, unthinking of anything except the next step.

"We're clear, sir," a mounted infantryman loomed out of the murk ahead. "We're clear of the pass."

"You'll get a break soon, men," Andrew promised. Brigadier Yule intended to rest through the day and march at night. They plodded on, boots rising and falling, men bumping into one another in the dark, muttering, cursing, yet covering the ground.

Dawn lit the eastern horizon, a broadening band of saffron-red between the dark earth below and the rainclouds above—a mixed promise of more rain and hope of redemption. When the advance guard reached the Waschbank River, the column eased to a thankful halt. Yule ordered the wagons to form a laager, and the men threw themselves down, most sleeping in full kit and ignoring the intermittent rain.

Andrew frowned as he heard the distant rumble. "Listen!"

"That's thunder," Lieutenant Sinton said, glancing at the river. "Let's hope the river doesn't flood."

"It's not thunder," Andrew corrected. "That's gunfire. Artillery."

"Where's it from?" Sinton asked. "Nobody's firing at us."

"It's a good few miles away," Andrew drew on his experience. "Maybe ten miles or more. The hills distort the sound."

Brigadier Yule rode past with his staff officers grouped around him. He stopped beside the Malverns for a moment, looking exhausted and drawn with fever. "That will be General White fighting Cronje's commando. We will lend him a hand."

Within twenty minutes, Yule wakened the column and marched them towards the sound of the guns. The men obediently followed, some staggering with weariness, others grumbling, and a few striding towards the battle, determined to do their best.

"Why march toward a fight when nobody's bothering us?" Private Jenkins asked.

"So the officers can win medals, promotion and glory," Conway replied.

"Ah, thanks, Cons. I feel better now that I know."

"It's stopped!" Sinton said. "The firing has stopped!"

"Halt!" Yule held up his hand.

The column stopped. Men strained to listen. There was silence except for the sough of the wind.

"You are right, Lieutenant Sinton. Return to the camp beside the Waschbank."

With sentries posted, Andrew slept fitfully, to wake every half-hour. Sometime in the middle of the afternoon, he saw the calm blinking of a heliograph across the rain-smeared miles and heard a signaller running to Brigadier Yule.

"Message from General White, sir!" The signaller sounded excited.

Yule was awake and fully dressed. He snatched the pencil-written message from the signaller, scanned it twice and raised his voice.

"Bugler! Sound the alert! Cooks! Prepare breakfast for the men! Officers to me!"

Andrew joined the rush of sodden and half-dressed officers gathered around the brigadier.

"We have a message from General White," Yule explained quietly. "We are to march on without delay to meet a column from Ladysmith under a local volunteer named Colonel Royston."

The officers murmured about the distance still to cover and the weariness of the men. Andrew looked back at C Company, sprawled exhausted on the sodden ground, and exchanged worried glances with Captain Boswell.

"Without delay, gentlemen," Yule repeated. "I presume that General White has intelligence of Erasmus' commando pressing close behind us."

Andrew was not alone in looking over his shoulder at the road to the gloomy pass. He had not seen a Boer since they left Dundee.

"Prepare your men, Gentlemen," Yule ordered. "We march in half an hour."

Yule's half-hour was overly optimistic as the column prepared itself; the drivers gathered the oxen, and the men folded and loaded tents while the cavalry and mounted infantry fed and cared for their horses.

Andrew and Boswell checked their companies as the column marched on, trudging across the miles as the weather deteriorated. Periods of torrential rain turned the ground to liquid mud and forced men to walk with their heads down and rifles inverted so the rain did not pour down the barrels.

"Join the army, the sergeant told me," Conway said. "See the world, the sergeant told me. Make new friends and live a life of leisure in sunny climes defending the bloody Empire, the sergeant told me."

Wet and miserable, the infantry dragged one reluctant foot after another, passing the occasional fallen ox or horse and peering into the teeming rain ahead.

"Walk on, boys!" Andrew ordered. "Warm quarters and hot food in Ladysmith!"

When a pencil-thin twenty-year-old man staggered and fell, gasping that he could not walk another step, Andrew and Corporal Harwood hoisted him onto Moshie and pushed on. Within an hour, another man collapsed, and Andrew dismounted and gave him Letsie.

"You'll have to walk, sir," Corporal Harwood sounded concerned.

"If the men can walk, so can I," Andrew said.

"If you say so, sir," Harwood replied.

"Keep moving, men!" Andrew ordered, snarling at the lazy and encouraging the genuinely weak.

Lieutenant Sinton stepped to Andrew's side. Unshaven, with his eyes sunk into deep pouches and his saturated uniform clinging to his sparse frame, he had aged in the last few days.

"The men are suffering, sir!"

"They'll make it," Andrew said. "Push them on! If they fall behind, the Boers will snap them up, or they'll die of cold and wet. Push them on!"

"Yes, sir!" Sinton said, looking upwards as the rain hammered down on the dripping, cursing column.

Andrew was unsure how many days passed in marching through the rain and mud before a cavalry patrol splashed up to Yule and reported the road was firmer ahead. "We're approaching Ladysmith, sir!"

"Smarten yourselves up, C Company!" Andrew ordered, and heard every other officer and NCO in the column echo his words. From a shambling collection of bedraggled refugees, Yule's column transformed into a military force, proud of the battle they had won and the hardships they had endured.

"Backs straight, men!" Andrew shouted. "The Ladysmith

garrison have come out to see us. Show them we are C Company of the Royal Malverns, the best company in the best regiment in the British Army!"

"The best regiment in any army," an anonymous voice sounded from the ranks.

"I stand corrected," Andrew replied, smiling. "The best regiment in any army!"

Yule led his column past the cheering garrison and into Ladysmith. Andrew saw his men march proudly, with the miseries of the journey already behind them. He wondered if the victory of Talana and the shared endurance of the march would strengthen them as men and soldiers, and then wondered what the future held.

He stepped away from the column and watched the men march past, yet his mind was on the chance meeting with Jacoba Fourie.

When I last served in South Africa, I met quite a few Boer women, but never one quite like her. I admired her practicality and directness, yet many Boers share that quality. Something else, a different, elusive quality, intrigues me.

Andrew shrugged, shook his head and smiled. It did not matter; he would never see her again. He resolved to write to Mariana as soon as he settled into his quarters that night.

"Heads up, lads! That's the way!" Andrew deliberately altered the direction of his thoughts as he chased away the memory of Jacoba Fourie.

CHAPTER 14

DUNDEE AND LADYSMITH, NATAL

NOVEMBER 1899

Jacoba eased her wagon into the laager and began to unyoke the oxen. She checked her wheels and decided the new spoke was adequate, but she should plane it further and paint it to match its fellows. She nodded, stood, and ordered some servants to care for the oxen.

"Where is Commandant-General Joubert?" she asked.

A dark-haired, bearded man eyed her, lifted his hat and gestured to a large tent in the centre of the laager. "Slim Piet is in there," he told her.

"Thank you, *meneer*."

Leaving the servants to care for the oxen, Jacoba walked to the tent, her skirt snapping against her legs with every stride.

Petrus Jacobus Joubert was a sixty-eight-year-old, heavily bearded man with calm eyes and a shrewd view of the world. Joubert had an impressive military record, having led the victorious Boer forces in the battles of Ingogo, Laing's Nek, and

Majuba in the previous war with Britain. He had also been successful in the Malaboch War against the Bahananwa tribe. Yet despite Joubert's successes, Jacoba did not think he looked like a warrior.

The Commandant-General of the Boer armies was smaller than most of his compatriots. His voice could change from a stentorian roar to high tones that seemed out of place in a military commander.

"*Goeie middag, mevrou* – Good afternoon, madam," Joubert stood and raised his hat politely when Jacoba entered his tent.

"Good afternoon, Commandant-General," Jacoba greeted him formally.

"I see you managed to evade the British," Joubert said with a smile.

"Nearly." Jacoba explained what had happened with Andrew.

Joubert nodded. "You met a good *Rooineck*," he said slowly. "I remember a young officer of that name from the last war we fought with the British. He could be a relative." Joubert sighed. "I do not like killing," he admitted, "but sometimes it is necessary to do a small evil for a greater good. I hope the Lord will understand."

"I am sure He will," Jacoba replied.

"We will find out when He calls us to His judgement seat," Joubert said, unsmiling. "I will pass the word not to kill a British officer wearing your scarf. We will try to keep him safe until we capture him."

"Thank you, *meneer*," Jacoba said. She could not say she felt a bond with the British officer.

Joubert nodded. "We should preserve what good we can. What intelligence have you gathered for me?"

Jacoba removed a small notepad from inside her skirt. "I have spoken to most of the Hollanders who farm in this part of Natal, from Dundee and Glencoe to Ladysmith," she said. "Here are their names, and I have put a cross beside those who might join us."

"*Danke*," Joubert studied the list. "You have been busy, Jacoba." He looked up. "We will ask these people where their loyalties lie. If every true Boer comes with us, we'll sing the *Volkslied* from the Low Veldt to Table Mountain."

PIET NOTICED THE NEW WAGONS AS HE RODE INTO THE laager. "We have newcomers in our midst," he said.

Hendrik nodded, dismounting and fondling his pony. "Three wagons," he said. "Two look like supply wagons, but the third is too lightly laden."

Piet narrowed his eyes and stepped back. "There is a woman in that wagon," he said. "Women always bring trouble."

Michal's face brightened with interest. "Women can bring other things." He pushed back his hat and tossed the blonde hair from his eyes. "She is well-favoured but too old for me." He looked away. "A woman that age will be married with a brood of children."

"I cannot see her man," Hendrik said, stepping closer and removing his hat. "Good day." He watched as the woman checked her wheels. "I see you have had to replace one of your wheel spokes."

"Yes," Jacoba agreed, glanced at Hendrik, and returned her attention to the wheel.

"Did your man replace the broken spoke?"

"I replaced it myself," Jacoba told him. She did not mention Baird.

Hendrik knelt beside her, smoothing a hand over the spoke. "It is good workmanship."

"It's a bit rough," Jacoba said, "but it works."

Hendrik touched the spoke. "If it works, then nothing else matters." He eyed her frankly. "Is your man with the commando?"

"I do not have a husband," Jacoba told him.

Hendrik nodded understandingly. "I understand," he said. "Losing your man is hard."

"I have never had a husband," Jacoba clarified her situation.

Hendrik frowned. "Why not?" he asked.

"You are very direct," Jacoba said, slightly annoyed.

"I am no youth to play silly word games," Hendrik replied. "Why have you not found a man?" He stepped back, looking her up and down. "You are a presentable woman."

Jacoba raised her eyebrows, unable to hide her surprise. "Thank you, *meneer*." She gave a little curtsey.

Hendrik lifted his hat politely. "You should have a good man to look after you."

"Do I need a man to look after me?" Jacoba asked.

Hendrik touched the wagon spoke. "Maybe you don't need a man to look after you," he said, "but you may want a man sometime."

"I may," Jacoba replied. "Sometime." She stepped away from her wagon. "I do not believe you are a single man."

"My wife died last year," Hendrik told her. "And my son."

"Ah," Jacoba said. "You will miss her. You will miss them both."

"I do. A man needs a wife," Hendrik replied.

"I have heard that is true," Jacoba said, holding Hendrik's gaze.

"What is your business with this commando?" Hendrik asked. "Do you know anybody here?"

"I have only met Commandant Joubert," Jacoba replied.

"And Hendrik du Toit," Hendrik lifted his hat again, bowing.

"Ja," Jacoba allowed herself a faint smile. "And Hendrik du Toit."

Hendrik replaced his hat. "Good day, Jacoba."

"Good day, Hendrik," Jacoba watched him walk slowly away.

Hendrik felt her gaze on him, wondering how long he would stay with the commando before he returned to his farm. He looked at the laager with its wagons, busy servants, oxen and groups of armed men and shook his head.

I do not belong here. I am a farmer, not a soldier.

"Hendrik!" Dannie shouted. "The British have left Dundee! We are going to take possession!"

Hendrik caught the men's elation as they rode into the little town of Dundee. Michal was laughing, waving his hat so his blond hair streamed out behind him. Piet was grinning, his teeth white against the dark beard and sun-browned face. Louis Grobler and his sons were staring around them, surprised that they had captured a British town, while Willem Mentz looked ready to shoot anybody who looked like a Rooineck.

Hendrik saw the sullen or scared faces of the citizens staring at the Boers as the victorious horsemen clattered through their town. Some riders dismounted as soon as they arrived in Dundee, kicking open doors and thrusting into houses despite the owners' protests.

"Come on, Hendrik!" Michal shouted. "Let's see what we can find before others take it all!"

"I am a farmer, not a robber!" Hendrik replied.

"Nonsense! We have conquered this *dorp*, and to the victor go the spoils!"

"No!" Hendrik shook his head. "We should not covet our neighbour's possessions!"

Michal laughed again, dismounted with a smooth, flowing motion, and ran into a shop. "Food, Hendrik! Bread and cakes and tins of meat!"

"I will not steal," Hendrik said. He watched as Wessels Commando scattered around Dundee, rushing into houses and shops and emerging with the prized possessions of ordinary people—clothes, jewellery, small items of furniture and as much food as they could carry.

"Biltong and bread keep you alive," Michal joked as he emerged from a shop with a long string of sausages draped around his neck, "but it is not enough for a hungry man." He grinned across at Hendrik. "You will not want to share our feast tonight."

Hendrik looked longingly at the bread tucked under Michal's saddle. His late wife had made bread every week, and the smell brought back many memories. He shook his head. "Stealing is against God's law," he said. "I will not profit from theft."

Michal nodded, still smiling. "You are a better man than I am, Hendrik." He called to the other members of his corporalship. "We will visit the British camp now and see what we can pick up. Where is Piet?"

"I saw him enter that house there," Willem pointed to a two-storeyed house behind a broad stoep.

"I'll get him," Hendrik dismounted. "You go ahead, and we'll catch up."

Michal grinned. "We'll get the best pickings!" he shouted, waved his hat and spurred along the street. His corporalship followed, some with items of men's or women's clothing trailing from their shoulders, all with items of food and a few busily chewing. The young Grobler boys were shouting excitedly, standing in their stirrups as they whooped down the street.

"Piet!" Hendrik opened the house door and peered inside. "Piet!"

The house was larger than Hendrik had realised, with rooms extending backwards and a wooden staircase stretching upwards.

"Piet!" Hendrik shouted again. He glanced into the front room. Careless hands had knocked down the furniture, yanking open drawers and opening cupboards to see what was worth stealing. Intruders had littered the floor with personal papers, books, family photographs and articles of clothing.

"Piet!" Hendrik heard noises upstairs and climbed heavily up, with the wooden steps creaking under his weight. He held his rifle in both hands, fearful of a British ambush. "Are you all right, Piet?"

Hendrik found a small landing with two closed doors. He pushed the first door open and saw Piet lying on a bed with his trousers around his ankles and his rifle lying on the floor. The woman beneath him had her eyes and mouth tightly closed. Piet's dogs lay at the foot of the bed.

"Get up!" Hendrik grabbed Piet by the shoulder and jerked him sideways. Piet fell to the floor, with the woman opening her eyes wide. Her mouth worked, making small, inarticulate sounds.

"Cover yourself, woman!" Hendrik ordered, yanking her long skirt down to her ankles.

"She only speaks English," Piet said, pulling up his trousers.

"We're leaving for the British camp," Hendrik did not mention the woman, unsure if she had been a willing participant. If the woman had been his wife, he would have shot Piet like a dog. "Come on!"

The British camp was like an Aladdin's cave of tinned food, tents and a fully equipped hospital, where doctors were still busy with British and Boer wounded. Even the wildest Boers respected the medical men, aware they treated both sides equally. Hendrik watched them for a moment and walked away.

"Come on, Hendrik," Louis said. "We can't help here."

When Hendrik lifted half a dozen tins of meat, Michal laughed. "I thought the Lord disapproved of stealing," he said.

"Stealing from civilians is wrong, but this is military equipment," Hendrik replied solemnly. "The British would have used everything here to support soldiers who would kill us. It is no sin to take the enemy's war supplies."

"I did not know the Lord made such fine distinctions," Michal replied. "I'll have to reread my Bible after the war."

"One must gain something from fighting," Hendrik said. He glanced at Piet. "As long as we do not take advantage of the weak and the helpless by our victories."

They sat in the middle of the camp, admiring their loot as others continued to rampage around. Michal removed his hat, swept back his hair and watched Piet feed his dogs with strips of biltong. "You are a strange man, Piet," he said. "You talk sparingly, and do not shoot much when we fight the *Rooinecks*."

Piet looked up, unsmiling, and his eyes were inscrutable behind a mane of shaggy hair. "No," he said, "I do not talk much, yet when I shoot, I do not miss."

Michal replaced his hat. "I have noticed that you never miss. I know you are not married. Do you have family in Transvaal?" he asked. "Or in the Free State?"

"I have family in the Republics," Piet replied after a long pause to think. "I have not seen or spoken to them for a long time."

"Have you always been a hunter?" Michal asked. He had not seen Jacoba arrive but noticed her listening to the conversation, busy with a fire and coffee pot. Hendrik was close by, watching Jacoba without speaking as he slowly filled his pipe.

Piet considered his words carefully. "I have always hunted," he replied. He waited a few moments as both dogs settled at his feet, panting, their tongues lolling from the side of their mouths.

"Did you ever farm, Piet?" Jacoba took over the questioning. "Where does your family farm?"

Piet fondled the smaller of his dogs. "My people were always Trek-Boers," he said. "Long before the Great Trek, they pushed beyond the frontiers into the wild lands. They were one of the first to explore Africa past the boundary of the Dutch East Indies Company, up to the Great Fish River and beyond."

"They never settled?" Hendrik asked. "A man needs land to call his home. Land, cattle, and a wife. A man is not complete without a farm and a wife." He glanced at Jacoba and then away again. Jacoba did not respond.

Piet's smile was slow but spread over his face to his eyes.

"Many men would agree with you, Hendrik," Piet said. "My people preferred the space of Africa, exploring the next range of hills, seeing what lies beyond the rivers and having the Lord's great sky above. We are not tied to the land; we are part of it."

Hendrik thrust his pipe into his mouth. "It is a different life from mine," he said.

"It is a free life," Piet said, with his eyes gentle. "We have been in Africa for hundreds of years, and there is much more to see."

"The coffee is ready," Jacoba said quietly. "Every man needs coffee, whether he farms the land or hunts over it."

Piet smiled. "Ja. That is true, Jacoba. Coffee is the cord that ties us all together."

Michal was the first to laugh, with the others joining in as they gathered around the fire. Piet's dogs opened lazy eyes to watch him, decided he was not going far and remained where they were.

"We have captured our first British towns," Jacoba said. "Now on to Ladysmith, Pietermaritzburg and Cape Town." She lifted her mug. *Een vrije volk zijn wij,*" Jacoba said. "A free people are we."

COLONEL NEWLAND SAT COMFORTABLY IN AN ARMCHAIR IN the farmhouse central to the Malverns' quarters. They were a quarter of a mile from Ladysmith, nestled on the lower slope of a hill called Maiden Castle. Newland stretched out his legs. "That's the first week of this war over, gentlemen," he said. "We have defeated the Boers in two battles and captured two of their guns, inflicted considerable casualties on them and proved we are the better men." He paused to light his pipe, shook out the match and flicked it away. "On the other hand, they have invaded Natal, killed and captured some of our men, and now occupy Dundee with a pile of captured military stores."

The officers nodded, reasonably satisfied with the results of the war so far after the disasters of the previous encounters with the Boers.

Newland puffed out aromatic blue smoke. "We should be quite comfortable in Ladysmith. We have a sizeable garrison here, with some 12,000 men, including good-quality cavalry who gave the Boers the about-turn at Elandslaagte. We also have the

Imperial Light Horse, who are showing up well. You all know the infantry: us, the Gordon Highlanders, the Royal Irish Rifles, the Leicesters, Devons, Rifles and the rest."

Andrew nodded. The infantry was good quality.

Newland exhaled more smoke. "We have six batteries of field artillery and a battery of screw guns most suitable for fighting the Boers on the hills." He smiled at his battalion. "In short, gentlemen, we have a fine little army here, and heaven help Piet if he tries to attack us."

"We should attack him," Major Cradley suggested. "We have already defeated the Boers in two offensive engagements. We should use our momentum to give Kruger another bloody nose."

The colonel treated Cradley to a long stare. "That decision rests with General White," he said. "We will do our duty as he decides. Dismissed, gentlemen!"

Andrew left the meeting, stopped a few yards from the farmhouse and stared around. Mist shrouded the hills around Ladysmith, slithering from the heights to cling to the upper slopes, creating an aura of mystery that slightly unsettled Andrew. He thought of the brave, resolute enemy the British faced, men who had defeated British armies in the previous war and who were determined to fight for their independence. Andrew could not help his involuntary shiver.

CHAPTER 15

LADYSMITH, NATAL

OCTOBER 1899

Andrew strolled around the town. He knew Ladysmith was strategically important, but he found little aesthetically pleasing about the town. The Town Hall was probably the most significant building with its high clock tower, but even that would scarcely warrant a second glance in Britain. Although it was older than many towns in Southern Africa, Andrew thought Ladysmith still felt like a frontier settlement with an air of impermanence. It seemed an imposition on the landscape, a place that Africa could sweep away in an instant by flood, fire or civil disruption.

It did not take Andrew long to pace the town, for there were only two streets of tin-roofed houses, with a few stores, the ubiquitous church, the Town Hall, some trees for shade and suburbs of detached villas complete with gardens and verandas.

"What do you think?" Sinton asked. "There's not much to see, is there?"

"I think this place will be hard to defend," Andrew said. "These hills surround us, as hills surrounded Dundee. You'll remember we had to launch a major attack at Talana when General Penn-Symons failed to garrison the hills at Dundee." Andrew shook his head. "We should never have allowed the Boers to capture that hill in the first place."

Sinton nodded, examining the surrounding hills. "General White has put men on the closest heights, sir, but we don't have sufficient to garrison them adequately. Even if we did, the further hills dominate them."

Andrew lifted his binoculars. "I think Ladysmith will be the crucible of this war, Sinton. The Boers will want to capture the town, and the British will try and ensure they don't." He lowered his binoculars. "The eyes of the world will be on us."

Sinton laughed. "And all for an insignificant little *dorp* that people would pass through without comment in Herefordshire."

"People would say the same about Hastings or Waterloo," Andrew said quietly. "Wars give significance to places that only want to live quietly in the background of history." He turned away. "We can only hope future generations remember Ladysmith as a British victory."

Sinton looked askance. "Of course, we will win," he said.

"Of course we will," Andrew said quietly, hiding his doubts. "General White will probably remain on the defensive. The Boers outnumber us, and if Ladysmith falls, the whole of Natal will lie open. The longer we tie up the Boers in Ladysmith, the more time we'll have to build up our forces elsewhere."

"Will Britain be sending reinforcements, sir?" Sinton asked.

"Without a doubt," Andrew replied. "Let's hope they arrive quickly."

"I heard that Joubert is approaching us with his main army, sir," Sinton said. "He's left Dundee already. The Free State commandos are also on the west and north, converging on Ladysmith."

Rather than waiting for the Boers to attack, General White

sent his mounted men to patrol around the town. Andrew enviously watched General French's patrols leave Ladysmith. He already felt constricted, tied to the plodding pace of infantry, although his family connections were to the Royal Malverns. He listened to the reports, learning that the Boers had six separate camps around the town, with wagons in tight laagers and their horses tethered nearby.

"What the devil is that?" Andrew pointed to a huge fabric ball that soared into the sky.

"That's an observation balloon," Sinton explained, grinning. "The army has moved on since your days of fighting with pikes and matchlocks, sir."

"We'll have less of your cheek, young Lionel," Andrew growled, watching the balloon rise. He immediately appreciated the advantages that such an innovation presented. "The men in there will see the enemy without venturing close."

"That's right, sir," Sinton said.

"Unless the Boers shoot it down," Andrew said. "That basket doesn't give much protection from a Mauser bullet."

"Perhaps not, sir," Sinton agreed.

The balloon's observers and French's mounted patrols brought news of the enemy's dispositions, which alarmed General White and his staff. With the Boers gathering on Long Hill to the northeast, at Bulwana on the east of Ladysmith, and Pepworth Hill on the north, they nearly surrounded the town.

White decided on a pre-emptive strike before the Boers closed the ring to complete the investment. He gathered his senior officers and told them his plan, with orders to pass on details to their units.

"The colonel wants us, sir," Sinton said cheerfully. "Things are happening out there."

Andrew put down the letter he was trying to compose to Mariana. "Thank you, Sinton. Let's see what the colonel wants."

Colonel Newland stood beside a large, hand-drawn map as he addressed his officers.

"General White does not agree with a passive defence," he told them briefly. "He is planning to attack Joubert. A reconnaissance in force, he calls it."

The officers glanced at each other and at the map, which contained all the information the patrols and observation balloon had gathered.

"The general has decided that the Malverns will be part of the attack," Newland said. "Ensure your men are fit and prepared."

"What's the plan, sir?" Major Cradley asked.

"The general's first idea was to attack on Sunday when the Boers observe a day of rest." Newland smiled. "They are a very religious people when they're not abusing Uitlanders or attacking our colonies. However, the staff officers thought attacking on the Sabbath would increase the Boers' dislike of us or strengthen their beliefs, so we're moving on Monday instead. That's the 30th of October."

Andrew took note of the date.

"It's an ambitious plan, so listen carefully," Newland said. "The main attack will consist of six infantry battalions, including us, with artillery support. Colonel Grimwood will be in command, and we will push the Boers from Long Hill, five miles to the northeast."

Andrew took notes of the units involved as Newland continued, stabbing the stem of his pipe on the map beside him.

"Our patrols tell us that Lucas Meyer commands the Boers on Long Hill."

Andrew did not know the name, but Newland continued. "Meyer lived in Ladysmith as a young man and fought against us at the Battle of Ingogo during the last Transvaal War. He also commanded the Boers at our recent victory at Talana. He does not care for the British."

"We don't care for him, either," Captain Boswell said to a cheer from the younger officers.

"Simultaneous to our attack, Colonel Ian Hamilton will

command another column of four battalions, supported by cavalry and artillery, to Pepworth Hill in the north. He will contain the Boers there, exploiting any successes once Grimwood has pushed away Meyer's commando."

Andrew remembered the difficulties of the previous British successes and hoped the men could accept the inevitable losses. No victory was ever straightforward.

"French's cavalry will protect Colonel Grimwood's right flank," Newland continued. "Thirdly, and finally, Colonel Carleton will make a night march with two battalions, plus artillery, to Nicholson's Nek, seven miles away. Carleton will remove any Boers and guard the nek to support our cavalry in pursuing the fleeing Boers."

Andrew remembered the lost opportunities of Talana and Elandslaagte when the Boers retreated with little hindrance. General White had absorbed the lessons and intended to thoroughly rout the Boers this time. He nodded his approval.

The Malverns lined up at eleven on Sunday night, with the officers and NCOs ensuring the men had water bottles and ammunition.

"I want the men to carry extra ammunition," Andrew said.

"The colonel stipulated only thirty rounds each, sir," Sergeant Kenny reminded him.

"I know," Andrew said. "I want fifty rounds per man."

"The men will complain about the weight, sir," Kenny said and hesitated.

"Fifty rounds a man," Andrew said, "and some food. These expeditions against the Boers have a habit of extending."

"If you say so, sir," Kenny looked doubtful. "The lads won't like it."

"I don't care a twopenny damn what they like," Andrew snapped, then relented. "If we're involved in a skirmish, Sergeant, a Lee-Metford can shoot off thirty rounds in ninety seconds. They're a lot different from the old Martinis. Even fifty rounds are insufficient."

"Yes, sir," Kenny said and passed the news on to the men. Andrew ignored the resultant groans and complaints. The NCOs would deal with such small matters, and he'd prefer his men alive and grousing than dead or captured because they ran out of ammunition.

"We've got a long night ahead of us," Andrew told C Company. "Follow orders, look after your comrades, and fire low if we meet the Boers."

The men nodded. The veterans of Talana and Elandslaagte knew what lay ahead, while those who had never experienced combat either boasted of what they would do or remained very quiet.

Colonel Grimwood gave the order to advance and led the column to the northeast, with the infantry following, stumbling in the dark.

"Keep the men together," Colonel Newland ordered. "March in quarter column. The younger recruits might be nervous in the dark, and having comrades nearby will reassure them."

Andrew closed C Company up, ordering Lieutenant Sinton to the rear with an experienced corporal to push any stragglers back into the ranks. He felt vulnerable in such a tight formation, momentarily expecting a torrent of Boer musketry. The night pressed down as the Malverns marched, with the column coiling before and behind them.

"If I commanded a Boer commando," Andrew said to Boswell, "I'd love a target of British soldiers marching in quarter column. Most of these men are townies who had never been away from publics and streetlights until they joined the army."

"And even then, it was barrack blocks," Sinton continued the theme, "with kindly sergeants to guide them." He grinned. "They would get lost if they walked a hundred yards away from the column."

Not only the recruits fumbled in the dark. When dawn cracked the eastern horizon, the Malverns halted beside Long Hill and looked for the neighbouring units.

"Where the hell are they?" Andrew asked. "There should be six battalions of infantry here, plus artillery. I can't see half that number of men, and no guns!"

"Lieutenant Sinton!" Colonel Newland snapped. "Find the other regiments and locate the guns, for God's sake!"

"Sinton!" Andrew handed him Moshie. "You'll be faster mounted." Sending Sergeant Kenny to ensure nobody straggled, Andrew kept his men together while Sinton trotted into the dark.

"Baird!" Colonel Newland said. "Take a patrol forward and see where the Boers are."

"Corporal Harwood!" Andrew said. "Bring your section and come with me. Kenny, look after C Company."

Andrew led Three Section forward to the hills. In the now grey light, rocks and scrubby trees looked like crouching Boers, so the men were understandably jumpy as they ascended the slope. They held their rifles in white-knuckled hands, listening for unknown sounds and peering to see movement.

"The Boers should have pickets out," Andrew said. "Extended order, lads, but keep in touch with each other. Don't stray."

The wind rose slightly, hissing through the rough grass and rustling the thorn bushes. Andrew pushed up his helmet to hear better and stared up the hill. He could not see anybody.

"Everybody lie down!" Andrew ordered in a harsh whisper. "Down!"

Wondering at the order, the patrol lay on the grass, holding their rifles ready to fire if the enemy appeared.

"Wait here," Andrew removed his helmet. "If I am not back in fifteen minutes, Corporal Harwood will take you back to the battalion." Taking a deep breath, he strode forward. After a hundred paces, he raised his voice and spoke in Afrikaans.

"Burghers! Where are you?"

When there was no answer, Andrew strode forward another hundred paces and tried again.

By then, the light was strong enough to see clearly. Andrew scanned the slopes through his binoculars, grunted, and returned to his men.

"Right, lads! There are no Boers on this hill. Back to the column."

Lieutenant Sinton arrived simultaneously with Andrew. "There are only three infantry units with us, sir," he reported. "And no artillery or cavalry."

Andrew said nothing, although he wondered if Colonel Grimwood's inexperience at handling anything larger than a battalion had contributed to half his command wandering off in the night.

Colonel Newland frowned and sent Sinton with the news to Colonel Grimwood.

"Your intelligence confirms what other patrols have discovered," Grimwood said primly, sending Sinton back.

The musketry came from an unexpected direction as Boers on the far side of the Modder Spruit opened fire on Grimwood's brigade. Already confused by the night march and the disappearance of half their numbers, the British infantry recoiled.

CHAPTER 16

LADYSMITH, NATAL

NOVEMBER 1899

"B, D and E Companies, about turn!" Colonel Newland was at his best in action. "Volley fire by the command of your company commander! A, C and F Companies, stand fast!"

Andrew heard similar commands from the neighbouring battalions as the Boer fire began to inflict casualties. "Stand fast, C Company," he shouted as the buglers reinforced Newland's commands. "Open order!"

C Company took defensive positions and waited for Grimwood's commands. Andrew paced behind the men, attempting to look calm. He thrust his empty pipe between his teeth as Sinton approached him.

"What the devil is Colonel Grimwood doing?" Sinton asked.

"I don't know," Andrew snapped. "Look after your platoon!"

"Yes, sir!" Sinton replied.

"Lie down, men, and find some cover!" Andrew ordered as

another man grunted and crumpled, holding his chest. He saw the rest of the Malverns slide to the ground as three companies replied to the Boer fire with hopeful volleys.

"There are no Boers on Long Hill," Andrew reminded. "Lieutenant Sinton, my compliments to Colonel Newland *and* ask permission for C Company to fire on the Boers attacking us."

Sinton ran on Andrew's last word, jinking from right to left to put the Boer marksmen off their aim.

"Steady, men!" Andrew shouted as some of the younger men looked shaken. "We'll get our chance to retaliate soon enough."

Mauser bullets zipped past, ploughing into the ground or cracking against the rocks, raising splinters and leaving a distinctive blue streak. Feeling very vulnerable, Andrew rose and paced among his company, reassuring them by appearing calm, although his heart was racing. He moved from rock to rock and scrubby tree to scrubby tree, trusting to luck to keep him safe.

"Sir!" Sinton skidded to a halt beside Andrew. "The colonel says to face the Boers and return fire, sir!" He hesitated for a second. "He also says you have to get under cover, sir."

"Good advice for us both!" Andrew dragged Sinton to the ground. "What exactly did Colonel Newland say?"

Sinton flinched as a bullet furrowed the earth beside him. "He said, tell Captain Baird to get his fool head down before the Boers shoot it off, sir."

Andrew forced a smile. "It's good to know the colonel cares about us," he said, ordering the company to about turn.

"Volley fire!" Andrew shouted. "On my word! Aim! Fire!" He knew the Boers were nearly impossible to see behind the rocks but hoped some of his veterans might glimpse the corner of a slouch hat or the barrel of a Mauser. At any rate, a volley of eighty rifles might diminish the enemy's fire.

"Load!" Andrew heard the rattle of eighty men pulling their rifle bolts. "Aim! Fire!"

A second volley crashed out without noticeable results on the

Boers' positions. Their fire came as thick as before, although without causing casualties, as the Malverns lay behind cover.

Andrew glanced over his men, knowing that being under fire without retaliating was one of the worst experiences a soldier could endure. Firing back, however ineffectually, always raised morale and helped the men feel like soldiers rather than living targets. He counted the volleys, subtracting each one from the fifty bullets his men carried.

They heard the deep boom a second later and saw a long tongue of flame leap from Pepworth Hill.

"What the devil?" Sinton asked.

"Heavy artillery!" Andrew explained. "The Boers must have one of their big guns on the hill."

"Where did the shell go?" Sinton looked around the Malverns.

"They are too close to fire at us," Andrew said. "They must be bombarding Ladysmith."

"How about the civilians?" Sinton looked shocked.

Andrew grunted. "Maybe the Boers believe their shells don't kill civilians."

The British firing died down as officers scanned Pepworth Hill for signs of the enemy.

"Individual firing," Andrew ordered his company. "Only fire if you see a definite target." He lowered his voice. "Where's Colonel Grimwood? He should be taking control of this action."

"I haven't heard anything from him since the Boers fired on us," Sinton said.

Andrew saw Sergeant Kenny aim with studious concentration, then deliberately squeeze the trigger of his rifle. He raised his head slightly and grunted in satisfaction.

"Got you, you devil!" Kenny said, working his rifle bolt.

"Well done, Sergeant!" Andrew praised, and swore as a bullet slammed into the ground at his side. "That came from Long Hill! The Boers are on both sides of us!"

"Can we move against Pepworth Hill, sir?" Major Cradley

asked. "I could lead three companies to clear the facing slopes of the Boers."

"We'll stay put and wait for orders, Major," Newland replied. "I am sure Colonel Grimwood knows what he is doing."

Captain Boswell glanced at Andrew and winked to show his opinion of Grimwood.

The Boer artillery fired irregularly, targeting Ladysmith, with some lighter pieces firing at the now-static British infantry.

"Are we going to lie here and be shot at all day?" Private Conway asked.

"Obey orders and fire if you see a blasted Boer!" Corporal Harwood replied.

"All I can see is rocks and bloody bushes," Conway said.

"Then save your ammunition and keep your fool mouth shut," Harwood snarled.

"The Boers are on both sides of us, sir!" Sinton reported.

"I noticed," Andrew replied. He heard Major Cradley ask permission to advance again, with the same reply.

"Wait for Colonel Grimwood's orders!" Colonel Newland replied.

Andrew heard heavy firing from the far left, where Carleton's force was at Nicholson's Nek.

"I hope Carleton is having better luck than we are," Boswell echoed Andrew's thoughts.

"So do I," Andrew replied. "And where the devil is French with the cavalry?"

As Grimwood's men sat tight, the Boers fired on them from Pepworth Hill on the left, Long Hill, and Lombard's Kop on the right, keeping them pinned down.

"Listen!" Sinton said. "There's another heavy gun!"

"That came from Ladysmith," Boswell said. "It must be one of ours!"

While Grimwood lost control of his advance, a train from Durban had brought a few hundred seamen with four 12-pounder cannon and two 4.6-inch naval guns. The British artillery replied to the Boer Long Tom that was pounding Ladysmith and terrifying the civilians.

"At least we are firing back!" Sinton said.

"Go on, boys! Hammer the Boojers!" Private Conway shouted.

The artillery duel continued in the background as the British infantry lay under the hail of Boer musketry. While most men tried to hide behind rocks or in depressions in the ground, a few returned fire. Andrew did not see the heliograph flash from Ladysmith; he only heard the runners address Colonel Newland.

"Message from General White, sir! He says we've got to retire to Ladysmith!"

Newland checked his battalion before he replied. "Very well. Bugler! Sound the retire! Move back by companies. C Company, take the rearguard!"

Andrew could feel the collective relief as the infantry heard the news. Some stood at once, looking towards Ladysmith, while most waited for orders as their NCOs and officers had trained them. As they stood, the Boers seized their opportunity and increased their fire, causing casualties and hurrying the withdrawal.

"C Company! Don't stand!" Andrew shouted. "Remain where you are! Volley fire on my word!"

Andrew organised his men, with one platoon facing the rear as the rest withdrew. While some men grumbled at retreating from the Boers, most were happy to escape the musketry, seeing no profit in lying still under constant fire. Andrew noted the men who wanted to stay and fight it out, remembering their names as he shepherded his company back, firing the occasional volley to discourage any Boer attack.

"Number Five Platoon, stand fast. Number Six Platoon, withdraw to that copse of trees!"

Andrew saw the Boers massing on the hills, some on horses but most on foot. He could not count the numbers.

"Why does Joubert not order a charge?" Sinton asked. "With

us in disarray and half the men discouraged, he could turn a withdrawal into a rout!"

"I don't know," Andrew replied. "Just be thankful for small mercies! Bring back Five Platoon to the trees and watch Private Morgan; he's limping badly."

"Yes, sir," Sinton said and paced to Five Platoon.

While some units retreated at speed, Colonel Newland kept control of the Malverns, ensuring they withdrew in order, with the rearguard constantly facing the enemy. After an hour, they reached the British artillery, who continued to fire at the Boers, altering their targets from the riflemen on the hills to the guns.

"*Shabash* the gunners!" Sergeant Kenny shouted as they passed the artillery.

"Somebody has to look after the PBI," a wiry bombardier responded. "You're no bloody good on your own!"

"You bloody try it sometime!" Conway stepped toward the bombardier until Corporal Harwood hustled him away.

With Boer musketry and artillery hammering them, the British retreat lost some cohesion. Men began to hurry, looking over their shoulders at the enemy. A few officers mounted their horses rather than remaining with their men.

Andrew felt a ripple of unease pass through C Company.

"Halt!" he roared. "We'll give Piet a farewell message so they know the Malverns will return!"

"Yes!" Private Conway shouted. "We'll be back to get you, Boojer bastards! We're the Malverns! The Royal Malverns!"

"Royal Malverns!" Private Hobart took up the chant. "Royal Malverns!"

"Open order!" Andrew knew the old shoulder-to-shoulder formation felt more secure for the young soldiers but only provided a solid khaki target for the Boers. "Fire two volleys on my command!"

C Company waited, holding their Lee-Metfords and glowering at the hillside where the Boers stood.

"Fire!" Andrew shouted, pacing behind his men.

The volley crashed out. The men reloaded with a rattle of bolts. The Boers retaliated, and Andrew shouted again. "Fire!"

The second volley sounded, and then Andrew gave the order to withdraw by platoons.

"The remaining platoon fire before you retire." *It might help to keep the Boers' heads down and diminish their musketry,* Andrew thought.

Private Reilly gasped and spun, holding his side. "They've shot me!" he said, giving a twisted smile. "The buggers have shot me!"

"Medical orderlies!" Andrew shouted. He knew the Boers would care for any wounded men but thought it better for morale if stretcher-bearers brought casualties back to the regimental hospital. He lifted Reilly's rifle, took his ammunition pouch and fired at the Boers.

C Company withdrew slowly, carrying their casualties, firing regular volleys and hoping they were doing some damage. Andrew kept the men under control and admired the gunners, who stood in the open as they fired round after round of shrapnel at the Boers.

How the devil did things go so badly wrong?

Two field batteries, the 13th and the 53rd, covered the infantry's retiral, each withdrawing alternately as the other blasted the Boers with shrapnel. When the infantry was relatively safe, the gunners also retired.

"Baird!" Major Cradley appeared from the main body. "Take a platoon and hold the Boers for another ten minutes. The guns will remain until you reach them."

"Yes, sir," Andrew replied. "Six Platoon! Remain where you are. Five Platoon, withdraw by sections! Lieutenant Sinton will give the word!"

The men of Six Platoon looked at Andrew without expression. They had heard Cradley's orders and knew their captain had no choice.

"Right, men," Andrew said. "You all heard the major. Find some cover and keep your heads down until I tell you to move."

The men obeyed, glad Andrew did not expect them to expose themselves pointlessly to Boer marksmen. They shifted to rocks and scrapes in the ground, staring up at the surrounding hills and the bleak plain where predatory riflemen were watching them.

Andrew checked his watch, carefully noting the time. Major Cradley had stipulated ten minutes, which seemed like a long time when the platoon was alone, with the rest of the army steadily retreating to Ladysmith. Andrew knew that every minute increased the distance between his men and the battalion's main body.

"Watch the flanks, boys. Make sure the Boers don't cut us off."

"Is it volley fire, sir?" Corporal Harwood asked.

"Volley fire be damned," Andrew replied. "Fire if you see an enemy, but don't waste bullets." He remembered Kenny's reluctance to issue the men with extra ammunition and wondered how the sergeant felt now.

Seeing the platoon isolated, the Boers crept closer. Mauser bullets hissed around, burrowing into the ground and cracking from the rocks. Andrew ducked behind a boulder, lifted Reilly's rifle and fired at a movement in the rocky hills above. Without observing the result of his shot, he worked the bolt, fired again and glanced over his platoon.

The men were sitting tight, saving their ammunition yet firing whenever they saw movement. Sergeant Kenny lay prone behind a scrubby bush, staring at a patch of vegetation three hundred yards away.

"I saw something move there, sir," Kenny said.

"The Boers have worked out that it's safer for them to move just after we fire," Andrew said. "They move as we work the bolt. You fire, and I'll watch the spot. If anybody's there, I'll nail him."

Kenny nodded, aimed and fired. Andrew saw the sudden

movement in the bushes, the hint of a slouch hat and squeezed his trigger. When he saw a man jerk upright, Andrew ducked back down to avoid the inevitable Boer retaliation. He heard the Boer bullets whistle past, saw one knock a chip from the boulder behind which he lay, and replied with three quick shots. Andrew reloaded, thrusting bullets into his box magazine and tossed away Reilly's now empty ammunition pouch. A Boer saw the movement and shot the pouch before it hit the ground.

An artillery shell landed behind the platoon, exploding with a shower of shrapnel that screamed over them. Private Jones yelled as a piece of jagged metal embedded in his side. He fell, writhing, and tried to pluck it out.

Andrew swore and looked for the British gunners, hoping for covering fire. Believing all the infantry had withdrawn, the gunners had pulled back.

"We're on our own, sir!" Harwood shouted. "How much longer?"

Andrew checked his watch. An unbelievable fifteen minutes had passed since Major Cradley had given his order. It seemed like fifteen seconds. "Now!" he replied. "Withdraw by sections, with the covering section firing as the other leaves."

"The Boers are behind us, sir!" Sergeant Kenny reported.

Andrew glanced over his shoulder. Kenny was correct. He saw half a dozen men in slouch hats running across the track and throwing themselves behind rocks.

"We're surrounded!" Jenkins shouted.

Andrew made a rapid decision. He could either form a defensive circle and fight it out, facing inevitable defeat by a constantly increasing Boer force as the British retired to Ladysmith, or break out before the numbers behind them grew too large.

"Khaki!" one of the Boers shouted. "Surrender! Hands up!"

"I'm damned if I'll surrender!" Corporal Harwood said as Kenny waited for orders. "What do we do, sir?"

CHAPTER 17

LADYSMITH, NATAL

NOVEMBER 1899

"We break out!" Andrew said. "We go for the throat! Fire at the road behind us, lads; empty your magazines and reload!"

Andrew led the way, hoping to clear the road and discourage the Boers from blocking Six Platoon's path.

"Fix bayonets!" Andrew shouted. He knew the Boers seldom waited to face the bayonets and hoped his bellow discouraged them from trying to prevent the platoon's retiral. As the men obeyed, Andrew searched for ammunition. Instead, he found the scarf that Jacoba had given him.

That Boer woman gave me this scarf for luck, Andrew remembered. *I need all the luck I can find to get my men clear.*

Smiling at his foolishness, Andrew wrapped the scarf around his neck.

"Ready, men?"

"Yes, sir!" Sergeant Kenny replied.

"On my word, we'll charge down the road and kill everything that isn't British. We can't stop for casualties, but the Boers will care for them. That includes me. If the Boers shoot me, leave me!" Andrew glared around the circle of Six Platoon.

Some of the men were gasping, others taking deep breaths. They looked nervous, angry, grim-faced, or scared.

"How about Franks and Stanton, sir?" Corporal Harwood indicated two wounded men.

"Can you walk, Franks?" Andrew asked.

"I can try, sir." Franks held a bloody bandage to his left knee.

"If you remain behind, the Boers will look after you," Andrew explained. "If you leave, they might shoot you."

"I'd prefer to try, sir," Franks said.

"Very well. And you, Stanton?"

"He can't walk, sir," Conway replied. "I can carry him."

"If you carry him, the Boers will shoot you both," Andrew said.

"We can't leave him, sir! We've been together since we were recruits!"

Andrew had to make an agonising decision. That was the price of command. "I'm sorry, Conway; we'll have to leave Stanton behind."

"Sir!"

Stanton lay on the ground, his eyes wide as he silently pleaded for relief from pain.

"I want to keep you both alive!" Andrew said. He turned away, hating himself, although he knew he had made the correct decision.

Andrew heard the tiny voice. "Don't leave me, sir!"

"Ready, men!" Andrew deliberately roughened his voice. "Run for that rocky outcrop!" He pointed to a clump of large boulders a quarter of a mile down the road. "We'll consolidate there. On the count of three! One, two and three!"

The men charged out, roaring, their bayonets flashing in the clear African light. Andrew swore, knowing he was putting himself in considerable danger as he shouldered his rifle.

"Come on, then, Stanton!" Stooping, he lifted the wounded man, holding him in both arms.

Stanton was lighter than Andrew expected. He shouted as Andrew scooped him from the ground and made small whining noises as Andrew stumbled in the wake of his men. He saw two Boers rise to fire at the onrushing Malverns. Corporal Harwood shot at the first and finished him with a savage lunge with the bayonet. The second ran away, losing his hat in his panic, as Six Platoon shouted abuse at his retreating back.

"Come back and fight!"

The Boers on the flanks fired as Six Platoon ran past. Two men fell, one with a bullet through his head and the other, Private Morton, yelling and holding his thigh. The others raced on, roaring, dodging and swearing.

Andrew followed, wondering when a Boer bullet would fell him and how it would feel.

Stanton was breathing heavily, gasping with pain as Andrew nearly fell and recovered.

"With you, sir!" Conway took hold of Stanton's left arm. "We'll get you safe, Paddy, son!"

"Keep going, sir!" Sergeant Kenny encouraged.

Andrew felt the breath rasping in his throat as he neared the rocks.

"You saved him, sir!" Conway helped Andrew place Stanton on the ground. He was grinning.

"We lost two men," Andrew said. "Mason is dead." *Why did the Boers not shoot me? I was moving at half Mason's speed.*

"Franks is coming, sir," Kenny said. "Shall I bring him in?"

Franks crawled towards the rocks, favouring his wounded leg and grimacing with pain. Andrew saw the first Boer bullet strike Franks on his uninjured leg and then another on his right arm. He rolled on the ground, yelling, until a third shot hammered into his chest, killing him.

"The murdering bastards!" Harwood said. "Frankie was no threat to them!"

"What now, sir?" Kenny asked. Franks had been one of them, and now he was dead. Kenny would mourn a lost colleague later.

Andrew glanced at the road towards Ladysmith, littered with discarded British equipment and an occasional khaki corpse or dead horse. "Now we dash again."

"Where to this time?"

Andrew surveyed the road through his binoculars. The Boers had recovered from their surprise and were firing at the rocks, knocking chips from the boulders and forcing the platoon to keep under cover.

"Head for those scrubby thorn trees," Andrew said. "The road dips beyond that, which will give us some cover." He measured the distance. "It's only about two hundred yards, but the Boers might be ready for us this time."

The men gathered round, grim-faced.

"I'll carry Paddy, sir," Conway volunteered.

Andrew shook his head. "No," he decided. "I'll take him."

I was lucky last time, but luck doesn't last forever.

"Come on, Stanton."

"Thank you, sir," Stanton spoke through eyes dulled with pain.

"How about Morton, sir?"

Morton lay still. The Boer bullet had smashed his femur and opened the femoral artery. Morton had bled to death as Six Platoon gasped for breath.

Andrew ducked as a fusillade of Boer shots crashed against the rocks, ricocheting around Six Platoon.

"Bloody hell!" Jenkins said. "Somebody out there doesn't like us!"

"They're coming down the hill!" Corporal Harwood shouted.

Andrew unslung his rifle and looked uphill, where the Boers moved from rock to rock, pausing only to fire. "Send them back, men!"

"Individual firing!" Sergeant Kenny said. He fired, worked the bolt of his rifle and fired again.

Andrew fired, checking his men as he pulled back the bolt. He thrust his hand into Stanton's ammunition pouch for cartridges.

"Thank you, Stanton."

Andrew heard the crash of artillery and saw the shell burst in the air a hundred yards up the hill, spreading an arc of shrapnel on the Boers beneath. Another shell exploded, and another, with each shell supporting Six Platoon.

"Sir!" Corporal Harwood shouted again. "Look at the trees, sir!"

A battery of British artillery had galloped to the trees and unlimbered, facing the enemy. Behind them and approaching fast, Lieutenant Sinton led C Company.

"Keep firing!" Andrew ordered. "Withdraw by sections; get to the guns!" He watched Sergeant Kenny lead his men away first, jinking and weaving to disrupt the Boers' aim.

"Extended order!" Sinton ordered. "Advance against the Boers! Cover Six Platoon's retiral!"

Andrew saw the remainder of C Company advancing from rock to rock, firing steadily. He waited until the artillery fired another salvo.

"Right, men! Head for the guns! Up you come, Stanton!"

Supporting the now quiet Stanton, Andrew strode to the artillery with his men running before him. He heard the spatter of musketry, the sharp cracks of the Mausers and the flatter bang of the British Lee-Metfords. A single fountain of dirt rose beside his legs, and then he was at the guns. Sinton greeted him with a broad grin, and the gunners stared.

"How did you do that, sir?" Sinton asked.

"How did I do what?" Andrew replied.

"You just walked through the enemy fire, sir," Sinton said. "Without a scratch. I saw you do that earlier. I was watching through field glasses."

"I was lucky," Andrew replied.

"You were, sir," Sinton said. "You must have a guardian angel looking after you."

Andrew nodded. "Maybe I had." He touched Jacoba's scarf, remembered her words and smiled. *I am not even slightly superstitious, but I should not have survived so many Boers shooting at me. Thank you, Jacoba.*

Andrew remembered Jacoba's skill in repairing her damaged wagon, and her direct speech.

I quite took to that woman; she was very like Elaine. I wonder how she would get on with Mariana. They are both South African frontierswomen on opposite sides of a war, yet with many more similarities than differences.

Shaking away the memory of Jacoba's bold, dark eyes, Andrew organised his men for the withdrawal into Ladysmith.

"Move by platoons," Andrew ordered, "and support the guns."

The artillery lieutenant nodded to him. "It's nice to be appreciated," he said.

MICHAL FRETTED IMPATIENTLY AS HE WATCHED GRIMWOOD'S column retreat to Ladysmith, with the men visibly hurrying through high clouds of dust. "Look at all that khaki," he said. "They are ripe for us to pluck them."

Hendrik took the pipe from his mouth, glanced at the massed Boers and nodded. "Ja," he said. "We could ride down and scatter them to the Lord's four winds."

"Then why doesn't Commandant-General Joubert order the attack?" Michal asked.

Hendrik considered the question for a moment, still holding his pipe. "He will have his reasons," he said. "I do not know. I am a farmer, not a Commandant-General."

"I will ask him," Michal decided. "He is only a man like the rest of us."

"Ja," Hendrik agreed, replacing the pipe in his mouth. "He is only a man."

Michal saw Piet taking careful aim from behind a rock, squeezing the trigger and nodding.

"Did you hit a Rooineck?" Michal asked.

"I killed a man," Piet replied without emotion.

When Michal approached Joubert, he saw a man talking to him angrily and recognised Commandant Christian de Wet.

"*Los jou ruiters, General! Los jou ruiters!* Loose your horsemen, General! Loose your horsemen!"

Joubert slowly shook his head. "No. When God holds out a finger, don't take the whole hand."

Michal stood for a moment, shaking his head, and returned to Hendrik.

Maybe the Lord was offering his whole hand, and we only took the finger.

"Did you ask him?" Hendrik asked.

"No, Christian de Wet asked my question." He told Hendrik what Joubert had said.

"The Commandant-General may be a wise man," Hendrik said. They watched the British disorderly retreat, with only the rearguard and a battery of artillery firing to keep back the Boers.

"We should have attacked," Michal said. "Joubert is too old and pacific to be the Commandant-General."

"We defeated them," Hendrik reminded. "Content yourself with that, Michal. Perhaps the Lord did not want us to kill the British. With our guns firing on Ladysmith, they must surrender soon, and we will have our independence without Rooineck interference."

Michal took a deep breath. "That may be so," he said, "but we should have hurried the process by smashing the British army."

Hendrik stood up and lifted his rifle. "Let's return to the laager. I hope this war ends soon, Michal. My farm needs me."

"The war is only a few weeks old," Michal said. "It could last for months yet."

"That is what I am afraid of," Hendrik said. "What do you think, Piet?"

Piet stared at the retreating British army. "Weeks, months, years is all the same to me. Hunting khaki is easier than hunting springbok or eland. They move slower and are not as intelligent."

Michal laughed, and they returned to the Wessels Commando's laager.

THE MALVERNS WERE GRUMPILY QUIET AS THEY RETURNED TO their camp, with the defeat weighing heavily on them.

"Glad you made it, Baird," Colonel Newland said as Andrew brought C Company into camp. "I want a casualty report from every company commander. And a written report of their company's part in the battle. Dismissed."

As the officers walked away, Andrew looked at Boswell, who rolled his eyes. "A written report! It's like being back in school!"

Andrew nodded. "We're meant to be soldiers, not blasted clerks. I haven't got the time to waste scribbling nonsense on a bit of paper."

"The army's changing," Boswell said. "Soon, we'll be writing orders to give to the NCOs in the middle of battle." He grinned as his customary good humour returned. "Maybe we should helio the Boers and ask them not to fire until we finish our reports."

Andrew found the atmosphere in Ladysmith subdued as the British realised the extent of their defeat. All the euphoria of Talana and Elandslaagte drained away as men counted their casualties and remembered the ease with which the Boers had halted their attack. Andrew listened to two NCOs discussing the day's events.

"They diced us without breaking sweat," Corporal Harwood said. "If it wasn't for the guns, they'd have wiped us out."

"They made some bad mistakes, though," Sergeant Kenny replied. "They must have outnumbered us three or four to one. If Joubert had unleashed his horsemen when we were retreating, he could have massacred us."

"Did you see the captain?" Harwood asked. "Carrying poor old Stanton through the Boer fire as if he was out for a stroll through Link Common. Bullets falling all around him, and he was whistling *Goodbye Dolly Gray* like he didn't care a button for the Boers."

"I saw him," Kenny replied. "He's got the devil's luck, that one. He survived Isandhlwana in the Zulu War and Majuba as well, and now this. There's something unnatural about that man."

"They called him Up and At 'Em in the old days," Harwood said. "I think his name should be Lucky Andy."

Andrew grunted and walked quickly away. He did not know how the Boers had missed him but knew such things happened in war. He had seen shells explode in a group of men, killing everybody except one man, who was untouched. He had seen a bullet pass right through a man's head without causing any real damage, while a thorn scratched a fit and healthy soldier, who sickened and died the following day.

Andrew touched his scarf, remembering Jacoba's words:

"Here, Captain. Wear this for luck." *She hesitated again. It may keep you safe in times of trouble. And it may help you to remember me."*

Andrew shook his head. *Pure coincidence,* he told himself. *All the same, I'll wear this scarf next time we're in action. I'll take all the help I can get.*

"Did anybody hear what happened to Carleton's column?" Andrew asked. "I know Hamilton guarded our flank as we retired, and French's cavalry got itself lost."

As the day wore on, news came in from Carleton's column, and it was not good. Their expedition had started with a night march, with the 10th Mountain Battery backing the Irish Fusiliers and the Gloucestershire Regiment. They made steady progress, with Carleton sensibly halting them periodically to ensure they were on course.

When the column neared Nicholson's Nek, Carleton decided to also occupy a hill called Tchrengula, left of their line of march and south of their target. Unfortunately, as they climbed the hill, something panicked the pack mules, which stampeded, carrying away the spare ammunition with the mountain guns and both heliographs. A lesser man might have abandoned the expedition, but Carleton continued. He occupied Nicholson's Nek with his men, without any artillery and only what ammunition they carried in their packs, which was twenty rounds a man.

"Twenty rounds a man," Andrew repeated. "Hardly enough for a skirmish!"

"Magazine rifles eat up the ammunition, sir," Sinton said. "If I ever have an independent command, I'll ensure the men carry spare ammo."

Andrew nodded. "You're learning."

Despite the mules' noise, the Boers were unaware of Carleton's presence until dawn, when they opened accurate rifle fire from the surrounding, higher hills. The British fired back, but with no artillery and limited ammunition, fate had stacked the odds against them. From their height, Carleton's men could see Grimwood's column retreating, so they knew they had no support or reason to occupy the hill. Their ammunition was steadily decreasing, and the surrounding Boers picked off the defenders one by one.

"Carleton was in a bad situation," Sinton observed.

The fighting was confused, with small parties of men holding out separate from their companions. With no ammunition and only eight men remaining, Captain Duncan of the Gloucestershire Regiment hoisted a white flag to surrender his handful. The Boers celebrated, convinced that the entire British force had given up. Perhaps believing that it was more honourable to surrender than fight on after his subordinate had shown a white flag, Carleton gave in. Over 950 British soldiers became prisoners, with the Irish Fusiliers furious to be included in the Gloucesters' surrender.

In Britain, the defeats became known as Mournful Monday.

It's not been a good day," Andrew said when the news of Carleton's capitulation spread around the Officers' Mess.

"That's a thousand men fewer to defend Ladysmith," Captain Boswell agreed. "And the Boers are rapidly closing the ring. They'll have completely surrounded us in a couple of days."

Andrew began to fill his pipe. "We'll be under siege, then." He thought of the other sieges in which he had been involved, either as one of the besieged or in the relieving force. "Let's hope the government sends a decent general to wallop the Boers and get us out of this mess."

"We could break out," Boswell suggested.

"And hand Ladysmith as a prize to Joubert?" Major Cradley shook his head. "General White won't do that. He'll sit tight and dare anything Joubert can do." He grunted. "We could be in for a hard few days or weeks." He leaned back in his chair. "I hope nobody expects to see their wife or sweetheart for a while!" He laughed without humour, for every officer present knew that Cradley was a bachelor whose only love was the regiment.

Andrew thought of Mariana and quickly removed Jacoba's scarf from his neck.

CHAPTER 18

LADYSMITH, NATAL

NOVEMBER 1899

"There is some good news," Major Cradley said. "General White is sending away the bulk of the civilians, meaning we'll have fewer mouths to feed."

"General French is also going," Boswell said. "A cavalry commander is better out of an invested town. He can do more good in the open spaces than behind barricades."

"We'll miss the mobility," Andrew said soberly. "But so will the Boers."

Watching refugees leave a threatened town was always unpleasant. Andrew had recently seen frightened civilians flee from Mandalay in the Burmese War of the 1880s and, more recently, from Johannesburg. Ladysmith was no different.

After the defeats of Mournful Monday, the population of Ladysmith knew the Boers would close the ring and invest the town. Most of the army accepted this fact, checked their rifles, and waited for the inevitable with that fatalism that seemed inherent to the Victorian British soldier. The civilians were not so phlegmatic and rushed to escape before the siege began.

General White ordered C Company of Malverns to assist the police in keeping order at the railway station. Andrew organised his men as crowds gathered inside the station, desperate to catch the last trains from Ladysmith. There were Black Africans with a handful of clothes who crammed onto open trucks, excitable, voluble Indians with huge piles of clothes, possessions and even furniture, and well-dressed white women who ushered their children onto the carriages.

"Who are these men, sir?" Corporal Harwood indicated the dozens of white men who also wished to flee Ladysmith. "You'd think they'd stay and fight."

Andrew nodded. "I agree with you." He watched as the native police herded the Blacks and Indians with ungentle knobkerries. "Take your section down and help the ladies, Corporal!"

"Yes, sir!" Harwood responded immediately, pushing through the raucous mob as he hauled back a group of European men who attempted to board one of the carriages.

"Women and children first!" Harwood roared, manhandling a portly man who had pushed in front of a young mother and her children.

"Get your hands off me!" the portly man shouted. "You damned blackguard! How dare you lay hands on a gentleman? Don't you know who I am?"

Andrew strode forward, determined to support his corporal, but Harwood could look after himself.

"I've no idea who you are," Harwood replied. "But I know what you are, and it's a term I won't use in front of a lady. Get back!"

Andrew stopped, watching Harwood at work. The corporal ordered his section to hold back all the white men until the women were safely aboard. Only then did Harwood allow the men to enter the carriages, one at a time and under his stern glare.

"And if I see any of you trying to displace a lady, I'll have you off the train at bayonet point, and you'll remain in Ladysmith to fight the Boers!" Harwood roared, momentarily forgetting to be polite in front of the women and children.

Andrew knew that higher command had ordered French and his aide, Major Douglas Haig, to leave Ladysmith. He watched them board the last train from the station, heading for Pietermaritzburg. There was no crowding onto an open truck for them but an escort into a quiet carriage with underlings saluting.

A smartly uniformed stationmaster slammed shut the carriage door on the white male civilians, blew a whistle and waved a green flag to allow the final train to leave Ladysmith.

"Rats leaving the sinking ship, sir," Harwood commented as the train disappeared into the night.

"Every person fewer means less food for us to find," Andrew said quietly. "We'll be hard-pressed to feed everybody in the town if the siege lasts long."

We're alone now, with the Boers closing in.

Not long after the last train steamed south, the Boers blasted the railway line.

"Joubert has cut us off," Sinton said.

"He has," Andrew agreed. "The Boers have challenged the British Empire, and now they'll have to either invade Cape Colony and hope the Cape Dutch rise to help them or ask for one of the Great Powers to assist."

Sinton's grin was crooked. "How about us here in Ladysmith, sir?"

"The eyes of the world will be on us," Andrew said. "Britain cannot let the Boers capture another significant town, and Kruger knows that as well as we do. Our national prestige is at stake. If the Boers take Ladysmith, one of the Powers may be encouraged to support them."

Sinton took a deep breath. "It's a lot at stake for a little nothing town that nobody had heard of last week."

Andrew glanced at the ring of hills that enclosed the town. "It is," he agreed. "And it's up to us to keep Ladysmith British."

ANDREW LEANED ON HIS RIFLE, SURVEYING THE DISTANT heights. "We hold the immediate hills around Ladysmith," he said, "and the Boers control the higher hills beyond. They can see everything we do in the town, yet our observers in the balloon can watch them watching us. This is the strangest of wars."

Lieutenant Sinton produced a map from inside his tunic. "I've created a plan of the defences," he said. "Ours and theirs, from what our patrols and the balloon observers have told me."

Andrew studied the hand-drawn map. To the northwest of Ladysmith, White had positioned guns on King's Post, and, following the defensive preparations in clockwise order, there was Observation Hill and a row of trenches and redoubts leading to Helpmekaar Hill on the northeast. Next came the gruesomely named Cemetery Ridge, more redoubts on either side of the snaking Klip River, and Caesar's Camp on the long Platrand Ridge, with the prominent Wagon Hill. Within the defences on the southwest were Highlander's Post and Maiden's Castle, then Rifleman's Post on the west beside King's Post.

"There are a lot of gaps and weak spots in the defences," Andrew said.

"The Boers are all around us." Sinton jabbed his finger on the map. "They've occupied every hill in the outer ring and cut the telegraph and the water supply."

"They can't stop the heliographs," Andrew said and smiled. "And unless they dam the Klip River, we'll have plenty of water." He looked at the surrounding hills, suddenly ominous as dark clouds rolled over the summits. "If nothing else, we'll have plenty of water."

CHAPTER 19

LADYSMITH, NATAL

NOVEMBER AND DECEMBER 1899

Hendrik sat beside the fire, with the men politely making room for him. He raised his hat and shook them by the hand.

"I am Hendrik du Toit from Soetwaters," Hendrik introduced himself. "I am in the Wessels Commando."

The men nodded and gave their names, waiting to hear the purpose of Hendrik's visit to their fireside.

"You men are from northeast of Pretoria, I believe," Hendrik said.

"Every one of us," the oldest man acted as spokesman, eyeing Hendrik over puffs of blue smoke from his pipe.

"Do you know the woman named Jacoba Fourie?" Hendrik asked.

The men studied him, one cutting a strip of biltong before he put it in his mouth and another adjusting the sights of his rifle with pliers.

"We know Jacoba Fourie," the spokesman replied, holding Hendrik's gaze with his steady eyes.

Hendrik took out his pipe and a tobacco pouch. He nodded and offered the pouch to the spokesman and the other men. One man accepted and filled his pipe.

"What is she like? Is she from a respectable family?"

The spokesman nodded as one of the men offered Hendrik a mug of coffee. "Ja," the spokesman said. "Her father was Willem Fourie, and her mother was Rachel, my second cousin. They were good people, hardworking, helpful to the neighbours, and always attended the church."

Hendrik sipped at his coffee, listening to the spokesman. "Yet Jacoba is a single woman," he said.

"Ja, she is single," the spokesman agreed.

"Why should that be?" Hendrik asked.

One of the other men smiled. "Jacoba Fourie is a strong woman," he said. "She is too strong for her own good. What man wants a wife who could lift him with one hand?" He laughed, with some of the others joining him. "She is destined to be a *Bokkeoppas,* a goat herder."

Hendrik listened without comment. "Thank you for your help," he said, "and for the coffee." He stood up, lifted his hat politely, and stepped away, his face thoughtful.

ANDREW STEPPED INTO THE SHELTER OF A WALL AS ANOTHER shell from the Boers' Long Tom exploded inside Ladysmith.

"The Boers seem determined to reduce the town to rubble and matchsticks, sir," Sinton said.

"If they continue to pound us, there will be nothing worth capturing," Andrew agreed.

"I wish they would just attack us," Sinton said, "then we could at least fight back."

"I think they are trying to wear us down," Andrew said. "Joubert knows that a direct assault will lead to heavy Boer casualties. This way, he spares the lives of his men." He nodded to the heights from where the Boer artillery fired. "We should attack the hills and destroy their guns."

Sinton nodded. "I think Mournful Monday shook General White, sir. He's no longer keen on offensive operations. It all depends on a relieving column now."

They entered the hospital, full of wounded and sick men. Andrew stepped to Stanton's bed and asked the medical orderlies how he was progressing.

"As well as can be expected, sir," the orderly gave the expected reply.

"Look after him," Andrew said. "He's a good man."

The orderly gave a weak smile. "We look after all our patients, sir."

"What's your name?" Andrew asked.

"Briggs, sir," the orderly said.

"Well, Briggs. I'll be back from time to time to check my men," Andrew said. "I expect to hear nothing but praise for you. If I hear anything else or any of my men sicken, I'll ensure you spend the remainder of the war cleaning out latrines with your fingers!" Andrew knew the medical orderlies did not have a good reputation and drove his point home. The rankers claimed the initials for the Royal Army Medical Corps, RAMC, stood for "Rob All My Comrades," and Andrew was determined to protect his men from any malpractice.

Nodding a final warning to Briggs, Andrew stalked out of the hospital, glad to be free of the smells and suffering.

HENDRIK STOPPED TO WATCH AS JACOBA DROVE HER WAGON into the camp, turning it expertly before she halted the oxen.

"You drive very well, *Mejuffrou* Jacoba," Hendrik said, lifting his hat.

"*Danke, meneer,*" Jacoba replied. She placed her whip in its stance and stepped towards him, tipping back her hat so the sun highlighted her strong jaw and high cheekbones.

"You are a very capable woman," Hendrik said.

"You told me that already," Jacoba said, smiling.

Hendrik nodded. "It is as true now as it was then," he replied.

Jacoba inclined her head at the attempted gallantry. "Did you stop for a reason, Meneer du Toit? I am sure you must have something more interesting to do than talking to me."

"Our duties here are minimal," Hendrik told her. "We take turns to watch the Rooinecks, fire at them if we feel inclined, and guard the camp."

"I understand," Jacoba said. She called on a servant to tend to her oxen. "And you decided to alleviate your boredom by talking to me because a woman's time is less important than a man's."

Hendrik smiled. "I am never bored talking to you, Mejuffrou Jacoba."

"Oh," Jacoba stepped back slightly, reading him, seeing the genuine interest. "You will be missing your farm, Meneer. And Jacoba will be sufficient."

"I am missing my farm, Jacoba," Hendrik admitted.

"Some men are already creating excuses to return home," Jacoba said. "They have a sick wife, a sudden flood, or an outbreak of murrain. Would you do that, meneer?"

Hendrik contemplated Jacoba before he replied. "No. Are you testing me? And my name is Hendrik."

"Yes," Jacoba replied. "I heard you were asking questions about me."

"I was," Hendrik said.

"What did you discover, Hendrik?"

"You are from a respectable family," Hendrik said. He examined the wagon, noting the rifle at the front, within easy reach of the driver.

"You will have heard I am only fit for herding goats," Jacoba said.

"I do not see a goat herder," Hendrik replied. "I listen to what people say, Jacoba, but make my own mind up." He saw a flicker of surprise in Jacoba's eyes.

"Sit beside me, Hendrik," Jacoba invited, patting the back of her wagon, "tell me about your farm. Is it a *hartbeeshuise*?"

Hendrik slowly shook his head. A *hartbeeshuise* was the most basic house on the veldt, a rectangle of pole-and-mud walls pierced by tiny windows for light. The simplest consisted of a single room, while others might have as many as three rooms, with a kitchen at the back. The roof was usually flat and made of thatch, shingles or corrugated iron, held down by heavy stones.

"No," Hendrik understood that Jacoba was testing his suitability as a husband. "I have a stone-built house with an upper storey and a fine orchard of peach trees."

Jacoba pulled her hat forward to shade her face from the sun. Boer women liked to maintain their peaches-and-cream complexions by wearing poke bonnets. Headgear like Jacoba's was highly unusual for a woman, but after a lifetime of rejection and scorn, she had decided her complexion was unimportant if no man wanted her.

"That sounds like a good farmhouse," Jacoba said. "Was your wife happy there?"

Hendrik knew Jacoba was asking if his wife had a happy marriage. "Ja. Ruth was a contented woman. She made the best *mampoer* – peach brandy – from the Limpopo to the Cape."

Jacoba shifted slightly, with her hip pressing against his. There was not much space on the back of the wagon. "I make fine *mampoer*," she said quietly. "And bread."

"I am sure you do," Hendrik said.

They both looked up as the Creusot gun fired, and the shell whistled past them to land on the outskirts of Ladysmith, throwing up a cloud of dust and rubble.

"It is a terrible thing to destroy what people have created," Hendrik said.

"Sometimes it is necessary," Jacoba said. "*Een vrije volk zijn wij*, A free people are we." She eyed Hendrik. "When the destruction is finished, you can return to your fine farm as a free man."

"Soetwaters is a fine farm," Hendrik agreed. "All it lacks is the touch of a good woman."

"A woman can make a difference to a farm," Jacoba agreed.

They sat in silence for a while, with Jacoba's mind racing and Hendrik puffing at his pipe. Eventually, he stood, tapped out the ash, and lifted his hat to her.

"Good night, Jacoba. I hope we understand each other."

"Good night, Hendrik." Jacoba watched him walk away with a slight smile on her face.

Boswell looked up from his month-old newspaper. "The Americans seem to support the Boers in this war, which is surprising given their revolution against tyranny."

Sinton raised his eyebrows. "The Americans wanted their independence, sir, like the Boers do."

"They are similar in that," Andrew agreed. "But the Americans fought for the slogan no taxation without representation."

"A principle rather than a slogan," Boswell reprimanded gently.

"Just so," Andrew said. "But either way, it's something the Boers do not accept and one reason we have slid into this war. The Boers are fighting for a freedom they deny to all non-Boers in their land."

"Do you mean the native tribesmen, sir?" Sinton asked.

"They treat the black people as slaves," Andrew said, "and tax the Uitlanders while denying them the vote. British, Jews, Catholics and Blacks cannot vote or hold any public office."

Sinton nodded. "The Boers are scared of losing their power in the land they created," he said.

"That could be the reason," Andrew agreed. "The Transvaal government has a law that every Boer must own a rifle, while Uitlanders are banned from rifle ownership. Only Afrikaans is allowed in official documents, and Kruger controls every government monopoly."

Boswell shrugged. "A bit arbitrary," he allowed, "but no worse than some other nations."

"Kruger banned public meetings outdoors and can close down any newspaper he dislikes, which means any of which he disapproves, so no press freedom." Andrew began to stuff tobacco into his pipe. "Add inferior education for non-Boers, arbitrary arrests, government corruption and mistreatment of the natives, and we have a highly unpleasant neighbour." He paused for an instant. "I saw a little of their work in Jo'burg."

"A little, but enough from what you told me," Boswell said.

"Enough," Andrew agreed. "We saw the other side of our Afrikaner opponents."

"I thought you liked the Boers, sir," Sinton said.

Andrew considered before he replied. "I am not sure if like is the right word," he said. "I respect them as adversaries and know they won't murder our wounded. I could respect the men I met back in 1880."

Boswell nodded. "That's something, at least." He scanned the surrounding hills through his binoculars. "I hear that General Redvers Buller has arrived to lead the relieving force, and all of Britain expects great things."

Redvers Buller was one of late Victorian Britain's military heroes. A Devon man, he made his name and gained a Victoria Cross during the Zulu War of 1879, afterwards serving in the Egyptian and Sudan campaigns. He was friendly with the Queen, although less so with the Prince of Wales, but after Sudan, the War Office appointed him to a desk job, and he saw no more active service until the outbreak of the Boer War in 1899.

"I served under Buller in Zululand," Andrew said. "Twenty years ago. He was an active commander of irregular cavalry before he became famous. We'll see how long he takes to penetrate the Boer defences."

"Not long, hopefully," Boswell said.

Then we might receive some mail, and I'll know how Mariana and the children are. Andrew refused to think of Major Charlie Dixon. He knew Mariana better than to distrust her. *Don't I?*

Andrew scanned the hills again, wondering if the Boers were up there, watching him.

Colonel Newland smiled at his officers. "Well, gentlemen, General White has assigned every unit their position in Ladysmith's defence. He has decided that the Malverns will be a mobile reserve, ready to move to whatever position most needs help." The colonel halted to allow his words to sink in.

"I'd prefer a definite defensive position, sir," Major Cradley said. "That way, we'd learn the ground and be better prepared to withstand an attack."

"I see your reasoning, Cradley," Newland said. "However, we are British officers and won't shirk whatever duty General White sets out for us."

"Of course not, sir," Cradley agreed.

"The good news, gentlemen," Newland continued, "is that we will also be available for any offensive movements the general makes. That is all. Dismissed."

"So now we know, sir," Sinton said.

"We'll have to maintain C Company's fitness and training," Andrew said. "I want every man to be familiar with the geography of Ladysmith and our surroundings and ready to move at a moment's notice."

"Yes, sir," Sinton agreed.

"Create a flying column, each platoon alternately, with

seventy rounds of ammunition, full water bottles and extra rations. The lieutenant and NCO to have a map and compass."

Sinton did not dispute the extra ammunition. "Where will I get the maps from, sir?"

"Draw them," Andrew told him bluntly. "Use your excellent map as a blueprint. The Quartermaster will have compasses; if not, ask him to find some."

"Yes, sir," Sinton said.

"That's all for now," Andrew told him. "If I think of anything else, I'll let you know. Get to work."

"Yes, sir," Sinton replied.

They both ducked as a shell from the Boer Long Tom landed a hundred yards away, throwing up a spray of dust and rubble.

"They're shelling the town regularly now, sir," Sinton said.

"I noticed," Andrew said dryly.

"Maybe they believe all the civilians left on the last trains."

"Maybe," Andrew replied. "If they are watching us through their field glasses, they'll see the civilians in the streets."

"Yes, sir," Sinton hesitated. "In that case, they are deliberately attacking civilians."

"Yes," Andrew agreed. "War is never as simple as history books make out."

"No, sir," Sinton replied. "If you'll excuse me, sir." He saluted and trotted towards the Malverns' quarters.

"Don't run!" Andrew called after him. "The men might think the shelling makes you nervous."

Andrew walked on, determined to inspect Ladysmith's perimeter so he would know every location where General White might send C Company.

He stopped when Lieutenant Leslie stepped from the shadow of a house to keep step with him. "Did your little Boer friend get back safely to Joubert?" Leslie asked with his ready smile.

"I hope so, Lieutenant," Andrew replied. He heard footsteps

behind him and stopped, guessing that Leslie's followers were nearby.

"I am sure she will be safe." Leslie's smile broadened. "These people look after their own kind."

Andrew could sense the presence of Leslie's companions but refused to turn around. "You had no right to abuse a civilian, Lieutenant." Andrew put an edge in his voice.

"We worked together in the Transvaal, sir," Leslie reminded him. "You know I understand the enemy. I hope you have not turned into a pro-Boer." Leslie stood in front of Andrew with his arms akimbo.

"A what?" Andrew asked. Leslie was nearly accusing him of treason.

"A pro-Boer," Leslie repeated. "I'd hate to have to report you to General White, sir. It's not a duty I'd enjoy."

Andrew heard three men breathing behind him, one heavily, as though he was out of condition.

"What the devil is a pro-Boer?" Andrew temporised, feeling for the revolver at his belt.

"It's the term for a man who supports the Boers," Leslie explained. "I am sure you are still loyal to the Queen, sir."

"No," Andrew replied. "I am not a pro-Boer. Why do you ask such a foolish question?" He prepared to defend himself.

"You helped that Boer woman," Leslie replied, his smile fading.

"We are here to fight armed men," Andrew said. "We don't make war on unarmed women."

"She might have been a spy," Leslie pointed out.

"Do you have proof she was a spy?" The breathing behind Andrew had calmed down.

"No," Leslie admitted. "We might have found some if you had not interrupted our questioning, sir."

"Innocent until proven guilty," Andrew said. "British law is the same in Southern Africa as in Britain."

Leslie pursed his lips. "That is so, sir," he said, nodding

slowly. His smile returned. "Now I know the reason for your actions, Captain Baird, I assure you I have no ill feelings towards you." He held out his hand. "All forgiven, I hope?"

Andrew took Leslie's hand in a firm grip. "I am glad we've sorted that out," Andrew said. "We have enough to do with fighting the Boers without squabbling among ourselves."

"Good," Leslie said. "May I introduce Sergeant Lambeth and Troopers Jones and Ritchie, sir? They are also loyal men."

The men behind Andrew stepped forward, smiling. Lambeth was broad-shouldered and flint-eyed, while Jones was the swarthy man Andrew had noted earlier. Ritchie was heavily built, full-faced and saluted with a flourish.

"You men can go about your duty now," Andrew said. He did not trust any of them as they marched away.

CHAPTER 20

LADYSMITH, NATAL

DECEMBER 1899

C Company had been on duty in the redoubt for three days and nights, keeping their heads below the parapet in case of Boer marksmen. They were tired and edgy, snarling at one another for imagined slights, waiting for the dawn as the bugles in Ladysmith sounded the Stand-to.

"There's no need to keep all the men on the wall," Andrew said. "The intelligence was mistaken. The Boers are not going to raid this sector."

Lieutenant Sinton looked relieved. "Yes, sir."

"Post one man every ten yards, and the others can rest. That way, they'll be fresher if the Boers do attack. Change the sentries every two hours."

"I'll do that, sir," Sinton said.

"You and Sergeant Kenny take turns on duty until the relief arrives," Andrew said.

"How about you, sir?" Sinton asked.

"I'll sleep when I need to." Andrew knew that although he appeared calm, he was tense inside. He forced a grin. "Carry on, Lieutenant."

"Yes, sir," Sinton replied.

The Boers greeted the dawn with half a dozen rifle shots that ricocheted from the wall and whined overhead.

"Welcome to another Ladysmith day," Sinton said, holding onto his sun helmet. "Piet bids us all good morning."

"Here's our relief coming now, sir," Kenny reported. "A company of the Devons." He shifted uncomfortably. "They think they're the only regiment in Ladysmith, sir."

Although the army always had an inter-regimental rivalry, Andrew found it more pronounced within Ladysmith. The Devons, in particular, seemed to resent the high reputation of the Gordon Highlanders and Royal Malverns and took every opportunity to emphasise their supposed superiority. The regular British and local Colonial forces were also mutually antagonistic, leading to disputes among the men.

"Everybody's nerves are getting strained, Sergeant. Ignore the shine and get the men ready to leave."

The few moments of confusion when one unit replaced another could be dangerous, as the Boers fired into the overcrowded redoubts. Andrew organised the transition carefully, moving men section by section. The Boers fired a few shots, with the bullets thudding harmlessly into the sandbags, and then C Company retired to their camp, and the Devons were in position.

"Thank goodness for that," Sinton said. "I'm heading for a stiff drink in the Officers' Mess, sir, then I'm going to sleep for five straight hours."

Andrew smiled. "I'll join you for the drink."

The shell landed twenty yards from the Malverns' Officers' Mess, shaking the building and sending a hatful of stones against the side window. Two of the four windowpanes cracked, and one broke, sending sharp shards of glass inside the room.

"Oh, I say!" Captain Boswell complained. "Mind the crockery! Those Boer fellows are getting rather above themselves now, don't you think?"

"Just a little," Andrew agreed, brushing glass from his lap as he rose from his seat. "That was a little too personal for my liking."

"We'll have to do something about that blasted gun," Colonel Newland said. "It's bad enough being stuck in this dead-end town without Piet throwing stones at the windows as well."

"General White agrees with you, sir," Major Cradley suggested. "He said that morale in Ladysmith will suffer if the Boers continue to bombard us without any retaliation."

"Good," Newland replied. "In the meantime, could somebody find a glazier in this place? Or at least get that window boarded up. It's causing a draught!"

"These Boer guns on Gun Hill are a headache," Andrew said.

"We've been urging Sir George White to do something about them since the siege started," Cradley said. "I think he's finally coming round to our way of thinking."

"Ever since they moved that damned six-inch Creusot from Pepworth Hill to Gun Hill, it's been a blasted nuisance," Boswell said. "The Boers call it the Franchise to mock the Uitlanders."

"The men call it the Stinker, sir," Sinton said.

"They only call it that when officers are listening," Andrew said, smiling. "They have other, less savoury names when they think we're out of hearing."

"You remember the Stinker bombarded the Imperial Light Horse camp on the 2nd," Cradley said. "The Boers dislike the Light Horse Uitlanders."

"I believe the feeling is mutual," Andrew said dryly.

"More importantly," Cradley continued, "the Boers also shelled our hospital in the Town Hall. They must know it's a hospital, and it's big enough not to miss with its clock tower. They murdered a wounded sapper and injured nine patients."

"The dirty scoundrels!" Boswell's face darkened. "The Natal

Carbineers were black affronted at that. That big lad there, Lieutenant Whatshisname, was furious! He shook his fist at Long Tom and said, 'May God Almighty help the first Boer who asks me for quarter!'"

"I can believe a Uitlander would say that," Andrew said.

"We're going to attack Gun Hill and blow up the Stinker," Cradley said quietly. "White's Chief of Staff, Sir Archibald Hunter, is in command."

"Hunter had a good record in the Sudan, sir." Andrew guessed that Cradley was leading up to something.

"Hunter is a fighting officer," Cradley said. "General White wants the attack to be an all-Colonial affair, with the men drawn from the volunteer South African units, led by experienced British officers."

Andrew felt Cradley's eyes boring into him. "I see, sir."

"You are an experienced British officer, Baird," Cradley reminded him, "and you have worked with Colonial units in the past."

"I have, sir," Andrew admitted.

"You led the Natal Dragoons in the Zulu War and the last Transvaal War," Cradley said.

"Yes, sir," Andrew said again.

"You also did some intelligence-gathering work before the war with Lieutenant Leslie of the Imperial Light Horse," Cradley said.

"I did, sir," Andrew admitted.

"Good," Cradley said, smiling. "Then that's settled. You will lead a unit of the Imperial Light Horse. I'll try to team you with Lieutenant Leslie's desperadoes as you know him."

Andrew felt a twinge of unease but could not disobey an order. "Yes, sir," he said.

"You'll hear the details later." Cradley leaned back, looking satisfied. "The general wants the Creusot Long Tom destroyed, and as much other damage as possible. We don't intend to hold the hill or push off the enemy, just destroy the gun. The Colonial

Volunteers want to show they are as good as we are and end this senseless bickering."

Andrew nodded. "We'll have to go up the hill on foot, sir," he pointed out. "We'll need wire cutters for the barbed wire defences and heavy hammers to smash the gun."

"That's the spirit!" Cradley approved. "Get together with Archie Hunter and the Imperials. See what you can work out. Off you go, now."

Andrew knew that military life was never straightforward. He would have preferred to fight alongside men he knew, but at least he had shaken hands with Leslie and some of his men, which should help.

Hunter had arranged a meeting of the officers, with Andrew standing at the back, surveying the men who would make the assault.

Major John James Macfarlane of the Natal Carbineers nodded to Andrew, recognising a fellow Zulu War veteran. Macfarlane was also a Justice of the Peace and mayor of Pietermaritzburg. At Macfarlane's side were Captain Foxon, a magistrate, and Captain Shepstone, a surveyor. Behind them stood Lieutenant Bartholomew, who farmed at the Mooi River and had more in common with the Boers than with any town-bred Briton, and the pale-faced Lieutenant Rodwell, who had vacated his civil servant position only a few weeks before. Lieutenant Sparks was the chairman of the Ladysmith Town Board and was naturally angry at the damage to his town. Lastly, there was Colonel William Royston, the commandant of the Natal Volunteers.

Andrew took a deep breath at such a gathering of Natal's great and good, feeling some strange respect that they were prepared to put their lives on the line to defend their homes.

Hunter greeted the Colonial Volunteers with a steady stare. "You gentlemen have an arduous and highly important task ahead of you," he said. "We will attack Gun Hill and disable the enemy artillery that is so troublesome to Ladysmith."

The men nodded, with Lieutenant Sparks pressing his lips together.

"We are not going to charge up firing our rifles and yelling like madmen," Hunter said. "Nor will there be any artillery support. We will use the element of surprise."

The men nodded. Most had been hunting in the wilder parts of Natal and knew more about stealth than any British soldier.

"You all know your enemy," Hunter said, "and you have personal scores to settle, particularly you Uitlander fellows of the Imperial Light Horse."

The men stirred and grunted, with a few nodding in vehement agreement.

Hunter's command was around 600 strong, mainly Colonials from Natal, with the Natal Carbineers, the Border Mounted Rifles, and the Imperial Light Horse all contributing. The British contributed officers and Royal Engineers with wire cutters, explosives, and sledgehammers.

"You're with us, then, sir," Leslie said as Andrew surveyed the Natal volunteers.

"You're with me, rather," Andrew replied. He checked the twenty-five men that Leslie commanded. They all carried their single-shot Martini rifles, with cloth wrapped around their equipment to prevent noise. "Keep together, keep silent, and don't shoot unless I give the order," Andrew said.

"We know the Boers," one man said.

"So do I, and I am in command," Andrew reminded. "You call me sir." He waited until the men looked away before giving more instructions.

Hunter's force marched from Ladysmith shortly after nine on the night of the 7th of December. As they passed the outer pickets, the watching Devons wished them a quiet good luck, and then the velvet night wrapped darkness around the silent men. In theory, only the officers knew the object of the raid for fear of Boer spies passing on the information. However, the men were aware of the threat from the Boer artillery and guessed where they were headed. Hunter led them along the Helpmekaar Road towards the north side of Gun Hill.

The Corps of Guides supplied half a dozen local men who knew the route intimately. They marched over an area of flat ground, with loose stones underfoot and a profusion of mimosa trees that loomed through the dark like tall Boer sentinels. The guides helped them over half a dozen *dongas* to the foot of Gun Hill.

"No sign of Brother Boer yet," Leslie said.

"They don't keep a good night watch," Andrew told him.

Hunter gave brief, final instructions to the intense men.

"Two hundred men will advance straight up the hill, with sections on each flank and two platoons in the rear. One platoon will follow immediately behind the assault party as a mobile reserve. The second will lie prone and form a horseshoe at the base of the hill. This final reserve will ensure the Boers to the east do not interfere with the stormers."

Hunter continued, "While we are destroying Long Tom, Colonel Eustace Knox of the 18th Hussars will hold the Boers' attention."

Andrew nodded. The plan seemed sound and not over-complicated.

The moon set early that night, but a myriad **of** stars punctured the sky. They passed Lombard's Kop, and at a signal from General Hunter, they veered from the road and headed for Gun Hill. The volunteers advanced in two groups, intending to meet at the base of the hill for the final advance.

Andrew had examined Gun Hill through his binoculars, but it seemed different when they reached the lower slopes. It was steeper, with loose, sliding rocks on a gravel base above a lower level of thigh-high grass.

Andrew wrapped his lucky scarf around his neck and looked at the long, dew-damp grass. While British infantry would lie still with infinite patience, he wondered how the volunteers from Natal would cope. He saw them crawl to find rocks for shelter and concentrated on the men he commanded. Nobody had dropped out, and all stared upwards at the slope, where the Boers and Long Tom the Stinker waited for them. At half past two, the units met.

"The Boers must be asleep," Leslie said.

"Let's hope so," Andrew said. He checked his watch. It was half past two in the morning.

General Hunter led the way, with the men swarming up the hill behind him. The ground was rough, with loose boulders and uneven patches to trip the unwary. Andrew noticed the Colonials moved smoothly, with less noise than a British unit. The Natal Carbineers eased up the hill on the right, while the Imperial Light Horse were in the centre and the Border Mounted Rifles on the left flank. In place of a bayonet, each man carried a Bushman's Friend, a government-issued knife.

As the hill grew steeper, some of the men dropped on all fours yet continued to move forward, heading for the artillery that had caused such mayhem in Ladysmith.

"*Wie is daar?* Who is there?" Andrew heard the challenge as the Imperials were halfway up the hill. He saw the outline of men, their broad hats distinct against the starry sky.

"Friends!" one of the Imperials replied in Afrikaans. "From the Modderspruit camp!"

The sentries hesitated, peering downhill until the Colonials reached them.

"Rooinecks!" a youthful Boer yelled, high-pitched, but it was already too late.

One sentry scrambled away, and then the attackers were on them with clubbed rifles and Bushmen's Friends. The struggle only lasted moments, and the advance continued, swamping or scattering groups of isolated sentries.

"Come on, men!" Hunter was still in front, with the Colonials rushing up the final few yards before the alarm spread to the Boers around the guns.

Hunter was a fraction too late. The Boer defenders grabbed

their rifles and fired downhill, with the bullets hissing and whistling around the Colonials.

"Get down and return fire!" Hunter shouted. "Volley fire!"

The Natal men responded, throwing themselves to the ground and firing at the muzzle flares.

"It's a reverse Majuba!" somebody shouted.

Andrew wondered if somebody would make that same comparison every time one side or the other stormed a hill. He lay with his men, noting how the Natal volunteers aimed and fired. Many had experience hunting game in Natal and were as expert shots as any Boer.

Three Boers rose from a small sangar ten yards in front of Andrew.

"Khaki!" the first shouted. Starlight glinted on the barrel of his Mauser as he pointed it at Andrew's chest. The second man knelt, bringing his rifle to his shoulder with near-military precision, and the third stepped forward.

With no time to move, Andrew steeled himself for the savage blow of two Mauser bullets.

"*Nee!* No!" the third man shouted, adding something Andrew could not understand. "*Die serp!* The scarf!"

Both men altered the angle of their rifles before they fired, with the bullets flying wide.

Andrew flinched, and all three Boers retreated at speed.

"Why did they do that?" Leslie shouted.

"Individual fire," Andrew ordered, too concerned about success to worry about details.

The closest Imperials aimed and fired until Colonel Edwards of the 5th Dragoon Guards, commanding the Imperial Light Horse, gave the expected order.

"Fix bayonets!"

Andrew knew the Boers were reluctant to face bayonets. He watched the Colonials tap their rifle butts against any handy rocks, creating a sound like the snick of bayonets being slotted home. Some volunteers tied their Bushman's Friends to the barrels of their carbines.

"Charge!"

General Hunter was first at the gun emplacement, with the Colonials only a few yards behind.

The Boers had a skeleton defence of sixteen men, who proved no match for the rush of aggressive Uitlanders and Colonials. Andrew was with the leading surge, seeing the defenders flee, even as more Boers arrived to bolster the defence. When they realised the British had captured the guns, the Boer reinforcements turned and fled.

"Form a defensive perimeter to guard the position," Hunter ordered. "Do your stuff, Engineers! Blow these guns to blazes! Baird, keep your men handy for a close guard."

Always interested in watching experts at work, Andrew studied the engineers' methods. While some removed the breech block from the Boer guns, others rammed gun cotton down the muzzle, hammered the screw to render it unusable, and plugged the breech and the muzzle. Without pausing, the engineers circled gun cotton around the barrel and stepped back, ready to destroy the gun.

The entire operation took only twelve minutes by Andrew's watch.

"The Boers have put some real work into this emplacement," Andrew said.

The engineer officer nodded. "When they declared war on us, we thought we would be fighting a gaggle of High Veldt rustics," he said.

"No wonder our artillery did not stop the bombardment," Andrew said. The guns were sited behind walls thirty feet thick and sat on solid iron wheels placed on steel rails to cope with the recoil after firing. A massive arch covered each weapon to protect it from dropping British shells.

"Blow it!" the engineer officer ordered. "You'd best move

your men back, sir. There will be a lot of debris and muck flying about."

When Andrew obliged, the engineers detonated the gun cotton. The explosion flashed orange, white and yellow across the hill's summit.

"And that's that," Hunter said with satisfaction. "Let's get back to Ladysmith before Joubert wakes up."

The Colonials and Uitlanders were reluctant to leave, with many clustered around the smoking wreckage of the guns and others shouting challenges to the Boer camps on the lower ground around the hill.

"Come on, men!" Andrew ordered his detachment. "We've won this round; let's leave before we have to fight our way back to Ladysmith." He ignored Leslie's curious stare. The incident with the Boers firing wide already seemed an age ago.

CHAPTER 21

LADYSMITH, NATAL

DECEMBER 1899

"That was a most successful encounter," Sinton said. "Have you read what *The Bombshell* says about the Gun Hill expedition?" *The Bombshell* was Ladysmith's siege newspaper.

"I have not," Andrew replied, and Sinton handed the newspaper across, pointing to the article.

> *£1,000 reward. Whereas on the night of the 8th December last some evil-disposed person or persons did wilfully destroy and carry away certain heavy guns from Lombard's Kop, Natal. The said guns being the property of the ZAR, anyone giving information that will lead to the recovery of the guns, and to the punishment of the offenders, will be rewarded as above.*

Andrew grinned. "A little bit satirical," he said, "but anything that raises the townsfolk's morale is good."

When the raiding party returned at half past three in the morning without a single casualty, half the garrison in Ladysmith seemed to be on hand to cheer them in.

"The Natal volunteers and Uitlanders have proved they can fight," Andrew said.

"Now all we need is a smashing victory by Redvers Buller, and we can dictate peace terms, sir." Sinton retrieved his newspaper.

"Our secondary attack was not so successful," Andrew reminded him. A diversionary attack at Limit Hill returned with casualties as Boer riflemen fired on the British daylight withdrawal.

"General White congratulated everybody," Sinton continued. "We captured and destroyed a 4.7-inch howitzer and a six-inch gun."

"I know," Andrew said quietly. He checked his watch. "Time to inspect the company," he said, leaving the Officers' Mess. As Andrew closed the door behind him, he remembered he had left his pipe. He turned to retrieve it and stopped when he heard Leslie's distinctive voice.

"The Boers should have shot him," Leslie said. "He was right in the open, with two of the brutes aiming at him from only a few yards away, yet they both missed. I think the Boers know our esteemed Captain Baird is a pro-Boer, maybe even a spy passing information to them."

"Nonsense!" Sinton laughed. "Captain Baird is the most loyal man you will ever meet. He's no more a pro-Boer than I am. No, Lieutenant Leslie, the Captain was wearing his lucky scarf."

"Wearing his what?" Leslie asked.

"His lucky scarf," Sinton said. "He wore it on Mournful Monday and walked right through a Boer fusillade without a scratch, even carrying a wounded man."

"His lucky scarf?" Leslie repeated. "You mean that brightly coloured thing he had around his neck?"

"That's the ticket," Sinton replied. "It acts as a talisman."

"Superstitious nonsense!" Leslie scoffed.

"Maybe it is," Sinton said, smiling, "but how else can you explain it?"

"I don't need to explain anything," Leslie said.

"Nor do I," Sinton replied. "I'll just accept that it works for the Captain."

Andrew walked silently away, pleased at Sinton's loyalty but unsure about Leslie.

THE BOER SEARCHLIGHT PROBED THROUGH THE DARK, searching the fringes of Ladysmith for any further British incursion. Twice, a rifle cracked, the sound intrusive in the stillness, but Hendrik ignored the shots, guessing some nervous sentry, Boer or British, had squeezed the trigger at an unknown sound or shifting star shadow. He leaned against a tree, motionless as he watched the besieged town.

Michal stamped his feet on the damp ground, staring through the clear, moonless night towards the hills that ringed Ladysmith. "Damned Rooinecks! They blew up our guns!"

"We'll get them fixed," Hendrik soothed him. "Joubert is sending them to Pretoria, and they'll be back as good as new." He sucked at his pipe and slowly exhaled a cloud of dense blue smoke. "It wasn't the Rooinecks, it was the Natal volunteers and Uitlanders." He caught Jacoba's glance. "You don't like the Natal volunteers, do you, Jacoba?"

Jacoba walked across to join them, with her long skirt swishing through the grass. She perched on a rock just outside the ring of light from the low cooking fire. "I don't like the Natal volunteers," she confirmed softly. "And I hate the Uitlanders."

Hendrik raised a bushy eyebrow, surprised at the intensity in Jacoba's voice. "Hatred is a strong emotion," he said mildly. "What have they done to you, Jacoba?"

"They encroach on our land, dig their mines where we used to farm, bring in strange natives from far lands and build the world's most ugly city on the Witwatersrand. More and more of them come in until we feel like strangers in the land we tamed."

Hendrik nodded, puffing smoke as his gaze never strayed from Jacoba's face. "All this is true," he agreed. "Yet there is more, I think."

"There is more," Jacoba controlled her passion.

"I am listening," Hendrik said quietly.

"We are all listening," Michal said, sitting with his back to a rock, his legs stretched before him. He removed his hat, brushed back his hair, and smiled. "You have an audience, Jacoba. Even Swart Piet is here."

Piet nodded. "I am also listening," he said.

"*Een vrije volk zijn wij* – a free people are we," Jacoba said. "When my grandfather arrived here with the Voortrekkers, the land was empty. There was neither native kraal nor civilised dwelling on the veldt. My grandfather found a place where he could not see the smoke from his neighbour's farm and broke the land. When the Voortrekkers had settled, the British searched for gold and diamonds and came with grasping, greedy hands."

"Ja," Piet agreed, cleaning his rifle. "They are a grasping, greedy people who believe they have a right to other people's countries. They fight this war to make rich men richer and control our land."

"You are not a farmer, Piet," Michal observed. "You are a hunter. If the British conquered the republics, you would move north, away from them."

Piet rubbed a cloth along the barrel of his rifle. "The Rooinecks would follow," he said quietly. "Rhodes wants the British to control Africa from the Cape to Cairo and then stifle us. They would recreate the whole world in their image, with their laws, language and ideas."

"You are right," Jacoba said. "We must stop them here, with the Lord's help." She eyed the saturnine Piet, sensing the hunter's fire within him, so different from the calm farmer's eyes of Hendrik or the lively, youthful enthusiasm of Michal.

"We will stop them," Michal said. "We defeated them before, and we are stronger now, with powerful artillery and better rifles." He tapped his Mauser.

Jacoba smiled as Michal replaced his hat, pushing it low over his forehead.

"The Rooinecks have a large army," Hendrik said. "Their General Buller is coming to try and relieve Ladysmith. He is an experienced soldier."

"We'll beat him," Michal said. "British soldiers cannot shoot straight and cannot think for themselves. They must have an officer to tell them what to do." He smiled, showing bright teeth. "Every time the officer orders, 'fire!' we just lie down, and the bullets pass right over us."

Jacoba allowed herself to laugh, feeling herself relaxing. Men and women had avoided her all her life because she had done the work of a man on her father's farm. Now, she was in the company of three very different men who seemed to accept her for who she was. Jacoba realised she was happy.

"You are very confident, Michal," Jacoba said.

He is a handsome young gallant, she thought, *and he knows it. Girls will throw themselves at Michal's feet. He will get his pick of women, much to their fathers' despair, for such a man will never be satisfied with just one when conquests are so easy.*

"Listen!" Piet held up a hand. "I hear something!"

The corporalship relapsed into silence, for Piet's hunter's ears were attuned to danger.

Hendrik reached for his rifle, which lay within easy reach as Jacoba lifted her head and Michal removed his hat. They all listened intently, hoping the pickets were alert.

"Who is on duty tonight?" Jacoba asked.

"Isaac Malherbe's corporalship," Michal replied quietly. When danger threatened, he looked older as efficiency replaced his youthful enthusiasm. "A dozen good men. Isaac will have two men on guard while the others rest. What did you hear, Piet?"

"Men walking," Piet said. "British army boots on the ground, and somebody talking."

"In Afrikaans?" Jacoba asked.

"I could not say," Piet replied.

They relapsed into silence until Hendrik nodded. "Ja," he said, nodding. "I hear something up Surprise Hill."

"Go closer, Piet," Michal ordered. "Hendrik and I will rouse the corporalship. Jacoba, this is no place for a woman if the British attack. Go inside the laager."

The shout came from Surprise Hill, the roar of excited men, followed by a burst of rifle fire.

"The Rooinecks have attacked again!" Jacoba said. "They are attacking our howitzer on Surprise Hill! Go up, Michal! Take up your corporalship and chase them away!"

Joubert had placed a 4.7-inch howitzer and a supply of ammunition on Surprise Hill, from where the Boers fired on Ladysmith.

"Come on, men!" Michal ordered. They heard more musketry from above and a long, agonised scream. "What is happening up there?"

Hendrik followed Michal to the foot of the hill and began to scramble upward with the others of the corporalship at his side. They climbed silently, automatically moving from cover to cover. They were all naturally fit from farm work and outdoor living and wanted to reach the top to push back the British.

The explosion was louder than anything Hendrik had heard before.

"The Rooinecks must have destroyed our howitzer!" Louis Grobler shouted. "They are blowing up all our guns!"

"There will be hundreds of them," another man sounded doubtful. "Like there were on Gun Hill."

"Keep going!" Michal ordered. "We are not alone. Malherbe's

corporalship will already be on its way, and Corporal Tossel will join us."

"The British will be waiting," the first man said. In the dark, Hendrik did not recognise the voice or the man's shape.

"Rooinecks cannot shoot," Michal reassured him. "Move on! We will hold the British until the Pretoria Commando comes around to block their retreat to Ladysmith!"

"Corporal!" Piet warned. "Somebody is running down the hill!"

Hendrik crouched behind the closest bush, listening to the sounds of scrambling feet and harsh breathing.

"Don't shoot!" Piet warned. "It's one of Tossel's men!"

"What's happening?" Michal hissed, standing up before the running man. "Stand still and tell us!"

"Rooinecks!" the man gasped. He was a Pretoria with wide, frightened eyes that darted from side to side. "Hundreds of Rooinecks came out of nowhere. They bayonetted the gunners, shouting 'Rule Britannia' and 'Come on, the Rifle Brigade!' Hundreds of khaki Rooinecks!"

"You were on watch," Michal accused. "Why did you not warn the gunners?"

"They came out of the dark, and there were too many of them!" The man was nearly in tears. "Nobody told me it would be like this!"

"You know now, you coward!" Michal said. "You left the gunners to die! I should shoot you where you stand!"

"No, Michal," Hendrik touched Michal's arm. "He is broken. Let him run."

"Ja," Michal said. "It would waste a bullet." He led his corporalship upward, with the men sober at the news and the sound of British voices spurring them on.

"Spread out!" Michal said.

"Who are you?" A Boer loomed out of the gloom, staring at these strangers climbing the hill.

"Michal Rheeder's corporalship," Michal said. "Who are you?"

"We are Malherbe's corporalship," the reply came. "We are alone up here. The Pretoria Commando have not left the camp."

The two corporals exchanged brief greetings and advanced together up the hill.

A double explosion sounded from the gun emplacement above, with the intense flash momentarily robbing the corporalship of their night vision.

"The Rooinecks have dynamited our gun!" Piet said.

"Come on, boys," Michal said. "We'll push the British back to London!"

The Boers pushed up the hill, desperate to wreak vengeance on the British destroyers.

"Halt! Who goes there?"

Hendrik heard a soldier roar the challenge immediately in front of the Malherbe corporalship. The Boers replied with a ragged volley and dashed uphill.

"Storm! Storm!" a Boer shouted.

Hendrik heard loose stones rolling down the slope and hurried footsteps retreating uphill.

"The British picket has done its duty, and the Rooinecks are going to warn the others," Michal said.

The Boers found a dead British sergeant lying beside a thorn bush, with two bullets in his chest. His eyes were wide open, and his badges proclaimed he was from the Rifle Brigade.

"Move on," Michal stepped over the body and continued the advance. He stopped as outbreaks of firing began from the Boer garrisons on Bell's Kopje and Thornhill's Kopje, both adjacent to Surprise Hill.

"We have them in a crossfire," Piet said.

"We'd better be careful," Hendrik warned. "A Mauser bullet doesn't know the difference between a Boer and a Briton, whoever pulled the trigger."

Most of the bullets hissed above the climbing Boers as smoke and dust from the ammunition dump and howitzer drifted across the slopes.

More British appeared, slipping and sliding among the rocks, smoke and dust from the explosion, just as rolling clouds obscured the stars and cut the faint light.

Boers and Rifle Brigade fired simultaneously, with the crackle of musketry deafening on the slopes of the hill. A man yelled, and somebody shouted, "To me, Rifles!" and "Rifle Brigade!"

Hendrik fired back, aiming for the voices. He heard Piet's muted grunt as he fired.

"Got one," Piet said calmly.

A bullet whined past Hendrik, knocking chips from the rock at his side. He fired by instinct, worked the Mauser bolt and lay still, peering into the dark. The British had vanished. He heard the soft hiss of the rising wind and a wounded man groaning. Whether Boer or Briton, he did not know; men in pain sounded much the same.

As the British fire intensified, the Boers recoiled, withdrawing downhill with scrambling feet and muted curses.

"Don't run!" Michal warned. "Stay together, Rheeder corporalship!"

"Here!" Piet indicated a *spruit* that eased down from the summit. The corporalships slid into the bed, searching for a suitable position to see the British above them.

The Rifles were alert and either saw or heard the movement, for a blast of rifle fire hammered at the *spruit*. Most bullets lifted dirt and stones from the lip, but one hit Samuel van Zijl of the Malherbe corporalship in the throat. The rifleman was so close the muzzle flare set Samuel's beard alight, and the flames lit up the agony of his face as he slumped down. One of his companions made him as comfortable as possible as the Boers hurried on.

A voice sounded from Bell's Kopje, inviting the Rifle Brigade to advance in that direction, and then a chorus of musketry greeted any man who followed the false command.

Michal smiled at the deception. "The British will withdraw soon," he said. "We'll wait in the *spruit* and fire when they come down the hill."

The Boers spread along the *spruit*, each man choosing a spot that gave him a clear field of fire. They heard the British above them, with officers blowing whistles and calling for their men and the rankers talking loudly.

"Good old Rifle Brigade!" somebody shouted, and others repeated the slogan. Hendrik smelled tobacco smoke and saw the brief flare of cigarettes as men lit cigarettes or pipes, certain the night had been a success, and the fighting was over.

"Wait!" Malherbe said.

The Boers waited, listening to the tramping feet as the Rifles marched downhill.

"Wait!" Michal repeated the order.

Fifty yards. Thirty. Twenty.

"Ready!" Michal said, with the Rifle Brigade's noise masking his voice.

Fifteen yards. "Fire!" Michal and Malherbe spoke together.

The Boers' bullets slammed into the unsuspecting British column. Hendrik saw men stagger back, spin or crumple under the force of the shots.

"Rifle Brigade!" a man called out. "We're the Rifle Brigade! Cease fire!"

"The poor fellows think we are British firing into them by mistake," Hendrik said.

"Keep firing!" Michal shouted, working the bolt of his rifle.

Hendrik fired, saw his target fall, worked his rifle bolt, and fired again. He heard somebody among the Rifles shout, "Charge!" and saw a body of British soldiers rush forward with their swords fastened to their rifles. An officer led them, encouraging his men with hoarse commands. Hendrik fired and saw the officer stagger, recover, and charge on, holding a revolver in his right hand.

"I'll get him," Piet said, aimed and fired.

The officer spun, stopped for a moment and continued, still shouting, with bloodstains spreading across his chest.

"What sort of men are these?" Michal asked.

A youngster from the Malherbe Corporalship fired, and the officer fell forward into the *spruit*. Some of the Rifles entered the watercourse and killed or wounded a few Boers while the main column continued their planned withdrawal to Ladysmith.

"How many bullets do you have left?" Michal asked his corporalship.

"Only three," Hendrik said. "We did not have time to pick up extra ammunition."

"Cease firing!" Michal said, with Malherbe giving the same order.

The Boers remained still, harbouring their ammunition in case the British returned. Hendrik heard somebody slide into the *spruit* and turned, ready to fight.

"I thought you might need this," Jacoba poured a mug of coffee. "It is cold out here."

"*Danke*, Jacoba," Hendrik sipped the coffee. "You be careful if the British come again."

Jacoba peered to the east. "Dawn is coming," she said.

"The coffee was welcome," Hendrik said. "Have you enough for Piet and Michal?"

"I have," Jacoba said. "Who were the Rooinecks?"

"The Rifle Brigade," Hendrik replied.

Jacoba smiled. "I hoped it was not the Royal Malverns. My Rooineck friend is with them, and I want him as a handsupper."

"Why is he important to you?" Hendrik asked.

Jacoba lifted her chin. "He treated me like a woman," she said. "He was the first man to do that."

"Ever?" Hendrik asked over the rim of his mug.

"Yes," Jacoba replied. "And now I have three more men in this corporalship who are," she struggled to find the word, "friends." It was less than she meant.

"It is good to have friends," Hendrik said solemnly. "I will not shoot your British friend if I recognise him."

"Thank you," Jacoba replied.

When the dawn broke, Hendrik saw scores of bodies scattered on the hill, mostly British but with some Boers among them. The British had all been shot, while many Boers bore the wounds of bayonets.

"War is a terrible thing," Hendrik said.

"Ja," Jacoba looked at the dead men with neither malice nor interest. Yesterday, these men had been alive, vital, breathing young men in the prime of life. Now they were dead, and their families would grieve. "War is a terrible thing. The wrong people die, and the greedy people prosper."

Piet looked across at Jacoba. "You said your family were Voortrekkers, and somebody told me that Willem Fourie is your father."

"He was," Jacoba's mouth tightened as she spoke.

"Was? Is he dead?"

"He is dead," Jacoba replied shortly.

"You have my condolences," Piet told her. "I did not know he was dead. How did he die?"

Death could come in many forms on the veldt. It could be a hunting accident, a fire, a raid by native tribesmen or a fall from a horse. Living lonely, isolated lives, there was nobody to call for help if a man lay injured.

"A Uitlander swindled him of his farm," Jacoba said. "He had no reason to live."

Piet nodded. "I understand," he said.

Hendrik touched Jacoba's shoulder in a brief expression of sympathy that both understood.

"Is that why you dislike the Uitlanders so much?" Hendrik asked.

"It is one reason," Jacoba said.

"What happened?" Hendrik asked.

"When the rinderpest struck in 1896," Jacoba's eyes darkened as she remembered. "It hit my father's herds harder than most. He lost all his cattle and had nothing to sell in the market."

"The rinderpest is a terrible blight," Hendrik understood. "I lost beasts as well."

Jacoba sighed. "The banks refused a loan, but a Uitlander offered money at a high rate of interest. Father agreed and bought more cattle, but the rinderpest killed them all. The Uitlander demanded his money, and when Father could not pay, he took our farm."

"It is a bad thing for a man to lose his land," Hendrik sympathised.

"The farm was Father's world," Jacoba said. "He moved to Johannesburg, but his heart was broken, and he died within the year. Mother followed." She looked up. "That Uitlander did not break any laws, yet he killed my parents as surely as if he put a rifle to their heads."

Hendrik touched Jacoba's shoulder. "You have suffered a grievous loss," he said quietly.

"We both have," Jacoba replied, slowly aware that Hendrik understood a little part of her.

Hendrik nodded and stepped back, eyeing her stocky, capable figure. "You are a strong woman," he said thoughtfully. "A fine woman." He lifted his hat, held her gaze for a long moment, turned and walked away.

Jacoba watched him, seeing her father in the way he moved, and felt something stir within her. *No,* she told herself. *That cannot be.*

When Hendrik turned again, Jacoba did not look away. They surveyed each other, and Hendrik nodded.

Ja, Jacoba admitted to herself. *It can be.*

CHAPTER 22

LADYSMITH, NATAL

DECEMBER 1899

"The Rifles lost fifteen men on that raid on Surprise Hill," Andrew said. "A bit more costly than the Colonials' show, but they achieved their object and must have given the Boers a fright."

"I hear that Buller is on the move," Sinton reported with satisfaction. "He is advancing with thousands of men. He will break through Louis Botha's cordon and relieve Ladysmith."

Andrew nodded. "We'll be pleased to see him."

"I'll make sure the men are smartly presented to welcome Sir Redvers to Ladysmith!" Sinton said.

"You do that," Andrew agreed.

Hunger was beginning to gnaw at the Ladysmith garrison as the siege dragged on and food supplies diminished. The cavalry wondered about their horses as fodder dwindled.

"The men are getting hungry, sir," Sinton said. "I heard the supply officer wants to slaughter the officers' horses for food."

HOLDING FOR THE QUEEN

"I'll be damned if he's getting his claws into my Basutos," Andrew growled. "I'd rather eat the supply officer than my horses."

"I doubt that's legal, sir," Sinton murmured.

Andrew found a small field near the Vaal River and paid two local boys to care for his horses. "I might be on duty elsewhere," he told them, spinning a half-crown in the air. "I will give you a shilling a week each to feed and water Letsie and Moshie, plus this half-crown extra if they are in good condition when I need them."

The boys nodded eagerly, watching the sun reflect from the spinning silver coin.

"If anybody tries to take the horses away for any reason, tell me," Andrew said. "Do you know who I am?"

"You're Captain Andrew Baird of the Royal Malverns," the older boy said immediately.

Andrew tossed him the half-crown. "Look after my horses," he said.

The Malverns manned the outposts, grew used to the Boer shellfire and waited for news from the south. Buller's name was on everybody's lips; Sir Redvers Buller was coming; Buller would save them; Sir Redvers was the man for the job; he would defeat the Boers and teach Botha about real soldiering. The heliograph flashed messages back and forth, keeping Ladysmith informed, and excitement rose when Buller announced he was advancing.

The men waited eagerly but when the news eased through, it sobered the garrison and sent morale plummeting.

"Buller failed to get through," Colonel Newland said quietly to the Officers' Mess. "The Boers cut him up badly at Colenso." He waited for a moment before continuing. "The Boers also defeated Methuen at Magersfontein and Gatacre at Stormberg, all within a week. The press in Britain is calling it Black Week."

"Three defeats in a week, sir. Good God," Andrew stared at the colonel. "That puts Majuba in the shade."

"We lost thousands of men," Newland said. "Kruger must be

dancing in the streets of Pretoria. He'll expect us to throw in the towel, as we did after Majuba. The foreign press is jubilant, naturally, anticipating that the Boers will push us right out of South Africa."

Andrew felt a slow slide of depression and anger. Britain had experienced several military defeats in his lifetime, from Isandlwana at the hands of the Zulus to Maiwand in Afghanistan and Gordon's death in Khartoum. However, they had never had three such calamitous defeats in one week.

"What did Her Majesty say, sir?" Sinton asked.

"Much what you would expect," Newland told him with the only hint of a smile he had shown that day. "When somebody – I do not know who – spoke about the Boers winning the war, she replied, "We are not interested in the possibilities of defeat; they do not exist.""

Andrew nodded. "Thank God for Queen Victoria."

"Thank God indeed," Colonel Newland said. "Excuse me, gentlemen, I have work to do." He squared his shoulders and left the Mess.

"There is worse," Major Cradley said when the colonel had gone. He lowered his voice as if ashamed of what he had to say. "Sir Redvers Buller advised General White to surrender."

Andrew flinched. "Buller did that?"

The officers gasped or shook their heads in disbelief. Buller was a living legend, a man with a reputation as one of Britain's best fighting generals. Nobody could imagine Sir Redvers Buller ever contemplating surrender, let alone suggesting it to another officer.

"I have a transcript of Sir Redvers' message," Cradley said quietly. "It was in code, thank God, but the deciphered message is all too plain." He stood and addressed the silent room.

"I don't have to tell you not to let the men know this, gentlemen."

The officers listened as Cradley read from a sheet of paper. "This is the message Sir Redvers sent:"

"I tried Colenso yesterday but failed; the enemy is too strong for my force, except with siege operations, and these will take one full month to prepare. Can you last so long? If not, how many days can you give me in which to take up defensive positions? After which I suggest you firing away as much ammunition as you can and making the best terms you can."

Andrew listened, hardly believing any British general would advise another to surrender.

"Good God," Andrew said. "That's not the Redvers Buller I remember."

"That's the Redvers Buller we have now," Cradley replied. "And there was another signal." He produced another slip of paper. He read the second message aloud.

"Whatever happens, recollect to burn your cypher, and decipher and code books, and any deciphered messages."

Andrew shook his head again. He had been in many difficult situations with the army but never felt as bad as that moment.

"The rank and file must never hear the contents of this message," Cradley reminded. He replaced both messages in a heavy file, which he closed. "The men still retain their faith in Sir Redvers," he said. "They view him as a personally brave officer, which he undoubtedly is."

"Need I ask what General White's reply was, sir?" Andrew felt his heart beating rapidly as he waited for the answer.

Cradley smiled for the first time. "Sir George is a fighting Irishman," he said. "He signalled: 'I hold Ladysmith for the Queen.'"

Andrew breathed out softly. "Thank God for Sir George."

"There will be no surrender with General White in command," Cradley said.

"What happens now?" Andrew asked.

"The War Office has removed Buller as Commander-in-Chief in South Africa and appointed Field Marshal Lord Roberts in his place. Buller remains in command of the army in Natal."

Andrew nodded. He knew such a move would end Buller's

career, but that was irrelevant compared to the lives that had been lost. "Bobs Roberts is a good man," he said.

Cradley nodded. "The government is also sending more reinforcements, calling up the reserves and accepting offers of volunteers from the colonies: Australia, New Zealand and Canada."

Andrew nodded. "These defeats have shaken the War Office," he said. "How about the Indian Army, sir? They are excellent soldiers and more experienced than any in Britain. The Guides, the Bengal Lancers, Skinner's Yellow Boys and the Sikhs are the best cavalry in the world."

"No," Cradley shook his head. "None of the Indian regiments. The government has decided this will be a white man's war."

Captain Boswell grunted. "I'd rather have a regiment of Sikhs with me than some fresh-faced yeomanry from the Home Counties. Did the government ask any Indian veterans before making that foolish decision?"

"I doubt it," Cradley replied dryly. "However, there is nothing we can do about it. All we can do is defend Ladysmith, for I expect the Boers to launch an attack soon when their morale is high and we are hurting from the defeats."

"We'll be ready, sir," Boswell replied. "After all, we're holding for the Queen."

"That we are, Captain Boswell," Cradley said. "That we are."

SUNDAYS WERE QUIET DAYS IN LADYSMITH. THE BOERS, Christian to a man and woman, refused to fight on the Sabbath and Ladysmith's garrison and civilians enjoyed the day of rest with various sports, from football to polo.

"Football, anyone?" Sergeant Kenny shouted. "We have a little Sunday league going, each unit playing the other."

Thirteen keen footballers from the Malverns volunteered at once, with two disappointed when Kenny relegated them to the substitutes' bench. Andrew had played rugby at school many years before, but the subtle arts of Association football were beyond him. His role was to watch and encourage.

The Malverns' first game was against the Manchester Regiment, a hard-fought affair that ended in a three-nil victory for the Manchesters.

"That referee was blind in one eye!" Conway said bitterly as the Malverns limped disconsolately off the field.

"As well he was," the jubilant Manchesters' captain said. "Or we'd have won by another three goals at least. You Malverns did nothing but foul and hack!"

Sergeant Kenny ushered Conway away before he swung a punch at the Manchester man and started a riot.

"That's only our first game," Andrew consoled Conway. "There are more to come."

Later that day, the Gordons played the Devons, and inter-regimental rivalries became more heated.

Andrew watched the game from behind the Gordons' goals, for the Devons were favourites to win the tournament. He winced as both sides put in a series of hefty tackles, with men falling and clutching bruised and bloody shins and ankles.

"You Scots lads think you're a better regiment than us," a tall Devon taunted as his side went one up. "Well, this isn't the bloody Dargai Heights, and the Boers chased you off Majuba the last time you fought them."

A Gordon defender grabbed the bait and headbutted the Devon, resulting in a general melee with punches and kicks thrown on both sides until the referee, a lithe cavalryman, intervened.

When the referee sent the Gordons' defender off, the Devons celebrated with loud cheers, which produced more resentment. The spectators joined the fun, with a few skirmishes on the touchline.

"Enough!" General White appeared. "We'll have no more. The game is abandoned. Indeed, the tournament will end here."

He watched as both sides slouched away, exchanging hot words and dire threats over their shoulders.

"I'm glad we got one game, anyway," Sergeant Kenny said. "We would have won the next one, sir."

Andrew nodded. "I think so," he said, hiding his worry about falling morale and disputes within the garrison.

"THE ROOINECKS MUST GIVE UP NOW," HENDRIK SAID. "We have defeated them on every front and hold Kimberley, Mafeking and Ladysmith under siege. Surely, they can see there have been sufficient deaths."

"We can only hope so," Michal said, chewing on a strip of biltong.

"The Rooinecks are a stubborn breed," Piet shrugged. "If they want to continue the fight, I can shoot more of them."

"What do you think, Jacoba?" Hendrik asked.

Jacoba held a mug of coffee in her hand as she sat beside the fire with her head down and her terai hat pushed to the back of her head. "I do not know what to think," she said. "The more Rooinecks we shoot, the more they produce from their damp little island. But Piet is right; if they want to continue the fight, we can continue to shoot them."

"We shot plenty at Colenso and Magersfontein," Michal said.

"Yet they do not seem inclined to go away," Jacoba said. "Unlike many of our men. Have you seen how many are returning to their farms or the towns?"

Michal nodded. "Ja," he said. "Cowards and traitors. We should not let them leave."

Hendrik looked up, faintly smiling. "Would you suggest we shoot them too, Michal?"

Michal held Hendrik's gaze for a few seconds before replying. "I do not know the solution, Hendrik," he admitted. "Everybody was eager to fight when this war started, but the rain and long weeks of besieging Ladysmith with no result have blunted their resolve. Our numbers are diminishing as men drift back to their homes."

"Then we must strike while we still have sufficient men!" Jacoba spoke fiercely. "The longer this war continues, the more men the British will gather. We had hoped our friends in Germany, France, the Netherlands, and Russia would help when we showed that we could win this war, but what do they do?"

Hendrik sipped at his coffee. "We have volunteers from these countries," he said.

"A few score mercenaries," Jacoba dismissed them with a wave. "Men who get themselves killed fighting differently from us."

"The Americans also send us men," Hendrik said.

"Mostly Irishmen who fight the British for their own cause," Jacoba said. "The Americans are too busy fighting in the Philippines to help us."*

"What would you do, Jacoba?" Piet asked.

When Jacoba looked up, Hendrik saw the fire in her dark eyes. "I would not slowly strangle Ladysmith," she said. "I would strike it now before any more men desert our army. I would hit the Rooinecks when they are still reeling from Colenso and Magersfontein and then push at Buller before he recovers from his defeat."

Hendrik watched Jacoba stand as she spoke, gesturing with her hands as she made her points. He nodded, placing his mug at his feet. "Ja," he said. "You have passion, Jacoba."

"Passion?" Jacoba looked at him.

Piet nudged Michal and nodded away from the circle of firelight. "Come, Michal. We are not needed here."

Michal frowned. "What do you mean?"

---

* At the end of the US-Spanish War, the USA annexed the Philippines, leading to a three-year war. Over four thousand US and twenty thousand Filipino combatants died, with 200,000 civilians.

"Come, Corporal Rheeder," Piet gripped Michal's shoulder in an iron hand. "Leave these two good people together."

Hendrik waited until he was alone with Jacoba. "You spoke with passion, Jacoba," he said. "It comes from inside you."

"I care about our land," Jacoba said.

"You are a fine woman," Hendrik told her. "A woman with passion and conviction. You would make a fine wife."

Jacoba stiffened with a mixture of nervousness and disbelief. "I would need a good man to ask me first," she said.

"If I asked you," Hendrik replied, "what would you say?"

"Are you asking?" Jacoba countered, playing for time as she pondered her reply.

"Ja," Hendrik said. "I have a good farm with sweet water and a house that needs a woman's touch."

"How can I resist such an offer?" Jacoba replied with a smile.

"You will become my wife, then?" Hendrik said.

"I will become your wife," Jacoba replied. "But not because of your good farm or your sweet water." She closed her eyes. For most of her life, she had dreamed of a man asking to marry her, yet she had never thought it would be in an armed camp in the middle of a war. Jacoba smiled. Why not? She had always been different from other women, so why not in courtship? When she opened her eyes, Hendrik was smiling at her.

"I will be the best wife I can," Jacoba promised.

Hendrik nodded. "I will be the best husband," he said. "But first, we have to defeat the Rooinecks."

Jacoba studied Hendrik across the dwindling bonfire. He was tall and more wiry than muscular, while the lines on his face and forehead spoke of hardship and experience. "No," Jacoba said. "We don't have to wait."

Hendrik filled his mug with coffee from the pot on the fire. "Would you prefer to marry before the war ends?"

"Ja," Jacoba said. "Why should we wait, Hendrik? The war could last for weeks, even months. We have agreed to marry, and there is a *kerk predikant* in the camp."

"There is," Hendrik agreed.

"If Oom Joubert can take his wife to war, surely Hendrik du Toit can marry his woman on campaign." Jacoba's smile disguised her inner turmoil. "Besides, Hendrik, if we wait, you might change your mind."

Hendrik smiled slowly. "My mind is made up. Any man would be proud of a wife like you."

Every man of the Rheeder Corporalship attended the simple wedding ceremony three days later, with scores of others from the Wessels Commando watching from a respectful distance. Joubert agreed to give Jacoba away and looked more comfortable in that role than as a fighting general. Mrs Joubert watched from the back of a wagon, ensuring everything was done to her satisfaction. Hendrik was not alone in wondering if she was the power behind the Commandant-General's throne.

When the *predikant* finally pronounced Hendrik and Jacoba as man and wife, the corporalship clapped, shook Hendrik's hand and politely kissed Jacoba.

"Will you be going to your farm, Jacoba?" Michal asked.

"I will go to our farm when Hendrik does," Jacoba replied. "The day that we defeat the British."

Joubert smiled softly. "Pray to the Lord that day comes soon."

When the crowd diplomatically dissipated to leave Jacoba and Hendrik alone, she looked down at the ground, uncharacteristically diffident. "We will sleep in my wagon tonight," she said.

"That will be best," Hendrik agreed.

"Hendrik," Jacoba said and suddenly looked up, her eyes challenging as if she had arrived at a decision. "I have never been with a man before."

"That is surprising," Hendrik said. "I can't imagine any man who would not want to be with you."

Jacoba took a deep breath. "Shall we go into the wagon?"

"Ja," Hendrik said and stretched out his hand for her.

CHAPTER 23

LADYSMITH, NATAL

DECEMBER 1899 - JANUARY 1900

The shell landed in Ladysmith's main street, blasting a crater in the road and spreading dirt and stones over a ten-yard radius.

"Brother Boer is getting serious now," Sinton said.

"He's increased his shelling since the 16th of December," Andrew agreed. "That's Dingaan's Day to the Boers."

"What's Dingaan's Day?" Sinton asked.

"They also call it the Day of the Vow, when the Voortrekkers defeated the Zulus at the Battle of Blood River in 1838," Andrew said. "We are proud of the 24th Foot's defence of Rorke's Drift and handed out Victoria Crosses. At Blood River, the Voortrekkers defeated between 15,000 and 30,000 Zulus with old muzzle-loading muskets, and they were civilians, not trained soldiers. We are dealing with a formidable people, Sinton."

"They are indeed formidable," Boswell joined the conversation. "Between the Boers and disease, we're having a sticky time."

Andrew knew that around 850 of the Ladysmith garrison were down with dysentery and enteric fever, weakening the defence and causing men to wonder who was next to fall sick. The Boer shelling was desultory but sometimes effective, killing a pair of gunners in the main street on December the 16th and five cavalrymen on the 18th.

Soldiers and civilians alike learned to listen for the whistle of the descending shell and the mighty crump of the explosion.

"Maybe they think they'll bombard us into surrender," Boswell said. "If so, they don't know General White."

"They don't," Andrew agreed, "but I don't like to think of the civilians facing the same dangers we do."

"I hope your lucky scarf keeps you safe from shells and disease as well as bullets," Boswell said. "Some people are envious of you."

Andrew touched the scarf around his neck. "I was never a superstitious man," he said, "but now I wear this scarf every day. I wonder what the Boer woman would think if she knew I was one of her sworn enemies."

Boswell laughed. "She'll be back across the Vaal weeks ago," he said. "I doubt she'll even remember you."

"Probably not," Andrew said. "I'm going to check the men."

"Is it that time already?" Boswell sighed. "What a fag. I'd better do the same. B Company will miss my cheery presence."

As the shells landed and illness spread, Ladysmith's food supply diminished. At the beginning of the siege, food had been plentiful, but rations steadily decreased, and men began to feel the first pangs of hunger.

"Murcot!" Andrew said quietly as he faced the private in a

corner of the camp. "My sources tell me that you are the best forager in the company."

Murcot was a swarthy, lithe man with a broad Worcestershire accent. "I wouldn't say that, sir." He looked evasive, as if he had spent much of his life avoiding police officers and gamekeepers.

"No? What would you say?"

"Nothing, sir," Murcot said.

"Nothing," Andrew nodded. "Well, Murcot, Private Smith, my soldier servant, has gone down with fever, and I need a replacement. That's you."

"Me, sir?" Murcot looked even more uneasy.

"You, sir. And your first duty is to forage for your officer. See what food you can find for us both."

"Yes, sir," Murcot said. "What would you like, sir?"

"Anything you can find, Servant," Andrew said. "Particularly eggs. I heard that the Imperial Light Horse have a secret supply of eggs."

"Eggs are hard to find, sir. One of the Colonial chaps has a small henhouse that he keeps locked so his hens lay two eggs daily, but he charges huge prices for them, sir."

Andrew grunted. "I haven't reached the stage when I can afford to pay siege prices for eggs, Murcot, but keep him in mind if things get desperate."

"I will, sir," Murcot said.

Andrew closed his eyes, thinking of eggs. He always had eggs for breakfast back home in Berwickshire. Two eggs, either boiled or poached, fresh from the bantam hens that ran loose around the farmyard. He liked nothing better than fresh, soft-boiled eggs, and the clucking and scurrying of bantam hens was one of the most cheerful sounds in the world.

Andrew realised that Murcot was still standing at attention in front of him. "Off you go then, Murcot. Dismissed."

Andrew heard a discreet cough and saw that Sinton was standing nearby.

"May I speak to you, sir?"

"What's the matter, Sinton?"

Sinton sounded nervous. "I am due on picket duty tonight, sir, and I wondered if I could borrow your scarf."

"Are you feeling the cold?" Andrew asked and then grinned and handed the scarf over. "I am not sure I believe in the scarf's powers," he said, "but if it makes you feel better."

"Thank you, sir," Sinton said. "I'll bring it back tomorrow."

"Try not to get bullet holes in it," Andrew advised.

When Sinton returned uninjured the following morning, other Malverns' officers wanted to borrow Andrew's scarf until he wondered if he should charge to hire it out.

"It's not a magic talisman," he told Sinton as they sat in the Officers' Mess.

"It works as one," Sinton said. "Not a single officer has been even slightly wounded when they wore it." He coughed slightly. "Here's the colonel, sir."

"Baird!"

"Sir!" Andrew came to attention as Colonel Newland strode towards him.

"The garrison on Platrand is short of men with this damned fever. You're the duty officer tonight, so you've drawn the short straw. Take C Company and reinforce the garrison."

"Yes, sir," Andrew saluted.

Platrand was a significant ridge to the south of Ladysmith. Although only 600 feet high, it occupied a strategic position. Two and a half miles long, scattered with boulders and alive with flowering thorn bushes, Platrand was only three thousand yards from Ladysmith, with no defences between.

"If Joubert captures Platrand, we can't hold Ladysmith," Colonel Newland said. "Their artillery could dominate the town and blow us to kingdom come."

White had sent a garrison to occupy the ridge at the beginning of the siege, and they remained in stubborn defiance of anything the Boers could do.

"Take extra ammunition," the colonel said. "The Boers have

been studying the ridge these last few days, and we've seen Commandant de Villiers nearby. He leads the Harrismith Commando and is a thrusting sort of fellow."

"That sounds ominous, sir. Who is the present garrison?"

"The Manchester Regiment is on the eastern side at Caesar's Camp, where we had our first camp, and the Imperial Light Horse holds the west, Wagon Hill. Three companies of the Rifles are in the centre." Newland produced a large-scale map and pointed out the defensive positions. "We also have entrenchments on the reverse slope, with solid emplacements for the 42nd Battery, R.F.A., under Goulburn."

Andrew nodded, studying the map. "Where do you want me, sir?"

"In the centre, Baird," Colonel Newland said. "Reinforce the centre and be prepared to shift your men to either flank if the Boers attack."

"Yes, sir," Andrew said.

"Platrand may be busy. There are some fatigue parties already on Wagon Hill," Newland said. "The sappers are digging pits for another couple of 4.7-inch naval guns, with the Gordons as escort."

"It sounds like General White is gearing up for a battle, sir."

"I agree, Baird, so keep your men alert. We don't want another disaster after Mournful Monday and Black Week."

C Company were quite happy to march to the southern perimeter after their spell in reserve.

"It's about time we had a chance to shoot back," Murcot said. "I'm sick of acting as a target for Oom Kruger's guns."

Corporal Harwood laughed. "You're a big enough target for anybody's guns, Murcot! You must have put on two stone since the captain appointed you his soldier servant!" He prodded Murcot's stomach. "You'll have to get back to real soldiering to lose that! You could give birth any minute."

Murcot good-naturedly joined in the platoon's laughter.

"If we see any Boers," Andrew reminded, "keep your heads down, aim and shoot low. They're masters of fire and movement, but many of us learned our trade against them. We're better than them."

C Company moved on through the soft dark, passing the toiling seamen driving the oxen with the 4.7-inch guns.

"Move that starboard beast, Petty Officer! It's steering off course!"

"Aye, aye, sir!" the Petty Officer replied. "Come on, you blasted lubber! Steer small!"

Andrew smiled. The Navy could always be relied upon to do its best, whether at sea or hundreds of miles inland.

The watchful Gordons' escort allowed the seamen to bring up the guns while they kept a lookout for prowling Boers. They greeted the Malverns with the expected good-humoured banter. C Company responded in kind, with Conway quickest at barbed comments that had the Malverns laughing.

"Here we are, lads!" Andrew said as a Rifles guide indicated their redoubts for the next few days.

"There you go, Malverns," the Rifleman spoke with a thin London accent. "Make yourselves at home. You'll get no sleep tonight with the sailor lads shouting and the sappers digging holes all over the place."

"How far away are the Rifles' positions?" Andrew peered through the dark. The top of Platrand was an undulating plateau, with a breeze blowing the long grass and the vague shapes of earthworks and sangars at strategic points.

"The closest to you is four hundred yards away, sir," the Rifleman indicated a solid lump in the darkness. "We have pickets all along the ridge."

"Thank you, Rifleman," Andrew said. "You'd better return to your mates."

"Yes, sir," the Rifleman saluted and trotted along the ridge, automatically keeping back from the skyline.

As C Company settled in, Andrew was impressed by the

seven-foot-high defences, with sandbags on top of the stones and loopholes for rifles.

"Brother Boer will have a hard time shooting through that," Sergeant Kenny said.

Andrew agreed. The British Army was learning how to cope with the Boers' musketry. He toured C Company's position, posted sentries and pickets, and allowed the remainder of the men to sleep.

The noise of the sappers and gunners gradually diminished as night eased into morning. The stars faded in the lightening sky while a breeze rustled the grass, causing nervous sentries to see Boers in every half-sensed movement.

Andrew completed his rounds. "Anything to report, men?"

"All quiet, sir," Corporal Harwood reported.

"All quiet," the other pickets echoed.

Andrew lifted his binoculars and scanned the slope to the south. The Boers were out there, somewhere, with Commandant de Villiers desperate to capture the ridge. Andrew touched his scarf, hoping his luck held. He saw the flickering lantern light from the new 4.7-inch gun emplacement, where the seamen were putting finishing touches to the defences and two men huddled over a Hotchkiss. One lit a cigarette, the tiny flare of the match momentarily visible.

Andrew looked away, returning his gaze to the slope below. Was that movement? Something brushing against a thorn tree? Andrew adjusted the focus, feeling his heartbeat increase.

"Halt! Who goes there?" The challenge came clearly from the Imperial Light Horse forward picket on Wagon Hill. "Identify yourself!"

CHAPTER 24

WAGON HILL, LADYSMITH

JANUARY 1900

The reply came quickly as a dozen Boer riflemen fired from lower down the hill. The picket retaliated with a volley, and then pandemonium broke out.

"Bugler!" Andrew shouted. "Sound the alarm!"

There was no need for the bugle as the gunfire woke C Company. Men rushed to their firing positions, ready to repel an attack. Andrew peered to his left, where muzzle flares gave brief vignettes of the action on Wagon Hill. He saw the lanterns around the 4.7-inch gun suddenly extinguished and guessed somebody had kicked them over. The Hotchkiss fired three times, four, with the yellow-white flashes harsh against the velvet dawn.

Shouts came from Wagon Hill—the hoarse cry of men readying to fight, the sharp commands of officers and NCOs, a man roaring in pure Buchan Doric to rouse the Gordons, and the Afrikaans of the Boers whose stealthy advance the alert Corporal Dunn had stalled.

"C Company!" Andrew shouted. "Face your front!"

The Malverns were already awake, holding their rifles, staring into the night-time dark.

"Do we fire, sir?" Lieutenant Sinton asked.

Andrew stared at the confusion of flashes, unable to distinguish friend from foe. "Not yet," he replied. "Wait until we can identify the enemy."

Having been fired on by British artillery at Talana, Andrew did not want his men to fire on British soldiers.

"If the Boers attack us, let them have it," Andrew said. He touched his scarf again, cursing himself for his superstition.

The firefight continued, flaring up in various places, dying away, only to start again—sometimes spreading across the breadth of Wagon Hill, and at other times only in isolated pockets.

Andrew swore, feeling frustrated at his inability to help the defence. "Aim at the muzzle flares low on the hill," he decided. "They must be Boers. We might get them in flanking fire and distract the others. Volley fire at the NCOs' and officers' commands." He knew that even the veterans might fire away half their ammunition in their eagerness to fight, and there was little chance of replenishment at night.

"Down to the right, sir," Murcot said. "I hear something."

Andrew glanced at Murcot, trusting his poacher's instinct. "Three Platoon, fire a volley down to the right, then take cover below the parapet!"

Three Platoon's volley crashed through the dark, adding to the confusion. The reply came with a scattering of individual shots that thudded in the sandbags or smashed against the stones.

"Aim for that man on the right," Sergeant Kenny said. "Three Section, on my word: fire!"

Eight Lee-Metfords fired, eight muzzle flashes split the night, and eight men immediately ducked behind the parapet. Boer bullets thumped back, both adversaries invisible to the other.

The British Hotchkiss fired again, a staccato banging through the night. Somewhere, a man screamed, long and high-pitched in his agony.

"Cease fire," Andrew ordered. C Company obeyed, men working their rifle bolts as they lay against the sandbags or rocks, grinning at each other. They were happy they had fired at the enemy without incurring any casualties. The battle on Wagon Hill continued in a series of isolated skirmishes, each intensely important to the men involved.

"What's happening out there, sir?" Sinton asked.

"I'm not sure," Andrew replied. "I'd guess the Boers tried a night attack like ours on Gun Hill and Surprise Hill, but our sentries were alert and stopped them. Now they are attacking our positions, and we're holding out."

"What do we do, sir?" Sinton asked.

"We sit tight and fight off any Boer attack until we can see what's happening," Andrew replied. "Ian Hamilton and General White will have heard the noise, and they'll send somebody to see what's happening."

"Here they come again!" Conway shouted, and a torrent of bullets crashed and hammered against the sandbags and walls.

"Individual firing!" Andrew roared. "Aim for the flashes!"

Within ten seconds of Andrew's order, C Company was in a hot skirmish with the surrounding Boers. Andrew paced inside the wall, offering encouragement and advice. One over-eager private raised himself up for a better view, and a Boer bullet hit him in the centre of the forehead, killing him instantly.

"That's Private Healey gone," Kenny said and raised his voice. "Keep your heads down, lads!"

When the Boer firing died away, Andrew ordered, "Cease

fire!" and cautiously raised his head. A dismal, misty morning revealed the scene on Platrand. The summit of Wagon Hill was about half a mile from west to east and 300 yards south to north. The British held on, although the Boers were all around them.

On the opposite side of the ridge, the Manchesters sat snugly within well-built defences on the much larger Caesar's Camp. The Manchesters had repelled every Boer attack, with the 42nd Battery, Royal Artillery, Royal Navy and Natal Naval Volunteers providing efficient backing.

"Bloody Manchesters probably bribed the referee!" Sergeant Kenny grunted.

Andrew frowned when he saw a cluster of khaki bodies around one Manchester outpost. The Boers had achieved a minor success but would be hard-pressed to make more headway against the stubborn defenders.

Between the two extremes, Bester's Ridge slithered southwards down to Bester's Valley, offering cover to the attackers with scrubby plants, scattered boulders and broken ground.

Andrew returned his attention to Wagon Hill, where the Boers had made their most significant effort. He could see the defences were not as substantial as on Caesar's Hill, but the garrison was holding out. The Natal Naval Volunteers and their 3-pounder Hotchkiss gun, with the Royal Navy's 4.7, nicknamed Lady Anne, and a twelve-pounder, also held firm.

Although both ends of the ridge were still in British hands, Boers and British hotly disputed the long stretch in between. The Boers had made inroads and sat tight behind rocks and in hidden gullies.

Andrew realised that his C Company, with a few hundred Rifles, was on the stretch where the Boers dominated. The British outposts were islands surrounded by thousands of Boer riflemen, now backed by eighteen artillery pieces.

"This day could get interesting, Sinton," Andrew said.

"If the Boers capture the ridge, sir," Sinton replied, "I can't see how Ladysmith will hold out."

"We'd better make sure they don't capture it, then," Andrew said.

"Yes, sir."

The Boer guns began an intermittent bombardment of the British positions, with shells landing randomly across the ridge.

"The Boers haven't coordinated their guns with their infantry," Sinton pointed out.

"Let's hope they never do," Andrew replied.

They heard scattered firing from other points on the Ladysmith perimeter. "Diversionary attacks," Andrew said casually. "Our defences will deal with them. They want Platrand."

"They won't get it," Sinton said. "General White will recognise the diversionary attacks and reinforce us here."

"This is the Boers' crucial attack," Andrew decided. "If we win today, we'll hold Ladysmith until Buller arrives." He did not mention what might happen if the British lost Ladysmith. The Boers would pour south through Natal, picking up any Hollanders who were waiting to change allegiance, and the reinforced army would fall on Buller.

A Boer shell crashed on C Company's redoubt, followed by another, and then the sentries on the south wall shouted the alarm.

"Here they come!"

The Boers moved skilfully as always, firing and jinking from rock to rock, with C Company firing and ducking away.

Andrew grabbed the deceased Private Healey's rifle, jumped up, fired and ducked. Boer bullets hissed and cracked over the defensive wall, knocking off chips of stone and ricocheting high above the men's heads.

"They're getting close!" Sergeant Kenny shouted.

"Fix bayonets!" Andrew roared. "Let them see the steel, boys!" He knew bayonets scared the Boers, so the sight of scores of shining, sharp blades above the parapet might dissuade them from attacking. Andrew nodded as the men snicked home the long blades and thrust them above the sandbags.

"We're waiting for you, Boojers!" Conway shouted.

"We need more loopholes in the wall, sir," Sinton said.

"We'll make them once we've driven this lot back," Andrew promised. He saw another man stagger, swearing as he held a hand to his bleeding face.

"They're falling back, sir!" Corporal Harwood shouted.

"Help them on their way!" Andrew ordered.

C Company rose to the wall and fired after the retreating Boers.

"The bayonets worked, sir!" Sinton said.

"I don't think so," Andrew replied. "Look to the north!"

Coming up the slope from Ladysmith, dismounted men of the Imperial Light Horse led a long column of the King's Royal Rifles to reinforce the garrison. Further along, a company of Gordon Highlanders and men of the Rifle Brigade hurried to help the Manchesters while Ian Hamilton led more Gordons to Wagon Hill.

"General White recognises the importance of this hill," Sinton said.

Andrew saw the muzzle flare from British artillery and the orange flashes of explosions on Platrand's western slopes, discouraging Boer reinforcements from advancing that way. Ten minutes later, British artillery bombarded the Boers on the southeast.

"White knows his job," Sinton approved, as the Boers scattered under a hail of vicious shrapnel.

The Boer artillery tried to retaliate, with the huge shells from a Long Tom howling down. Andrew saw the explosions near the British battery, but the gunners had positioned their artillery well and continued to fire. A Naval 4.7 on Cove Redoubt, a few miles away, targeted the Long Tom, which soon stopped firing.

"Saint Barbara's pets are doing well today," Andrew murmured.

"Saint Barbara, sir?" Sinton asked.

"Saint Barbara is the patron saint of artillerymen," Andrew replied, touching his lucky scarf.

"I see, sir," Sinton replied doubtfully. "I didn't know the gunners needed a protective saint."

Trusting to luck and his scarf, Andrew stood at the highest point of the redoubt and watched events along the Platrand. The British artillery had effectively stopped the Boer reinforcements from joining the men on the hill, while Andrew saw a few Burghers away to the south.

"The Boers are not so keen now," Sinton said.

"They'll be even less keen in a moment," Andrew said. "Look what's coming up the hill."

Captain Carnegie of the Gordon Highlanders had seen the Boers wavering and ordered his company to fix bayonets and clear the summit. The Gordons cheered, with the bayonets glinting in the early morning sunlight. Somebody shouted the inevitable, "Remember Majuba!" as the Gordons swept forward. The Boers recoiled before the Highlanders, who recaptured the outposts the Manchesters had lost during the night and fired at the retreating enemy.

"That's the way, Gordons!" Andrew roared.

"You'd better get down, sir," Sinton sounded anxious.

When a bullet whined past his head, Andrew realised the Boers had been firing all the time he had watched their movements. Sinton and half the company were watching him curiously.

"You'd best come down, sir," Sinton repeated. "Your luck won't last forever."

Andrew slipped beneath the shelter of the wall. "The Gordons are here," he said.

The desultory fighting around C Company's position continued. Andrew had the men create more loopholes in the wall, with small niches in which to stand as they fired. After a few hours, the British artillery ceased firing, and a few Boer reinforcements filtered back onto the ridge.

"That's the end of round one," Andrew said. "We've held the initial Boer attack, but they have a foothold on the hill."

"What happens now?" Sinton asked.

"Now we'll have to clear them off the hill before dark," Andrew said. "Or Joubert will add reinforcements during the night."

CHAPTER 25

WAGON HILL, LADYSMITH

JANUARY 1900

Andrew heard increased firing from Wagon Hill and wondered what had happened. Much later, he learned that as the Imperial Light Horse reinforced the Wagon Hill garrison, Hamilton's Gordons headed southeast to outflank the Boers, only to meet heavy and accurate fire from the neighbouring Mounted Infantry Hill. They found cover and returned fire, joined by the King's Royal Rifles, with both regiments pinned down and immobile under Boer fire. Although British artillery tried to dislodge the Boers, the infantry could not progress.

"The Boers are coming again!" Sergeant Kenny warned, as hundreds of Boers stormed southwest Wagon Hill, with one group heading for C Company's redoubt.

Andrew checked his watch. It was one o'clock in the afternoon. They had been fighting for hours, and neither side seemed willing to concede territory.

"The Boers are still after the guns, sir!" Sinton shouted.

"Give the gunners a hand, boys!" Andrew ordered. "Pour flanking fire into the Boer attack!"

C Company obeyed, firing through the loopholes as the Boers targeted the gun emplacements on Wagon Hill. Andrew's counter successfully diverted some Boers to concentrate on the Malverns.

"Permission to lead a bayonet charge, sir?" Sinton asked hopefully.

Andrew considered for a second. "Denied, Sinton. This is no time for glory. I want you to hold on here."

"Sir!" Sinton protested.

Andrew knew defending a redoubt was easier than charging across broken ground, where the men could become scattered and lose cohesion.

"Take command of the outpost, Lieutenant," Andrew ordered. "I'll take a platoon out there."

"Sir!" Sinton protested again.

"Ensure the men don't waste ammunition, Lieutenant!" Andrew ordered. "I want Five Platoon to join me. Sergeant Kenny, send them over. Corporal Harwood, you are with me!"

The selected bayonet men gathered inside the redoubt, eyes gleaming as Andrew told them what to do.

"We're going over the wall at the north side away from the Boers," Andrew said. "We'll circle the redoubt and fall on their flank."

The men nodded, licking their lips as they contemplated the coming action.

"Take off all surplus equipment," Andrew ordered. "Dispense with anything that rattles or makes a noise. Just take the rifle, bayonet and fifteen rounds of ammunition."

The men obeyed, revelling in their new freedom of movement.

"Keep in a body," Andrew instructed. "If anybody gets separated from the rest, return to the redoubt. The password is Hereford."

The men nodded, some testing the sharpness of their bayonets.

"Right, follow me."

Andrew carried a rifle and bayonet, with nothing to mark him as an officer, for the Boers targeted the officers first. He touched his scarf and led the men across the wall, keeping low. The platoon followed, with only a few men scuffing stones as they circled the redoubt. Andrew signalled for them to crouch as he surveyed the slopes, then moved forward, hoping to get close to the enemy before he charged. The less open ground Five Platoon had to cover, the fewer casualties the Boers could inflict.

The Boers scrambled forward, firing and moving with a hunter's skill. Andrew took a deep breath.

"Charge!" he roared. "Get them with the bayonet!"

Five Platoon stormed across the broken terrain, yelling like demons to unnerve the enemy and give themselves courage. Andrew saw one Boer turn toward him with his eyes open in horror. "No!" the man said, and Andrew thrust his bayonet into his side. The man's face contorted as the blade sank in. Andrew twisted and withdrew, crashed his rifle butt against the Boer's jaw and moved on.

Five Platoon followed, roaring as the Boers retreated before them. Few Boers waited for the bayonets, although a few further in the rear fired a final shot before fleeing.

Andrew saw one tall, heavily tanned man aim his rifle directly at him, then frown and turn away without firing.

My lucky scarf has saved me again, Andrew thought.

The British around the gun emplacement cheered as the Malverns' flank attack broke down the Boer attack.

"Back to the redoubt, lads!" Andrew called.

Five Platoon retired, some shaking with reaction, but only one man was lightly wounded. Andrew counted them back, heard the password "Hereford" called and glanced over his shoulder. That lone tall Boer stood beside a mimosa tree, studying him.

Andrew raised a hand in salute; the man responded, and both turned away.

After the successful bayonet charge, the men were in high spirits, and Andrew allowed them a few moments to let off steam before calming them down. The Boers fired a few shells at the Malverns' redoubt, and then the weather worsened, with heavy rain and strong winds adding to the men's discomfort.

"God help any wounded men lying out there in this," Sergeant Kenny said as the rain dripped from the brim of his pith helmet.

"When I was young," Corporal Harwood said, "I believed Africa was always hot and sunny."

"You got taught a lot of nonsense when you were young," Kenny said. "A recruiting sergeant told me the army was a good career, and I'd be an officer within a year."

Harwood smiled. "A year? The recruiting sergeant told me it would only take six months."

Kenny laughed. "If I were you, I'd blacken that man's eye."

"Yes, Sergeant," Harwood replied. "You were the recruiting sergeant."

Kenny laughed, shaking his head. "I know. You've disappointed me, Harwood, only making two stripes rather than becoming a general."

"Yes, Mama dear," Harwood lifted his head. "There's trouble out there again, Sergeant."

As an outburst of musketry sounded, Andrew stepped forward, blinking the rain from his eyes as he peered into the storm. "Sit tight and keep alert, men. Lieutenant Sinton, take a patrol and find out who's making that infernal racket."

Sinton returned in fifteen minutes. "All under control, sir. The Boers attacked our lads on the southwest, but we repelled them."

As the storm intensified, Andrew checked the ridge. Although the British outposts held on, the Boers controlled the ground between them. For all the day's effort and bloodshed, the position had not altered.

"Sir!"

Although the heavy rain reduced visibility, Andrew saw a column of British soldiers advancing to the ridge. Through his binoculars, he saw they were fresh troops, relatively neat and clean if dripping wet from the rain. Every man had his bayonet fixed and looked to his front. Andrew frowned, unable to discern the regiment until he recognised the officer leading from the front.

Colonel Park. That must be the Devons.

"That's the Devons, sir," Harwood confirmed. "They're based on the opposite side of Ladysmith. Colonel Park must have force-marched them right across town."

As Andrew watched, the Devons formed up, and the colonel shouted one word: "Charge!"

A lieutenant echoed the colonel's words. "Company! Double! Charge!" He ran forward with the leading company at his heels, bayonets lowered as they advanced along the ridge.

A second company followed the first, and then a third. Hundreds of Devons charged across the open ground, with Boers firing at them from concealed positions.

"It's the bloody Light Brigade!" Kenny breathed.

"Come on, the Devons!" Corporal Harwood shouted.

The Boers held their positions until the Devons were around fifteen yards away, when they broke and ran.

"Fire at them, C Company!" Andrew shouted.

The Malverns lined the walls and loopholes, firing into the now panicking Boers. The other British outposts followed, bowling down the retreating enemy, cheering as they realised they had held the ridge and won the battle.

"*Shabash* the Devons!" Kenny shouted.

When the last Boers fled from the Devons' bayonets and the

garrison's bullets, Andrew had time to wonder how he had survived. A Boer had him squarely in his sights, yet had not pulled the trigger. He fingered his scarf again.

"I saw your pet Rooineck on Platrand," Piet said as the corporalship slouched around the fire, dejected after their reverse. "I only had to squeeze the trigger, and he was dead, but I refrained. Your scarf saved his life."

Jacoba nodded. "I hope he does not take too many Boer lives."

"It was a bloody day on Platrand," Hendrik touched the stained bandage on his head. "We lost many of our best and bravest."

"Two men of the corporalship died," Michal said. "I do not know how many Rooinecks we killed."

The men were quiet, mourning their losses as they stared into the hissing fire. Piet's dogs curled up at his feet, sensing his sadness.

"Keep your heads up, men," Jacoba said. "We must have hurt the Rooinecks as badly as they hurt us. They have resorted to killing their cavalry horses for food, and every day, more sick soldiers enter their hospital. All we need to do is keep them confined in Ladysmith, and they must surrender."

"What about Buller?" Piet asked. "He has built up a large army since Botha defeated him at Colenso."

"General Buller has the hardest task of any British officer in South Africa," Jacoba said. "The British demand victory from him, yet he must push through a defended ring of hills. We did not break through one hill at Platrand. Buller faces a dozen Platrands before he can relieve Ladysmith."

"Ja," Hendrik eyed his wife. "You are correct, Jacoba. You are the best soldier of us all. Maybe you should lead the corporalship like Madame Joubert leads the army."

Only Michal did not laugh. Every man present suspected that Joubert's determined and steely-eyed wife was the power behind the throne. In a masculine-dominated culture, no man would ever challenge Madame Joubert.

"Have you been inside Ladysmith that you know so much of what happens there?" Michal asked.

Jacoba hesitated before she replied. "I have been inside Ladysmith," she said.

"Why?"

"To see what is happening," Jacoba replied. "I bring little bits of food to the garrison and bring out little pieces of information to Joubert." She smiled. "The information is worth more than the food."

"I wish you would not go," Hendrik said. "It is dangerous putting your head inside the jaws of the British lion."

"It is not dangerous," Jacoba replied. "I am safe. The British do not make war on women, and they welcome the little food I bring." She smiled. "I speak to an infantry corporal and an officer's servant every visit. They believe I am a Hollander from a farm behind our lines."

"Be careful," Hendrik said.

"The British do not make war on women," Jacoba repeated. She smiled. "Anyway, I have a pass."

"A pass?" Hendrik repeated.

"Everybody over twelve in Ladysmith has to have a pass," Jacoba said.

"How did you get one?"

"I gave a woman six eggs, and she gave me her pass," Jacoba said. "They are hungry in Ladysmith."

Hendrik smiled slowly, although his eyes were troubled. "If the British catch you, they may think you are a spy."

"I am a spy," Jacoba replied, "but the British don't make war on women."

"The British will do anything to win a war," Hendrik said.

"That is how they won their empire. They only follow rules if the rules benefit them. Be careful, Jacoba."

"I will," Jacoba said, smiling. She was unused to having somebody care about her and lingered for a moment before moving away. When she suddenly turned around, Hendrik was still watching her.

Dear Lord, I have the husband I have always hoped for.

CHAPTER 26

LADYSMITH

JANUARY 1900

The people of Ladysmith greeted the returning Devons like heroes. Men and women cheered the jubilant soldiers, patted them on the back and presented them with welcome cups of hot tea.

"Hail the conquering heroes!" a man roared. "The finest regiment in Ladysmith."

Harwood watched, smiling, as the Malverns returned to their quarters. "Good lads, the Devons," he said. "That bayonet charge will make them as famous as the Gordons after Dargai."

"Quite right," Sergeant Kenny approved. "There were many brave men on that hill, with the Devons, the Gordons and the Imperial Light Horse teaching Brother Boer how to fight."

"We did our bit, too," Harwood said. "And the Imperials lost a lot of men holding the hill."

"So did the Boers," Kenny said. "They're a tenacious bunch, I'll give them that."

When the casualty reports came in later the following day, Sir George White claimed his men had inflicted around seven hundred Boer casualties. With a truce to gather the dead, British stretcher-bearers helped the Boers retrieve their bodies and remarked on the grief among the Boers at the men they had lost. The British admitted losses of 175 killed and 250 wounded.

"I doubt the Boers will try another assault like that," Andrew said. "They are more careful of their men than we are."

"If they come again," Sinton said, "we'll be ready for them. We know they're scared of the bayonet."

Andrew nodded. "We do," he said. "We also know better how to cope with their defensive tactics. They are nervous of their flanks and don't like artillery."

"Neither do I," Sinton admitted.

Andrew grinned. "No sane man does. Well, Sinton, I'll turn in now. You're duty officer for the company tonight. Good night to you."

"Good night, sir," Sinton said.

Andrew retired to his tent, nodded to Murcot and undressed for the night. He placed his pistol belt near the cot in case of an emergency, leaned Healey's Lee-Metford against the tent pole and lay down, suddenly intensely weary as the events of the Platrand unfolded in his head. Andrew guessed he would sleep poorly as the images returned in his dreams. He touched his scarf for luck, draped it above the rifle and fell asleep.

The bugle sounded reveille, shattering the relative peace of the night. Andrew jerked awake to see Murcot at the foot of his bed with a battered tray holding a mug of coffee and a hunk of fresh bread and cheese.

"Well done, Murcot," Andrew reached for the coffee. "I knew I was right to make you my servant. How the devil did you manage to get bread like this?"

"I met a farmer's wife," Murcot admitted. "She's a bit broad in the beam for my taste but friendly. She's a Hollander from some outlying farm and brings me bread and mealie flour, sometimes biltong."

"You are a marvel, Murcot," Andrew told him. "What do you give her in return?"

"A few pennies from the regimental kitty, sir," Murcot said, "and I've promised that when we break out of Ladysmith, we'll put a guard on her farm to ensure there's no looting."

Andrew nodded, chewing the bread. "We'll make sure and do that," he said. "What's the farm called?"

"Sweetwater, sir," Murcot said. "I can't find it on the map, so it must be a tiny place."

"I'll pass the word on to the colonel," Andrew promised. He rose from his cot and began to dress. "Did you move my scarf, Murcot?"

"Your scarf, sir?" Murcot looked confused. "No, sir. I brushed and pressed your uniform but didn't see your scarf."

Andrew felt a sick slide of dismay. He had come to depend on that scarf. "Look for it," he ordered.

They searched the tent without success, and Andrew's enquiries failed. The scarf had vanished.

"It's only a scarf, Baird," Major Cradley reminded him. "I am not turning the battalion upside down for a blasted scarf."

"Of course not, sir," Andrew agreed. He told himself he was being superstitious in granting his survival to an item of clothing and a few words from a passing woman.

"I am sure it will turn up, Baird," Cradley said kindly.

"Thank you, sir."

As the siege returned to its monotonous routine, with snipers firing at the sentries and Long Tom landing the odd shell around the town, Andrew wrote a long letter to Mariana. The blockade meant very little mail could get in or out, but Andrew wrote as if she would read his words the next day. When he finished, he re-read the letter, added a final few endearments and assured Mariana the war could not last much longer. Andrew did not mention Charlie Dixon. With his wife's letter out of his mind, he wrote to his mother, asking her to contact Mariana. He hinted that he was worried without giving details and hoped his mother could read between the lines.

Let's hope this war is over soon, Andrew thought. *Surely, Joubert will realise he can't break our defences, and Buller will smash his way through to relieve us.*

Sealing the letters in stout envelopes, Andrew added the addresses, smiling at the familiar names. He imagined himself back in the old farmhouse beside the gently flowing River Tweed, with the mouldering tower house of Corbiestane at the side and green fields stretching to the misty distance, interspersed with lines of noble trees. The memories brought visions of his wife and children, Simla and Iain. He closed his eyes, visualising his family in their home and wondered when he would see them again.

"Are you all right, sir?" Murcot asked. "You looked worried there for a minute. I am sure we'll find your scarf, sir."

"My scarf?" Andrew pulled himself back to the present. "Oh, yes, thank you, Murcot. I wasn't thinking of the scarf." He checked his watch. "Nearly time for the afternoon parade. Warn the men I am coming, will you? I don't want anybody on a charge after the last few weeks."

Andrew knew Sergeant Kenny was too experienced an NCO to allow any laxity in C Company. It was better for a sergeant to snarl at the men than to have them on a charge that could see them on fatigues or blight their future promotion.

On his way to inspect C Company, Andrew handed his letters to one of the eager native runners.

"The fee is ten shillings, isn't it?" Andrew asked.

"A pound," the man demanded, grinning.

"That's extortion!" Andrew said.

"A pound!" the man held out his hand, and Andrew, sighing, paid the piper.

❊

"The helio's been active, sir," Sinton said when Andrew later visited the Officers' Mess. "Bobs and General Kitchener are busy in Cape Town, and the Queen sends Ladysmith her best."

Herbert Kitchener became famous after defeating the Mahdi's armies in the Sudan. In many British eyes, Kitchener's victory at Omdurman had avenged Gordon's death in Khartoum in 1885.

"With Sir Redvers on one flank and Bobs and Kitchener on the other, we should have the Boers in a vice," Andrew said hopefully.

Both looked up as another Boer shell landed on the outskirts of Ladysmith, sending up a column of stones and dirt.

"The sooner Buller comes, the better," Boswell said. "Or the Boers will reduce the town to rubble and dust."

"And us to skeletons," Sinton added. "We don't all have such expert foragers as Murcot working for us."

"He's a rare find," Andrew agreed smugly.

The situation in Ladysmith deteriorated as the siege dragged on. Lack of food took its toll on the garrison, with the men weakening daily. Andrew gave most of the food Murcot brought to the increasing number of sick in the hospital and watched helplessly as an average of five men a day died of disease.

Despite the weakness caused by the lack of food, some men grew restless, with the occasional soft chorus of "Oh, why are we waiting?" heard among the ranks.

"I can't say I blame them, sir," Sinton said.

"Nor can I," Andrew agreed, "although Buller has a hell of a job on his hands. He's facing thousands of the best riflemen in the world in entrenched positions, backed by superb artillery and with no room for manoeuvre. He can't outflank them, and the Boers overlook every move he makes."

"As do the newspapers," Sinton murmured. "It must be frustrating having reporters with no military experience scrutinise every decision and criticise every minor setback."

Andrew nodded. "That reporter fellow Churchill seems to

consider himself a military genius." He shook his head. "I'd send him away under military escort and lock him up until after the war."

Sinton smiled. "He certainly likes to push himself forward," he agreed. "In his eyes, it's Winston Churchill fighting the Boers single-handed."

Boswell looked up as his servant bustled into the Mess, saluted, and delivered a rapid message.

"Heliograph message, sir! Sir Redvers is trying again!"

The news soon spread around the town.

"Buller's trying again!"

Officers, men, and civilians dared to feel a surge of hope as the breeze carried the crackle of musketry, dying away, increasing to a crescendo, and fading again.

"Maybe this time, sir," Sinton said.

"Maybe," Andrew agreed cautiously.

"There's a good viewpoint on Cove Hill, sir," Sinton suggested, and Andrew joined the stream of hopeful officers who clambered up the grassy height to stare to the southwest. Interested officers with field glasses crowded the hill, all staring towards the south. Sinton produced his long, leather-covered telescope.

"This telescope is more powerful than any binoculars, sir," Sinton boasted. He glanced around the hill summit. "If Brother Boer lands a couple of shells here, sir, he would decimate Ladysmith's leadership."

Andrew agreed, but with the fate of the siege at stake, the officers ignored the danger and remained on the hill.

"That hill is called Spion Kop," Andrew said. "It looks like Buller's grabbed it."

"He has, by Jove!" Sinton adjusted his telescope. "Even with this telescope, I can't see details, but I think Brother Boer is running away!"

Many officers gave a subdued cheer as they saw Boer wagons hitched up from their laager at the foot of the hills.

"The Boers are retreating, by God!" a man shouted. "Buller must have broken through!"

Andrew exchanged glances with Major Cradley, who had joined them.

Despite the distance, a fluky wind carried the occasional rattle of musketry.

"It's not over yet," Cradley said quietly. "You remain here, Baird. I'll return to base and send up runners, and you tell them what's happening."

"Yes, sir," Andrew said.

"Lieutenant Sinton will take command of C Company in your absence," Cradley said. He lowered his binoculars. "Take Sinton's fancy telescope and keep me informed of events."

"I will, sir," Andrew promised. He found a suitable vantage point and readied himself for a long day on the hill.

Andrew saw Boers running down the hills, singly or in small groups. When they reached the level ground at the foot of the hill, they moved away, some at great speed. Andrew grunted in satisfaction, knowing the Boers were retreating from a British advance or occupation of Spion Kop.

When they reached the laager at the foot of the hill, many retreating Boers hitched oxen to their wagons and rolled away, with others milling about the laager, seemingly unsure what to do.

"Buller's broken through at last," a captain of the Devons said. "I always thought he would. He's a good man, Sir Redvers!"

Andrew forgot the time as he watched the drama unfold. Gradually, the Boer flow down the hill decreased, and Andrew saw a few men return on horseback or foot.

"What the devil is happening now?" the Devon captain said. "Are these men mad? Can't they see they've lost the battle? They'd best get away before our lads advance on them with the bayonet."

Andrew watched, saying nothing as a chill of foreboding gripped him. Buller had not won the battle yet.

The number of Boers retreating diminished to a trickle, and an increasing number returned to the battle. Andrew saw a few men in authority turning back those descending. The wagons halted, and some turned around.

"The damned Boers have stopped running!" the Devons' captain spluttered. "By God, if my men were there, we'd be at them with the bayonet. We won the battle on Wagon Hill, and we'd clear that blasted hill as well. Let the Devons at them, I say!"

Andrew nodded wordlessly. He could not see the actual battle but could read the signs by the behaviour in the laager and at the base of the slope. Rather than retreat, the Boers were now swarming back uphill, with wagons and groups of horsemen hurrying to the fight. The sound of firing increased as the wind shifted, then died away.

"What's happening over there?" the Devons' captain asked. "What the devil is happening?"

"I'm damned if I know," Andrew replied.

When Major Cradley's runner arrived for news, Andrew told him all he knew and watched the man scurry back downhill, one hand on his pith helmet to keep it in place. The runner stopped twice to catch his breath, and Andrew knew that lack of food was affecting the man's fitness.

We'll have to end this siege soon. The men are suffering. If the Boers make another determined attack, like on Wagon Hill, we won't have the strength to repel them.

Soon, only wounded men trickled away from the hill. More Boers arrived, climbing uphill purposefully with rifles in their hands. Andrew felt the despair return.

The Boers have repulsed our attack. They've held on.

"What's that fool Buller playing at?" the Devons' captain lowered his binoculars. "Can he not defeat a handful of rustics? If he's the best we've got, then God help the army, and pity help the Empire, I say. This is a fine pickle!"

Andrew nodded slowly. "It is a fine pickle," he agreed. He knew the Boers had won the battle.

The defeat of Spion Kop was worse because of the early signs of success. Andrew felt the Malverns' morale slump as the news spread. Men, already weakened by lack of food and the constant strain of the siege, heard of Buller's repulse with dismay. The defenders looked around at the surrounding hills with their Boer garrisons and wondered at the future.

As if to press home their victory, the Boer Long Tom continued to bombard Ladysmith.

"What now?" Sinton asked.

"Now we continue as before," Andrew said. "We hold for the queen."

"Yes," Sinton agreed. "But how long for, sir?"

Andrew could not answer.

CHAPTER 27

LADYSMITH, NATAL

FEBRUARY 1900

Without sufficient food for the horses, White retained a single mounted squadron for each cavalry regiment and released the remaining horses to fend for themselves. For days afterwards, distressed horses wandered the streets of Ladysmith, some torn by barbed wire and searching for their keepers. Equally distressed cavalrymen hugged their abandoned animals, sneaked food to them and hid their tears.

"It's about time this blasted siege ended," Andrew said, turning his head away. He hated to see animals suffer. He checked Letsie and Moshie every day, fought his guilt, and ensured both animals had at least the minimum of food.

On the 10th February, the garrison began to slaughter the horses for food.

"Colonel Ward is in charge of food supplies," Sinton said.

"He's made one of the railway's engine sheds into a food factory, and he's making soup and sausages from horse offal."

Andrew nodded. "Every little helps," he said. "Murcat has taken to harvesting the mealie crops near the Boer positions, bringing me sacks of the damned things."

"I know," Sinton said. "My men told me you give most to the hospital."

As hunger bit and stress rose, men's tempers shortened, and they argued over minor issues. Their conversations were brief, and attention spans and stamina decreased. With ammunition diminishing, Ladysmith's artillery only fired one or two shells daily in return for the Boers' bombardment. Prices rose, with eggs becoming a luxury item and cigars sought by only the most well-heeled officers. Enterprising men left the perimeter every night, foraging for whatever they could find, with occasional skirmishes with Boer patrols.

And all the time, the Boers watched from the surrounding heights.

"The Rooinecks have been busy around here," Michal said. "They have taken half the mealies in the fields and most of the fowls."

Hendrik removed the pipe from his mouth. "They are hungry in Ladysmith," he observed.

"My little soldier friends tell me the garrison is slaughtering the cavalry horses." Jacoba sat at his side, their hips touching.

"Good," Michal said. "The hungrier they are, the more likely they are to surrender. Since we stopped General Buller's latest advance, the Rooinecks in Ladysmith must think of giving up."

Piet looked up from cleaning his rifle. "Let's help them make up their minds. We can hunt the hunters."

Michal grinned, removed his hat and brushed back his long

hair. "That is my idea. The Rooinecks will be too busy hunting for food to expect us."

"Be careful," Jacoba said. "A lion is most dangerous when it is hungry."

Hendrik held her hand for a second. "We'll be careful," he said. "We've hunted Rooinecks before and know their habits."

Michal took six men to hunt for foragers. They left the laager before dark, rode to an abandoned farm and dismounted. Leaving the horses knee-tethered in a sheltered field, Michal led his men to a stone wall overlooking a broad field of mealies.

"The Rooinecks have raided this field for the last three days," he said. "I think they will return tonight."

Piet tapped his rifle. "There will be fewer going than coming," he said without smiling.

The wall was of rough stone, with larger boulders at the base and smaller stones leading to a relatively flat coping at the top. Each man chose a position that afforded him a view of the field, settled down and waited for night. Hendrik made a hole in the wall to peer through.

"If the Rooinecks come, we will slaughter them," he said.

Michal laughed. "We'll teach them to keep inside Ladysmith's defences."

The corporalship marked out ranges in the field and lay still, waiting for darkness. Insects inspected them, with flies buzzing around their heads. The light faded and died.

"Somebody's coming," Piet hissed.

The corporalship was instantly alert, listening for every sound. Hendrik smelled tobacco smoke and heard the rattle as a careless boot kicked over a stone.

"Twelve men," Piet hissed.

Hendrik nodded. Twelve unsuspecting British soldiers blundering towards half a dozen Boer riflemen. He calculated that the first Boer shots would hit at least four of them, leaving the survivors confused and shocked. The ambushers would have time to fire another shot before the British reacted, accounting

HOLDING FOR THE QUEEN

for at least two more. Even when the British retaliated, they would be firing at men behind a stone wall.

Hendrik nodded. The ambush should be over quickly, with at least six British casualties and no loss to the Boers.

"Ready!" Michal signalled by lifting his hand.

Hendrik saw the shadowy shapes enter the mealie field. He counted the twelve men, moving more quietly than he expected from British soldiers, and some carrying sacks for the mealies and short carbines rather than long rifles.

Cavalrymen, then, rather than infantry. Either that or the Rooinecks have learned that shorter weapons are handier at night. We have taught them well.

Michal dropped his hand, giving the signal to fire.

"Fire!" the voice shouted in English, and shots cracked out from the farmhouse behind the Boers.

Bullets crashed into the stone wall and hit two of the Boers. Willem Mentze staggered forward, open-mouthed with shock.

"They're behind us!" Michal yelled as the men in the mealie field dropped to evade the fire.

"Fire back!" Piet shouted, firing at the muzzle flares.

From a well-organised ambush, the scene had degenerated into chaos, with the British on both sides of the corporalship and bullets screaming and whining around them.

"Cease fire!" a man shouted, and the British stopped firing. "Burghers! You are surrounded and outnumbered! Will you surrender?"

"*Nee!*" Michal replied. "No!"

The British fired another volley, with the men in the field running closer.

Another of the Boers roared as a bullet ploughed into him, smashed the collarbone, and continued, exiting by ripping a large hole and splintering his shoulder blade. He fell sideways, writhing in pain.

The Boers fired back until the British from the mealie field vaulted over the stone wall and stood over them with naked bayonets.

"Surrender, Boers," a soldier said in Afrikaans. "Your war is over."

"We will fight!" a man said, and the speaker lunged forward with his bayonet. He thrust the blade into the nearest man, who yelled and grabbed at the rifle. The soldier withdrew and plunged the bayonet in again, twisting to enlarge the wound.

"That's done for you, Piet!" he said.

Hendrik felt the blade slide inside him. He tried to scream, but no sound came. He saw the soldier withdraw his bayonet, with the blood dripping onto the ground, and then nothing.

"Hendrik!" Michal shouted.

Urged by the jabbing British bayonets, the corporalship raised their arms in surrender.

"Up!" the lieutenant in charge of the British shouted. "Drop your rifles and stand up!"

The Boers stood, hands raised, staring at these Rooinecks.

"Who are you?" Michal peered at the British, unable to make out the regiment. He saw the bright scarf around the officer's neck and gasped. "It is you!"

"Get the Rooinecks!" Michal heard Dannie's voice from behind and the rush of running feet. The British hesitated, fired a few shots and ran, with Dannie van Niekerk leading a charge of determined men.

With the tables turned again, Michal grabbed his rifle and followed the retreating British, firing into the mealie field in the hope of avenging Hendrik.

"There's more of them!" Dannie shouted as another British unit appeared. "Return to our lines!"

Michal saw moonshine gleam on hundreds of British bayonets and pulled back, with his men following, glad to have escaped with only three dead.

❄

"Where's Hendrik?" Jacoba asked. "Where's my husband? Did you leave him with the Rooinecks?"

Piet glanced at Michal before he replied. "We have bad news, Jacoba," he said.

Jacoba straightened her back. "Tell me," she said, taking a deep breath.

"He is dead, Jacoba," Piet told her quietly. "A Rooineck bayonetted him as he lay on the ground."

Jacoba nodded, unable to comprehend the news. "No, Hendrik is not dead."

"We saw him killed," Piet said. "The Rooineck bayonetted him twice."

"It is true, Jacoba," Michal said. "I led him to his death." It was the first time the responsibilities of command had affected him.

"Did you see the Rooineck?" Jacoba asked quietly. She knew she would cry later, but not in front of these men.

"It was dark, but we saw him," Piet said.

"What was he like?" Jacoba asked so softly that Michal barely heard her.

"He was a tall officer who spoke our language," Piet said, "and he wore your scarf."

"My scarf?" Jacoba repeated. She took another deep breath and repeated quietly. "He wore my scarf?"

"Yes," Piet said.

Jacoba looked away. "I want the man who murdered my husband killed. I want the Royal Malverns destroyed, wiped out, every last man of them."

Piet nodded. "Hendrik was a good man. One of the best."

"He was my husband," Jacoba said. *I will never find another.*

CHAPTER 28

LADYSMITH, NATAL

FEBRUARY 1900

The Boer artillery on Bulwana fired again, with the shell screaming overhead to land on the outskirts of Ladysmith. The garrison and citizens watched the dust raised by the explosion, shrugged, and continued their daily routine.

The garrison knew the shell took twenty-one seconds to travel from Bulwana to Ladysmith and had organised warning signals. The Natal Carbineers devised a unique bugle call when Long Tom fired, men waited with loud whistles, and some stood ready with semaphore flags. The shells were no longer a surprise, and everybody knew what to do. Young boys and girls waited for the explosion and ran to the crater or ruined building to collect pieces of the shell to sell in the town.

Andrew tossed a shilling to an eager—if dirty-faced—boy who proudly presented him with the nose cap of the latest Long Tom shell. "Thank you," Andrew said solemnly. "Now you'd better wash your hands and face, or your Mama will be angry."

The boy grinned. "She won't be," he said. "She'll use the shilling to buy bread so I can get as dirty as I like." To prove his point, he took a handful of dust from the ground and rubbed it over his face.

Andrew hid his smile, wondering what Mariana would say if Iain came home dirty-faced and how his children were progressing.

"What are you going to do with that, sir?" Sinton asked.

"Give it to Iain, my son," Andrew said. "Little boys like this sort of thing."

Sinton grinned. "I used to collect birds' eggs," he said. "And insects. My mother didn't mind the eggs, but she didn't like the insects."

"Mothers are strange creatures," Andrew said solemnly, watching a file of Malverns pass, with tattered, faded uniforms, broken shoes and near-skeletal appearance. "The men look about done," he said.

"The siege is taking its toll," Sinton said. "If you'll excuse me, sir, I am duty officer."

As Sinton left, Murcot stepped out of Andrew's tent.

"Eggs, sir," Murcot said proudly. "I managed to get you six eggs."

"Six eggs!" Andrew repeated, sitting up on his bed. "You are a marvel, Murcot. There is no other word for you!"

"Thank you, sir!" Murcot unwrapped the parcel he carried and placed the eggs, one at a time, on Andrew's small folding table. "I got eight, sir, and took the liberty of keeping two for myself and Private Conway. He and I have been chums ever since India, sir. We were on the Grim together and marched along the Great Trunk Road."

Andrew smiled. If Murcot admitted keeping two eggs for himself, he had probably obtained a great deal of loot for Conway and himself. Well, good luck to him, Andrew thought.

Anybody who could find six eggs in Ladysmith after months under siege deserved a few perquisites.

"There's more news from the south, sir," Murcot said. "General Buller has attacked again. I don't know any more than that."

"Thank you, Murcot." Andrew was unsure which was more important to him at that moment, having six eggs or Sir Redvers moving against the Boers. "I'd better find out what's happening, I suppose." He struggled out of bed, rubbed a hand over his tousled hair and yawned. "Put the eggs somewhere safe, and I'll have two for my breakfast, soft-boiled."

"Very good, sir," Murcot said.

Andrew walked the short distance to Colonel Newland's quarters, noting the fresh craters where the Boers had landed their shells. The road seemed longer every day as hunger bit, and the soldiers he passed were gaunt, with uniforms that hung on skeletal frames. He heard the grumble of artillery in the distance and knew Buller was still pushing at the Boer defences.

Another Boer shell landed, throwing up the usual quota of rubble and smoke. Early morning civilians stepped into shelter, watching the destruction with minimal interest. They had seen it all so often before, and it only mattered to the householder directly affected. Finding food was more important. Food, disease, and Redvers Buller's progress dominated everybody's thoughts, with hunger uppermost.

Colonel Newland was with General White and greeted Andrew with a curt nod.

"Have you heard the latest, Baird?"

"Only a brief word, sir," Andrew said. "I heard that Sir Redvers is trying again."

Newland held Andrew's gaze. "Trying and making heavy weather of it, I'm afraid. He had initial success but withdrew, according to the reports we are getting."

By now nearly inured to disappointment, Andrew listened to reports of Buller's third attempt at breaking through the Boer lines. The action at Val Krantz had not been as big a disaster as

Colenso or a slaughterhouse like Spion Kop, but with the same result. The Boers had held the British attack, and Buller had withdrawn.

Andrew sighed. "Sir Redvers is a persistent man," he defended the general. "Some men would have given up after a single failure. General Buller is in the mould of Robert the Bruce, trying repeatedly until he succeeds. Maybe his next attempt will be his Bannockburn."

General White heard Andrew's words, eyed him, nodded but said nothing.

"The van Collier brothers are playing the cat and banjo in the west as well," Newland said. "We have the van Colliers, the de Wets and de la Rey causing all sorts of trouble."

"Van Collier?" Andrew remembered the name. "He was a formidable opponent in the last Boer War, sir."

"He'll be trouble if we don't contain him," Newland said, facing General White.

"What now, sir?"

"We keep the flag flying," White replied briefly. "That's our duty. We hold Ladysmith for the Queen and keep the flag flying."

"Of course, sir," Newland replied.

"How is your battalion, Colonel?" White asked.

"As well as any other, sir," Newland said.

"Good. The Boers will be cock-a-hoop over inflicting another reverse at Val Krantz, so we should give them something to think about. Send out a strong patrol and disrupt one of their outposts. I don't care which one; just ensure we have something to cheer up the garrison."

"Yes, sir," Newland said. "I'll lead it myself, sir."

"Do that, Newland," White agreed.

"The Devons, Gordons and Manchesters won all the plaudits on Wagon Hill," Newland said. "It's time the Malverns did our bit." He glanced at Andrew. "Captain Baird, you take over Sentinel Outpost on the west; you had your fun on Platrand."

"Yes, sir," Andrew could say nothing else. He thought of the eggs waiting for him and sighed. They would still be there when he returned, something to look forward to after a long day on the perimeter.

Sentinel Outpost was one of the better positions, with a solid sanger and deep dugouts if the Boers decided to shell them, and a fine field of fire in front. C Company eased into the position, with the men keeping below the parapet and grousing cheerfully.

"Take the left flank, Sinton," Andrew ordered. "Sergeant Kenny, you have the right flank, and I'll look after the centre."

They saw the Malverns' patrol pass, with Colonel Newland in front and two hundred men behind him. They looked tired as they stumbled towards the Boers.

"The colonel might be better waiting for dark," Sinton murmured.

Andrew nodded. He kept C Company busy, checking the wire defences were tight, adding broken glass to the booby traps and white-painted range markers in front of the entrenchments.

"I want bottles and cans tied to the wire," Andrew added. "Anything that rattles or makes a noise. We don't want the enemy to sneak up on us in the dark. You lads who served on the Northwest Frontier will remember the Paythans' tricks. We got their measure, so we also out-think the Boers."

After twenty minutes, Andrew stopped pushing the men. They were already staggering with fatigue and hunger.

"That's enough, lads. Hold your positions."

The men stopped immediately, with some leaning on the wall for support.

Andrew grunted. *Let's hope the Boers don't attack. The men are as weak as kittens.*

JACOBA STOOD UNDER THE RAIN-BATTERED MIMOSA TREE, talking to the lean corporal from the Devons. "I have bread and a bag of mealies," she said, hiding her hatred of anything British as she thought of Hendrik.

"You're a good lass," the corporal handed over a small bag of medical supplies. "Is your sister no better?"

"The medicines are helping," Jacoba said. "The sooner this war is over, the better. Is your General Buller not going to advance soon? These damned Boers are robbing us dry."

"We're waiting for Buller all the time," the corporal told her. He looked closer. "Have you been crying? Your eyes are red and puffy."

"It is the wind," Jacoba said. "And I am worried about my sister."

"Of course," the corporal said. "You'd better get back to her."

"Yes. Is it safe? Are there any patrols out? I don't want to be shot by mistake."

"You'd better be careful," the corporal told her. "A couple of companies of the Royal Malverns are out, heading northwest."

Jacoba felt something twist inside her when she heard the name. *The Malverns.*

"Thank you," she said. "I'll watch out for them. Heading northwest, you say?"

"Best keep clear, miss," the corporal warned.

"Thank you," Jacoba said. She favoured the corporal with a forced smile. "I'd better head back."

C COMPANY HEARD THE FIRING IN THE EARLY AFTERNOON, A sudden eruption of musketry that told of an ambush or an attack.

"That's the colonel at work!" Private Jenkins said. "Give them hell, Colonel!"

"That's Mauser fire," Corporal Harwood corrected quietly.

C Company listened as Lee-Metfords replied to the Mausers, and both merged in a chaos of gunfire.

"Take your positions, men," Andrew ordered, scanning the surroundings through his binoculars.

"What's happening, sir?" Sinton asked.

"It sounds as if the colonel's run into trouble," Andrew replied. "Keep the men alert."

"Yes, sir," Sinton returned to his position.

The firing became less intense but continued intermittently with occasional furious outbreaks.

"Should we try and help, sir?" Sinton asked.

"It's on the far side of the town," Andrew replied. "Our duty is here. If we leave or weaken our post, the Boers may raid or even mount a major attack. We remain fast."

"Yes, sir," Sinton said, still staring toward the gunfire.

Andrew heard the firing fade into a few isolated shots and listened to the pipes as a company of Gordons marched out of Ladysmith to help the Malverns. Half an hour later, a heliograph message flashed, and a signaller hurried to Andrew.

"Message from Major Cradley, sir," the signaller reported. "Colonel Newland's force was ambushed with many casualties. Major Cradley orders us to remain here and wait for orders."

"Thank you." Andrew passed the message on to his men.

"The Boers will be riding the crest of a wave now," Andrew said to Sinton. "They've stopped Buller again and ambushed one of our patrols."

The Boer sniping began a few minutes later, with an increased artillery barrage that hit the town and the military camps on the fringes.

"That one must have been close to the Malverns' camp," Sinton said as one of Long Tom's shells exploded outside the town.

"It looked like a direct hit," Andrew replied. He faced his front, waiting for the Boers to attack.

※

Piet crouched behind a rock with his rifle steady. "Here they come. Your information was correct, Jacoba."

"The British trust me, and their soldiers like to talk to a helpless farm woman." She held a rifle for the first time in the war.

"Wait until they come close," Dannie ordered.

Jacoba nodded. When she lifted a rifle, Piet glanced at Michal and raised his eyebrows but said nothing. He also missed Hendrik and understood Jacoba's cold rage.

The Royal Malverns approached, marching more slowly than usual for British soldiers. Some men were lagging as if reluctant to advance or lacking the strength.

"Wait," Dannie mouthed.

Jacoba sighted along the Mauser barrel, targeting the colonel who rode in front. She felt the tension and excitement among the waiting men. She thought of Hendrik with his quiet eyes and the slow smile that said so much.

Piet could have been carved from rock as he waited, with Michal's face set and serious, Dannie concentrating, and Louis Grobler flanked by his sons. Jacoba thought the boys did not look so young now, with the sights and sounds of war having matured them.

"Fire!" Dannie shouted.

Jacoba squeezed the trigger. She had hunted on her father's farm since she was old enough to hold a rifle and rode the Mauser's recoil like a veteran. She saw the colonel jerk backwards as her bullet smashed into the centre of his chest.

"That's for Hendrik," she said, blinking away sudden hot tears. She worked the bolt and searched for Andrew, scanning the officers one by one.

He's not there.

Another officer came into view, a captain attempting to bring some order into the chaos the Boers' ambush had wrought. A dozen men lay on the ground, some kicking and writhing, others still. The officers and NCOs were taking control, ordering the men to extend into open order, find cover and return fire.

Jacoba lost the captain in the confusion, found him again, and aimed, ignoring the running, firing rankers. Many Malverns were firing back, with bullets cracking and whining around the Boers' position.

Jacoba kept her aim steady, centred her foresight on the captain and fired. The officer spun as the bullet slammed into his shoulder. Jacoba calmly worked the bolt, aimed again and fired a second time. The captain looked puzzled for a second, then crumpled.

"Keep firing," Dannie shouted as the Malverns began to retreat, platoon by platoon, with the rearguard firing volleys at the ambushers.

"Don't follow!" Dannie ordered. "Don't expose yourself to their fire."

As the Malverns retreated, Jacoba checked the Boer casualties. The ambush had lasted fifteen minutes, carpeting the ground with khaki, yet only one Boer was wounded. Jacoba smiled, then began to cry. She did not want to kill Rooinecks. She wanted Hendrik back.

CHAPTER 29

LADYSMITH, NATAL

FEBRUARY 1900

"At least I have my eggs," Andrew said as he returned to the Malverns' camp after a day of bitter disappointment.

"No, sir," Murcot said. "Sorry, sir, but the Boers shelled the camp while you were on the perimeter. They hit your tent."

"No eggs left?"

"Not even one, sir," Murcot said.

Andrew shook his head. "Was any of my kit saved?"

"Yes, sir." Murcot's expression did not alter. "Most of it. I found another tent."

"Tents are in short supply, Murcot. Where did you find it?"

"The Rifles had a spare, sir," Murcot said.

Andrew nodded. "Did they know they had a spare?"

"I didn't ask, sir," Murcot replied.

Andrew grunted. "I didn't think you had. Thank you, Murcot. That's the only bit of good news on a bad day."

"How many did we kill?" Jacoba asked.

Piet pondered the question for a second. "I'd say about thirty," he replied. "Thirty men."

"Good." Jacoba wrote the number in a small notebook. "Every dead Rooineck is a little payment for Hendrik. Every dead Rooineck and every dead Malvern soldier."

"There were wounded as well," Michal said.

"I am not interested in wounded," Jacoba said. "They might recover."

"They might not recover until the war ends," Michal said.

Jacoba glared at him. "Dead men cannot recover," she said. "I want to strike at the Imperial Light Horse next, the Uitlanders. They are on the western perimeter."

"We are under Adriaan Wessel's orders," Michal replied. "We need his permission if we are to attack anybody."

"I asked him," Jacoba said, "and he agreed."

"This is my corporalship," Michal reminded her. "I make the decisions."

"Then you can decide to attack the Uitlanders," Jacoba said.

"When the time is right," Michal said.

"You are too cautious, Michal." Jacoba's voice rose. "You are like Commandant-General Joubert. We should strike now and keep striking!" Snatching off her hat, she threw it on the ground and faced him, eyes wide and hot with anger. "Why do you not want to attack the men who killed Hendrik?"

Michal took her arm. "Come with me, Jacoba, and I will show you," he said, lifting the binoculars he had taken from a dead Colonel Newland.

Michal led her to the top of the nearest hill, from where the whole of Ladysmith spread before them, with the balloon high above and the smoke and dust clearing from the latest shell burst. Louis Grobler stood nearby, scanning the town through a long telescope.

"Show me!" Jacoba demanded impatiently.

"You see the British defences?" Michal asked. "The deep entrenchments, the gun emplacements and the barbed wire?"

"I see them," Jacoba replied shortly.

"Can you see the Town Hall in the middle of Ladysmith? The taller building?"

"I know the Town Hall," Jacoba replied.

"A troop of the Imperial Light Horse have moved opposite. They are right in the centre of Ladysmith," Michal said, passing over his binoculars. "We would have to break through the defences to get close. Other Uitlanders are based on Platrand, and we have tried there already."

Even with the binoculars, the men in Ladysmith were too far away to be distinct. Jacoba snorted with frustration. "I can get through the defences with my bags of food," she said. "Many of the sentries know me."

"No." Michal shook his head. "General White has given new orders that nobody is to pass."

Jacoba swore. "Then we will wait until the Uitlanders come to us," she said.

"I have a man watching," Michal indicated Louis. "When Louis gets tired, his elder son will take over."

"I will wait," Jacoba decided. "When we have them, I will kill everyone."

"Unless they surrender," Michal said.

"I will not have any handsuppers," Jacoba told him.

Michal looked at her, opened his mouth to speak and closed it again. "Come on, Jacoba," he said.

Jacoba led the way back to their camp with her shoulders straight as a guardsman, her face rigid and her heart breaking.

"Buller's attacking again, sir," Sinton said, smiling.

Andrew nodded, refusing to allow himself to hope. "Pray for his success this time, Sinton."

"I pray for his success every night, sir," Sinton replied. "Dundonald's cavalry are doing great things around Hussar Hill and Hlangwane, according to the helio reports."

Andrew consulted the map. "Buller and Dundonald have some difficult country to negotiate before they are close to Ladysmith," he said.

"Yes, sir," Sinton said, "but they are pushing on. The infantry is attacking the hills, with Dundonald's cavalry and Barton's 6th Brigade guarding their flank. Buller's artillery is also hammering the Boer positions. Sir Redvers is making sure there won't be another Spion Kop."

Andrew looked over the depleted and disheartened Royal Malverns. The Boers had killed Colonel Newland and Captain Boswell as well as twenty-seven men, with another fifteen wounded.

"I hope Buller breaks through this time," he said. "The men have just about had enough."

"They'll still fight," Sinton said.

"They'll still want to fight after losing the colonel and poor old Boswell," Andrew agreed, "but between hunger and sickness, they're weak as babies."

The garrison heard Buller's guns as the British pushed at the Boer lines, using new techniques of rolling artillery barrages and a combination of infantry and cavalry attacks to capture Boer positions on hill after hill.

Day after day, Buller's heliograph flashed his movements to Ladysmith. The garrison waited, fighting hunger and disease.

As Buller's men pushed painfully closer, Andrew read the heliograph messages with rising hope. He wrote another letter to Mariana, slanting the news to remove the negatives, added that he missed her and would be home as soon as the war ended, and gave it to a native carrier to take to the relieving force.

"Two pounds," the native demanded, grinning.

"The standard fee is one pound," Andrew protested.

"There are more Boers between Ladysmith and the British now," the native said.

Andrew sighed, aware the native's task was dangerous. He handed over two pounds, grinned and added another half-crown. "Here, keep out of the Boers' path."

The man closed his fist around the half-crown. "They won't catch me," he promised with a grin. "I am a Zulu!"

News from Roberts' advance gradually reached Ladysmith as the heliographs passed messages from front to front. The garrison learned that the British had relieved Kimberley on February the 15th, with the Australian Horse first to enter the town.

"That won't please Piet," Sinton said.

"No," Andrew agreed.

They spoke in short staccato sentences, as talking was an ordeal for hungry men. They needed all their concentration to survive without wasting energy on conversation.

The observers in the balloon reported that many of the Boers around Ladysmith drifted away after Kimberley's relief, with the men in the trenches and outposts noticing fewer men opposing them.

"There are still plenty of Boers out there," Major Cradley said. With the death of Colonel Newland, he was temporarily in command of the Malverns. "If we were stronger, I'd advise General White to try a breakout." He indicated the wan, gaunt men who stood behind the barricades. "We no longer have the strength to march five miles, let alone march and fight a battle."

Andrew nodded. "Joubert's tactics of containing and besieging us might not be glorious, but they are effective. We couldn't fight off an attack by schoolgirls." He caught Cradley's frown. "We'd do our best," he said. "It all depends on Sir Redvers Buller."

"It all depends on Buller," Cradley agreed.

"Why are these men leaving?" Jacoba asked, watching a trickle of riders leave the Boers' camp.

"They are returning to their farms," Michal said.

"Why?" Jacoba demanded.

"Either they have a sick wife or a sick animal, or they think they've done enough fighting for the Republics."

"We have not won yet," Jacoba said. "The British still have armies in the field. Ladysmith has not surrendered, and Buller and Roberts could invade the Republics."

"We cannot force men to stay," Michal said.

"Look at them all!" Jacoba shouted. "They're running like sheep!" She pointed to the Boers riding away and the men loading up wagons. "Cowards! Come back and fight!"

Piet removed the pipe from between his teeth. "You are wasting your breath, Jacoba," he said. "They have had enough."

"Cowards!" Jacoba repeated, shaking her head.

"Enough, Jacoba," Michal gently took her arm. "You will not stop them from leaving; you are only hurting yourself."

Jacoba shook her arm free. "Don't they want to fight for our freedom?" She raised her voice again. "Come back and fight, cowards!" She strode to the nearest rider. "Where are you going, *meneer*?"

The man was about thirty, with a neat beard and a deeply tanned face. "Back to my farm," he replied offhandedly.

"Why? We have not won the war yet!" Jacoba grabbed the reins of his horse.

"Let go!" the man flicked the reins free.

"You coward!" Jacoba shouted as the man rode away. "Coward! We have not won the war yet!"

"Leave him, Jacoba," Dannie stepped to Jacoba. "Let him go. Men like that will only weaken the commando."

"He has fingers to pull a trigger," Jacoba said. "He can shoot the enemy!"

"What would you have me do?" Dannie asked.

"Shoot the cowards," Jacoba said. "Make an example of two or three, and the others will remain behind."

"We cannot do that," Dannie said.

"I would do that," Jacoba told him.

Dannie shook his head. "I would not," he said.

Jacoba watched the slow drift from the camp. "Soon, there will be no fighting men left in the camp," she said. "You will have to rely on the women to win this war."

"If all the women are like you, Mrs du Toit," Dannie said, "we would sweep the British into the sea."

Jacoba strode away, with her skirt snapping against her legs.

Dannie watched her go. "She's grieving for Hendrik," he said.

Michal nodded. "I know," he replied. "I do not know how to help her."

"Time and the Lord will find a way," Dannie said. "Or her mind will snap."

"Please, God, it is the former and not the latter," Michal replied.

CHAPTER 30

LADYSMITH, NATAL

FEBRUARY 1900

General Buller had learned from his earlier disasters and worked out how to defeat the Boers. Combining infantry, cavalry and artillery, Buller fought from hill to hill, pushing the enemy back at each encounter. The Boers fought stubbornly, inflicting casualties, but the British finally had their measure.

"The Boers can't stop Sir Redvers now," Sinton said. "He'll be here any day."

The news entered Ladysmith through the winking heliographs and reports by the men in the observation balloon. The defenders learned of the British sixty-gun barrages that hammered the Boer trenches and the British losses when Boer riflemen punished them for daylight advances over open ground. Men waited for the heliograph and commented on each scrap of news.

"Buller has withdrawn to the far side of the Tugela," Sinton reported. "The Boers have pushed him back again."

"Buller has advanced again, capturing another hill!"

"The Boers are holding firm!"

"Sir Redvers has outflanked them!"

Rumours and facts alternated in Ladysmith as contrasting reports brought elation or despair. Andrew listened and tried not to allow either emotion to affect him. He listened to Sinton's words and repeated lines from Rudyard Kipling's poem *If*.

"If you can meet with triumph and disaster
And treat those two impostors just the same;
Yours is the Earth and everything that's in it."

"What?" Sinton replied. "What do you mean, sir?"

"I mean, no campaign always goes smoothly," Andrew said. "Don't listen to the nay-sayers. I have more trust in Sir Redvers than most."

"Yes, sir," Sinton replied.

Andrew pieced together details of Buller's movements. After initial advances, the army had withdrawn across a Royal Engineers-built pontoon bridge at Hlangwane. On the night of the 26th of February 1900, the Engineers dismantled the bridge and re-erected it beside Monte Cristo with the army pouring across.

"Thank God for the Engineers!" Sinton said. He had lost weight during the siege. His uniform hung loosely on his wasted body, while his cheekbones were sharp above eyes sunk into deep, dark hollows.

"Unsung heroes, those Engineer lads," Andrew agreed. "And some clever dick sapper erected a signpost on the north side saying: 'To Ladysmith' in big letters."

Sinton laughed. "They don't need a signpost," he said. "All they need do is follow the smoke of burning buildings and the smell of disease."

Andrew nodded. Ladysmith had been a neat little town when he first arrived, but the Boer artillery had left piles of rubble in the streets where houses had once stood. With accustomed black British humour, the garrison had given individual names to each Boer gun that bombarded the town. As well as Bulwana Tom, there was Puffing Billy, Fiddling Jimmy, the Meddler, and Silent Susan, a six-inch Creusot whose shells arrived without warning.

Although the Long Toms had not done as much damage as the Boers hoped, disease had taken more toll on the garrison and population than battle casualties. Andrew was constantly aware of the stench of unwashed soldiers and overfull latrines from the enteric- and dysentery-stricken men. Lack of food created lassitude and weariness, with men too weak to talk as they staggered to their posts and stared, hollow-eyed, towards the encircling Boers.

"Buller had better come soon," Sinton said. "The men are about done in."

Andrew agreed. Often underweight and undersized through chronic poverty before they joined the army, many British soldiers lacked resistance to disease.

The Boer shelling augmented their customary sniping of the outposts. Well used to both, the garrison kept their heads down, gave the usual warnings and thought about eating. Food dominated their lives, with the sporadic Boer attacks a distraction from gnawing stomachs. Dysentery and hunger had left the garrison wasted, living on a biscuit and a half a day with foul water from the Klip River.

In the south, Buller's stubborn attacks continued, with his massed artillery supporting coordinated brigade-strength infantry attacks that captured hill after hill from the Boers.

On the 27th of February, the anniversary of Majuba, Buller's army captured three hills in succession, with the Royal Scots Fusiliers holding Pieter's Hill despite intense and accurate Boer musketry.

"The Boers are on the retreat," a jubilant, if worn-faced, subaltern shouted. "Buller has broken through!"

After months of disappointment and frustrated hopes, Ladysmith's garrison was unsure whether to cheer or scoff. Many viewed the news with suspicion, and others were too weak to care if the Boers were leaving or not.

Civilians and soldiers could all hear the rumble of Buller's guns as he rolled through the Boers' defences. The noise mingled with peals of thunder that echoed from the surrounding hills so that men were unsure what was natural and what was man-made. Flashes of lightning added to the drama, reflecting from gun barrels and temporarily blinding men on the perimeter defences.

Andrew stood in the basket of the observation balloon with his binoculars fixed on the retiring Boers. "There they go," he said. "They're only about four miles away, and we don't have a horseman with four legs strong enough even to harass them."

Sinton held onto the edge of the basket with his left hand. "The artillery horses are too weak, and the cavalry horses are all eaten. We don't even have the strength to pull the Navy's big guns to the north side to fire at them."

"All the same, we've survived," Andrew said. "Somehow."

"Somehow," Sinton lowered his binoculars. "Do you think people will talk about the siege of Ladysmith? Maybe teach it in schools like they do with Lucknow and Cawnpore?"

"My father was at the relief of Lucknow," Andrew said, "yet it already seems like ancient history." He forced a grin. "We must win this war now. Kruger must realise he can't defeat the British Empire. He attacked us when we were at our weakest, and he failed. Now we have Buller and Roberts pushing at his armies." Andrew glanced at the surrounding hills, shrouded in mist and rain. "Buller will be here in a day or two, and after that, we'll be in the ascendancy."

"There's your man waiting for us below," Sinton said.

Andrew saw Murcot on the ground far below and signalled for the balloon operators to lower them.

"Sir!" Murcot looked excited when Andrew stepped from the basket. He threw a hurried salute.

"What's the matter, Murcot?" Andrew asked.

"Terribly sorry to disturb you, sir, but Major Cradley ordered me to tell you there are horsemen on Bulwana Hill."

Andrew glanced at Sinton. "Horsemen? Are the Boers going to try a last assault before Buller arrives?" He checked his pistol belt was secure. "Has the major sounded the Stand-to, Murcot?"

"Not yet, sir," Murcot said. "He's gathering the officers first." He grinned. "They're not Boers, sir."

"Our horsemen?" Andrew asked.

"Yes, sir. Colonials, sir. Natal Carbineers and Imperials, sir. The Imperial Light Horse."

"Good God," Andrew said, unable to comprehend the news. "Good God in heaven. Thank you, Murcot. Come on, Sinton, we'd better report to the major."

Leaving the balloon area, Andrew straightened his back and stepped forward. Other men were doing the same, with all eyes on Bulwana Hill. Officers stood in the street with their binoculars raised while men muttered and pointed at the distant specks, more in hope than expectation.

"They're ours, I tell you," Private Hobart said.

"No; it's another Boer trick," Jenkins said. "They're going to lure us out and then hammer us with Long Tom. I wouldn't trust them as far as I trust you."

"Look!" A grey-haired major with a salt-and-pepper moustache pointed. "They're leaving the hill."

"Bugler! Sound the alert!" a thin-faced subaltern shouted to a teenage bugler with the eyes of an old man.

"Belay that!" a Royal Naval lieutenant countermanded. "They're friendly!"

"Are they friendly, sir?" Corporal Harwood asked Andrew.

"They are, Corporal," Andrew lifted his binoculars and focused on the tiny figures that seemed to crawl down the hillside, although he knew they would be moving as fast as their horses could carry them.

"Somebody better tell those lads there are trenches full of Boers between them and us," Sinton murmured.

"I don't think they care," Andrew said. "I don't think they care a damn for Boers, devils or Kruger himself!"

Andrew watched the Natal Carbineers and Imperials ride down the hill, avoiding the scattered rocks with impressive skill and seemingly careless of any Boer retaliation. The officers were in front, riding like centaurs, with men's hats flying off, some dropping their blankets or any other equipment that might hamper their speed. When a man fell, his fellow riders left him to roll on the ground and powered on, desperate to reach Ladysmith.

"Come on, gentlemen," Sinton said. "Let's go to the perimeter! They seem to be heading for Wagon Hill."

Andrew lost sight of the riders as he moved toward Wagon Hill, but he could not mistake the outburst of cheering. The Naval Brigade on the guns were shouting, all weakness forgotten as the colonial horsemen swept past the defences.

Andrew watched the Natal Carbineers and Imperial Light Horse ride around the town, waving and shouting. He checked his watch. It was five in the afternoon.

"Halt!" a sentry called, aiming his rifle as duty demanded, but smiling broadly. "Identify yourselves!"

"The Ladysmith Relief Column!" a strong voice replied.

"Pass, friend!" the sentry called. "And welcome!"

As the horsemen pushed into Ladysmith, soldiers and citizens alike emerged from trenches, dugouts, houses and sangars to greet them. Soldiers leaned on each other for support as they cheered, with women crying and others watching through unbelieving eyes.

Andrew was at the back of the crowd when Major Gough, in charge of the horsemen, met General White. The general had aged during the months of siege. He looked grey, weary and as emaciated as any of his men as he greeted the burly, well-fed riders.

White gave a short speech Andrew thought he must have been rehearsing for weeks. "I thank you, men, one and all, from the bottom of my heart, for the help and support you have given me, and I shall always acknowledge it to the end of my life. Thank God we kept the flag flying."

"Give them toco, boys!" somebody shouted, and the seamen fired their 4.7-inch guns at the Boers on Bulwana Hill, ignoring their shortage of ammunition.

"Dear God, it's true," Sinton said. "Buller has reached us. The siege is over."

Andrew nodded. *Maybe we'll get some mail now, and I'll hear from Mariana.*

CHAPTER 31

LADYSMITH, NATAL

FEBRUARY AND MARCH 1900

"They'll be celebrating in Britain," Sinton said as the officers checked each other's uniforms before General Buller's official entry into Ladysmith.

"No doubt Mariana will tell me all about it," Andrew said. "I haven't had a letter from her for months. I have a lot to catch up on."

I am sure Mariana's friendship with Charlie Dixon is perfectly innocent, but I want to hear from her.

The garrison lined the route into Ladysmith for Buller's relieving army. On the one side were the defiant defenders, gaunt, hollow-cheeked survivors of hunger, vicious skirmishes and disease. On the other were the relievers, stalwart, bronzed men who had fought half a dozen brutal battles to reach the town, pushing through the most challenging territory in South Africa against stubborn opposition.

The Devons, heroes of Wagon Hill, stood at attention to

salute Sir Redvers Buller, a fellow West Countryman, beside the Irish regiments and the Gordon Highlanders, whose pipes screamed to the hills. The relieving Royal Scots Fusiliers greeted the Gordons with broad grins and handshakes, which the Gordons returned with interest. Pipers tried to outdo pipers in playing, but then the column passed, and another regiment took their place. The Royal Malverns stood, with their ranks much depleted and the memory of the recent ambush seared into their collective soul.

The relieving infantry looked shocked at the garrison's condition and threw food and tobacco to the civilians, who nearly wept with gratitude.

When the relieving ceremony ended, Andrew dismissed C Company and retired to his tent, weary but happy.

"Did you hear the news, sir?" Sinton asked.

"Not until you tell me," Andrew replied.

"Our cup runneth over, sir," Sinton was nearly dancing. "We've had a major victory in the west as well. On the 27th of February 1900, Kitchener forced the Boer General Cronje to surrender at Paardeberg with over 4,000 prisoners."

"That is good news indeed," Andrew agreed. "Maybe we'll win this war soon."

"If Buller pushes on now, and Bobs invades the Orange Free State, we could finish it in a few weeks," Sinton said. "All they have now are these guerrilla bands, the de Wets, de la Rey and the van Collier brothers."

"We've fought this sort of action before," Andrew said. "Guerrilla bands are a nuisance, but they only hit outposts. They can't win a war." He sat on his chair. "You are right, Sinton. The war should be over soon."

"BULLER HAS REACHED LADYSMITH," ADRIAAN WESSELS SAID, riding up to where Michal's corporalship sat under the shelter of three dripping trees. The remainder of the Wessels commando waited fifty yards away, shoulders bowed under the pelting rain. "He has relieved the town."

Jacoba nodded. "We heard," she said. "We saw some of the men running back to the Transvaal. So much for their proud boasts about driving the British into the sea."

"We must run too," Adriaan said. "We can't fight Buller's thousands alone."

Michal lifted his head. "I don't want to retreat," he said, glancing at Jacoba.

"Stay then," Adriaan shrugged. "I'll tell your family how bravely you died."

"We're not dead yet," Jacoba said softly.

"Look around you," Adriaan said.

The Boers were in full retreat, running northward and westward away from Ladysmith. The proud commandos galloped through the rain and mist, men drove wagons, and individuals left the army to return to their farms, villages or towns.

"They are defeated," Adriaan said. "We are defeated."

"I am not defeated," Jacoba told him quietly.

"Nor am I," Michal said. He nudged Piet, who sat silently with the rain dripping from the brim of his hat. "How about you, Piet?"

Piet watched the retreating men before he replied. "I am not defeated," he said, "but one rifle, or a dozen rifles, cannot stop an army."

"We can try!" Jacoba said wildly. "We must try!"

"Ja," Piet said. "We can try." He closed his mouth with a snap, took his pipe from his pocket and began stuffing tobacco into the bowl.

"I am ordering the commando to move north," Adriaan said.

"Then do so," Jacoba said. "Run away from the Rooinecks. Go on! Run!"

"I order you to join me!" Adriaan said.

Jacoba shook her head. "I will only obey my corporal," she glared at Michal. "Are you running too, Corporal Michal?"

Michal saw Adriaan twitch the reins of his horse, watching the Boer army disintegrate.

"I am not running," Michal said.

"You see, Adriaan?" Jacoba said. "We are not all cowards!"

"I am no coward," Adriaan said. "And neither am I a fool to remain behind for the British to kill!" Pulling at the reins, he trotted away to join his commando. A few men lifted their arms in farewell to Michal's corporalship, but most turned their heads and trotted away.

"I am also going," one of Michal's corporalship said. "It is foolish to wait to be killed."

"I will join you," Louis Grobler agreed. "I am sorry, Michal, but I have a wife and family. Come, boys!"

One by one, the others left until only Michal, Jacoba and Piet remained under the trees.

"How about you, Piet?" Jacoba asked.

"I have no wife and family," Piet replied, puffing calmly at his pipe.

"I have no husband or family," Jacoba said. "I have nobody to mourn if I die. Do you have a girl, Michal?"

"I had a girl in Pretoria," Michal said with a faint smile. "And one in Johannesburg and another on a farm in the west. I have not seen any of them since the war began, nor heard from them."

"You have nobody then, Michal," she said.

Michal removed his hat, scratched his head and shrugged. "Not yet," he said.

"Then we have nothing to lose," Jacoba decided. "We will continue to fight whatever others do."

The remnants of the corporalship watched the Boer retreat as hundreds of wagons and thousands of men fled from the British, who allowed them to leave without firing a shot.

"Botha is organising a rearguard!" a Boer stopped to shout. "He is looking for volunteers!"

Louis Botha had taken charge of the siege after Joubert fell from his horse. Jacoba lifted her head as a flicker of hope lightened her defiance. "Where is Botha?"

Louis Botha was a steady-eyed, sombre man. Natal-born, he had fought with the Krugersdorp Commando and then with Lucas Meyer and had successfully commanded Boer units at Colenso and Spion Kop.

"Botha knows how to defeat the Rooinecks," Jacoba said.

Michal stood up. "Ja. Now that Joubert is ill, Botha will take command of the Transvaal army."

"The Transvaal army is running away," Piet said sourly.

"Botha is not," Jacoba's hope rekindled. "He is the man who captured that interfering journalist, Churchill."

"That was Field Cornet Sarel Oosthuizen," Piet corrected.

"Botha was involved," Jacoba snapped. "Where is he?"

Michal pushed back his hat. "Not many of us are left, but we will still show the British how to fight." His grin had lost its youthful impulsiveness, but the desire remained.

GENERAL WHITE LOOKED WAN AND SICK AS HE FACED Andrew across the width of his desk. "I am no longer in command here, Captain Baird. General Buller has taken over Ladysmith's garrison."

"Yes, sir. But Major Cradley suggested I ask your permission before speaking to Sir Redvers."

White sighed. "Have you not seen enough fighting, Baird?"

"I want to end the war, sir," Andrew replied. "And the quickest way is to defeat the Boers and capture Pretoria."

White's smile revealed a depth of weariness. "And you believe Field Marshal Roberts cannot win without you."

Andrew stiffened to attention. "I am sure he can, sir, but I'd like to help."

"Ask Sir Redvers, Baird," White said with a weary smile. "Tell him I granted permission."

"Thank you, sir," Andrew saluted and marched away.

Despite the arrival of Buller's army, Ladysmith seemed quiet without the excitement of the siege. Andrew guessed that the town had experienced its fifteen minutes of fame and would now sink into the obscurity it enjoyed before the war. The citizens would repair the shell-scarred buildings, the sick and wounded would move on, and the Klip River would flow past another sleepy colonial town. The siege would remain in the participants' memories, in regimental accounts, and as a footnote in history books.

Nothing else.

Buller frowned at Andrew. "You want what, Captain?"

"I want permission to take a unit of men, infantry or mounted, to join Roberts' army, sir. It would only be a token force, but sufficient to show the enemy that we have combined our forces."

"You've got a nerve!"

Andrew had served with Buller during the Zulu War twenty years before. Buller had been a dashing commander of irregular horse when he won his Victoria Cross. His name had been on everybody's lips as a hero of the same stature as the defenders of Rorke's Drift, a man who restored some of Britain's pride and prestige after the disaster of Isandhlwana.

The man who sat opposite Andrew was overweight, with nervous, indecisive eyes and a flabby neck. Years of soft living had altered the bold horseman.

"We fought together in Zululand, sir," Andrew reminded tentatively.

Buller started. His eyes narrowed as he shuffled through his memory, and a slow smile spread across his face. "So we did, by God! You were known as Up-and-at-'em, if I recall."

"That's right, sir," Andrew admitted.

"That was twenty years ago, Baird, and you are still only a captain in a line regiment?" Buller looked surprised.

"The Royal Malverns is a quality regiment, sir."

"Oh, indeed, I meant no disrespect to the Royal Malverns. Fighting Jack Windrush served with them, didn't he?"

"General Windrush is my father, sir," Andrew said.

Buller frowned at the difference of surnames, then dismissed it as unimportant.

"Why only a captain, Baird? I remember you as a thrusting officer with unlimited potential. I had you marked for great things."

"I left the army, sir," Andrew said. "I only returned during the Chitral nonsense and the Pashtun Revolt of '97."

"I see." Buller scribbled something on a pad. "I can't send a mere captain to Roberts. He's a strange little fellow and might take that as an insult."

Andrew did not reply. He knew the British Army was divided into two factions, one half supporting Field Marshal Roberts and the other following General Wolseley. Roberts' star was now ascending, and Buller had been a protégé of the failing Wolseley.

"If I decide to send a unit to support Roberts, the commander would be a major at least," Buller continued.

Andrew felt his hopes dive. He was condemned to wasting more time in Ladysmith.

"I've spoken to Major Cradley," Buller said, surprisingly, "and he agrees that you are better utilised on horseback rather than as an infantryman."

Andrew started. "Sir?"

"You heard me, Baird," Buller said. His sudden smile surprised Andrew again. "Major, or rather brevet Lieutenant-Colonel Cradley, put your name forward for a promotion to major. General White approved it. The War Office will agree in their own sweet time."

Andrew tried to appear unemotional. "Yes, sir. Thank you, sir."

Buller's eyes were bright again, enjoying Andrew's astonishment. "I know your record, Baird. You commanded mounted men in the Transvaal War, worked along the Irrawaddy in Burma and fought in Chitral and on the Khyber, as well as Elandslaagte and Talana in this present war."

Andrew stood mute. He saw the old devil-may-care Buller behind the uncertainty: the Redvers Buller he had known in Zululand.

"I have written orders for you, Major," Buller said, suddenly formal again as he handed over a sealed package. "I will tell you them verbally first. I want you to raise a mounted unit from the colonial forces and any fit British volunteers. Name them the Natal Dragoons. Find Roberts' force, then obey whatever orders he gives you." Buller frowned at Andrew from behind furrowed brows. "Try to avoid the enemy until you reach Field Marshal Roberts."

"Yes, sir," Andrew replied.

"One last thing." Buller smiled again as he held out his hand. "Congratulations on your promotion, Major Baird of the Natal Dragoons."

CHAPTER 32

NATAL AND ORANGE FREE STATE

MARCH 1900

Finding suitable men for the Natal Dragoons proved more challenging than Andrew had anticipated. He first approached the Imperial Light Horse, knowing local knowledge was vital. Where he had hoped for a dozen experienced men, the commander only released four: Lieutenant Damien Leslie, Sergeant Lambeth, and Troopers Jones and Ritchie.

"You're welcome to them," the colonel said with a twisted smile. "And the best of British luck to you."

Only three more Natal men volunteered, and Andrew was slightly despondent when he approached Brevet Colonel Cradley.

"You'll want to rob the Malverns of my best men," Cradley said with a rueful smile.

"Yes, sir," Andrew replied.

"General Buller doesn't seem keen to move at present," Cradley said, "and the war will be over soon."

"Do you think so, sir?" Andrew asked.

Cradley nodded. "As soon as Roberts captures Pretoria, Kruger will surrender," he predicted. "Your little unit won't see any action, and my men will be back in the fold in a few weeks."

"Maybe so, sir," Andrew agreed diplomatically.

Cradley nodded. "What do you call yourself? The Natal Dragoons?"

"Yes, sir. That was the name of the unit I led in the Transvaal War."

"I see," Cradley said. "All right then, Baird. Cherry-pick my best men."

"Thank you, sir. I only want volunteers."

"You'll want men who can ride and shoot, I presume?"

"That's less important than attitude, sir," Andrew replied. "I can teach riding and shooting. I want men who will keep going when things seem impossible."

Cradley grunted. "You won't find many men like that."

"No, sir," Andrew agreed. "I don't want many men. Just the best sort."

Andrew already had men in mind when he approached the Malverns.

"Attention, lads! It's Captain Baird!" Sergeant Kenny shouted.

C Company came to attention when Andrew approached, with some men chewing and swallowing and others trying to hide their smiles.

"That's not the captain!" Corporal Harwood said. "That's the major!"

The men laughed, and on a signal from Kenny, they began to cheer.

"Come on, lads, three cheers and a tiger for the major!" Kenny shouted.

Andrew stopped, unsure how to react. He had never sought popularity, but C Company seemed to genuinely like him. He stood as the men cheered, some throwing their helmets in the air and others grinning widely.

"Thank you, men," Andrew said. "How did you know? I've only learned myself!"

"Murcot told us, sir," Corporal Harwood told him.

"How the devil did you find out, Murcot?" Andrew asked.

"Colonel Cradley's servant saw the documents, sir, and he told me," Murcot replied.

Andrew nodded. He envisioned a network of servants and clerks exchanging information before most officers learned what was happening. The Boers did not need an intelligence service; they only needed to befriend one of the servants to learn what was happening.

"Well, men, if you know about my promotion, you'll also know I am leaving the regiment."

"You'll be back, sir," Hobart said. "Once a Malvern, always a Malvern!"

Andrew smiled. It was harder than he expected to say goodbye to the men he had fought beside for so many months. "I'll be taking the Malverns with me," he said. "I want some volunteers to join the Natal Dragoons. The pay is slightly more than you earn as an infantryman, but the work is harder. We'll be riding to harass Oom Paul's commandos, meeting them on their own terms, riding to battle and scouting for the army."

The men were quiet when Andrew stopped talking. He knew that for many, the regiment was the only home they knew. It gave them security, regular food, clothing, and companionship.

"I'll give you time to think," Andrew said. "You know where to find me if you decide to join."

Andrew retired to his tent in the Malverns' camp and sat at his table, reading through Mariana's letters, for some mail had come through at last.

Mariana and the children were all well, which was reassuring, but Mariana had mentioned Charlie on far too many occasions for Andrew's peace of mind. He noted gaps in the dates and guessed the war had delayed some mail. Finally, he lifted a letter from his mother.

As always, Andrew's mother was straight to the point. She dismissed everyday domestic affairs in a two-line paragraph and centred on Mariana.

"Your wife seems to be with a person named Charlie Dixon more often than is healthy. Your father knows a major of that name, who is currently occupied in purchasing horses for the war effort. I will travel up to Berwickshire to visit Mariana to ensure everything is all right, and your father will pull strings to remove the major from his present situation."

Andrew read the suppressed worry in his mother's words. He was unsure he welcomed his father's influence, although he knew the general meant well. Andrew put the letter aside and lifted one of Mariana's missives for a second read. Mariana had written a long, involved story about Simla and Iain's latest mischief-making exploits. The children were proving a bit of a handful, despite Charlie's help, and needed their father's guidance.

"Sir?" Murcot stood before him, looking uncharacteristically uncomfortable.

"Spit it out, Murcot." Andrew put his finger on his place.

"What is it, Murcot?"

"Will you still need me when you leave the regiment, sir?" Murcot asked.

Andrew frowned. He had not considered Murcot's place. "Would you want to join me, Murcot?"

"Yes, sir, but I've never ridden a horse in my life."

"We'll teach you," Andrew reassured him. "I'll be glad to have you along."

"Thank you, sir." Murcot looked relieved.

One by one, men from C Company came to see Andrew. Sergeant Kenny stood at attention, looking very apologetic as he explained he would prefer to stay with the Malverns.

"I've given it much thought, sir, but I only know the regiment. My father fought beside your father, sir, and I was born into barrack life."

Andrew understood. "That's quite all right, Kenny. The Malverns need you. Anyway, I've recommended you as a Company Sergeant Major. You've been doing that job unofficially for months, so it's time you got the pay and perks that accompany it."

Kenny smiled. "CSM! Thank you, sir! Thank you very much!" He saluted smartly, turned on his heel and marched out.

Andrew compiled a list of his men. Between the Imperials and a few other Natal men, with a dribble of British volunteers, plus Murcot, he had sixteen men. Andrew looked up as somebody scratched at the fly of his tent.

"Come in!"

Corporal Harwood entered, standing to attention as if on parade.

"Yes, Harwood?" Andrew asked.

"Permission to join the Natal Dragoons, sir?"

"Granted," Andrew replied without hesitation. He considered Harwood one of the more promising junior NCOs in the regiment.

"Thank you, sir," Harwood said. "Hobart and Conway also wish to join, sir."

Andrew pondered for a moment. Hobart was vocal but a good soldier, while Conway was a brawler and a troublemaker.

"I'll have a quiet word with Conway, sir," Harwood read Andrew's hesitation.

"Give me your opinion of Conway, Corporal," Andrew ordered.

"He could start a fight in an empty barn, sir," Harwood said cheerfully, "but he finishes them, too. I'd rather have him at my back than most men in the company."

"All right," Andrew agreed. "Try to keep him under control."

"I will, sir. Thank you, sir," Harwood saluted.

Andrew had little time to train his Dragoons. He used the

experienced colonial horsemen as examples to teach the uninitiated the basics of horsemanship and despaired at the results.

"You will be riding against men who have been in the saddle since before they could walk," he told the shame-faced Dragoons. "You must learn, and learn quickly, if we are to meet them on anything like equal terms."

After seven hard days of training, most men could remain on horseback for a gentle walk without falling off. Two of the infantry volunteers decided to return to their units rather than spend half their day picking themselves off the ground. One other broke his leg when the horse threw him and ended up in hospital. The others persevered, slowly becoming adequate horsemen.

"You leave tomorrow," General Buller said at last. "I am sending General Hamilton and a division to help Roberts. You will accompany him with your men."

"Yes, sir," Andrew said. He knew he had barely trained his Dragoons and they were no match for a Boer commando, but he had had enough of being confined in Ladysmith. He wanted the open spaces of the veldt. And besides, the war was all over bar the shouting, and soon he would go home to Mariana.

And I'll find out about Major Charles blasted Dixon.

MICHAL PACED SLOWLY AROUND THEIR CAMP, LISTENING TO the sounds of the African night and enjoying the brilliant stars. This Africa was the land he knew and loved, with the satisfying scent of the grass and the peace of the veldt stretching as far as creation. All it needed was the distant lowing of cattle, and Michal would be at home. Instead, there was that persistent moan he could not identify.

A leopard growled somewhere, too far away to be a threat, and anyway, Michal knew the animal was hunting for more tender prey than his tough hide. He cradled his rifle in the crook of his arm, worked the bolt to ensure it was loaded and walked on. He completed the circuit of their camp and returned to his original spot.

Piet was asleep beside the fire, his bearded face relaxed and peaceful, and his rifle within easy reach at his side. Jacoba was inside her wagon, the cover tightly laced as always.

Michal frowned. The noise came from within the wagon.

"Jacoba?" Michal hissed from outside the wagon. The sound continued, a sigh followed by a gulp. "Jacoba? Are you all right?"

When there was no reply, Michal scratched at the canvas. "Jacoba? I'm coming in." Unlacing the cover, he peered inside. Jacoba lay on her side in her rough bed, sobbing. Michal stared for a moment, unsure what to do. Leaning his rifle against the wagon wheel, he slipped inside the wagon.

"It's all right, Jacoba. Everything will be all right." Crouching at Jacoba's side, he touched her shoulder. When she started, he whispered, "It's only me, Jacoba."

"Hendrik?" Jacoba turned around, her face puffy and wet with tears. "Hendrik? Are you back?"

"No, it's me," Michal said. "It's Michal."

Jacoba stared at him, recognising who he was. "Get out!" she screamed, struggling to sit up. "Get out of our wagon! Get out!" Her voice rose to a shriek as Michal retreated hastily and nearly ran out of the wagon. Jacoba lunged at him with clawed fingernails, catching the shoulder of his coat without doing any damage. "Get out!"

Piet watched Michal scramble to safety. "Best leave her to cry it out," he advised. "She's missing Hendrik." He lay down again, pulled his rifle closer and fell asleep.

Michal retrieved his rifle, took a deep breath and continued to pace around the camp as the fire died to glowing orange embers. A jackal howled in the distance, echoing the emptiness of his thoughts. He remembered how vulnerable Jacoba had looked as she lay curled on her bed, and something stirred inside him.

She is a good-looking woman, Michal told himself. *Hendrik was too old for her.* He shook his head. *No, Jacoba is my colleague and a fighting woman.*

Michal resumed his patrol, identifying and dismissing every night sound, listening for the noise of any approaching British patrol and sniffing the air for their tobacco smoke. Yet all the time, his mind wandered back towards Jacoba. He had been with many women, but none like her.

Why did I not notice Jacoba before Hendrik took her?

ANDREW HALTED HIS MEN OUTSIDE BLOEMFONTEIN, THE capital of the Orange Free State. "We won't enter the town," he said.

"Why not, sir?" Sinton asked. "Bobs captured Bloemfontein on the 13th of March."

"Typhoid," Andrew explained. "It's rife, and some of our men haven't recovered their strength from Ladysmith yet. They might not have the resilience to fight off the germs."

"As you wish, sir."

"We'll camp here," Andrew said. "I'll report to Field Marshal Roberts."

Roberts was old, white and gentle-voiced, a small Indian-born Irishman. Andrew thought Roberts did not look like a victorious general until he met his gaze. Roberts' eyes were steady as he studied Andrew from head to foot.

"How many men in your unit, Captain?"

"Thirty, sir, a mixture of Colonials and British regulars."

Roberts nodded. "Experienced?"

"Everybody has come through the Ladysmith siege or relief, sir, and some Malvern regulars were involved in the Pashtun Revolt on the Frontier."

"We never have sufficient mounted men or horses for them," Roberts said. "You'll be acting as scouts when we move. In the meantime, keep your men healthy. Typhoid is rife in Bloemfontein."

"Yes, sir. We've camped outside the town to avoid the disease."

"Keep your men alert. We are having some trouble with irregular bands of Boers. You'll have heard of de Wet, and there are also the van Collier brothers from the far west."

"I have heard of them, sir," Andrew said.

Roberts sighed. "The van Colliers have been troublesome since we started this campaign, Baird."

"Yes, sir," Andrew said. "I remember them from the previous war with the Boers."

"Do you, indeed?" Roberts replied. "Well, Major, if you meet them again, shoot straight. They're troublemakers."

"I'll pass that on to my men," Andrew promised as the memories of that previous campaign resurfaced.

CHAPTER 33

NATAL AND THE ORANGE FREE STATE

MARCH TO MAY 1900

When Jacoba emerged from her tent just before dawn, Michal avoided her until he judged her mood. She took a deep breath of the morning air, stretched and smiled. "Is there no coffee in this country of ours?"

Piet stirred the fire to life. "Give me five minutes, Jacoba," he said.

Michal kept a respectable three-yard distance. "Good morning, Jacoba."

"Good morning, Michal," Jacoba favoured him with a smile and no mention of the previous night's drama.

Michal thought it best to keep silent about the tear marks on her face.

"What are we doing today, Corporal?" Jacoba asked as Piet handed her a mug of strong coffee.

"Riding around Ladysmith's defences, looking for a weakness," Michal replied, relieved Jacoba was in a better temper.

"Ja. We'll keep the garrison on their toes," Jacoba said. "Remind them that not all Boers have run away."

Piet lifted his head. "Hoofbeats," he said, "coming this way."

"Khaki?" Jacoba asked, stepping towards the wagon and reaching for her rifle.

"Maybe. One rider, approaching fast."

Michal worked the bolt of his Mauser. "How far away?" He scanned the horizon, knowing that sound travelled fast, so they would have plenty of time to find a defensive position against a single rider.

"Two miles. Perhaps more," Piet finished his coffee. "I'll have a look."

The lone rider trotted straight to Jacoba's wagon, removing his hat when he realised she was a woman.

"I am looking for Corporal Michal Rheeder," the rider said without dismounting.

"That's me," Michal lowered his rifle and emerged from behind a rock.

"I have a message for you, Corporal." The man was dusty from hard riding, with bandoleers crossed across his chest and veldt sores spotting his exposed wrists.

"Speak," Michal said.

"Things have changed in Ladysmith," the rider did not dismount. "General White is too ill to continue and has returned to Britain. General Buller has taken complete command of the garrison and has sent General Hamilton and a division to help Field Marshal Roberts."

Michal nodded without comment.

"Buller has created a new unit of mounted men, the Natal Dragoons, with a Major Baird as commander. It is a mixture of Uitlander, Natal and British troops."

"Major Baird and the Uitlanders?" Jacoba interrupted. "Which Uitlanders?"

"A mixed bunch," the messenger said, patting his now restive horse. "Excuse me, I have others to see."

"Major Baird? Is that Andrew Baird?" Jacoba lifted her head, but the messenger was already riding away.

"It might be the same man," Piet said quietly.

Michal shouldered his rifle. "We'll follow," he said.

"Ja," Jacoba said. "We will follow, and we will kill Andrew Baird, the man who took my scarf and murdered my husband."

ANDREW LED HIS NATAL DRAGOONS IN FRONT OF ROBERTS' army, watching for a Boer ambush or dust on the horizon.

"Extended front, men," Andrew ordered. It was good to be mounted again, in command of his own unit, with mobility and freedom, although he was still restricted by orders from above, still tied to the army. He glanced at his men. The Colonials rode like men born to the saddle, leaning back in their long stirrups with the bandoliers crossing their chests and the slouch hats on their heads. The British recruits could not match their level of competency, although they were already looking more comfortable on horseback as long as the ground was fairly even.

It takes patience and practice to make a horseman, Andrew told himself. *Give them time, and they will get better. But will the Boers give them time?*

Satisfied his men were all right, Andrew swivelled in his saddle to watch Field Marshal Roberts' army march. Roberts had left all the sick and wounded in Bloemfontein and headed towards the Transvaal with a proud show of British military power. Bands led the infantry in their worn woollen khaki while teams of horses pulled the artillery. Roberts hugged the railway, marching towards Pretoria, with French commanding the cavalry well to the left and in advance of the central column. General Ian Hamilton was also already on the move with the right wing, pushing against any Boers on the Winburg, Kroonstad and Ventersburg roads.

"I hope Kruger gives up now," Sinton said. "He's provoked us with his invasions, but we've raised the sieges of Ladysmith and Kimberley. Mafeking is holding out, and we're thrusting through the Orange Free State. Kruger can't stand against Roberts here and Buller in Natal."

"I hope you are right," Andrew said. "We have a hundred and twenty miles to cover before we reach Kroonstad, the next major destination."

The Dragoons rode three miles ahead of Roberts' central column, scouting the land, inspecting farmhouses for hidden commandoes, and having occasional skirmishes with small bands of Boers.

Boer resistance melted before Roberts' slow but inexorable advance. Andrew was grateful for every quiet day, for it gave his Dragoons time to gel into an efficient fighting force.

Every day that passes helps; every skirmish gives my men experience in this form of fighting.

The Boers retreated steadily, doing what they could to delay the British advance. They blew up water tanks, bridges and pumping stations, destroyed the railway line and occasionally stood, only to withdraw when Roberts approached.

The crack of a Mauser sounded across the veldt, with the bullet whistling well to Andrew's left.

"Did anybody see where that came from?" Andrew shouted.

"There's a small house over there," Harwood pointed to his left.

Andrew studied the house through his binoculars. It nestled beside a copse of fruit trees, with a small fruit garden in front and some neatly fenced fields on either side.

"Leslie!" Andrew shouted. "Take your section and inspect that farm."

Andrew had never learned to like Leslie, but he thought it best to treat him respectfully and include him as much as possible. He was also one of the Dragoons' best horsemen.

Leslie left at a gallop, with his section spread out behind him. Andrew watched them approach the farmhouse in a line, surround the building and dismount. Leslie paused momentarily to adjust something at his neck before leading his men forward. The Mauser cracked again, with the "buck-up" sound distinct, and then Leslie's men closed. Despite his dislike for the man, Andrew could admire Leslie's professionalism as he moved quickly from cover to cover, always with half his men covering the others.

The Mauser fired again, and Leslie led a rush inside the farm. Andrew heard more shooting, a few shouts and then silence, broken by a man's laughter.

"Take charge of the Dragoons, Sinton," Andrew ordered. "I'll see what's happening." He trotted Letsie across the intervening ground as Leslie's men emerged from the house.

"How many Boers?" Andrew asked as he dismounted.

"Two," Leslie was grinning, pleased with himself. "We captured a Mauser." He displayed the rifle, well-kept except for a scrape across the butt.

Andrew frowned as he noticed the scarf around Leslie's neck. "Where did that come from? That's my scarf!"

Leslie's smile broadened. "I thought it was familiar, sir," he said. "I found it inside the house. One of the Boers was wearing it." Removing it from his neck, he handed it to Andrew. "Here you are, sir, with my compliments."

"Thank you, Leslie." Andrew stuffed the scarf in his pocket. "How the devil did a Boer get hold of my scarf?" Stepping past Leslie, he entered the farmhouse.

The boy lay on his back, with his mouth and eyes wide open and a bullet hole through the centre of his head. Blood pooled beneath him. Andrew estimated him to be ten years old at most.

"Dear God, the Boers are fighting us with children," Andrew breathed.

When Andrew entered the next room, he found the second Boer.

The man must have been wounded in an earlier encounter,

for bandages swathed his stomach and both arms. He lay on his bed with two fresh bullet holes in his chest.

"Was this man dead when you found him?" Andrew asked quietly.

"No, sir," Sergeant Lambeth replied immediately. "He tried to shoot us."

"What with?" Andrew asked. "You only found one Mauser in the house."

"He had it," Lambeth replied.

"Then why shoot the boy?" Andrew asked.

"He tried to shoot us, too," Lambeth sounded uneasy.

"That's right," Leslie appeared behind Andrew. "This bandaged fellow had the rifle, and he fired first, and when we shot him, the other Boer grabbed the rifle and fired. We didn't see he was only a child until after we returned fire. It was self-defence."

Andrew knew both men were lying, but he could not prove it. "I see. I want a written report, Leslie, as soon as you can. I don't like killing wounded men and children."

"No more do I," Leslie said, shrugging. "It goes against the grain, but what choice do we have when they fire at us?"

"We had no choice," Lambeth said, and Ritchie and Jones nodded in support.

"Which one had my scarf?" Andrew asked.

Lambeth looked confused until Leslie answered. "The boy," he said. "He must have sneaked into your tent and stolen it when you were asleep."

"Somebody certainly did," Andrew agreed. "We'll give these people a decent burial before we leave."

The Dragoons erected crosses above both graves, wrote the date on a piece of paper, left it inside the house for any relatives to find, and rode away from the farmhouse. When Andrew looked back, the place looked lonely under the vast sky, with the fruit trees forlorn and the fields swept bare of livestock by the competing armies. He thought he saw a small figure running from an outlying barn but could not be sure. It was just one more incident in the war, one more tragedy in the overpowering horror of political disagreements.

"Come on, Dragoons!" Andrew shouted and rode on to scout for Roberts' army as it marched towards Pretoria.

"Did you hear?" Michal asked as he sat beside the fire. "The Natal Dragoons murdered a wounded man and a young boy."

Jacoba faced him across the flames. "Who? When?"

"I don't know the names," Michal said. "The Natal Dragoons are scouting for Roberts' force. They broke into a farmhouse north of Bloemfontein and shot a wounded man and his nine-year-old son."

"How do we know this information?" Jacoba asked.

"The little daughter was in the barn," Michal replied. "She saw them go into the house. A man with a Vierkleur scarf led them."

"Baird!" Jacoba said. "Andrew Baird is killing children now." She gripped her rifle. "I trusted that man."

"War changes people," Piet said, stuffing tobacco in his pipe.

"He chose to become a soldier," Jacoba replied. "He chose to kill people for a career."

"Roberts is marching towards Pretoria," Michal said quietly. "If Botha stands to defend our capital, we might meet the Natal Dragoons there."

"We will travel light and ride hard," Jacoba said. "I won't need the wagon."

"That is a good decision," Piet said. "The wagon is a burden."

"Mount up," Jacoba turned her back on the wagon. "We have *Rooinecks* to hunt."

CHAPTER 34

ORANGE FREE STATE

MAY 1900

Roberts' march northward continued, scooping up prisoners and easing the Boers from their strongholds with only token resistance.

Andrew's Natal Dragoons cautiously approached the small village some thirty miles north of Bloemfontein, with each man expecting strong Boer resistance. The Dragoons held their rifles ready, checking the land around them, listening for the crack of a Mauser.

"Where the devil are they?" Sinton asked. "Don't they want to defend their towns?"

"Extended order," Andrew said, glancing to the right and left. "Watch for ambushes." Lifting his binoculars, he scanned the village's outskirts, house by house, searching for movement, the flash of sunlight on a gun barrel or a rifleman's slouch hat. Only when he was satisfied it was safe did he signal the Dragoons to ride forward.

Nobody challenged them as they entered the fringe of the neat, prosperous-looking village, although Andrew sensed people watching from behind shuttered windows and half-closed doors. One woman scurried away, looking fearfully over her shoulder, and a young girl stared at them before tying coloured ribbons around her straw hat.

"She's wearing ribbons of red, white, blue and green. That's the Vierkleur's colours," Sinton said. "She's a Boer sympathiser."

"We're in their heartland," Andrew replied. "Of course, she sympathises with the Boers. I would do the same."

The Dragoons rode through the town without meeting any resistance and signalled that it was safe for the main army to follow. The Guards marched in the following day.

Brandfort was next.

"The Boers have four thousand men ready to defend Brandfort," Leslie said.

"That's a fair number," Andrew replied. "Who told you that?"

Leslie smiled. "One of the prisoners was willing to talk," he said.

Sergeant Lambeth laughed. "More than willing," he added.

"Where is he now?" Andrew asked.

Leslie's smile broadened. "With the other prisoners," he said.

"In future, bring any prisoners to me," Andrew ordered. "I'll question them." He hardened his voice. "I don't want any mistreatment."

"Of course not, sir," Leslie looked pained at the suggestion.

The Boers at Brandfort resisted, with a party of two hundred defeating the stubborn resistance of twenty-five men of Lumsden's Horse. When the Guards approached the following day, the Boers retreated, and the British occupied the town. There was a short skirmish as No. 9 Field Battery hammered the last of the Boers, and when the dust settled, the advance continued.

One day, the Dragoons acted alone; the next, Roberts attached them to the Mounted Infantry, continually gathering experience and learning from the colonial horsemen. On the 5th of May, the West Australians reached the Vet River to find Boers dug in on the far bank. The Dragoons were spectators as British artillery pounded the Boers, who remained in place for once. General Hutton flanked them to the left, and the Tasmanians, Canadians, and New Zealanders fought their way over the Vet and stormed a Boer-held kopje.

"These colonial lads are good," Sinton approved.

"Better than us in many ways," Andrew agreed. "We can learn a lot from them."

Although the Boers rarely stood and fought, they delayed Roberts' advance. As the railway probed northward to the Transvaal frontier, it crossed more rivers after the Vet. Andrew marked each on the map: the Zand, the Vaalsh and the Rhenoster. At each river crossing, the Boers hacked out trenches and defended them with riflemen. Roberts was a canny veteran, and rather than attack head-on, he sent his mounted units, including the Natal Dragoons, on wide outflanking movements. Yet each time the pincers looked like closing, the Boers ran, and the mounted units grasped at empty air.

"How the devil do they know we are coming?" Sinton asked.

"How many farms did we pass?" Andrew asked. "Every woman and old man in those farms will support their fighting men in the commandos."

To add to the army's frustration, the Boers blew up the bridges, with the mercenaries of John McBride's Irish Brigade proving adept at destruction. Although they were termed Irish, most of McBride's men were United States citizens of Irish ancestry.

Despite the delays, Roberts pushed inexorably onward, pushing the enemy before him. The Natal Dragoons participated in the skirmishes, learned from the various colonial units and became more proficient at their job.

The town of Boschrand fell without a struggle, and then pretty Kroonstad on the Vaalsh River became the next major prize.

Roberts made a spectacle of Kroonstad's capture, partly because President Steyn had recently fled the town. The Field Marshal arranged a parade through the streets, with his mainly colonial bodyguard in the van. The staff officers and foreign attachés were next, followed by the Imperial Yeomanry.

The Natal Dragoons were not part of the procession, and Andrew watched the parade with his mind thousands of miles away. His mother's latest letter had mentioned that Major Charles Dixon had joined the Imperial Yeomanry and might soon be leaving the UK.

Send him out here, Andrew thought. *Send Charlie blasted Dixon to me.*

"Sir!" A lean Imperial Light Horse lieutenant threw Andrew a smart salute. "The Field Marshal requests to see you, sir."

"Thank you, Lieutenant. Lead on." Andrew mounted Letsie and followed the Light Horseman.

When Andrew arrived in the Field Marshal's tent, Roberts looked as old and genial as ever, a philanthropic grandfather rather than Britain's most successful general. He greeted Andrew like an old friend before becoming businesslike.

"We'll halt at Kroonstad and consolidate the supply lines," Roberts said. "The Boers don't seem willing to seriously contest our advance, but they are a nuisance in the rear. We have marched 128 miles from Bloemfontein, and the Boers are threatening every mile of railway."

"Yes, sir," Andrew agreed.

"Baird, take your Dragoons and guard the railway here." Roberts indicated a section of line ten to fifteen miles to the south.

"Yes, sir," Andrew nodded. He had enjoyed the exhilaration of constantly advancing through enemy territory, but now it was back to the grind of routine patrol work and worrying about Mariana.

※

HOLDING FOR THE QUEEN

MICHEL WATCHED FROM THE STREET AS THE ZUID-Afrikaansche Republiek's *Volksraad* – the parliament – opened in Pretoria. In addition to the delegates from the Republic, consuls and attachés attended from various countries. Some wore military uniforms and others sported stiff formal clothes.

"Do these men know we're fighting a war, and the British are approaching?" Jacoba asked. "Roberts could bombard Pretoria in a few weeks and set these buildings ablaze."

"The British don't do that," Michal said.

"We did it to Kimberley and Ladysmith," Jacoba reminded, "and they have more guns than we do."

Michal shook his head. "The Rooinecks are a hard, grasping people, but not vindictive. They won't make war on women and children."

Jacoba's mouth pressed into a hard, thin line. "That depends on which face they wish to present. When Captain Baird helped me, I thought he was a gentleman, but he bayonetted Hendrik, shot a little boy and killed a wounded man on his bed."

Michal turned away, unable to respond. The truth could sometimes be too harsh to accept.

When Jacoba looked inside the building, she saw President Kruger wearing the white gloves and sash that proved his position. She also saw the *Vierkleur*, the Republic's flag, covering one of the chairs, with black crepe and wreaths of immortelles across others.

"Why is that?" Jacoba asked an official.

"The *Vierkleur* covers Cronje's chair," the official explained sadly. "The British captured him and his army at Paardeberg. We put black crepe over the chairs of Joubert, Kock and the rest because they died in the service of the Republic."

"I did not know Joubert was dead," Jacoba said. "All the good men are dying."

"He is dead," the official confirmed. "Yet the Republic lives on."

"*Een vrije volk zijn wij,*" Jacoba said. "A free people are we."

"We are," the official agreed softly. "And now I must close the door so the *Volksraad* can debate matters of state."

"Thank you, meneer," Jacoba said. "It is good to know our government is still working despite the British attacks."

"*Een vrije volk zijn wij,*" the official said. "And always will be."

ANDREW WATCHED GENERAL HAMILTON LEAD A STRONG force to capture the small town of Lindley and returned to his thankless task of patrolling the railway line. He had the Natal Dragoons move in groups of five, within sight of each other for mutual support. They rode parallel to the railway, always watching and hoping to meet a commando. As the British patrolled, the Boers struck at will, blowing up the line, ripping up the tracks and vanishing into the veldt.

Andrew organised his men, with the colonials mixed with the British, the stronger riders beside the weaker. He split them into mutually supporting groups, spread them into extended order to cover a wider area of the countryside, and patrolled his section of the track. He placed static pickets at two of the most crucial points, built rough sangars, cleared a firing zone for a three-hundred-yard radius, and placed white-painted range markers.

For all the patrolling and effort, Andrew's Natal Dragoons did not encounter the enemy, and each day left the men tired, dusty and frustrated.

Andrew learned again that hunting Boer commandos was like catching water in a sieve. Wherever the British were, the commandos were not, except for the occasional lightning ambush and retreat. The Dragoons listened for the drumbeat of hooves in the night, the blast of dynamite on the line and the rattle of musketry on an isolated sentry post.

"How the devil can we fight these men if we can't see them?" Sinton peered into the immensity of the veldt.

"How many attacks have the Boers made on our section of the line since we arrived?" Andrew asked.

"None," Sinton admitted.

"Exactly," Andrew said. "Our methods are deterring the Boers, so our unit is successful. We cannot speak for others."

Sinton grunted. "I'd rather have an open fight than just deter them. We know they are out there, somewhere."

Andrew nodded. "There's a lot of somewhere for them to hide. If we send out patrols, we'll be playing hide and seek on their home territory."

"Hopefully, they'll make a final stand. Bobs will smash them, occupy Pretoria, and they'll see sense and surrender. Then we can all go home," Sinton said. "We don't have sufficient men to patrol the entire track. We'd need thousands more, with watchtowers and patrols."

Andrew agreed. "We'd have to build a Hadrian's Wall the full length of the railway, with milecastles and forts for the garrison."

Sinton pushed back his hat and mopped the sweat from his face. "This isn't war; it's tig for adults."

Andrew grunted. "We faced the same problem fighting the dacoits in Burma and the Pashtun along the Frontier." He shaded his eyes and peered into the seemingly limitless veldt. "I believe the Americans have a similar difficulty in the Philippines."

"Maybe that's a common factor to every Empire," Sinton said. "I imagine the Arabs faced recalcitrant Spanish and Basques; the Ottomans would have trouble in Greece and the Balkans, and the Mongols would experience resistance in China."

Andrew grunted again. "The Mongols didn't have any trouble. They massacred everybody that stood in their path. We won't do that."

"No," Sinton said. "We treat war like a game with rules and expect the enemy to act accordingly. Anything else is just not cricket."

After days of frustrating patrolling without seeing a single Boer, the Dragoons were ordered back to the front.

"What's the date, sir?" Corporal Harwood asked.

"It's the 22nd of May 1900," Andrew replied.

"We've been at war for seven months," Harwood said. "That's long enough for anybody. Surely, Oom Paul will throw in the towel soon. He must know he can't win."

Andrew listened, peered over the vast expanse of the veldt and hoped Harwood was correct. He thought of Mariana, wondered when he would hear from her, and returned his attention to his duty.

After his pause at Kroonstad, Roberts advanced again, marching for Johannesburg.

Andrew felt the new purpose among his Uitlanders as the Natal Dragoons scouted ahead of the army again.

"We're going home," Leslie told him with his usual ready smile. "Back to the City of Gold, where the Boers started all this trouble."

"Kruger is sure to fight for the gold," Sinton said. "That's where all the Transvaal's wealth originates. He'll fight one last battle to defend Johannesburg; we'll smash him, and that will end the war."

"These people don't think like us," Andrew reminded. "They are people of the Book and the land, not of the counting-house. Many will see the gold as a curse; remember that the love of money is the root of all evil, and it is easier for a camel to pass through the eye of a needle than a rich man to enter heaven."

Sinton was quiet for a few moments. "Maybe so, sir, but even Kruger needs gold to buy Mausers and Krupp guns for his commandos."

Andrew nodded. "That is true, Sinton," he conceded.

Two days after Roberts left Kroonstad, General French sent his cavalry across the Vaal River into the Transvaal. Andrew's Dragoons were in the vanguard, and as his men splashed through the river, he knew he was part of history.

Kruger had declared war on the Empire, Kruger had invaded British territory, and Kruger's armies had besieged British-owned towns. The Empire had struck back. They had held the initial Boer thrusts, relieved the sieges and, despite initial setbacks, had defeated the Boer armies. In addition, Roberts marched through the Orange Free State, captured and occupied the capital, and chased the government and its army out of the country.

When they saw the Vaal, the Dragoons gave an involuntary cheer. Unlike most rivers they had crossed, the Vaal was broad and clear, a welcome sight to men used to the Tyne and the Spey, the Severn and the Wye.

"Now it's the Transvaal's turn," Sinton said with satisfaction as troop after troop of British cavalry crossed the Vaal and spread out on the northern bank, with Roberts's observation balloon, or Spy Balloon as the men termed it, floating above.

"Kruger must react now," Leslie said. "Or maybe we've broken him already."

The same day British cavalry crossed into the Transvaal, Roberts announced the annexation of the Orange Free State to the British Empire.

"That should provoke Oom Paul into action," Sinton said.

"Maybe that's Bobs's idea," Andrew replied. "Bring the Boers to an open battle rather than this guerrilla warfare. Keep it a clean and honest war between fighting men."

In addition to annexing the Free State, Roberts changed its name to the Orange River Colony and sent French's cavalry westward, seeking the right flank of the Boer army he expected to defend Johannesburg.

"Here we go, men!" Andrew said. "We're with General French!"

Andrew knew that Louis Botha and Koos de la Rey commanded the enemy forces, both experienced fighting men, so the oncoming struggle would not be easy.

When a range of hills loomed ahead, Leslie grinned. "That is the Klipriversberg," he said.

"If I were the Boers, I'd make my stand here." Andrew

scanned the hills through his binoculars, looking for the now familiar signs of enemy activity.

"Over there, sir," Sinton pointed to the hill known as Doornkop near the middle of the range. "Movement. Sunlight on metal."

"Doornkop," Leslie said quietly. "That's where the Boers captured Jameson back in '95. Were you here then, sir?"

Andrew shook his head. "I was up the Grim," he said. "On the North-West Frontier of India."

The Dragoons halted, heliographed their observations to Roberts and waited for orders.

Andrew spread a map on the ground, gathered his men around and explained the situation.

"Field Marshal Roberts has a two-pronged advance on Johannesburg," he said. "One column, with French's cavalry including us and Hamilton's infantry, is advancing west of the city, while General Tucker and General Pole-Carew are taking the main force along the railway line to the east."

"Will the Boers fight this time, sir?" Sinton asked.

"I think they will," Andrew replied, folding the map. He glanced at his men. "We're with the 1st Mounted Infantry Brigade for the present, lads."

The Natal Dragoons were beside two Canadian units when they forded the Klip River. The horsemen splashed through, with sunshine reflecting from water droplets and the men watching the far bank.

"Spread out," Andrew ordered. "Don't bunch!" On an impulse, he removed the scarf from his pack and tied it around his neck. "The Boers will be watching us."

The Dragoons moved slowly forward, trusting in Andrew's intuition. Working with the colonials had sharpened their techniques, so even Murcot, the worst rider, was now proficient in the saddle. They walked their horses on the north side of the river, waiting for an outbreak of musketry and the familiar, hated "buck-up" sound of Mausers.

Behind the scouts, the British cavalry moved in a broad column of khaki-clad men wearing sun helmets, some with lances or swords and others with carbines. The more experienced could also sense the enemy's presence. They all expected the Boers to fight fiercely for their country.

The Dragoons saw the muzzle flashes and heard the rumble of Boer artillery from Doornkop, but the shells landed near the cavalry in the rear. The ground rose in a score of dirt fountains, dust, shrapnel and pebbles scattered, and men struggled to control their panicking horses. Trumpets blared, officers shouted hoarse commands, and the column stopped.

The Boer artillery fired again, with the shells landing accurately between the scouts and the main body of cavalry.

Trumpets and bugles ordered a halt and then a retire.

"Back, lads," Andrew said. "Get out of range of the guns."

The Dragoons moved back, avoiding the still-smoking shell holes. Andrew saw the Canadians operating calmly, well-extended and with no sign of distress. He had never served with Canadians before and was immediately impressed by their demeanour.

They move like veterans, well-controlled.

The British artillery began a counter-bombardment, so the Dragoons and cavalry sat tight with shells screaming over them. An occasional Boer shell landed amongst them without causing casualties. The men stood beside their horses, impotent and frustrated.

"Come out and fight!" Conway shouted.

As French's cavalry waited, General Hamilton marched his infantry further west, kicking up dust and jeering good-naturedly at the cavalry.

"Maybe we should have stayed with the Malverns, sir," Sinton said as they watched their regiment march past.

"Our turn will come," Andrew consoled him. "The Boers are concentrating their artillery on us but can't defend the whole line in depth. The more we stretch their line, the weaker they'll be in any one place. By sitting tight, our cavalry keeps the Boer artillery occupied and allows General Hamilton's infantry to get into position."

Heliograph messages flashed from both wings of Roberts' army, with French and Hamilton confirming their positions.

Andrew attempted to read the distant flashes until Sinton translated the Morse code. "Hamilton is ready, sir," he said.

A moment later, French ordered most of the cavalry to withdraw, leaving only the Canadian Mounted Rifles and Royal Canadian Dragoons. The Canadians drew the Boer fire, preventing them from concentrating on Hamilton's advance on their left.

French sent for Andrew.

"You know Hamilton, don't you, Baird?"

"Vaguely, sir. I was with him at Majuba and again in Ladysmith."

French nodded. "That'll do. Take your men over to him as an extra mounted force. He might need more scouts."

"Yes, sir." Andrew knew his Dragoons would prefer to be on the move rather than sitting tight. Men of a retiring nature did not volunteer for irregular cavalry units.

Hamilton raised his one good arm when Andrew arrived. "Good to see you, Baird, although I don't think I'll need you. I've just sent the infantry forward."

Andrew saw the British infantry attack. Hamilton had sent two brigades, the 19th and 21st, with the Second Royal Canadian Regiment on the right and the Gordon Highlanders in the centre.

"Stand with me and watch the fun, Baird," Hamilton said. He sounded every bit as enthusiastic as he had been as a subaltern at Majuba twenty years earlier.

As the Canadians kept the Boer left occupied, the Gordons extended their formation and advanced with fixed bayonets. The Boers had set the dry grass ablaze, but the Highlanders marched into the smoke and flames without hesitation. Andrew watched the khaki-clad, kilted men advance, with billowing smoke now hiding and now revealing them. At eight hundred yards, the Boers fired, with hundreds of Mausers hammering the advancing Highlanders.

To the Gordons' right, the Canadians advanced over a ridge and up a slope of rocks, grass and bushes. Although the flames had reached this section of the ground, the Canadian infantry continued, jinking from cover to cover amidst the flames. Behind them, their machine gun section rattled at the Boers.

Andrew watched with his heart thumping, remembering the previous defeats when British infantry attacked entrenched Boer riflemen. Thin on the wind, Andrew heard the Gordons' pipes play with the old tune, *Cock o' the North*, encouraging the men.

"They're going to charge!" Andrew said quietly. "God help the Boers if the Gordons get at them with the bayonet."

He heard a loud cheer, and the Gordons changed their steady advance to a full-blooded bayonet charge, with the firelight reflecting on the blades and the kilts swinging. Ignoring the men who fell before the massed Boer rifles, the Gordons surged forward. They captured the position and put the surviving Boers to flight, although at a heavy cost of nearly a hundred casualties.

"Remember Majuba," Andrew said softly, ignoring Leslie's stare.

If any glory at Wagon Hill belonged to the Devons, the victory of Doornkop was wrapped in Gordon tartan and fringed with Canadian accents.

"Now for Johannesburg," Leslie said.

"On to Johannesburg," Andrew agreed. "The city of gold."

"Gold for some," Sinton said quietly. "That was another splendid victory, and we didn't fire a shot."

CHAPTER 35

TRANSVAAL

MAY 1900

Andrew watched Roberts' army march on, with the bright khaki of the City Volunteers and the newly arrived yeomanry regiments contrasting with the battered uniforms of the veterans who had spent months on campaign.

He knew the war had already changed the army. Although Indian regiments had fought alongside the British since 1757, Canadians, Australians, South Africans, and New Zealanders were now included under the British flag. Roberts, as commander-in-chief, led a genuinely imperial army.

"Johannesburg is next," Leslie said.

Conway sharpened his bayonet on a handy stone. "I heard the Boers have built a ring of forts around Jo'burg," he said. "Big bloody stone forts armed with big bloody guns and those nasty pom-poms."

Murcot grunted. "Have they? They'll come in handy if we have to defend our gold mines against the French."

Andrew watched an infantry battalion march past. The men were fresh from the United Kingdom and staggered under their full kit. Each man had a greatcoat wrapped around his waist, a blanket and a waterproof sheet in line with his shoulders, rifle, water bottle and ammunition. The combined weight was over sixty pounds, but nobody complained about the blanket during the freezing cold nights.

Once again, the Natal Dragoons scouted ahead, searching for Boer ambushes or traces of Boer commandos. When Andrew reached a ridge south of Johannesburg, he stopped to look at the city that spread ahead.

"There's the City of Gold," Leslie thumbed back his hat and pointed ahead. "The sooner we get it under British control, the better for everybody."

"Except Kruger," Sinton said.

Leslie laughed. "Except Kruger," he agreed.

Andrew was not impressed with his first distant view of Johannesburg. The tall chimneys could have belonged to any industrial town in Britain, while the spoil heaps from the gold mines looked no prettier than the slag heaps of the coal mines of Northumberland or Midlothian. The famous City of Gold looked dirty, industrial and ugly.

Roberts advanced cautiously, trusting to the massive siege guns he had especially requested from the United Kingdom to match anything the Boers could throw at him.

"What about these forts, then?" Sinton examined Johannesburg through his binoculars. "Why are they not firing at us?"

"Best ask Oom Paul," Andrew replied. "And thank your personal God."

"When do we charge in?" Leslie asked, holding his horse's reins.

"We don't," Andrew said. "We're scouting around in case the De Wet brothers, Botha or the van Colliers decide to raid."

Leslie looked disappointed. "If the Boers fight, we'll have the right to sack the town."

Andrew knew looting was a long-established perquisite of any army. "If we make the Transvaal a British colony, we'll be sacking our own town."

"It's not ours yet, sir," Leslie said with his habitual smile. "Until then, it's open season."

As the Dragoons waited impatiently for orders, Roberts reached an arrangement with Dr Fritz De Jong, the governor of Johannesburg. Rather than push into the city and risk ugly street fighting that might cost many lives and damage the gold mines, Roberts agreed that if Johannesburg surrendered, any fighting Boers could leave unmolested.

On the 31st of May, Roberts marched into Johannesburg, although some regular soldiers were unhappy that the Field Marshal allowed the Boer fighting men to escape.

Roberts treated the city to a full military parade, with burghers, Uitlanders and natives watching from the streets. Andrew's Dragoons were near the back of the column, with Leslie's men staring at the familiar places in triumph.

"That's another in the eye for Oom Paul Kruger," Leslie said jubilantly.

"We won't get to loot the town, though, sir," Lambeth replied.

Jones laughed, high-pitched. "Wait for Pretoria," he said. "The Boojers will fight for their capital, and we'll take what we fancy there."

Andrew expected larger crowds in Johannesburg's streets, and the few people who gathered stared in near silence. Only the Uitlanders cheered as the army trooped past. He saw a few Boers watching, with one elderly man in tears.

"Poor old fellow," Sinton said. "He must think all his dreams are shattered now with the British capturing the city."

Andrew lifted a hand in acknowledgement to the elderly

Boer. "Imagine how we would feel if the French or Russians marched through London."

Sinton nodded. "Yes, sir. But that will never happen."

"Please, God, you are right," Andrew said.

Roberts halted his army outside the courthouse and raised a silk Union flag his wife had made. The crowd had increased, black and white faces side by side, and the troops gave three hearty cheers for the Queen. When one defiant Burgher refused to remove his hat and cheer the Queen, an indignant Uitlander grabbed him by the throat.

"Hoi!" A tanned soldier pushed the Uitlander away. "He fought for his flag. You fight for none! I never saw you in the firing line."

Andrew watched with approval. The average British soldier respected the Boers as worthy opponents, particularly because they treated the wounded and prisoners well, unlike many of the men they fought on the Empire's fringes.

"Now on to Pretoria," Sinton said, "and surely that will end the war."

Leslie laughed. "I hope the Boers resist, and we can burn their little capital to the ground. That will show Oom Paul who is his master in Africa."

Andrew shook his head. "I disagree, Lieutenant. I want peace without any more bloodshed."

Leslie's smile did not fade. "With respect, sir, are you in the right job? A soldier's profession is shedding blood."

"A soldier's job is to defend his country," Andrew replied. Yet he wondered if Leslie was right. Was he in the right job?

MICHAL LEANED AGAINST THE TREE, TIPPED HIS HAT OVER HIS eyes, and surreptitiously watched Jacoba. She was not his usual choice of girl, that was certain. He liked the willowy, slender kind with heart-shaped faces, demure attitudes, and innocent eyes. There was nothing innocent or demure about Jacoba. Indeed, she was as aggressive and confident as any man and could handle a horse, a wagon or a rifle with the best of them.

Even so, Michal admitted, something about Jacoba appealed to him. Her face was not pretty, with its stubborn chin, and her open gaze was undoubtedly challenging. She was no youngster, being at least thirty, which seemed old to Michal's twenty-five. He shifted his stance to watch her walk past, with her skirt swinging and her feet firm on the dusty ground.

"Yes," Michal thought, there was something there. Jacoba had wide, child-bearing hips, he decided, which was what a man wanted. The more sons she produced, the better, for he would need help on the farm he hoped to create after the war and wanted a son to pass it to in the distant future. Michal's previous girls had been younger than him, playthings, really, while Jacoba was the sort of capable, strong woman who was good wife material.

Michal closed his eyes, imagining Jacoba as his wife. He knew she would be hard to control, but once she had borne him a couple of children, she would be too busy to disagree much. Now that she had lost Hendrik, Jacoba would be lonely.

Michal smiled, removed his hat and smoothed a hand over his long hair. Hendrik had been a good man, but he was better. He was younger and a corporal rather than a mere follower. Women liked leaders and active men. Michal stood up, pushing the hat back on his head, determined to make his case before Piet approached Jacoba.

Michal studied Piet. No, Piet was no competition. Piet was too old and had nothing to offer. He was another follower who owned nothing except the clothes on his back, a rifle, and a pair of dogs. As the only son, Michal was heir to his father's farm and all his possessions.

"Jacoba!" Michal called.

"Ja?" Jacoba turned to face him. Sun and wind had tanned her face, but a few months indoors and wearing a fine poke bonnet would soon restore the creamy-white complexion that Boer women valued.

"I have a proposition to put to you," Michal said.

"What is that?" Jacoba could see the question in Michal's eyes. She waited, eyeing him up and down.

"Michal Rheeder! Where is Michal Rheeder!" The rider was young and lithe as he trotted into the camp and pulled up with a flourish. "I want Corporal Rheeder!"

"That is me!" Michal replied.

"Piet de Wet is hunting Khaki. Will you join him?"

"Ja!" Jacoba replied for Michal. "We are coming!"

They were mounted within five minutes and followed the rider with spare horses trotting behind them.

"Where are we going?" Michal asked.

"Lindley!" the rider said.

The De Wet brothers kept the Boers' hopes alive despite the victories of Roberts, Buller, and Kitchener. Rather than face the British in full-scale static battles of the European mode, the De Wets utilised the Boers' mobility, firepower, and the vastness of the landscape.

Piet de Wet led a two-thousand-strong commando but greeted Michal's diminutive force as though he had been the answer to the Republic's prayers.

"Welcome!" Piet de Wet said.

"What is happening?" Michal asked.

"The British General Henry Colvile leads a detached force," de Wet explained. "Colvile's role is to catch any of us who evade Hamilton, but he has allowed his force to scatter. One battalion of yeomanry, the 13th, is lagging." De Wet grinned. "We have them in our net."

"How many British?" Michal asked.

"Hundreds!" de Wet said, smiling. "Colonel Spragge of the 13th Battalion of the Imperial Yeomanry will soon be a hands-upper in our hands. Or dead."

"What is yeomanry?" Jacoba was never afraid to admit her ignorance of military matters.

"Yeomanry are not regular Khaki horsemen," de Wet explained. "They are British countrymen, officered by, often, gentry—men with lands and power, gentlemen as they call themselves."

"I understand," Jacoba said.

"The British have not trained their cavalry to fight men like us," de Wet continued, "so they have called up their country squires and fox hunters to defeat us. The British call them the Imperial Yeomanry and have 20 battalions, each of four companies of 115 men."

"Are they good soldiers?" Michal asked.

"They are brave, but lack experience of Africa," de Wet replied. "The 13th is mostly Irish, with some very wealthy men, commanded by Colonel Basil Spragge." He smiled. "They are heading for Lindley, where we will meet them."

"Lindley is firmly on our side," Michal said. "Does Spragge not know that?"

De Wet looked innocent, although his eyes sparkled with mischief. "He believes Colvile ordered him to rendezvous there, but we sent the order. We have men working on the telegraph service."

Jacoba laughed. "What are we waiting for?"

"We'll allow Colvile time to plod clear," de Wet said, "and then we'll remove Spragge from our land."

Michal heard the firing as Piet de Wet led his commando towards Lindley.

"Marthinus Prinsloo is wishing Colonel Spragge a good morning," de Wet said.

The commando moved quicker to find Spragge dug in outside Lindley and determined to fight. Although the yeomanry were amateur soldiers, they were brave men, while Spragge was a professional and chose a good defensive position.

He had based his five hundred men northwest of Lindley in

an area of scattered kopjes, with sweet water in between and a stout farmhouse as a focal point. With the yeomanry based on the kopjes waiting for a Boer attack, Spragge sent messengers to Colvile.

"Will Colvile come to Spragge's aid?" Michal asked.

"I will leave Prinsloo here to deal with Spragge while I watch Colvile's column," de Wet replied. "If he returns, we will delay him."

Michal's handful joined Prinsloo's men surrounding Spragge's position. They moved in the dark, finding a position opposite one of the outlying kopjes and near a small, British-garrisoned ridge. When the first light of dawn came, the Boers opened fire.

Piet crouched behind a quickly constructed sangar with his rifle ready. He waited with all the patience of a hunter.

"You are not firing," Jacoba accused.

"I won't waste bullets," Piet said. "There is a gap between two rocks there. A Rooineck must pass that sometime, and when he does, I have him in my sights."

Jacoba stared at the kopjes, where tiny sparks of light showed where the British were firing at the surrounding Boers.

"Michal," Jacoba said. "I am going to move closer to the British positions. I will attract their attention, and you will fire."

"That's too dangerous!" Michal snapped.

Jacoba shook her head. "The British can't shoot straight."

"I don't want you to disprove that," Michal said.

They both looked around as Piet fired. "That's one," he said calmly, working the Mauser bolt.

British bullets hummed around them as both sides fired. The yeomanry had a Colt machine gun, which hammered at the surrounding Boers and forced them to keep their distance.

"Shall we storm them?" Jacoba asked eagerly. She fired at the muzzle flashes, hoping to kill a British soldier with each bullet.

"No," Prinsloo said. "I will not throw away the lives of my men. Henry Colvile is not marching to Spragge's relief, and the yeomanry do not have many supplies. We will hold them here until they surrender." He ordered the Boers to occupy some nearby farm buildings, which gave better cover from the British fire.

That day passed, and the next, as the 13th Imperial Yeomanry strengthened their defences by building sangars. Both sides sniped at each other without causing many casualties.

"At Doornkop, we made the British advance through burning grass," Jacoba reminded. "Let's burn Spragge out of his defences."

Prinsloo surveyed her through narrowed eyes. "I do not like the idea of burning men alive," he said.

"They won't stay to be burned," Jacoba told him. "They will flee the kopjes, and we can shoot them."

"Or they will surrender," Prinsloo considered the idea. "Horses do not like smoke, so a fire will drive them from their shelter. Deprived of horses, the British will have to give up."

Jacoba led the Boers in setting fire to the dry grass, mouthing her hatred of the British.

"The more Khaki we kill, the better," she said. "Burn them alive!"

Piet watched her through narrow eyes. "The wind will change," he said.

Jacoba ignored him as she crouched low behind rocks, lighting fires around the yeomanry's positions. She stamped her feet in frustration when a fluky wind sent the flames in the wrong direction.

"Even you can't go against nature, Jacoba," Piet told her.

When the wind altered direction the following day, the Boers tried fire again, and Jacoba watched the smoke coil around the kopjes.

"That should smoke them out," Piet said.

"I hope it burns them," Jacoba said. "I hope they burn!"

Piet eyed her, puffing at his pipe. "Maybe you do," he said. "And maybe you don't."

De Wet galloped in with the vanguard of his commando, dismounted with a flourish and approached Prinsloo.

"Colvile shows no sign of returning," he said. "I've left men watching him, but my commando is more useful here." de Wet had brought a machine gun and a few artillery pieces, which he soon brought to bear on the British positions.

Jacoba watched the Boer shells explode on the kopjes and the ridge. She nodded, smiling.

"That's for Hendrik," she said at each explosion. "That's for Hendrik."

Piet and Michal glanced at each other, and Piet began to scrape the bowl of his pipe clean.

"The hatred will die when the hurt eases," Piet said.

"I hope so," Michal replied. "She's damaging herself as much as the enemy."

Piet nodded slowly. "Maybe more. Hatred is corrosive."

De Wet's arrival brought a new energy to the Boers, who mounted a surprise attack on the forward British ridge. At first, the British gave way, and then the yeomanry countered, recapturing the ridge with superb bravery and wild yells.

"No, Rooinecks!" de Wet said. "You can't have the ridge." He sent his men around the back of the ridge.

When the yeomanry on the ridge realised the Boers surrounded them, they reluctantly raised their hands in surrender.

"Come, my Khaki friends," de Wet said, escorting the bewildered prisoners behind the Boer lines. "Your war is over."

Piet put a hand on Jacoba's arm when she lifted her rifle as if to shoot the prisoners.

"They did not kill Hendrik," Piet reminded.

"They are Khaki!"

"These men did not kill Hendrik," Piet gently pushed her rifle down.

The battle for the ridge continued with a successful yeomanry bayonet charge, followed by a British withdrawal under a heavy Boer artillery bombardment. When the Boers finally occupied the disputed ridge, Prinsloo attacked the southern side of the kopjes.

"Come on!" Michal said. "It's time we got more involved." He led the way up the closest kopje, moving from rock to rock, firing and moving again. The yeomanry fired back, but with shell and machine gun fire keeping them under cover, they could not organise an effective resistance.

Michal fired at a British soldier, saw the man spin, ducked as a bullet whined overhead and heard somebody shouting that they surrendered. While the dismounted Boers assailed the kopjes, de Wet led his mounted men to scoop up the British wagons and horses, leaving the yeomanry without transport. While small groups of men raised white flags from isolated positions, others tried to fight on until Spragge ordered a general surrender.

Jacoba watched the hundreds of disconsolate yeomanry huddle under watchful Boer rifles.

"Why did you invade our land?" she yelled at the confused men. "Why did you not leave us alone?"

Some prisoners looked at her, wondering what she was saying, until Michal touched her shoulder.

"Come, Jacoba," he said. "We have won the day. We should celebrate."

"I will celebrate when the last Khaki is out of our land," Jacoba said. She shook off his hand and raised her voice. "Did you hear me, Rooinecks? I shall celebrate when the last Rooineck is out of our land!"

CHAPTER 36

TRANSVAAL

JUNE 1900

"The de Wet brothers have been busy," Sinton said. "While Piet de Wet captured half our yeomanry, the other, Christiaan de Wet, snatched a supply convoy of 56 wagons and 160 men."

"Pinpricks," Andrew said, without believing his own words. "I don't like having these commandos behind us, though."

"We'll be in Pretoria soon," Sinton nodded ahead. "Colonel Mahon has relieved Mafeking, and General Buller has pushed through the Biggarsberg to retake Dundee and Newcastle, so we're winning on all fronts."

Andrew agreed. After weeks of consolidation and preparing his army, Buller had left Ladysmith, with Dundonald's cavalry to the fore, while the siege of Mafeking was finally over.

"All the Boers have is these little flea bites by de Wet and the van ColliersColliers," Sinton said.

Again, Andrew agreed. "We had the same in Burma," he said.

"We sailed up the Irrawaddy and captured Mandalay, but the Burmese dacoits irritated us for years."

"Pretoria, here we come," Sinton said happily. "It's only forty miles away. Let's hope the Boers stand so we can smash them."

"Let's hope they surrender so we don't have to," Andrew replied. He rode around his men, ensuring they all had full water bottles, food and sufficient ammunition if the Boers decided to make a stand.

"Right, men," Andrew said. "Mount up. Behave yourselves when we reach Pretoria. These burghers will be British soon, so treat them as you would our own people. No looting or any other nonsense."

The wilder of his men looked disappointed at Andrew's words.

"The war is nearly over," Andrew said. "The Boers gave us some hard knocks and proved a stubborn and brave enemy. They will be an asset to the Empire."

Trooper Jones grunted and spat on the ground at Andrew's words. Other Uitlanders looked equally sceptical.

Andrew led his Dragoons on towards Pretoria, towards the capital city of the Boer heartland.

THE VICTORY OVER THE IMPERIAL YEOMANRY HAD RESTORED the commando's hope, but visiting the Transvaal's capital drained it away. People filled the streets, heading north, away from the advancing British. Some men gathered outside the Raadzaal, the parliament building, hoping for help, but there was none. Michal saw people breaking into houses to loot.

"Take what you can!" one plump burgher said, "before the British take everything. Strip the city!"

"These people are defeated," Jacoba said. "They have no fight left in them."

"The news is bad on every front," Michal said. "The British

are pushing us aside; all we can do is defeat small parties and round up their amateur soldiers." He dismounted outside a church, with the others following. "Perhaps the good Lord can restore our faith."

"Stay outside!" Piet told his dogs, who settled down, tongues protruding.

Only Jacoba retained her rifle when they entered the simple church, where the predikant preached a service. Some people in the half-empty pews looked around as the corporalship entered, with Jacoba leaning her rifle against the wall at her side. She felt out of place in her veld-dusty clothes in that place of sombre peace.

The service was shorter than Michal expected, with the predikant sounding subdued as he tried to reassure his congregation that the Lord was still looking after them.

"There are mainly women here," Michal said when the service ended.

"Yes," the predikant replied quietly. "The war has been hard on the men." He nodded to a woman who sat alone in a pew near the front. "That lady lost her husband and two of her sons at Paardeberg. The British killed them all. The lady behind her lost a son at Spion Kop and her husband at Platrand. The woman in the corner does not know what happened to her men and hopes the British have them prisoner in St Helena."

Michal nodded. "The war is hard on women," he said, with a dawning understanding of the true cost of war.

"Every war is hard on those who wait and work and hope," the predikant replied. "The women who dread every message from the front, fearing bad news yet watch for dust on the veld in the hope the men are coming home."

"Our Republic is gone," a red-eyed woman mumbled as she passed Michal. "All we hear is defeat and retreat. Soon, the British will have Pretoria, and then we have nothing. They have taken the land the Lord granted us, which we wrestled from the wilderness."

"*Een vrije volk zijn wij*," Jacoba encouraged. "A free people are we."

"We are free no longer," the woman said. When she raised her head, Jacoba saw infinite sadness, and something behind it: anger and hatred.

"We will still fight," Jacoba said. "There are those among us who will continue to fight."

"You are in the House of God," the predikant reminded. "This is no place to talk about fighting."

"We will leave the church," Michal agreed. "Come, Jacoba."

Piet was already at the door, his hat in his hand, as he nodded uncomfortably to the predikant. "I have not been inside a church for years," he admitted. "I do not know what to do."

The predikant smiled sadly. "God is everywhere," he said. "He knows the goodness in your heart whether you are on the, in His house or on the battlefield."

"I have killed men," Piet admitted.

"The Lord knows that, too," the predikant told him. "Ask forgiveness, and He will grant it."

Piet hesitated momentarily, nodded again and stepped outside, replacing his hat.

Jacoba had gathered a small knot of women, some of whom looked enviously at her rifle and travel-stained clothing.

"We cannot all fight the enemy," one woman said. "I cannot ride a horse and shoot like a man. I am sixty years old, with three children and six grandchildren."

Jacoba realised the women were looking to her for encouragement and leadership. "There are other ways of fighting apart from shooting Khaki," she told them, moving away from the church. The predikant was correct; it seemed like sacrilege to discuss war in the shadow of God's house. "You can give information to the commandos. You can count the Rooinecks and tell the fighters where they are, what regiments there are and how many. You can sing the *Transvaalse Volkslied* and refuse to talk to the British. You can unsettle their horses and set them loose."

Jacoba searched for inspiration as they stood underneath a shady tree. The women gathered round, listening, some in mourning clothes, others dressed for church. They listened to Jacoba's words, nodding through their tears, eager to help, willing to do all they could for the Republic.

"The younger women, those without family, can fight as I do," Jacoba said as her imagination soared. "You can form a commando of women, an Amazon Corps, to fight the British." She remembered something Captain Baird had said. "The British do not make war on women, they say, so they would hesitate to fire on a body of female warriors."*

"When they shot my son, they made war on me," a thin-faced, sad-eyed woman in her forties said. "When they killed him, they killed most of me. What is left will fight them."

Seeing the gathering under the tree, more women joined them, with a few men standing at the fringes, uncomfortably aware they were not included.

"What do you want us to do?" a middle-aged woman shouted. "Tell us what to do!"

"Jacoba!" Michal shouted above the crowd. "We cannot stay here! Roberts' scouts are only a few miles away. We must leave the town!"

"Go then!" Jacoba said. "I will join you later!"

"The British will shoot you," Michal shouted. "Or send you to St Helena!"

"They don't make war on women!" Jacoba replied. "Go!" She wanted to speak to the women without men interfering. "Ride, Michal!" She watched as Michal pulled his horse around and trotted away. Piet held her gaze, lifted a hand in farewell and followed Michal, with the dogs at his horse's hooves and the dust

---

* The Boer women were extremely unhappy at the British occupation. Shortly before Roberts arrived in Pretoria, there was talk of an Amazon Corps to fight the advancing British, although the idea never took shape.

of his passage lingering for a few moments before it settled on the ground.

Jacoba watched the men ride away before she continued her conversation.

"All right, ladies," Jacoba said. "Most of us cannot fight the British like the men tried, with bullets and cannon, but we will make them unwelcome in other ways and encourage our men to keep resisting."

The women listened, some in tears, others with a dawning of renewed hope. One woman pulled her young son to her in undisguised fear as they heard the drumbeats of approaching hooves.

Jacoba finished talking and looked up. "Now get back to your homes, ladies, and get ready. Khaki is coming!"

ROBERTS' TRIUMPHAL ADVANCE THROUGH THE TRANSVAAL continued, with Pretoria next to fall. Andrew remembered the Transvaal's capital from his previous travels but had forgotten how attractive the town was. Pretoria was small, with a population of around twelve thousand, well shaded by trees, with church spires thrusting to an azure heaven, and even some industry to prove the Republic held more than farmers and gold diggers.

As Andrew rode through Pretoria at the head of his men, he noted the various architectural styles and the number of large, prosperous houses. Most of the shops remained open, with the proprietors hoping for a rush of business from Roberts' army, although the ordinary British ranker had little disposable cash.

Pretoria's streets were as wide as Andrew remembered. They were also dusty, as none were paved. Andrew rode down Church Street, wary in case an angry Boer had remained behind for a final shot at the invaders, but there was no resistance. Most of the inhabitants seemed to have remained, although Andrew noticed many more women than men among the sullen spectators.

"Look at all these broken people," Leslie said. He grinned. "They were laughing when they pushed us out of Jo'burg, but they're not laughing now!" He raised his voice to a shout. "You're not laughing now, are you?"

"Keep quiet," Andrew snarled. "It's bad enough for them watching us parade through their capital."

"It's not bad enough, sir," Leslie said. "We should make them sing *God Save the Queen* and swear an oath of loyalty to the Crown."

"If anything would make them dislike us more, that would do it," Andrew said. "Watch for snipers and keep your mouth shut, Leslie."

The army was in high spirits as it marched through Pretoria. That morning, an advance party had rescued scores of officers from a Boer prisoner-of-war camp. The Boers had held the officers in a long hut surrounded by barbed wire on the outskirts of Pretoria. Although the Boers had treated their prisoners well, the men were still glad to be free.

After the scouts had ridden through the town, Roberts led the main army into Pretoria. The British made a fine display, with over twenty-five thousand men, nearly six thousand horses, over a hundred pieces of artillery, and seventy-six machine guns. Andrew only glanced at the soldiers, preferring to watch the crowds who witnessed their arrival.

He saw weeping civilians watching the British alongside nutmeg-brown-faced men who he guessed had faced the invaders along the barrel of a Mauser a few weeks before. One group of women stood at the corner of Church Square, staring at the marching men. They were singing, and although Andrew could not make out the song, he guessed it was not *God Save the Queen*.

As Lord Roberts led the army into Church Square, the women removed their bonnets and replaced them with flat straw hats, each with a Vierkleur ribbon wound around the crown.

Leslie swore, glaring at the women, who returned his gaze with more cold hatred than Andrew had ever experienced. As the Dragoons came level, the women chanted a single phrase.

"*Een vrije volk zijn wij,*" they shouted. "A free people are we."

"We might have defeated the men in battle," Sinton said, "but the women don't like us."

"No, they don't," Andrew agreed.

The women stepped forward, defying the dusty, sweating, yet good-humoured soldiers who endeavoured to keep them in place. Each one sang at the top of her voice.

"Ken jy die Volk vol heldemoed
en tog so lank verkneg
Hy het geoffer goed en bloed
vir Vryheid en vir reg
Kom burgers! laat die vlae wapper
Ons lyding is verby
Roem in die sege van onse dapp'res
'n Vrye volk is ons!
'n Vrye volk, 'n Vrye volk
'n Vrye, Vrye volk is ons!"

Andrew listened to the words, recognised the spirit behind them and lifted his hat in a genuine, if ironic, salute. He translated the words as the women sang:

"Know ye the folk full of heroism,
And yet, so long oppressed?
It hath offered property and blood
For freedom and for righteousness.
Come, citizens! Let the flags wave
Our suffering is over;
Praise the victories of our braves:
That free folk are we!
That free folk, that free folk,

That free, free folk are we!"

Andrew halted his Dragoons to act as a barrier between the women and the passing soldiers. In response, they sang all the louder, shouting their defiance to the invaders.

Andrew ran his gaze over them. They were all ages, from teenagers to elderly grandmothers and great-grandmothers. They were mostly townswomen, but with some in traditional Boer clothes who may have come from the farthest reaches of the veldt.

As one woman stepped forward, staring into the face of an embarrassed Dragoon, Andrew recognised her. *That's Jacoba Fourie,* he told himself. *The woman with the broken spoke on her wagon.*

Andrew started as Jacoba nearly shouted out the Transvaal National Anthem with tears in her eyes and a glazed, near-hypnotised expression on her face.

She does not recognise me.

"Move on," Andrew ordered the Dragoons when the women stopped singing. He led his men into Church Square, where Roberts and his staff officers sat proudly erect on their horses. The British and Colonial troops filed into the square and stood to attention while somebody hauled down the Transvaal Vierkleur and hoisted the Union flag to cheers and tears from the British and Uitlanders in the crowd.

After Lord Roberts inspected the troops, he dismissed them. Some immediately sat beside the road.

"Thank God the war is over," one weary corporal said.

Andrew saw Jacoba step across to the corporal. "Tommy Atkins," she hissed in his ear. "The war has just begun. Free folk are we!"

As the corporal looked up in surprise, Jacoba stepped back. For a second, Andrew thought she was going to slap the man, but she turned away with her skirt flicking the corporal's shoulder. She walked away with her head held high, and Andrew noticed the women who had been with her scattered among the crowd.

What mischief are you planning, my little Boer virago? Andrew wondered.

"That's a brave woman," Andrew said to Sinton.

"They know they're safe," Sinton replied carelessly. "We don't shoot women."

Andrew nodded. "Perhaps not," he agreed, smiling as he thought of Jacoba fixing her wagon. "She is some woman."

Sinton laughed. "You'd better not let Mrs Baird hear you saying that."

"I haven't heard from Mariana for weeks," he said, closing his mouth hastily in case he said too much. However, Sinton was either too diplomatic to reply or had not heard, for he changed the conversation.

"I hope we free the other prisoners of war soon."

"So do I," Andrew said, glad of an escape. He tried to push thoughts of Mariana from his mind, but seeing Jacoba had once again reawakened memories of Elaine.

CHAPTER 37

TRANSVAAL

JUNE 1900

"Roberts has sent a brigade to free the prisoners," General Jacobus Herculaas de la Rey said. "We will not allow that to happen."

Michal had never met de la Rey but joined any commando that promised to continue the struggle. Better known as Koos de la Rey or the Lion of West Transvaal, Jacobus de la Rey was a veteran of the Basotho War of 1865, the war against Sekhukhune in 1876, and the 1880 war with the British. When war broke out in 1899, his victorious attack on a British armoured train in 1899 made him famous. He also fought at Modder River and Magersfontein.

At a time when the Boers were fleeing before the victorious British army and many men were returning to their farms, warriors such as de la Rey attracted the most resolute and defiant of the fighters.

"What shall we do, Commandant?" Jacoba asked.

De la Rey passed stern eyes over his men. "We'll take whatever action is best according to circumstances," he said.

De la Rey had a strong commando of some two thousand hard-bitten riders, many of them veterans, backed by four pieces of artillery. Posting pickets ahead to harass the British advance, de la Rey was determined to damage the enemy. He had positioned his men between the railway, the natural axis of the British advance, and the barbed wire enclosure in which the Boers held the British prisoners. Most of the three hundred prison guards were either old or very young men unfit to ride with the fighting commandos. With ten prisoners to each guard and news of Roberts' capture of Pretoria quickly spreading, the atmosphere was of tense excitement.

Michal led his small corporalship to the centre of the Boer force, determined to continue the fight. Piet was as emotionless as ever, staring across the veldt in the direction they knew the British would come, while Jacoba was trembling.

"Are you all right, Jacoba?" Michal asked.

"Ja," Jacoba replied shortly. "I am ready to kill Khaki."

Michal glanced at Piet, who shook his head warningly.

"We will get our chance," Michal said.

"Kill Khaki," Jacoba repeated, staring forward. Her knuckles were white against her tanned hands as she gripped her Mauser. "Kill Khaki."

"Here they come," Piet said quietly. "I hear a train coming."

The commando spread alongside the railway track, with men easing back their rifle bolts and a few saying a short prayer. Michal lay prone on the ground, rested his rifle barrel on a suitable rock and waited. He saw smoke in the distance and a rising ribbon of dust as the British brigade marched to free the prisoners.

"They must have the train to bring back their men," Piet said.

Jacoba nodded and laughed high-pitched. Her mouth was open, and her pink tongue licked at dry lips.

"Listen!" Jacoba lifted her head. "Gunfire!"

Michal nodded. The Boers looked up as their forward picket returned, galloping backwards within a blanket of dust.

"Khaki!" they shouted. "Khaki on grey horses!"

"Grey horses! That's the 2nd Dragoons!" de la Rey said. "The Scots Greys."

"I don't want the Scots Dragoons," Jacoba said. "I want the Royal Malverns!"

Michal glanced at the prison camp when he heard a rising noise. Prisoners stood on the roofs of their huts, cheering when they saw the Scots Greys trotting across the veldt, driving a group of Boers before them.

"Look!" Michal pointed to the prison compound. "The prisoners are escaping!"

The men on the hut roofs told their comrades what was happening, and hundreds of men charged forward. Ignoring the bewildered guards, they grabbed their belongings, scrambled over the wire fence and ran towards the advancing Dragoons.

"Fire at them!" Jacoba shouted. "Kill the Khaki!"

"Don't shoot!" de la Rey countermanded, holding up a hand.

The Boers held their fire.

De la Rey gave an order, and his artillery fired a salvo of warning shots to drive the prisoners back. Some men hesitated when the shells exploded, but most continued running forward.

"Stop firing," de la Rey ordered.

"Why?" Jacoba asked. "We are entitled to kill them! They will rejoin their regiments and fight against us! They are handsuppers, men who have surrendered!"

"I won't kill men who have no means of fighting back," de la Rey said.

As the Boer guns fell silent, Captain Maude's squadron of Scots Greys greeted the released prisoners. More men poured from the prison camp, jubilant at their release as de la Rey withdrew his commando.

Jacoba watched, nearly crying in frustration, as the British rescued the prisoners who flooded from the camp.

"They are hands-uppers!" Jacoba said. "They should not rejoin the army."

Colonel Porter rescued over three thousand prisoners, too many for the train to hold. Jacoba watched as more than two thousand released men trudged the thirteen miles back to Pretoria. Weak from imprisonment, malnourished and exhausted, they moved slowly to be housed in a special camp and fed and cared for until doctors deemed them fit to return to their units. While officers interviewed the men to find out where and why they surrendered, many slipped out of barracks to seek drink and infest the streets of Pretoria.

"We are handing victory to the British," Jacoba said as they rode away. "Every soldier we kill is one less to infest our land."

"We are a civilised people," Michal said. "We are not brute beasts to massacre unarmed men as they run to freedom."

"They are the Khaki!" Jacoba said. "They are the enemy of our blood!"

"They are men sent here by their queen," Piet said soberly. "They are like us, fighting for their country."

"Many of us have stopped fighting," Michal said. "Even some of our leaders are talking of surrender."

"Are you thinking of joining them?" Jacoba asked fiercely.

"No." Michal removed his hat, swept back his hair and gave her his old grin. Despite the new lines on his face and the deep weariness of his eyes, Jacoba thought he retained his old boyish spirit.

"I am glad to hear that," Jacoba said. "De la Rey said that if the Republic's leaders surrendered, he would trek north and found his own republic. Would you join him?"

"Not yet," Michal said. "I would fight here until there was no more hope."

Jacoba eyed him approvingly. "Good," she said. "The de Wets are still fighting the Rooinecks, as are the van Colliers."

"Then we shall join Piet or Christiaan de Wet," Michal said, laughing. "Our three rifles will surely turn the tide."

"Later," Jacoba said. "We can join one of the de Wets later."

"Later?" Michal was confused.

"Jacoba has some personal business to complete first," Piet understood. "Is that not so, Jacoba?"

"I must kill the man who murdered my Hendrik," Jacoba said. "I will kill Captain Andrew Baird."

"Jacoba will have no peace until she has dealt with Captain Baird," Piet said quietly to Michal. "Her mind will have no peace until then."

Michal thought of Jacoba's demands to open fire on the unarmed British prisoners. "We had better find Captain Baird," he said. "De Wet will have to struggle on without our help."

"He will miss our rifles," Piet said without altering his expression.

"He will have to wait," Michal said. "Jacoba's mind is more important." He felt Jacoba watching him and smiled inwardly.

She is a fine-looking woman and a good patriot. She will make me a good wife.

CHAPTER 38

TRANSVAAL

JUNE 1900

"De Wet has been busy," Sinton said. "He's attacked Roodewal Station and grabbed £100,000 of stores and burned hundreds of mailbags."

Andrew frowned. The British could always find more stores, but mail was more precious than ammunition or gold. Every soldier, from the newest recruit to the most senior general, looked forward to receiving letters from home, and caring families often sent small gifts and luxuries. Regular mail deliveries kept up morale, giving men a reason for enduring harsh conditions on campaign.

Maybe de Wet has stolen and burned Mariana's letters, which is why I have not heard from her for so long.

"We cannot communicate with Bloemfontein," Sinton said. "De Wet and the van Colliers have cut the railway line again. It's a damned unsportsmanlike, uncivilised, spiteful act." He tapped his rifle. "By God, sir, I'd like to have de Wet in my sights."

HOLDING FOR THE QUEEN

"He's well south of us," Andrew said. "We're heading north." He scanned the orders of the day. "It seems that some Boers are surrendering. We are taking away their rifles and allowing them back to their farms. Christiaan de Wet is causing trouble, but he's fighting a losing war."

"Boer resistance is crumbling," Sinton said with satisfaction.

"They'll surrender one by one until the sensible, peace-loving Burghers recognise that men like de Wet, the van Colliers and de la Rey are rebels against responsible British rule."

While de Wet was burning wives' and mothers' letters, General Buller pushed through the Boer positions at Botha's Pass and Alleman's Nek before marching into the Transvaal.

"We now have two British armies in the Transvaal," Andrew said, "and only scattered guerrilla bands opposing us."

The Natal Dragoons sat in their camp outside Pretoria, waiting for orders as the war raged without them. Increasingly irritated by de Wet's guerrilla actions, Roberts ordered more draconian action. Believing that farms close to the places where de Wet cut the railway line aided the enemy, he sent British soldiers to burn the houses and arrest the farmers.

"The farmers might be completely innocent," Sinton said.

"No Boer is completely innocent," Leslie contradicted Sinton. "They'll support de Wet."

When Roberts went a step further and placed Boer hostages on military trains, the British public protested. Roberts immediately stopped the practice, much to Leslie's disgust.

"We should do everything we can to win this war quickly," Leslie said. "I hope the civilians in Britain are as quick to criticise Roberts' methods when de Wet kills their sons."

"Forget de Wet for the present," Andrew advised. "We still have Botha to worry about. He's gathered most of the still-active Boers, and he's digging himself in about fifteen miles to the east."

"Is he going to stand and fight?" Sinton asked hopefully.

"It looks like it," Andrew replied.

"Then we can smash him," Sinton said. "I hope Bobs sends us to help rather than leave us mouldering in camp."

Andrew grinned. "Your wish is granted, Lieutenant. We leave in two days. I hope you've enjoyed your rest." He enjoyed the slow smile that spread across Sinton's face.

STRONG SUNLIGHT REFLECTED FROM THE TWIN STEEL RAILWAY lines, which announced the progress of civilisation. Only a few decades previously, the area had been a pristine wilderness, with perhaps some native kraals and herds of cattle. Now, two modern armies contested for supremacy.

Louis Botha had taken a position on a line of kopjes overlooking the railway line, effectively blocking Roberts' progress without firing a shot.

"Survey the land, Baird," Roberts ordered.

Andrew nodded and led his Dragoons to patrol in front of the army.

"Extended order," Andrew ordered. "Watch out for artillery or any mounted attacks."

After weeks of campaigning, the Dragoons were seasoned professionals and obeyed without question.

"Corporal Harwood, take three men and scout ahead." Andrew watched as Harwood selected Hobart, Conway and Kerr, one of the Natal men.

Andrew called up Sinton and Leslie and showed them their position on the map.

"The railway here stretches east to Middelburg, where the Transvaal government has retreated to, and on to the Mozambique border and Lourenço Marques," Andrew said. "That's the Boers' only lifeline to the outside world."

"If we cut it, the Boers are trapped," Leslie said.

Andrew grunted. "Lord Roberts is a few miles away with 14,000 men, seventy pieces of artillery and a few pompoms.

Surely more than enough to deal with the ragtag remains of Botha's army."

"It seems a long time since Black Week," Sinton said.

Andrew agreed. "The defeats of the early months of the war are behind us. A victorious end to the war is certain, and then it's home."

"Botha wanted to surrender, you know," Sinton said. "President Steyn of the Orange Free State persuaded him to continue the fight."

"The Orange River Colony now," Leslie said. "Roberts changed the name."

"The Boers haven't accepted the change," Sinton replied quietly.

Botha's five thousand Burghers, the die-hards who refused to surrender, gathered at the Donkerhoek Pass at the Magaliesberg range, ready to dispute the British access to the northern Transvaal.

"It's all over bar the shouting," Sinton said. "Botha doesn't want to fight."

Andrew was not so sure. He had sufficient experience of war to know that nothing was ever certain. The British were undoubtedly in the ascendancy, but Roberts' army was hundreds of miles from its supply base, with de Wet's men running riot, cutting the railway whenever they felt inclined.

Andrew scouted both sides of the Donkerhoek Pass, noting every Boer position before reporting to the Field Marshal.

"What have you discovered, Baird?" Roberts asked.

"Botha must be afraid you'll outflank him, sir," Andrew said. "He's spread his men right along the Magaliesberg, with the Donkerhoek Pass roughly in the centre. He's not in any depth anywhere, but stronger at the flanks than in the centre." He spread out his map and indicated the Boers' positions.

"He expects a flanking attack," Roberts said, half smiling as he pulled at his moustache. "He knows I don't like going through the front door."

"He has a front of around twenty-five miles, sir," Andrew said, "and I believe Botha commands the left flank and De la Rey the right."

"Thank you, Baird," Roberts said. "We'll give Botha what he expects and beat him at his own game." He lifted his voice. "Hamilton, you command 3,000 cavalry and 2,200 infantry. Take your men past the Bronberg Ridge south of De la Rey and capture Diamond Hill. General French, take your men, cavalry and mounted infantry to the north and outflank Botha. We'll take him in a pincer movement."

"Yes, sir." The two generals inspected the map before departing to organise their men.

"Pole-Carew," Roberts addressed the Cornishman, Lieutenant-General Sir Reginald Pole-Carew, a veteran of the Second Afghan War and Modder River. "You will remain opposite the Boers' centre as a decoy. Wait at the Pienaars River and have your artillery covering the road and railway. Move forward when French and Hamilton's columns meet behind Botha's lines."

"Yes, sir," Pole-Carew replied.

"Baird, go with Hamilton."

Andrew led his Dragoons to support Hamilton, ensuring he wore his lucky scarf. He anticipated and ignored Leslie's envious glance.

"Dismount your Dragoons and use them as infantry," Hamilton ordered. "They'll be better on foot than mixing their ponies with the cavalry chargers."

As always, Ian Hamilton was in his element in battle, with his eyes laughing as he strolled around his command, nearly inviting the Boers to shoot at him.

The Dragoons were unhappy at dismounting until Andrew tagged them onto the Royal Malverns, who most of them knew.

Sergeant Kenny saluted Andrew. "Did you miss us, sir?"

"Every hour of every day, Sergeant," Andrew replied.

He looked to the right and left as the infantry began to ascend Diamond Hill, another ubiquitous African ridge topped by a plateau. Although the Boers' defence lines were slender, they stretched beyond the British flanks.

"We'll have to push hard at the centre," Andrew said. "And move quickly, or we'll take casualties from both sides."

Sinton nodded, while Leslie looked slightly sick.

As soon as the British began the climb, Boer artillery opened fire, with the Mausers a moment later. The battle assumed the usual pattern of encounters with the Boers as infantry and dismounted cavalry moved against entrenched Boer riflemen.

"Here we go again!" Conway said. "We can't even see them; they can see everything we are doing and shoot us at will."

"Keep moving," Corporal Harcourt snarled. "The closer we get, the more chance we have of breaking their line."

Andrew saw bullets pinging against the rocks, slicing through the dry grass and burrowing into the ground. Another man threw up his hands and fell to lie still. Another life gone.

"They've caught us in a crossfire," Andrew shouted. "Watch your flanks, men, and push on!" He saw a Malvern corporal look suddenly surprised, staring at the red stain spreading across his stomach. The corporal dropped his rifle, crumpled to his knees and pitched face down on the grass. Another man screamed as a bullet hit his kidneys. He fell, kicking and writhing as his nearest comrade bent over him.

"Push on!" Andrew ordered as the Dragoons hesitated. He saw Hamilton's cavalry waver, with Boers on three sides firing into them and the sudden white flashes of artillery. Shrapnel hammered above, sending deadly sharp steel shards, and more men fell.

"Come on, Dragoons!" Andrew shouted, but the advance had stalled. Men were finding cover behind rocks as they returned the Boer fire. Andrew realised the initial assault had failed. Rolling into a natural depression, he focussed his binoculars on the far flank, where French's cavalry had also halted and was exchanging musketry with De la Rey's commando. In the centre, Pole-Carew's men sat still, waiting for the success of the flanking columns as his artillery wasted ammunition on the sparsely defended centre.

Andrew cursed. He wanted the battle to end quickly rather than have his men endure another long, drawn-out mutual killing match. He heard a cheer from his left and saw the 12th Lancers try a gallant charge, only for the entrenched Boer riflemen to mow them down before they got close. Lieutenant-Colonel David Ogilvy, the 11th Earl of Airlie, died then, killed by the bullet of an unknown Transvaal farmer. Despite the gallantry, the charge failed, and the Boers pinned the British back.*

"This is horribly familiar," Sinton said, crouching behind a rock. "We are down here, unable to move forward and unwilling to move back, and the Boers are above us, shooting at everything that moves."

Andrew grunted and raised his voice. "Keep under cover, Dragoons, and shoot whenever you see a Boer!"

The British inched forward as the day eased into darkness, with musketry and the groans of the wounded polluting the night.

"Sit tight!" Andrew ordered and chivvied the stretcher-bearers to find the injured men.

"Happy to be back with the Malverns, eh, Baird?" Colonel Cradley asked calmly as he toured his men shortly after ten. The fighting had faded away, so only an occasional shot punctured the night. Some men fell asleep behind their rocks.

"It seems so, sir," Andrew replied. "Sinton, set every fourth man as sentry and allow the rest to get as much rest as possible. The Boers don't normally attack at night."

"Permission to take a patrol up and see what I can do, sir?" Sinton asked half an hour later.

"Granted," Andrew agreed. "Don't get yourself shot."

Sinton took two ex-Imperials and one Frontier veteran with

---

* There is a monument to the 11th Earl of Airlie on Tulloch Hill above Kirriemuir in Angus.

him, as men more used to moving quietly at night, but a sudden outbreak of musketry told Andrew the Boers were alert.

"Not a hope of a night advance, sir," Sinton reported as he scrambled back down fifteen minutes later. "They have tripwires out, and their pickets are alert and waiting for us."

"At least we learned something," Andrew said.

The night passed slowly, with an occasional outbreak of firing from abortive patrols or nervous sentries. The following morning, Pole-Carew sent reinforcements, and Hamilton tried again, pushing men up the hill against the concealed Boer riflemen.

"Is this an example of an irresistible force meeting an immovable object?" Sinton asked as another attempted advance gained a hundred yards at the expense of a dozen casualties.

"The days of Magersfontein and Spion Kop are over," Cradley grated. "We know how they fight and know we can defeat them. Push on!"

The British advanced grimly, with Hamilton sending wave after wave of attacks up Diamond Hill. Andrew trusted to the luck of his scarf and glanced hopefully at the opposite flank. Heavy firing from the flank proved that French was also engaged, and Andrew wondered at the stubbornness of Boer resistance even when their defeat was inevitable.

Hamilton was equally stubborn. He progressed a few yards, consolidated his position, and advanced again, with the constant crackle of rifles a backdrop to every movement. Khaki-clad bodies freckled the hill behind the forward British line and the stretcher-bearers were busy.

"Push on!" Andrew saw a line of slouch hats in front as the Dragoons and Malverns rushed another ten yards closer to the Boers. He slammed down behind a rock, ducked as a bullet whistled above his head, fired at a careless defender and saw a slight wavering from the enemy.

"The Boers won't hold much longer!" Cradley shouted. "We have the beating of them!"

As the grim British advance closed on them, the Boers on

Diamond Hill withdrew, and the infantry scrambled to the top of the plateau.

The men cheered as they reached the summit, with the Boers retiring before them. It was a victory of dogged courage rather than a glorious charge.

"We've beaten them again!" Sinton said as the British took possession of the hill.

Andrew agreed. He counted his men and found one short. "Where's Trooper O'Hara?"

"Wounded, sir," Corporal Harwood reported. "The stretcher-bearers took him down the hill."

"Is he bad?"

"I don't know, sir," Harwood said.

"We'll find out later," Andrew said. He checked the time, swearing when he saw something—either a stray bullet or a chip of rock—had hit his watch. The case was dented, and the glass face cracked right across.

If my watch hadn't been there, the bullet would have hit me instead. Andrew fingered his scarf. *My lucky scarf worked again. Thank you, my little Boer lady. You may be a dedicated Transvaal Republican, but you've proved a true friend. I hope we meet again after the war.*

Even with Diamond Hill in British hands, the Boers elsewhere clung on through a long day and slipped quietly away after dark.

"Botha's not a fool," Andrew said. "He knows he must keep his army intact to retain some hope of fighting on. He has delayed Roberts, inflicted a couple of hundred casualties and withdrawn. We have pushed further towards the north of the Transvaal; both sides can be satisfied."

O'Hara and the other casualties might not agree. Is any victory worth the price of killed and wounded men?

CHAPTER 39

BRANDWATER BASIN, ORANGE FREE STATE

JULY 1900

After the hard-won victory of Diamond Hill, the British advance continued, pushing the remaining Boer army into the furthest corners of their territory.

"Baird!" Roberts summoned Andrew to his side. "I am transferring your unit."

"Sir?" Andrew replied. He had hoped to remain with Roberts' army until the end of the campaign.

"Your men and expertise will be better utilised in the Drakensberg with General Hunter," French told him. "I have made the arrangements to transport you there."

"Yes, sir." Andrew knew he could not argue with a field marshal. "When do we leave, sir?"

Roberts' kindly eyes surveyed Andrew. "This afternoon, Baird. I wish you all the best." He turned away to concentrate on other matters.

The Natal Dragoons were not happy about another long

move from the north Transvaal front to the north-eastern Orange Free State. The regulars groused but accepted the transfer with the philosophical phlegm of British soldiers, while the colonials were more vocal. The journey was long and frustrating, but eventually, the Dragoons joined General Hunter's army.

"Glad to have you with us, Baird," General Archibald Hunter knew Andrew from the raid on Gun Hill. "We've pushed the Boers hard against the mountains. Bring your officers to me."

Sinton and Leslie joined them as Hunter spread a map on his rickety campaign table.

"Look." Hunter spread a map on the table, weighed down the corners with stones, and showed the Dragoon officers their position. "The Boers have moved into the Brandwater Basin, a massive U-shaped valley, with the and Roodebergen ranges hemming them in. The Drakensberg is our ally, gentlemen; your men are used to operating among mountains."

Andrew nodded. "The Free Staters have trapped themselves, sir. With the mountains all around and the Caledon River at the foot, they have reduced their area of manoeuvrability, which is their greatest asset."

"Who is all here, sir?" Sinton asked.

"Everyone that matters from the Orange Free State," Hunter replied. "President Steyn, the de Wet brothers, Philip Botha, Marthinus Prinsloo and all the rest."

"How many men, sir?" Andrew asked.

"We estimate about four thousand," Hunter said. "I hope to bring them to battle here or round up as many as possible. We particularly want the de Wet brothers. We regard them as the most dangerous guerrilla leaders, along with the van Colliers, ranging free somewhere in the west." He grinned, with white teeth showing behind his moustache. "Christiaan de Wet is the Orange Free State's new Commander-in-Chief."

Leslie grunted. "Being Boers, they will all argue who is in charge. Every Boer believes he should be in command."

"That is one of their weaknesses," Hunter agreed. "I am positioning my men to surround the basin, with detachments moving towards the passes and neks to prevent a Boer breakout."

"Are your men all in position yet, sir?" Andrew asked.

"No," Hunter replied. "Some are still marching to the passes. Go inside with your men, Baird, and see what's happening," Hunter ordered. "I remember you from Ladysmith. You're no fool."

"Thank you, sir," Andrew had replied, although he realised Hunter was sending him into the forefront of battle, like Uriah the Hittite.

Is Hunter a friend of Major Dixon's? Andrew wondered, then recognised that tiredness made him stupid.

"I will expect your messages at eleven hundred hours, Baird. That's your allotted time. My messengers will be waiting for your helio."

"Yes, sir," Andrew said, recognising the dismissal.

When they entered the horseshoe of mountains, Andrew increased his caution, strengthening the scouts and warning everybody to watch for Boers. "An animal is at its most dangerous when cornered," he reminded his men. He looked around him at the surrounding peaks. "They call this the Brandwater Basin," he said. "I can't think why the Boers have ridden here. They've trapped themselves."

Sinton nodded. "They prepared for war, invaded our territory, abused our people in their country, stole our gold and looted our towns. In October last year, they seemed to be in the ascendancy. They tweaked the British lion's tail, and we responded with Buller, Roberts and Kitchener, the lion's teeth and claws."

"And this basin is where it ends," Andrew said. "General Hunter won't let them escape from here."

Hunter commanded a formidable force, including MacDonald's Highland Brigade, veterans of Modder River, Magersfontein and Paardeberg, a host of yeomanry and locally raised mounted units, the New Zealand Mounted Infantry and artillery batteries.

He also had the Lovat Scouts, a newly raised unit of ghillies and gamekeepers from the northern Scottish Highlands who were all expert trackers and first-rate shots.

"I think Hunter is slow in blocking all the entrances to the basin," Leslie said as the Dragoons moved slowly along a narrow nek.

"Maybe," Andrew conceded, agreeing with Leslie for once. He had examined the map and led his Dragoons over the roughest and least considered nek, trusting in their small numbers and fitness to negotiate the rough terrain. "In war, nothing is as easy as it looks to civilians, and nothing goes exactly according to plan."

"Hunter is terribly slow," Leslie repeated.

"He has terrible logistic problems," Andrew reminded, "and poor-quality maps to work with. The Lovat Scouts are helping him map the area, but other units are less reliable. That's why he's sent us in to help the Lovats." He looked over his shoulder as he heard a clatter behind him. "Be careful with that heliograph, damn it!"

The basin's interior was riven with river valleys, an uneven area of rough ground, in which the different Boer commandos camped wherever seemed more convenient for them. Smoke from their campfires drifted into the clear mountain air, sweet-smelling yet giving away their positions to the predatory Dragoons.

"We could attack some of the smaller commandos," Sinton said. "Make them believe Hunter's entire army is in the basin."

"Then what?" Andrew asked.

"They would attempt to flee, and General Hunter would flatten them," Sinton said.

"Hunter hasn't got all his men in position yet," Andrew reminded. "We'll just observe and report."

HOLDING FOR THE QUEEN

Jacoba watched the bustle as the Free State commandos spread across the basin, with every unit selecting a separate base and laagering its wagons around central fires. Servants outspanned the oxen, men knee-haltered the horses and allowed them to graze, and men sat in companionable groups, smoking and talking as the leaders discussed what was best to do.

"I wish the commandants would make up their minds," Michal said. "I don't like waiting."

"Nor do I," Jacoba agreed. "We should not be talking while Khaki is infesting our land. We should be shooting them!"

"I heard that." Christiaan de Wet had been passing as Jacoba spoke. He reined up his horse. "It's unusual for a woman to ride with a commando," he said, peering closer, "Jacoba Fourie, isn't it? Or rather Jacoba du Toit?"

"Yes," Jacoba said. "Jacoba du Toit."

When de Wet laughed, his neat beard seemed to leap with joy. "You organised the protest when Lord Roberts raised the British flag in Pretoria."

"I did," Jacoba admitted.

"And you thought of the idea of an Amazon Corps of women to fight the British," de Wet said. He nodded to Michal. "This basin is a trap, so I am leaving with my men. Do you want to join us with your corporalship, Michal Rheeder?"

"How do you know my name?" Michal asked.

"I know you have fought the Khaki since the beginning when others have given up," de Wet said. He looked around. "We have trapped ourselves in here, and the politicians do not know what to do. The British can use the dead ground and deep dongas to attack us, and we lack the space to evade their columns."

Jacoba nodded. "Even if we beat off a British attack," she said, "what good can we do here? The British can close the passes and hold us like prisoners."

De Wet smiled. "You have it," he said. "Are you with me when we leave?"

"We are," Michal said.

Jacoba watched as de Wet rode away. "There are things not being said," she decided. "I'll see what's happening."

"How will you find the truth?" Michal asked.

"I'll ask the wives," Jacoba replied with a rare smile. "Men confess things to their wives, and women talk to each other." An hour later, she returned, slid off her horse, and walked to Michal.

"The leaders, generals and commandants held a secret meeting," Jacoba told them. "After much argument, they decided to leave the basin, but I don't know where they are heading next."

Piet stuffed tobacco into the bowl of his pipe. "The British have us running from our shadows," he said. "We have too many generals, all with different ideas."

"We are leaving this bowl in three divisions. The divisions will leave over three successive days, with Christiaan de Wet in charge of the first," Jacoba said. "Christiaan de Wet's group will include President Steyn, Piet de Wet and Louis Botha."

"And it will include us," Michal said. "We are not staying here a moment longer than necessary."

Michal had camped his corporalship three hundred yards from de Wet's laager at Kaffir Kop. They watched the commotion as the commandos readied to leave the basin, with men mounting their horses and driving hundreds of wagons and carts towards the Slabbertsnek Pass. With de Wet in the lead, an array of commandos merged and headed up the unguarded nek in a long snake, five thousand yards long.

De Wet's column was the best-disciplined of any Boer force Michal had encountered. Scouts rode in front, then the fighters of the main force, with Steyn and the other politicians. Behind the politicians came the artillery with a powerful escort, the wagons, and a strong rearguard.

"We'll join the rearguard," Michal decided and merged with the efficient-looking men at the back of the column.

They rode up the entrance of the Slabbertsnek Pass, watching the long column of riders and wagons in front. Michal fretted at the slow passage, glanced at Jacoba and knew she felt the same.

"Somebody's watching us," Piet spoke without moving his head.

"Where?" Michal asked.

"A mile to the right, you'll see a copse of trees on the lower slopes. I saw the sun reflect on something there, either metal or glass."

"A British spy!" Jacoba hissed. "Watching us leave." She reached for her rifle.

"I'll tell the field cornet," Michal said and passed on the news.

Jan de Jong, the field cornet, was a flint-featured man in his thirties. He listened, glanced at the hillside and ordered his men to follow. "We will deal with the spy," he said. "Where there is one Rooineck, there will be more." Twenty-five of the Boer rearguard peeled off, hard-bitten veterans of conflict with the British who would shoot a khaki-clad soldier without compulsion.

The field cornet eyed the slope for a moment. "Ten men on the left side," he commanded, "ten on the right and the rest of us will attack straight up the middle."

Jacoba worked the bolt of her rifle. "If one of them wears a Vierkleur scarf," she said, "leave him for me. He murdered my husband."

De Jong passed the information on. "I lost a brother at Spion Kop," he said. "You can kill your Rooineck."

"THEY'VE SPOTTED US," SINTON WARNED AS HE SAW THE BOER rearguard split and a large body of men hurry towards the Dragoons' position.

Andrew lowered his binoculars. "They have. There must be six thousand Boers in the basin," he said. "Time to leave. We'll helio a message to General Hunter about the Boers heading for the nek and then get away."

"The Boers are coming fast," Leslie said.

"So they are," Andrew agreed. "Get back uphill and get the men ready to depart. Prepare the horses on the other side of the nek. Sinton, Murcot, Conway and I will remain here until the signallers send the message; we'll be with you immediately after."

Brightwood and Price, the signallers, were nervous when they saw the Boers heading towards them. "We've only got a small window to signal through," Brightwood said, pointing to a nick in the ridge, beyond which stretched the Orange River Colony where Hunter's signallers waited for the signal. Andrew's men were on a knoll above a group of trees with an extensive view over the basin.

Andrew checked his watch, swore when he remembered a Boer bullet had damaged it, and asked Sinton the time.

"Ten to eleven, sir," Sinton said.

"We can't signal until eleven," Andrew said. "That's the prearranged time."

The Boers were climbing rapidly towards them, moving from cover to cover and keeping low. Andrew nodded to Sinton. "Take the left flank, Sinton; I'll take the right. Murcot and Conway, you pin down the lads advancing right towards us."

Sinton fired first, sending a bullet ricocheting from a rounded boulder and over the shoulder of a too-casual attacker, and the Boers retaliated with half a dozen shots, all of which whined above Sinton's head.

Majuba, Andrew thought and stilled his nervous laughter. *Why does every skirmish and battle in this war remind me of Majuba?*

He fired twice in quick succession, seeing the Boers on the left flank throw themselves down. He worked the rifle bolt and fired again, more concerned with slowing down the approaching men than with hitting any of them.

Conway fired, swore and fired again. "Come on then, Boojers! Show yourselves, you bloody cowards!" He worked the bolt and fired a third time. "That's one less to fight for Oom Kruger!"

"What's the time, Sinton?" Andrew saw the signallers erecting the heliograph and remembered a similar scene in the previous Transvaal war.

"Seven minutes to eleven, sir!" Sinton shouted.

Still seven minutes before the signallers could heliograph. Andrew peered downhill, searching for movement. He saw a bush move against the direction of the breeze, took rapid aim and fired, worked the bolt and fired again, ducking down as three bullets crashed and whistled around him. He heard somebody groaning and knew he had found his mark.

My lucky scarf is still working, Andrew told himself.

Murcot shouted again, fired and ducked. "They're getting closer, sir," he said. "They're running up the hill like sailors to a brothel!"

Andrew felt something smash into his leg and glanced down. He already carried a wound on his left thigh and now saw fresh blood oozing three inches above his knee. *That must have been a chip from the rock,* he told himself. Another bullet whined past his right ear, and something burrowed into the ground at his feet. *They're getting closer.*

"What time is it?" Andrew yelled. He fired and began to reload, pushing bullets into his magazine one at a time.

"Three minutes to eleven, sir!" Sinton replied.

Andrew saw a rush of men on his right. Their slouch hats were the only indication they were Boers, as they all wore khaki clothing. *They must have looted our stores to get those uniforms,* Andrew thought abstractly.

Sinton fired and threw himself down as three Boers replied. "We can't hold them much longer, sir!"

Andrew glanced at the signallers, who were adjusting the heliograph mirror to get the best angle of the sun. Neither of them flinched when a Boer bullet chipped the rock beside them. Andrew slammed his now-full magazine into the rifle.

"One minute!" Sinton said.

Conway roared in pain and dropped his rifle, swearing. "The buggers hit my bundook, sir! They've smashed it to buggery and gone!"

Andrew heard the voice but was too busy aiming and firing to take any notice. He saw a Boer suddenly dash forward, took quick aim, fired and saw the man fall backwards with his mouth wide open in shock. Somebody fired from above and Andrew heard a yell.

"Natal Dragoons! Come on, the Dragoons!" Corporal Harwood half rose from behind a tree, fired and sank down again.

"Time!" Brightwood said calmly and began to work the heliograph. Andrew had scribbled a long message for them, giving details of the Boers' dispositions, numbers, and movements. The signallers sent the message by Morse Code as the skirmish continued beneath them.

Knowing the signallers were working as fast as possible, Andrew did not try to hurry them. Conway threw and rolled rocks down the hill, swearing at the Boers in a constant monotone. He attached the same copulative adjective to such a surprising variety of nouns that Andrew was impressed by his imagination.

The Boers were only seventy yards away, shifting between rocks, but Andrew, Murcot and Sinton were experienced in firing at moving targets, while Corporal Harwood had a better angle and caught them in a crossfire.

"Nearly done, sir!" Brightwood shouted.

"The Boers are above us!" Harwood roared.

Andrew swore. While he had concentrated on the Boers beneath them, another group had swarmed up the hill on their left flank.

"Brightwood! How long?" Andrew asked, flinching as a bullet zipped past his face. The Boers were closing in now, becoming bolder as they saw the small numbers that opposed them.

"All done, sir!" Brightwood shouted.

"Get out of it!" Andrew ordered. "Get up the hill and away!" He fired at the Boers on the left, worked the bolt, realised he was out of ammunition again and dropped behind a rock to reload. As he thrust the cartridges into the magazine, he heard Conway's shouting and a curious rumble.

"There's for you, Boojer bastards!" Conway shouted as he used his broken rifle to push a huge rock down the slope. The rock moved slowly, gathering more stones as it gained momentum until a small landslide descended on the approaching Boers.

Men leapt out of the way of the rolling stones, with Murcot standing, firing, working his bolt and firing again as the Boers frantically sought shelter.

"Well done, Conway," Andrew shouted. "Come on, lads! We're out of it! Head upwards!" He looked up to the nek, behind which Leslie would be waiting with the horses. It was seven hundred feet above them over a mixture of rocks and scree but with some bare patches and a few scattered trees. At that minute, the distance looked like seven hundred miles.

CHAPTER 40

BRANDWATER BASIN, ORANGE RIVER COLONY

JULY 1900

The signallers scrambled up, carrying the heliographs as they negotiated the slope. Andrew heard the rumble of Conway's landslide, with loose rocks crashing down and the yells of unfortunate men.

"Push on!" Andrew shouted. "Lieutenant Leslie is waiting with the horses on the nek!"

Andrew saw the Boers on the left flank moving to intercept them, most wearing British khaki, one young man bounding from rock to rock like a gazelle. The youngster's long hair flowed behind his hat, golden in the sunlight. Andrew wondered who he was for a moment, then powered on with the wound in his left leg nagging him and the breath rasping in his throat.

Sinton was to his right, slightly higher up the slope, slithering on an area of loose rock. Murcot was at his back, arms flailing as he tried to keep his balance. Boer bullets crashed and whined from the rocks, screaming this way and that.

Price yelled and grabbed at his leg. He looked over his shoulder, staggering as he struggled to carry the heliograph and his rifle.

"Dump the helio!" Andrew ordered.

"Sir?" Price queried the order, his face twisted in pain.

"Dump the helio!" Andrew repeated. "That's an order!"

Price looked shocked. "I can't, sir!"

"Your life is worth more than a blasted piece of equipment!" Andrew closed with the man and threw the heliograph to the ground, smashing it with his rifle butt. "Now get up that hill!"

Andrew saw that the Boer bullet had only grazed Price's leg, opening a wound that would fester unless cleaned and treated but would not yet incapacitate the signaller.

"Move!" Andrew shouted, very aware of the Boers pounding above them on the left.

"Catch us if you can, Boojers!" Conway taunted, rolling down more rocks and hoping to start another landslide.

"Save your breath for moving!" Andrew shouted. He looked upwards. The nek was still some four hundred feet away, with a thin grey mist creeping over the crest, blocking the sun. He only saw two Boers above them.

Sinton slid behind a tree, aimed his revolver and fired. The closest Boer staggered and fell. Sinton fired again, wounding the second Boer.

"Good shooting, Sinton!" Andrew shouted.

"Top of my class at Sandhurst, sir!" Sinton replied.

Corporal Harwood threw himself behind a rounded boulder, facing down the slope, gasping and sweating with effort. "You go on, sir! I'll hold them here."

"No!" Andrew said. "We'll all make it! Not far now." He saw Sinton on his left, holding a tree trunk as he caught his breath. "Keep moving, Lieutenant!"

Andrew heard the sudden shout of pain and saw Conway standing erect, holding his back with a curious expression on his face.

"They've got me," Conway said. He removed his hand, which was dripping with blood. "The buggers shot me." He turned to face downhill, and another bullet slammed into his chest, sending him staggering backwards, and then a third thumped into his stomach. Conway crumpled without another word to lie like a heap of khaki rags on the nameless African hill.

"Sir!" Andrew heard Sinton's voice as if from miles away. "Leave him, sir. He's gone!"

Andrew nodded. A thin mist crept over the nek, a hundred feet above, where Leslie would be waiting with the horses. One last effort, and they'd be there. Once on the nek, they could push the horses out of the basin and towards General Hunter's army.

One last effort!

Andrew glanced to his left, where Brightwood was helping the limping Price, and Harwood was crouching to fire downhill, spreading his shots to keep as many pursuers as possible under cover.

"Good man, Corporal!" Andrew shouted. "Now get moving! I'll cover you." He slid behind a thorn bush and faced downhill. He fired at the first movement he saw, rolled on his back to work the bolt and returned to his original position.

For the first time, Andrew had a clear view of his pursuers. He estimated about thirty Boers scrambling up the hillside, some firing but most making as heavy weather of the climb as the Dragoons had done. Andrew had expected the pursuit. He had not expected to see a woman among the Boers.

That's Jacoba Fourie, the woman who gave me the scarf and who led the singing in Pretoria. What the devil is she doing fighting with a commando?

"Sir!" Sinton shouted. "Come on! I'll cover you!"

Andrew fired another shot, deliberately avoiding Jacoba, worked the bolt, fired again and scrambled the final few feet to the nek.

"Leslie!" Andrew looked for the rest of his command and the horses that would carry them to safety. "Lieutenant Leslie!"

The nek was empty except for a grey, swirling mist.

Andrew looked around, but there was no sign of Leslie and the horses. "Sinton! Find Leslie! He might have taken the horses down the nek a little. Maybe we can't see him in the mist."

Corporal Harwood was lying on his stomach, firing downhill as the signallers sank onto the crest, keeping below the skyline.

Sinton scampered down the nek, kicking up loose stones. When he disappeared in the mist, Andrew peered around. The horses had left traces on the ground, with hoofprints heading back down towards the outside world.

"The lads have gone, sir," Harwood said, frantically reloading. "But the Boers haven't! They're getting closer."

Andrew nodded, firing to support Harwood. The signallers were gasping, with Price losing a lot of blood. Andrew realised his own wound was throbbing and beginning to stiffen.

"We can't wait here for the Boers to capture us," Andrew said. "Head over the nek. We'll lose them in the mist."

"Yes, sir," Harwood said. He fired three more rounds, rolled backwards, away from the edge, and stood up. "Come on, lads!" he said to the signallers. "Let's be having you. How's the leg, Price?"

"Not bad, Corporal," Price replied.

"Use your bundook as a crutch," Harwood said. "Brightwood and I will help you." He slung his rifle across his shoulder. "Mr Swinton will soon find the horses, and we'll have a nice comfortable seat for you."

Andrew peered into the mist. He saw the track winding downhill, too narrow and steep for any wagon and only negotiable by the most nimble of Basuto ponies. He could not see Leslie and the horses, and there was no sign of Sinton.

"Come on, men," Andrew said. "I'll take the rearguard."

They could not move quickly with an injured man but limped down the rough path. Andrew and Harwood took turns at the rear, circling every few steps to look behind them.

"Here's Lieutenant Sinton, sir!" Harwood said as a figure loomed ahead, the mist making him appear huge and misshapen.

Sinton was red-faced with exertion. "I couldn't see Leslie, sir," he reported. "Maybe he's taken the wrong turning."

"Maybe he has," Andrew said. *There are no wrong turnings up here. He's bolted and left us in the lurch.* "Come on, boys, we'll have to make it on foot. General Hunter is bound to have other patrols out!"

Andrew led them down the slope, moving in and out of the shifting mist. They supported Price, with Andrew hiding his wound as much as possible, although, after ten minutes, he felt the blood trickling down his leg.

The horses had left their mark on the track, and Andrew limped forward, still hoping to meet Leslie around every corner. His hope faded every few yards.

"I don't think Lieutenant Leslie has waited for us," Sinton said.

Andrew did not want to openly admit the possibility that a British officer would leave another in danger. "Something will have happened to him," he replied.

"That must be it, sir," Sinton agreed.

"Sir!" Harwood shouted from the rear. "The Boers are on the nek behind us!"

Andrew had expected the news. "Fire if you see them, Corporal," he said. "Keep moving, lads."

The mist thickened around Andrew's small party, encouraging them to hurry. Price gasped as he stumbled over a loose rock.

"Stick it, Pricey," Brightwood said, tightening his grip around Price's shoulders.

Andrew's small party slowed as the path narrowed further to a near-knife-edge with a precipitous drop on one side. Mist boiled upwards from the unseen bottom, with cold grey tendrils reaching towards the struggling men.

"At least the mist will help hide us from the Boers," Sinton said.

Andrew nodded. "Any help is welcome." He heard Harwood firing behind him, saw a Boer bullet plough a long furrow in the ground at his feet, and heard Sinton shout.

"They're ahead of us!"

Andrew looked forward, hoping Sinton was mistaken and Leslie had returned with the horses. His hope died when the figures loomed through the mist, strangely elongated but with the distinctive Boer slouch hats. Andrew swore as the Boers hurried up the nek, their voices distorted but floating before them.

"Sir?" Sinton looked quizzically at Andrew. "Orders, sir?"

Andrew thought rapidly. His handful of men were trapped on a narrow ridge with a more numerous enemy in front and behind. Andrew had little choice.

"Get down," he said. "Find some cover, and we'll hold out until help arrives."

They slid to the ground, huddling behind the many rocks to return the Boer fire. Andrew fired at shadowy figures in the mist, ducking as bullets whined and zipped around.

"They don't know how many we are," Andrew said. "Try and sound like an army."

It's a trick I've used before and might hold them off a little longer.

"Come on, C Company!" Sinton shouted. "D Company, take the right flank!"

The men yelled, shouting challenges that the mist swallowed as shots crashed and echoed.

After a few moments, the Boer musketry ended, and a man stepped forward, holding a white rag on the muzzle of his Mauser. Tall and young, he wore his slouch hat tipped back, and long blond hair lapped at his shoulders. Andrew recognised him from the assault up the hill.

"I would like to speak to your commander," the Boer shouted, raising his hat politely.

"I am Major Andrew Baird of the Natal Dragoons," Andrew said. He was aware of the long pause before the Boer replied. "Who are you?"

"I am Corporal Michal Rheeder, Major Baird, attached to Christiaan de Wet's commando."

"I will accept your surrender, Michal Rheeder," Andrew said. "Tell your men to throw down their arms and come forward with their hands up. When my relief arrives in a few moments, we'll escort you to General Hunter."

Michal shook his head, smiling. Andrew thought he looked young, except for the lines of strain and responsibility on his face. "No, meneer," he said. "We have you surrounded and outnumbered. You have no reinforcements coming, and you will have to surrender, or we will kill you and your men."

"We won't surrender!" Swinton shouted.

"Lieutenant Swinton has said all there is to say," Andrew told Michal. "We will not surrender."

"As you wish, Major Baird." Although Michal lifted his hat again, there was steel in his voice. He frowned at the scarf around Andrew's neck and withdrew with his rifle balanced over his shoulder.

CHAPTER 41

ORANGE RIVER COLONY

JULY 1900

"It is he," Michal said curtly as he unwrapped the white rag from his rifle.

Jacoba shuddered. "Captain Baird? The man who bayonetted my husband?"

"He is a major now and still wears your scarf, Jacoba."

"I will kill him," Jacoba said, standing so the mist shrouded her. "Major or captain, I want to kill him. I want nobody else to touch that Rooineck! He is mine to kill."

Jan De Jong frowned. "Why is that, Jacoba?"

"He killed my man. He murdered my husband," Jacoba said.

"It is war," the field cornet said. "Men kill each other in war." He edged back slightly, seeing the madness in Jacoba's eyes.

"He thrust a bayonet into Hendrik as he lay helpless on the ground," Jacoba said.

De Jong looked troubled as he glanced at Michal, who nodded.

"That is what happened," Michal said.

"I saw it happen," Piet confirmed quietly. "It was murder. Hendrik lay disarmed and helpless on the ground."

De Jong sighed. "Even good men can do evil things in war. Major Baird is yours to kill, Jacoba."

They looked up at a sudden commotion lower down the pass. The firing was intense for a few moments, died down to a few intermittent shots, and flared up again.

"Willem! See what is happening!" De Jong ordered.

Willem ran down the pass, sliding on loose stones but miraculously retaining his balance. He returned in a few moments.

"Khaki!" he said. "We have run into khaki and dispersed them, but many more are on the way."

"How many more?" De Jong asked.

"I don't know," Willem replied. "We have a hands-upper—a prisoner!"

"Fetch him," De Jong ordered.

Two Boers escorted the prisoner, a tall, bedraggled-looking man who looked around at his captors with wide eyes. He smiled at the Boers.

"What name do you bear?" De Jong asked.

"I am Lieutenant Damien Leslie of the Natal Dragoons, meneer, and I request you treat me fairly as a prisoner of war!"

"We will treat you fairly," De Jong promised.

"He is a Uitlander," Jacoba said.

Piet studied the prisoner through narrowed eyes. "I know this man," he said slowly, speaking around the pipe he held between his teeth. "His is a face I will never forget."

De Jong spoke directly to Leslie. "Are there more khaki soldiers coming?"

Leslie smiled. "Yes, meneer," he said. "General Hunter is approaching with his army—tens of thousands of men, infantry, cavalry and artillery."

"Baird must have sent a signal to General Hunter," Michal said.

"We'll have to leave before Hunter gets here," De Jong said.

"I want Baird first," Jacoba insisted, working the bolt of her rifle. "He murdered my Hendrik."

Piet removed the pipe from his mouth and jabbed the stem towards the prisoner. "Is this man Major Andrew Baird?"

"No; this man is Lieutenant Leslie," De Jong replied.

Piet nodded. "Then Major Baird did not murder your husband, Jacoba. I saw this man bayonet Hendrik twice."

Jacoba stared at Piet. "Are you sure?"

"The good Lord gave me eyes to see, and I saw this man bayonet Hendrik," Piet said quietly. "He was wearing a Vierkleur scarf."

"Then this man also murdered the Harebroeks, father and son," Jacoba's tone made everybody nearby stare at her.

Leslie looked from one to the other. "You made a mistake," he said, still smiling. "I didn't bayonet or murder anybody. It must have been Baird. He wears the lucky scarf, not me."

Piet began to clean his pipe. He pointed the stem at Leslie, shaking his head. "Do not add lies to your sins."

Everybody looked up as a young Boer ran up the track. "Jan! Khaki is coming!" The man looked agitated. "Thousands of them with mounted men and artillery."

De Jong nodded. "Return to De Wet's men at the Slabbertsnek Pass." He looked at Jacoba. "You will have to fight your Natal Dragoons another day, Jacoba. We don't want Hunter to trap us in the basin." He nodded to Leslie. "Let that man free. We have no room for prisoners."

"No!" Jacoba shouted. She looked at Piet and Michal. "We cannot let him go!"

"We must," Michal said. "A prisoner will slow us down."

When Jacoba saw Leslie's triumphant sneer, an image of Hendrik lying with a bayonet piercing his chest came to her. She aimed at him, compressing her lips.

"No, Jacoba," Michal pushed her rifle down. "We do not kill prisoners. Even things like this creature."

Jacoba glared at Michal and stormed away. Borrowing a scrap of white rag from a rider, she tied it on the end of her rifle and approached the waiting, wondering Dragoons.

"Is Major Andrew Baird there?"

"I am Major Andrew Baird," Andrew stepped forward with wisps of mist trailing from him. "We've met before, Jacoba Fourie."

"I am Jacoba du Toit," Jacoba said proudly. "I was Jacoba Fourie when we met, but I married Hendrik du Toit recently."

"Congratulations," Andrew said, wondering why Jacoba mentioned her private life. "I hope you have a happy marriage after this senseless war ends."

"One of your officers, Lieutenant Leslie, murdered my husband," Jacoba said.

Andrew heard the tremor in Jacoba's voice and saw the steel in her fine eyes. "Did Lieutenant Leslie kill Meneer du Toit in battle?" he asked.

"No. He bayonetted Hendrik as he lay helpless on the ground," Jacoba said.

"If that is correct," Andrew said, thinking quickly, "Lieutenant Leslie will stand before a court of law after the war and be tried, with witnesses to prove the facts. Until then, the law states he is innocent until proven guilty."

"Michal!" Jacoba shouted. "Bring Lieutenant Leslie here!" She faced Andrew again. "We are still under the protection of the white flag," she said.

Andrew knew many Boers had only a vague idea of the meaning of the white flag. "My men will not shoot," he promised. He saw Michal Rheeder propel Leslie in front of him.

"Here is your murderer," Jacoba said, pushing Leslie towards the small group of Dragoons.

Leslie stumbled forward, smiling.

Michal attached a white handkerchief to the muzzle of his rifle and lifted it as Leslie rejoined the Dragoons. Another dozen Boers appeared, with one tall, heavily bearded man leading them.

They appeared ghost-like in the mist, ethereal figures who could vanish at any time.

Andrew stepped aside to let Leslie pass.

"Where the hell were you when we needed you, Leslie?" Sinton snarled. "You were meant to wait for us with the horses!"

"Not now, Sinton!" Andrew snapped.

He saw, as if in slow motion, Jacoba remove the white rag from the muzzle of her rifle. Her mouth moved, the words seeming to be dragged from her throat.

"We do not shoot prisoners," Jacoba said. "But Lieutenant Leslie is no longer a prisoner, and I have removed the white flag!"

Guessing what was about to happen, Andrew opened his mouth to protest, but Jacoba lifted her rifle and fired.

Andrew saw the orange-white flash of the muzzle flare and the sudden shock on Leslie's face. The bullet struck him in the chest, the force knocking him backward. He roared as he fell, and Jacoba worked the bolt and fired again. Her second bullet entered Leslie's head under the chin and travelled upward to exit at the top of his skull in a welter of blood, brains and fragments of bone.

"No!" Andrew lifted a hand to stop his Dragoons from retaliating. He understood Jacoba's actions and knew the Boers could destroy his small command in seconds. He faced Jacoba. "You murdered that man!"

"I administered justice to a murderer and shot an enemy," Jacoba said. She replaced the white rag on her rifle. "We have spoken as friends, Major Baird, and we have spoken under the flag of truce. Next time we meet, we may be enemies and try to kill each other."

"I hope not," Andrew was very aware of the score of rifles pointing towards him and his small group. "I hope we can meet as friends after the war."

"It may be many years before you admit defeat, Major Baird," Jacoba said.

Andrew tried to ignore Leslie's crumpled corpse lying nearby. "You have lost the war, Jacoba."

"Major Baird," Jacoba said, "the war has just begun."

With a last look at Andrew, she backed away, and the other Boers followed, keeping their rifles pointing at the Dragoons until they vanished in the mist.

"What now, sir?" Sinton asked.

"Now we rejoin Hunter's army," Andrew said, remembering Jacoba's fine eyes. "Come on, lads!"

CHAPTER 42

ORANGE RIVER COLONY

AUGUST 1900

"Did you hear the news?" Sinton could hardly contain his excitement.

"Not yet," Andrew looked up from Mariana's last letter, "but I am sure you will tell me."

"Commandant Prinsloo surrendered to Hunter in Brandwater Basin," Sinton said. "Over four thousand Boers laid down their arms!"

Andrew closed his eyes. "That's good news," he said. "We can take a little credit for that, Sinton. The information we heliographed to General Hunter would have helped. Is there any news of the de Wets?"

"Oh, yes," Sinton said, smiling. "Piet de Wet surrendered, but Christiaan de Wet escaped with some other commanders and about 3,000 men between them."

"Christiaan de Wet is the man I'm bothered about," Andrew admitted. He returned to his letter, trying to convince himself that Mariana's friendship with Charles Nixon was innocent. "We won't get real peace here until we muzzle de Wet and the van Collier brothers."

"Bobs is approaching the frontier of Portuguese East Africa," Sinton said. "Once he reaches that, there will be nowhere for de Wet to run."

"Maybe," Andrew said. "He has the veldt." He looked up as Murcot approached.

"Yes, Murcot?"

Murcot saluted. "Sorry to disturb you, sir, but a Major Dixon and Major Buchanan have come to see you."

Andrew felt himself stiffen. "Have they indeed? Where are they?"

"I asked them to wait in the Officers' Mess, sir," Servant said. "I thought it best."

"You thought correctly," Andrew replied, feeling his heart race. "Excuse me, Sinton," he said, stepping towards the marquee that acted as the Mess the Dragoons shared with the Royal Malverns.

Two strangers lounged on cane chairs, diminishing the Malverns' meagre stock of champagne. Both rose as Andrew entered.

One was tall and broad, with a neatly trimmed moustache and a short row of medal ribbons. Andrew estimated him at thirty-five and well-heeled by the quality of his clothes and boots. The second was short, stout and fifty, with a red face.

"Major Nixon?" Ignoring the older officer, Andrew assessed the taller man, understanding how Mariana could be attracted to him.

"Yes. Major Baird?" The older man extended his hand. "I am Major Charles Dixon. This fellow is Major Buchanan. General Windrush sent me to contact you, Major. I believe it was to discuss remounts for your unit."

Taken off balance, Andrew shook Dixon's firm hand. "I believe you know my wife," Andrew attacked immediately.

"Mrs Baird is a lovely lady," Dixon replied enthusiastically. "We are on first-name terms, you know."

Andrew saw Colonel Cradley spirit Buchanan away. "I know," he said coldly. "You spent quite some time together, attending the theatre and taking my children to the seaside."

Dixon looked confused. "The theatre, Major Baird? You must have been misinformed. I have never been to the theatre in my life. I can't stand play actors and the like."

Andrew lifted his chin, wondering if duelling was still allowed in the British Army. He accepted a whisky from the mess waiter and sat down, with Dixon joining him. "Mariana mentioned you were with her at the theatre," he said.

"No, Baird, I was working when my wife accompanied Mariana to the theatre."

"Your wife? Mariana did not mention her presence."

Dixon shook his head. "Did she not? Charlie and Mariana have become fast friends. I am surprised Mariana did not mention her."

"Charlie?" Andrew felt relief flood him. "Charlie is your wife?"

"Yes, indeed, Major Baird. Her name is Charlotte, but everybody calls her Charlie. Did Mariana not tell you?" Dixon was smiling.

"Oh, dear God in heaven, my dear fellow!" Andrew rose to shake Dixon's hand again.

How the devil could I ever have doubted Mariana? Charlie is Dixon's wife. What a damned, distrusting fool I am. Those blasted missing letters!

Dixon looked up in pleased surprise. "Shall we discuss remounts, Baird?"

"Indeed, Dixon, after I buy you a drink and you tell me about Mariana and Charlie."

"My pleasure, Baird," Dixon replied. "Where shall I start?"

"At the beginning, Dixon, at the very beginning."

Piet sat halfway up a kopje, staring across the veldt to watch for British patrols. He saw a ribbon of dust rising in the west, raised his binoculars and gazed in that direction. Whoever made the dust was moving too fast for a British column, so Piet decided they posed no threat to what remained of Michal's corporalship. He patted the dogs at his feet and glanced down at the camp at the foot of the kopje.

Jacoba cleaned her rifle and replaced it in the holster beside her saddle. She ensured her horse was safe, pushed the hat to the back of her head and smiled, looking more relaxed than she had since she heard of Hendrik's death.

Jacoba eyed Michal as he washed in the river. When she first met Michal, he was little more than an enthusiastic boy, waiting for permission to run everywhere and expend his surplus energy. Now, months of war and hardship on the veldt had steadied and matured him. Jacoba watched Michal wade chest-deep into the fast-flowing river, ducking his head under the water to wash his hair.

He is a clean-living man, Jacoba told herself, *loyal to the Republic, tried and tested in battle. Handsome, too, now he's grown up. He has a strong jaw and a firm mouth.*

Jacoba pulled her hat forward over her face and watched Michal move, noting the fine muscles of his upper body. He had lost all his puppy fat and was lean, hard and deeply tanned.

Jacoba no longer worried that men had not found her younger self unattractive. She was no longer interested in the kind of men who had rejected her. Some would be back on their farms now, having fled from the fighting. Others would be languishing in prison camps in St Helena or Ceylon, having surrendered to the British. Only the real men remained, those who would fight despite defeats and disappointments, those who would remain to the bitter end.

Michal is one of the latter, Jacoba told herself. He was younger than her but had proved himself a man and had shown interest in her. She watched as Michal emerged from the water. She did not smile, examining him as she would examine a stallion she intended to purchase. *He is all man, with a horseman's thighs, good haunches and everything else that mattered. True, he is no Hendrik; nobody could replace Hendrik, but he could be an adequate replacement.*

Jacoba rose from her seat under the tree and walked purposefully forward.

"Jacoba! I did not see you there!" Michal instinctively covered himself.

"I was watching you," Jacoba told him. She stood opposite him, unsmiling.

Michal caught her interest. "I often watch you," he admitted.

"I know," Jacoba said. She held out her hand. "Come, Michal."

Piet looked away. He had no desire to intrude between a woman and her man, and he had seen that relationship forming many weeks ago. It was natural, a virile young man and a woman who had recently discovered her sexuality.

The ribbon of dust was much closer now. Piet focussed his binoculars, seeing a small, hard-riding commando of around fifty men, with outriders on either flank and two men a hundred yards in front. It seemed that the war had rediscovered Michal's corporalship.

Sighing, Piet rose and moved downhill. He did not have to whistle to his dogs, who followed at his heels, tails slowly wagging.

"We saw the smoke from your fire," the commando leaders said as they politely raised their hats and dismounted together.

"I saw the dust from your commando," Piet countered. His dogs sat on either side of him, contemplating these strangers.

The commando spread out and halted, each man holding his rifle ready for use. The dust slowly settled.

"We will camp beside you." The leading men were about forty, Piet judged, with the leathery, calm faces of farmers and the veldt-worn clothes of men who had ridden far and fast. Their rifles were well kept, and cartridges filled the bandoliers across their chests.

"There is good grazing for your horses and sweet water for you all," Piet said. "What name do you bear? I am Piet Stoffberg, and my companions are Michal Rheeder and Jacoba du Toit." He glanced over his shoulder. "Do not disturb them."

"We won't," the taller of the two men replied. "I am Jan van Collier, and this man is my brother Mannie."

"Your names and exploits are known," Piet said.

Jan van Collier snapped orders that saw four of his men climb the kopje to act as lookouts.

"We will continue the war," Jan van Collier said. "Are you with us?"

Piet nodded. "Ja," he said. "We are with you to the bitter end."

ABOUT THE AUTHOR

 Born in Edinburgh, Scotland and educated at the University of Dundee, Malcolm Archibald has written in a variety of genres, from academic history to folklore, historical novels to fantasy. He won the Dundee International Book Prize with *Whales for the Wizard* in 2005 and the Society of Army Historical Research prize for Historical Military Fiction with *Blood Oath* in 2021.

Happily married for over 42 years, Malcolm has three grown children and lives outside Dundee in Scotland.

To learn more about Malcolm Archibald and discover more Next Chapter authors, visit our website at www.nextchapter.pub.

Printed in Dunstable, United Kingdom

67620139R00214